NO TIME, NO AIR, NO EXIT . . .

It was too late. The person they had left behind in the corridors was doomed. Even if she could stop the airlock doors in time, they had no strength—no strength left, and no air. They could not go out and rescue their fallen comrade. Their only chance to survive was to let the door close and let their partner die.

Half-sitting, half-lying on the floor in Cago's arms, Hillbrane stared at the airlock doors as they came together. Locked, and sealed. Now it really was too late. She had no air with which to weep; she could only stare in mute misery. Somebody was on the other side of that door. Somebody had watched it close and seal, and seal their death penalty with it.

Somebody . . .

"Susan Matthews is a writer to watch—
and to keep away from explosives and sharp objects."
Debra Doyle, co-author of the *Mageworld* series

Other Eos Titles by
Susan R. Matthews

AN EXCHANGE OF HOSTAGES
PRISONER OF CONSCIENCE
HOUR OF JUDGMENT
AVALANCHE SOLDIER

COLONY
FLEET

SUSAN R. MATTHEWS

An Imprint of HarperCollinsPublishers

This is a work of fiction. Names, characters, places, and incidents are the products of the author's imagination or are used fictitiously and are not to be construed as real. Any resemblance to actual events, locales, organizations, or persons, living or dead, is entirely coincidental.

EOS
An Imprint of HarperCollins*Publishers*
10 East 53rd Street
New York, New York 10022-5299

Copyright © 2000 by Susan R. Matthews
ISBN: 0-380-80316-X
www.eosbooks.com

First Eos paperback printing: October 2000

Eos Trademark Reg. U.S. Pat. Off. and in Other Countries,
Marca Registrada, Hecho en U.S.A.
HarperCollins® is a trademark of HarperCollins Publishers Inc.

Printed in the U.S.A.

WCD   10 9 8 7 6 5 4 3 2 1

Dedicated to the memory of
Matthew Ames Stobie,
July 1999,
a warrior in the sight of God.

The race is not always to the swift,
nor the battle to the strong;
and his life was no less important to us
just because it was so short.

PROLOGUE
LAUNCH

Eamon Jasper approached the chief engineer's office with a feeling of accomplishment that was thoroughly mixed with the reservations that she had about her findings. She wanted more time. But didn't they always want more time? There was always a better solution, if only they had the time to find it. But once they found that, she would know that somewhere out there was a better solution yet. So she would see what the chief engineer had to say about this one, and let him make the call.

She called out her "Good morning!" as she neared the open door; and went in. Salter Beame was there, right enough, but he sat slumped at his desk with his head in his hands. Eamon stopped short in the middle of the room and took an involuntary half-step backwards. What was this all about?

"Waystation Five, Beame. It's the last one we needed, and it's close enough to the line of original course to be doable."

Something had to be amiss. Beame was a vibrant personality: two peoples' life energies in one body. Irrepressible. They said he never slept; that he'd absorbed his shadow-twin in his mother's womb, and that was why his eyes were not both the same color. But that was the sort of thing one said about chief engineers. You didn't get to head up an enterprise as complex and important as the final stages of construction of a colony fleet unless you were out of the ordinary. Half-admiring stories that made ambiguous fun of his personal characteristics were only one way of managing envy and frustration among the people who worked for him.

Beame looked up. His eyes were red; had Beame been crying? Beame, who only got excited about hardware? "Ask me if I've heard anything, then," Beame said, in a voice that seemed to communicate resignation to the question his appearance could not help but raise. "Go ahead. I'm listening."

Jasper thought for a moment, then shook her head, scarce conscious of the clattering of the beads that decorated the tens of thin braids that made up her coiffure. No. Beame didn't like talking about personal issues. She didn't want to hear anything that he might later wish he hadn't said.

She opened her portfolio and laid it on the desk before him, instead. "Here it is. It's got the weight class, nontoxic atmosphere, everything. It's not as beautiful as Waystation Three and it's smaller than Waystation One, but there is no perfection in the world. The point is that it's the fifth and it's within requirements. We can go now."

Beame paged through the report while Jasper watched anxiously. Of course there was uncertainty in the spectrophotometrology. There was always uncertainty, especially when they were dealing with something that was fully seven hundred light years from Earth, which made it approximately 699.99 light-years from the Pluto base. Give or take a half an hour. It had taken the old probes so long to get there, and so long for the information to get back; but the decision to send an autonomous fleet to seek for colony worlds had only been made in her lifetime.

"You're forgetting something."

Jasper felt her stomach muscles contract in involuntary reaction to the criticism. If only she could manage not to respect Beame quite so much as she did, she wouldn't be so helplessly dependent on his approval nor so vulnerable to his disapproval. She kept her voice neutral and professional, but she was cringing inside. "Yes?"

"Rainforest. You know Tonio wants Rainforest before we

go. He's out in the umbilicus right now, just taking it all in."

Taking all what in? Rainforest was still in the earliest of the preparation stages. They'd only located a suitable asteroid, that was all. Oh, and hauled it in to the shipyard beyond Charon and started to work on its interior, but it wasn't even sealed for atmosphere.

"The mission isn't to take ten Noun Ships and go." Beame knew that. He liked to encourage his scientists to challenge authority, that was all. So she would challenge him. "The mission is to take at least nine Noun Ships and identify five worlds profiling at eighty-five percent or greater of the long-term survival indicators for colonization. And we have nine Noun Ships."

Beame was staring at her with an expression on his face that she could not quite interpret. But she had a good string going. It created its own momentum; she was enjoying this.

"We have all the atmospheres and the water stores. We have the colonization party, it's all here, it's been here, you know it. And now we have a target for Waystation Five. So we should leave, because Fleet isn't getting any younger and we have a long way to go."

Then she waited, locked eye to eye with Beame, all but daring him to argue with her. Something seemed to cross his face, a shadow, an expression behind his expression; what could it be?

Had he been serious when he'd suggested that she ask him what he'd heard?

The moment passed. Beame stood up. "We'll go see Tonio with this. You can tell him. Come on."

It was a bit of a walk down the long corridor to the elevators, and from there to the trams. Beame was not in a talkative mood, but Jasper refused to let herself respond to his abstraction. She thought about her planet instead: Waystation Five. The last one they needed. It would take more than seven hundred years to get there. How many generations was that?

Would the flora and fauna that the Colony Fleet was to carry with it on the Noun Ships evolve during the long transit that they faced?

Would the species itself evolve?

The umbilicus was as busy as ever when they got there, but there was an odd sort of tension in the air; the sort of excitement that was associated with events both huge and horrible. No one greeted them; people looked at Beame and turned their attention elsewhere, a little too quickly.

Jasper started to worry.

The Fleet's senior administrator was Tonio Stuarda, and he stood at his favorite spot in front of the great observation wall, staring out into space at the Fleet that he managed. He had his arms folded across his chest, and the strong lights overhead picked up the silver that glittered in his tightly crimped blond hair.

He didn't turn around when they approached, though Jasper was certain that he must have heard them.

"Tonio," Beame said. "Jasper's people have got the last Waystation world. She says we can go now. What do you say?"

At the sound of Beame's voice Tonio started, and turned around quickly. Jasper saw his face; it was the color of the putty that the technicians used to secure the seams in the fabric lining the corridors.

Something was wrong.

"Beame." Why did Tonio's voice sound so choked? "I can't say how sorry I am."

But Beame only nodded. "I know. But it's done now. I've missed my chance. So I agree with Jasper when she says that it's time."

She should have asked him when he had suggested it. Now she could only guess at what might have happened—

"We know that you feel Rainforest is important, Tonio," Jasper said. "We don't disagree. But."

And damn Beame for being so coy about whatever it was that had happened. He had to learn to trust. They were to be shipmates in a fleet of forty thousand souls, embarking on the most audacious odyssey in the history of the human race. They had to be able to rely on one another.

"You know the political climate better than any of us. Earth could hold us hostage for years waiting for Rainforest. We need a clean break."

Beame's family was supposed to be joining him soon. That was right. Had their transport been denied? The space transit authority was subject to civil control, and the anticolonial movement grew stronger on Earth day by day.

Tonio nodded his head sadly. "Quite right, Jasper. I think we should leave. I think we should leave now, so it's good if we have the fifth colony."

Oddly enough this seemed to startle Beame as much as it did her. "Tonio—the bioset—it's not coming after all?"

The bioset, the organic materials required to set up the Rainforest environment. Once away from Earth's atmosphere, the freighter convoy would take months to get out to the Pluto shipyards where the Colony Fleet was mustered. It would be just barely long enough to get the Noun Ship ready to receive the environment as it was—but Tonio was nodding his head again, agreeing.

"You know what they say, Beame. Earth first. Let's clean up our environment before we spend any more resources on reproducing it for some colony or another. I can't tell you how sorry I am about your family, Beame. But twenty percent of the entire launch capacity we had is gone now too."

It was like the proverbial drop of catalyst into a flask of substrate.

She understood all too well, and all at once. Rogue nukes. Beame's family would have been near the primary point of departure for the Colony Fleet. A terrorist attack on Seaport Three's launch facilities would have destroyed the launch complex, the waiting shipments, the merged cities of the northwest Pacific coast all in one monstrous sequence detonation of stolen and antiquated nuclear weapons.

Anticolonials.

The governments still supported the Colony Fleet, but there

were too many people on Earth who were willing to force their agenda if they could not obtain it by lawful means. Because there were too many people on Earth.

"Well. Tonio." There were volumes in the two words Beame spoke. Just this once it seemed that he couldn't think of anything else to say; so Jasper filled in for him.

"We'll build you a minidome on Temperate, Tonio. Once we've launched. But we'd better launch. We have the psychological momentum. We've got to get out of here, or we may never leave."

There had been threats in the anticolonial rhetoric, emotional blackmail. *How can you turn your back on your home while your own family is starving in Ontario, in Alabama, in Sahar, in Manchuria? We need people who are willing to sacrifice to save their planet, not run away from it.* And most ominously, *We can't afford to waste our scarce resources on the dependents of people who care nothing about the planet of our birth.*

"There were mosses," Tonio said. The suppressed grief in his voice was terrible to hear. "Seventeen types. So beautiful. And now I will never see a redwood again."

There weren't redwoods in Rainforest to begin with.

But that wasn't the point.

"Issue the orders, Tonio," Beame said, and for a man who had just lost his family it was oddly enough as though he was comforting Tonio rather than the other way around. And Tonio had lost only Rainforest; but the bioset was symbolic of so much more. "Everything is ready now. We can finalize the outbound course once we come up to speed for the transit. Let's go."

Now.

Or perhaps never.

The mission of the Colony Fleet was too important to let fail for lack of courage to leave home, just because they were leaving everything they knew and loved behind.

"We'll get Ellyn and transmit the warning order," Tonio said. He had decided. "Jasper. If you could get a message to

Construction. Tell them we need the shipbuilder general, and we need her now."

Engineer, administrator, and technical master.

They would publish the departure instructions as a team.

"Right away, Tonio."

And the Colony Fleet would launch: to find new worlds of refuge for a species that had outgrown the world that had given it life.

ONE
NOUN SHIP

Hillbrane rolled off the low slatted bed to the cool wooden floor and rose to her feet in a swift graceful movement that her dance teacher would have applauded had she been there.

Stiknals.

She remembered.

She was in Stiknals, really and truly, and she hadn't been to Stiknals but the once in her life.

It was early yet by the clock, but she was awake now, and hurried to the shuttered lanai doors to greet the morning. It had been late when she'd arrived, too dark to see much of anything. She couldn't wait to see whether it was still as beautiful as she remembered it.

Already warm. Hillbrane stepped out onto the wide veranda, breathing deeply of jasmine-scented morning air. The grounds of the Stiknals Engineering Academy stretched out before her, green and beautiful; beyond the compound wall, the morning boats were already poling their way down the canal that served in place of a road in Stiknals. Yes, beautiful, the great trees heavy with humidity and flowers, the air breathing the soft fragrances of wood and water. At this early hour the canal's fragrance was still merely exotic, and not unpleasant. The water in the canals would stink by noon with rotting organic matter and rich silt, but the odor would fade again to an interesting perfume by evening. She remembered that.

She'd been here just once before, for First Sex. But that had come too soon after her parents' untimely death; she hadn't enjoyed it as much as she'd expected. Stiknals itself, though, Hillbrane remembered as a fantasy of warm nights and rich scents long after she'd returned to Temperate, looking forward to the day when the Comparisons would bring her back to this city of canals.

Now she was back. Her shuttle had brought her in to Subtropical during its night phase; she'd gone straight to bed, mindful of the need to maintain the time schedule common to the Noun Ships in order to maintain maximum mental productivity. According to the clock on this Noun Ship it was early morning, and therefore she should be hungry. She *was* hungry. Turning away from the scene before her—the misty sky, the long avenue of tree-lined canals, the jasmine that tumbled over the centuries-old walls—Hillbrane hunted through her room for the administrative call button. Breakfast. Pineapple, ripe as it never was on any other Noun Ship, and bananas fried in coconut milk. . . .

The call button was a toggle switch mounted near the door. Schematic Belvidere, then; Hillbrane noted it to herself out of force of habit. That told her where the bathroom was and whether there would be a tub as well as letting her know which piece of furniture concealed her connect station. There were only six or seven Schematics for Jneer dwellings on all of the nine Noun Ships, from Islands to Desert.

Hillbrane toggled the call, and waited.

"Admin, Aitch Harkover. How may we provide for you?"

Aitch Harkover. The title gave Hillbrane a little thrill; once the Comparisons were completed she would be an adult, she would take her place in the Jneer community, and no one would call her Hillbrane unless they had been explicitly invited to do so. Well, no Oway would call her Hillbrane, no matter what relationships she would build with her peers. Aitch Harkover. A grown woman, and a Jneer.

"I'd like breakfast, please." Yes, her mother had died when she'd been only fourteen, nearly eight years ago. Hillbrane had never forgotten. *Please and thank you, Hillibee, I don't care if it's just an Oway. Please and thank you, even to a Mech. A Jneer has no excuse for bad manners.*

"Of course. Immediately. We have your choice of menus available, Aitch Harkover, would you care to state a preference?"

Choice of menus. Hillbrane thought fast. She liked more than a simple third of her daily fuel at breakfast, even when that meant a light supper. Carb-heavy would work best for where she was; the cuisine of Stiknals was protein-sparing by tradition. "Carb-heavy, seven hundred. Please."

"Very good, Aitch Harkover. It will be ten minutes. You may wish to review the agenda while you're waiting, will there be anything else?"

Not for the moment, no. "Thank you," Hillbrane answered, and toggled out. Agenda. Agenda would be on the connect station. Now was probably a good time to connect, because it was only going to get warmer as the day progressed, and living quarters in Stiknals did without climate control—no cooling systems. Tradition.

She opened the wings of the rattan-work console that housed the room's connects. Invoking her agenda, Hillbrane crossed into the washroom to clean her teeth, listening all the while.

Aitch Harkover, Comparisons testing cycle three hundred. Sixty. Five. More than three hundred and eighty years since the Colony Fleet had set out on its mission; that meant more than three hundred and sixty-five years of tradition, of Comparisons Testing year after year. Three hundred and sixty-five years of twenty-two-year-old Jneers testing themselves against their peers to see who was to claim the technical direction of the Colony Fleet by right of superior analytical ability. Three hundred and eighty years since the hope of a dying world had launched Colony Fleet, and then fallen silent; and now approaching Waystation One at last.

She rinsed her mouth and rummaged for the comb that would be provided for her. An Oway had been in here while she'd slept; her kit had been unpacked, and local dress laid out for her on the valet stand in front of the toilet screen. It was the thinnest, lightest cotton she had ever seen, and it was—needless to say—local. Hillbrane was impressed. The local fabric on her home Noun of Temperate was fine enough, but hemp simply didn't work up as light and silky to the touch as cotton.

Orientation assembly at ten. Cases will be issued at fourteen. Meals on demand, debrief on day plus four, graduation day plus five. The time is five and one-half, standard Nouns time.

Her hair was combed, but Hillbrane wasn't happy with it; the humidity had teased each wheat-colored strand into a springy wire, and the woman who looked back at Hillbrane from the mirror looked like she was wearing a headdress of straws, with her hair standing out from her head. Setting the comb down with a grimace of disgust, Hillbrane stripped for a wash.

There were orchids in the shower, and the soap was scented with sandalwood, and the shower slippers that waited for her tucked neatly against the inside rim of the shower stall were beautifully crafted of split bamboo, cool to the touch. Silky.

Could there be anywhere nicer in the whole Colony Fleet to come for Comparisons?

Her hair was much easier to manage once it was wetted through and lightly dressed with fragrant oil. She plucked an orchid blossom from one of the plants in the shower and plaited it into her long thick hair. Her breakfast was waiting for her; the Oway had delivered it while she'd been in the shower. There was a single scarlet flower on the lid of her entrée dish, a fat swollen streak of golden pollen spilling suggestively from its throat. She tucked that one behind her ear.

Assembly, and then the cases would be released.

She wasn't really thinking about her Comparisons, though.

When she'd come to Stiknals for First Sex it had been because she had less genetic content in common with the Jneers of Subtropical than with those on any of the other Noun Ships.

It was arranged that way to maximize the genetic diversity of any unplanned and fortuitous pregnancies, but it meant that she hadn't met any of her First Sex partners before in her life, nor had she seen any of them again. This would be different. There were other people from Temperate here for Comparisons, removed as she had been from their native ships to minimize potential favoritism on the part of the evaluation staff.

First Sex had been almost more depressing than anything else; she'd been scared, insecure, deeply ambivalent, terrified of failure to perform.

She was older now. And she was back in Stiknals.

Once Comparisons were over she was going to find Selchow, and Axel, and Raleigh and do First Sex all over again . . . but right this time.

Raleigh Marquette stood on the threshold of the assembly hall with a fan in his teeth, knotting a cloth band around his forehead absentmindedly. It was hot, and the sweat stung his eyes. He carried the traditional palm-leaf fan, true enough; everybody did. But what did a boy from Temperate know about palm-frond fans? It just annoyed him. He didn't remember it often enough to use it to any particular benefit; it was just one more thing to carry around.

He had other things on his mind, much more pressing issues than the transitory physical discomfort of heat and sweat and stickiness. There were more than seventy others here in Assembly, waiting for the dean's address; which of them was it?

Because one of these people was his enemy.

He didn't know more than half of them, and hoped his enemy would be someone he'd never met. But there was no other way out of the situation for him or for anybody else. They were to be paired for the Comparisons, counted off by twos, and each of them would prepare their case analysis and then evaluate the case analysis that their antagonist had written.

Raleigh knew perfectly well what tradition demanded, but he could not afford the luxury of tradition. He had to be sure.

He had to win this. The alternative was unthinkable.

Some particular movement to his left caught his eye and Raleigh grinned despite his somber mood to recognize its source and its effect on him. Hillbrane. Hillbrane, tossing her beautiful patrician head, her glorious halo of tightly kinked blond hair tied up in a heavy braid down the back of her neck and decorated with flowers.

Red ones.

It didn't take much consideration on his part to decide him; he was already moving toward Hillbrane as he thought about it. There was space beside her. He should be there. She was one of the reasons he had made up his mind to the daring betrayal that he had planned, after all. He had to be sure of his position before he proposed a repro contract to any woman, and Hillbrane had admirers enough. He couldn't afford to let a rival get an edge.

Taking his place in a seat in the row behind her, just to her left, Raleigh tweaked her braid with a swift practiced gesture, studying the filigree work on the long high ventilation ducts as he did so. She started up with a nervous twitch, and he grinned, but frowned at the far wall immediately. It didn't have to fool her. It was just part of the game.

"Ar Marquette." Her tone was superior and icy; he knew she was playing. She wouldn't keep it up. She never could, with him. "Ever seen the moon rise over Stiknals from a flower-boat?"

No. But it sounded like fun. Raleigh smoothed the pretended frown from his brow and widened his eyes, blinking.

"Why, no, Aitch Harkover, ma'am. Whyever do you ask?" If he was lucky he knew. If he was lucky—but he wasn't leaving anything to luck. The stakes were too high.

"I've got a flower-boat on reserve, with your name on it. For after. If you don't think it might be too much of a waste of your time?"

"Not a bit of it, Harkover. I'll look forward to it." He kept his voice light and informal, of course, keeping his delight to

himself for the time being. They were in public, after all. And
even though she had just invited him for sex, he wasn't supposed to notice it until the time came, when he would be
naturally delighted—pleasantly surprised—at the treat being
offered him.

It only emphasized how much there was to lose.

He had the future to think of, and the future was on Waystation One. Everybody knew how important the colony was,
whether or not they shared his suspicions about what condition
Fleet would be in by the time it got to Waystation Two. He
had no intention of taking any chances. He would be there in
the colonization party; and Hillbrane would be there with him.

There was a stir of some sort at the front of the room.
Pulling his thoughts back together, Raleigh put on his best
"respectful attention" face; the dean was arriving to deliver the
remarks that marked the official opening of Comparisons.

Everyone stood on signal and recited the Creed.

*I am an engineer. It is my duty to ensure that this Fleet
stays on course, that resources are conserved, that science
goes forward. The best my mind can offer belongs to the Colony Fleet for the mutual benefit of all. I am an engineer. It's
my job.*

Once they were seated again, the dean—a slim black
woman of middle height and middle age, her hair crowned
with creamy trumpet-shaped flowers tinged with a delicate ros-
iness—stepped to the fore of the raised teaching platform.

"Welcome to the Subtropical Canals Engineering Academy,
young people. It's my pleasure to serve as your preceptor for
this crucial rite of passage."

Did she understand how crucial it really was? Could she
guess? It was unfair, really. When the dean had done her Comparisons, it had been just as it had been for years and years
and years again before—a rite of passage, but scarcely one
with life or death as its ultimate goal. Did she understand what
was at stake for this class?

Did Hillbrane?

Unsettled by a sudden sense of unease, Raleigh fought to

calm his nerves. It didn't matter. Hillbrane was in no danger, Hillbrane was brilliant—one of the sharpest minds Raleigh had yet encountered amongst this class. Hillbrane didn't need to know how important this actually was. She would be safe whatever happened. Hillbrane was Strategy-caliber, and Raleigh faced a future in Ponics—an ugly job for a Jneer, traveling out to the rest of Fleet to trouble-shoot the food production process among the Mechs, far away from the home comforts of the Noun Ships.

"Let's all agree on the following assumptions. I've made a speech about the role of Comparisons in ensuring that each of us finds a job that best matches our abilities and aptitudes. You've listened in polite silence, all the while wondering what the case you'll get will be like. I've spent some minutes trying to communicate what I wish I'd known when I was in your place, and you've promised yourselves that you'll never inflict such platitudes on the next generation when it's your turn on the speaker's platform. I've made a humorous remark, and you've laughed because it's polite, not because you thought it was funny. Yes or no?"

She was right, a response was expected. So Raleigh joined the sheepish laugh that murmured through the audience, and the dean nodded with apparent satisfaction.

"Now that that's out of the way, down to business. Your cases will be released at fourteen to individual rooms. You have two days. In two days and two hours you will transmit your completed case for review and receive your evaluation case. You have one day to prepare your evaluation. In three days and four hours you will transmit your evaluation."

Some of this had already been covered in agenda; some of it was just understood, from reports of other Jneers who had already completed their Comparisons. The dean was required to rehearse it anyway. Raleigh stifled a yawn that was equal parts boredom and nervousness: he wanted to be started, and he couldn't start. Not till fourteen.

"You will assemble on day four and stand ready to be called to defend your case before a panel of senior Jneers. That is, in the event that any unresolved issues remain after evaluation of your case."

She put a dry flourish to the tail of her speech that evoked a genuine laugh, this time. Everybody knew there would be unresolved issues. Ever since there had been Comparisons there had been "unresolved issues," ever since the first Jneers had realized that so long as nobody won, nobody lost. So everybody knew that defending their cases before the panel was an academic exercise.

Of course there would be unresolved issues.

It was all part of the game, but there was just enough uncertainty, just enough uneasiness in Raleigh's mind to edge his laugh with the sharp shrill hint of nerves. What if. What if. He couldn't be the only person who had seen the future.

What if he tried and failed?

What if it didn't work?

Raleigh refocused his attention on the speaker with an almost physical effort. He was not going to waste energy on unproductive anxiety-looping. He couldn't afford to.

"We'll be serving lunch in the banquet hall shortly; get a good meal into your furnace before you tackle your case. Good luck, young people, and may you all find your perfect place in Fleet."

What if he wasn't an engineer after all?

What if he was an Oway? What if he was a Mech?

Raleigh knew there was no margin for error. He wasn't going to take any chances. He'd run the game analysis, and he knew what he had to do.

Four hundred years of tradition was as nothing compared to the analysis of a true Jneer.

Strolling with Raleigh down the gravel path that divided the lush green lawn from the canal, Hillbrane luxuriated in the heavy air, the heavy fragrance of the flowers, the exotic odors of the canal itself. Raleigh seemed abstracted, a little moody; Hillbrane pointed out the beautifully colored fish that swam in the warm shallow waters of the tributary canal beside them.

"Look, Raleigh. There's your dinner. What do you think? Steamed in banana leaves, with lime juice? Or maybe curried, over rice."

The thin yellow cotton wrapped-skirt that he wore became him, the folds of his silk royal blue shirt more flattering to his otherwise somewhat underfleshed figure than the workshirts she usually saw on him. He looked very exotic, with a spray of flowers behind one ear. Of course he was exotic—a genetic mosaic, one blue eye, one brown—but exotic was more at home here at Stiknals than in the everyday environment of Temperate.

"Aitch Harkover. Hillbrane. Come on. Do you know what carp eat?" He shouldered her, in friendly fashion, and then seemed to realize that the water was on her side; because he put his arm around her shoulder, as if to ensure she didn't lose her balance. "Give me a nice piece of shark any day. With green chilies from Desert. After Comparisons, of course."

"And shark eat carp, so what's the difference?" But she was just teasing, and they both knew it. She and Raleigh had grown up together, bonded by mutual experience of deviance. Her parents were dead, not as though that was her fault, but it was deviant. And he was what he was. "You'll eat carp and like it. It's good luck. I'm buying."

He gave her shoulder a little squeeze, as if in appreciation of her offer—and of the sentiments behind it. "I'm willing to give it a try. But you're right. I'm nervous, Hillbrane, I wish this was all over."

Nervous she could understand. She didn't care how many times they were told that there was nothing to be nervous about: this was the last thing they would ever do as nonagers. That was intrinsically anxiety-provoking.

"Raleigh, you can do this in your sleep. I see a great success for you. Straight to Resource Allocation, my man, don't forget me when the time comes to allocate quarters. I think I'd quite like Islands, but so long as it's not Arctic I won't insist on Tropical."

Oddly enough Raleigh frowned at her joke; maybe it was in questionable taste. Raleigh really didn't have much chance at Resource Allocation. He'd be doing well to avoid Hydroponics, with his academic record; but since he knew that she knew that, it wasn't as if she was lying.

"I always wanted someplace a little cooler, myself." Maybe he wasn't frowning at her; he was staring off into the distance, his gaze seemingly fixed on something out beyond the compound gates along the arched bridge over the canal. "Altitude. That's my fantasy, Brane. Alpine meadows, a chalet, maybe a cow and some goats—"

"Stop it." He was teasing, now, she was sure of it. Goats stank. The Oways who raised the goats stank. It was a wonder that the goat cheese didn't stink as well, though there were some who claimed it did. "You'll settle for Seaboard and be grateful, good sir, or don't you like lobster, either?"

Seaboard, where the Seniors lived. Raleigh flashed her one of his brilliant smiles, but it was gone as quickly as it had come. Raleigh was shy of smiling because his teeth weren't perfect, but his smile itself was one of the most attractive things about him—in Hillbrane's mind, at least. Or in her hormones, or wherever exactly it was that such things were decided, she wasn't quite sure. Rational thought probably had less to do with it than anything.

Somewhere in her own genetic background there had to have been a gene line that was angular and skinny, thickhaired, triangular of face with that strong unapologetic nose, those feline cheekbones, that deeply incised upper lip that overruled the near-pout of the lower lip beneath it. That would explain the fondness in her heart for Raleigh, and the stimulating effect he frequently had on her pulse rate. Yes.

"Oh, look at the guests, Brane," Raleigh suggested, with a gesture of his head. Guests? Hillbrane followed the line of his fixed gaze—oh. Yes. So that was what had been distracting him. Lining the bridge over the canal, pointing, taking pictures—it was a tour group. Mechs.

Her heart shrank within her, shying away by reflex from the sight.

They were deformed.

Not all of them, of course, but even from where she stood Hillbrane could see that at least one of the Mechs on tour—the "guests" of the City of Stiknals—was emphatically not quite right.

"Don't stare, Raleigh, be nice." Taking his arm, she drew Raleigh with her down the gravel path toward the trees that shaded one of the pavilions that graced the compound lawn. "It may be the only time some of those people ever get to be out in the air. I can't see them all coming back for their honeymoons."

She didn't blame them for their deformities. Hillbrane considered herself blessedly free from the endemic and—truth be told—understandable prejudice against the Mechs. It wasn't their fault. It was their parents she blamed. There was no excuse for bringing an imperfect child to term. Prenatal genetic counseling was available to everyone; there were even traveling clinics that made the rounds of Noun Ships and the rest of the Fleet alike.

Why would anyone elect to dedicate valuable resources to a child that would be born handicapped, knowing as everybody did that Fleet's medical resources would not stretch to cover such voluntarily incurred requirements?

It was beyond Hillbrane's understanding.

"I don't mind them being here. I'm glad they're here," Raleigh claimed emphatically, but without complete conviction. "It's good luck to see Mechs before a test, isn't it? I wonder if I could get my picture taken with that one substandard, there."

He was right, as far as it went. It was good luck to see Mechs before a test. If nothing else it was a useful reminder of how important it was to do well, how vital to the Fleet a Jneer's skills were.

Mechs didn't live on the Noun Ships; there wasn't room for them.

The only time a Mech got to enjoy privileges Jneers took for granted was on holiday, on honeymoon, on school trips, so that they would all remember what the words meant: canals, jasmine, carp, pineapple. It was part of learning the vocabulary that was part of their common inheritance—and the reason why the Noun Ships had been commissioned in the first place.

"You don't have time, Raleigh. You know they'd all want their pictures taken with a Jneer. You wouldn't get away for two hours yet." Their cases would be released in less than two hours' time. It went without saying that they were all anxious to get started. A complete colonization scenario, environment, resources, limitations, and only two days in which to evaluate all of the intangibles and prepare a colonization plan—challenging enough, without the ultimate test of creativity.

What to leave out?

Because something had to be left out for the other, the Jneer who would evaluate the case, to find and point out as a deficiency. In the beginning the Comparisons process had pitted Jneer against Jneer, mind against mind, to test and validate the quality of each young person before they would be allowed to return home and continue to enjoy the quality of life that had been theirs since birth. But that was not the way of things now, nor had it been for centuries; what sense was there in so arbitrary and meaningless a test?

What sense was there in measuring performance against a test case that would be exhaustively prepared by the finest minds in the Colony Fleet in concert, before they ever got to the colony planets they sought?

Yet if one solution was superior, the other solution was inferior by default. By definition. The only way around it was to make sure one's solution was flawed.

If there were no winners and losers, no superior and inferior solution—if both test cases were flawed—then there was no ranking one Jneer over another: and both remained within their natal communities, both Jneers, both on the Noun Ships, to do the jobs for which they had been trained since they'd been born.

It wasn't as if there were too many Jneers. The population of the Noun Ships, Jneer and Oway alike, had never increased as quickly as the founders had anticipated. So it wasn't as if letting Jneers stay Jneers by practicing a harmless bit of ritual endangered the effectiveness of the Fleet in any way.

They had reached the scented shadows of the arbor. It was comfortable and comforting to walk with Raleigh; there was no need for meaningless conversation to fill the companionable silence between them. Hillbrane was glad Raleigh was here, to remind her of who she was and where she had come from. To keep her focused, grounded, centered.

"Well, a kiss for luck then," Raleigh suggested. "If I can't go have my picture taken. One for the case—and one for the evaluation—and—one—for the unresolved issues, if there are any—"

He smelled spicy with sweat, peppery and musky at once. It was familiar, and exciting. Hillbrane sighed, snuggling her head beneath Raleigh's chin happily.

"There'll be time for that later." At least more time. She didn't like to rush. Hurrying reminded her of the heady confusion of First Sex, and that wasn't a completely positive memory. "Come on. Let's go back to the dormitory. Cases will be out by the time we get there."

To work, then.

And a holiday after.

"If it wasn't so warm I'd race you," Raleigh said, and they walked back to the residence hall together to face the first part of Comparisons testing.

The Oway who coordinated the residence support on her floor—a tall and solidly built woman named Podile, who had the broad face and flat nose of the Islands—had brought the documentation package, and laid there on the top was the code Hillbrane was to use to call up her formats and keys on the workstation.

She was excited; nervous, but eager to get started.

The package Podile delivered was heavy and promising, mysterious in its plain wrapper, tantalizing in the shapes and sizes of the constituent elements that could be felt through the coarse cotton fabric that served as the package's wrapping.

Hillbrane broke the seals and laid the wrapper flat atop the rattan study table near the lanai doors.

This was it.

Astronomy. Atmospherics. Geologic survey. Resource lists, and on the bottom of the stack the biota forecast, the expected vegetation and animal life predicted for the world she was to conquer—or whose conquest she was to simulate.

Her fingers were trembling with excitement.

She took up the biota sheets and carried them with her to her workstation, where the simulation model would be waiting.

What world was this, that she was to be tested on?

Its size classed in the general range of the index world, the home world that had chartered the Fleet so many years ago. Bigger by a factor of thousands than the Noun Ships—even all nine, taken together, would make up only a fraction of the mass. All of that room . . . mostly under liquid seas, yes, and the liquid spectraled out as water with a rich broth of mineral salts in solution. A modest local sun, a handful of neighbor planets, a nearby constellation cluster that looked somehow familiar—

Waystation One.

Hillbrane forgot the simulation on her workstation, staring at the document in her hands with delight.

Waystation One.

The first of the colony worlds, the goal toward which the Colony Fleet had been traveling for nearly four hundred years, the first of five such destinations but still the first—only a matter of months away now, their goal within figurative sight at last—

Waystation One.

She recognized it now, its stellar neighborhood, its index features, the characteristics of landform and stage of planetary evolution that had focused the attention of the founders of the Fleet in this direction so many years ago.

Breathable atmosphere, pressure within tolerance, and oh, to touch the virgin soil after centuries of living on the same old terraformed rock, working with resources that had been put in place ages ago. Three land masses, active tectonics, local weather generators—there was no mistaking the world.

There was an attention-tone from the workstation, alerting Hillbrane to the fact that she was sitting in a daze at her desk with a piece of documentation in her hands and an idiotic grin on her face. She'd known that the test would focus on a colony world, and yet she had somehow never anticipated being tested on Waystation One itself.

Now that they were this close to the planet, though, it made sense that Waystation One should be subject to Comparisons. It wasn't an academic exercise any longer. The colony would leave the Fleet within the coming year. This was real. Live fire, in a sense.

As she looked a little more closely at the biota sheet, Hillbrane noticed some interesting information in the document, new information. The vegetation index seemed to hint at great grassy prairies; oxygen wouldn't be an issue, but there was more to it than that. Didn't the possibility of prairies hint at the potential development of animal life-forms—a herbivore, at the very least, that would be capable of exploiting the ecological niche?

Best not to assume so; that would be more speculative than Hillbrane generally found comfortable. The plan called for them to reach Waystation One before it generated any indigenous higher life-forms, so that the Colony Fleet would be free to import its own while the moral issues raised by potentially pushing a native life-form out of its proper place were still safely at the hypothetical stage. There shouldn't be much by way of vertebrate life on land, though a resource-rich ocean would be a plus as a potential source of protein.

Life exploded so quickly—speciation happened so fast—who could say for sure that Waystation One was to be the virgin world that had been sought? Granted that the evolutionary processes were slow in human terms, but why might not the critical point have been reached at a different time in the life of this planet?

This was just the test case, though, Hillbrane reminded herself. She was taking it more seriously than was necessary.

Waystation One had been presented to them because it was too obvious a part of their lives to not use, as close as they were. Her challenge was to concentrate on the problem she'd been given and not yield to distraction.

She imagined she could smell fresh air. She didn't know what that might smell like, but it would be air that she would know was fresh—not scrubbed and dosed and siphoned and recycled over centuries. Air that no human soul had breathed before.

She could feel the warm breeze on her face, a real breeze borne of the respiratory processes of a living planet, not an artificial air current artificially generated by cooling and warming different areas on the dwelling surfaces of the Noun Ships. She could taste water that came virgin to her lips, water fallen from the sky and melted out of glaciers, water that had not been drunk and excreted and recovered to be drunk and excreted and recovered yet again . . .

There was a signal at the door, and Hillbrane shook herself out of sensual reverie to pay attention. It was the floor Oway, Podile. Tea service to sustain the student until dinnertime.

Comparisons itself was enough excitement for now. Waystation One would wait. It had been waiting for them for all of this time already. She would stand beneath its azure-vaulted skies soon enough.

The interruption had been a useful wake-up call of sorts, an alarm going off: time to stop dreaming and get on with it.

Letting the case constraints fill her consciousness and focus her mind, Hillbrane set to work.

*   *   *

His case analysis had been transmitted in good time. The worst of it was behind him now, and Raleigh broke the snap-seal on his evaluation pack with a sense of relief and fatalism.

Over and done.

No going back on it now.

He couldn't change anything in his analysis now if he'd wanted to, so second-guessing himself was only a waste of time and energy that he needed to husband carefully over the next few hours if he was to hope to face the challenges still before him with grace and aplomb.

Events would take over from here on out, regardless of his attempts to perturb trajectory.

Pushing a stray lock of hair back behind one ear, Raleigh stared at the case he was to evaluate. He didn't want to read the evaluation case. He wanted to go off for a run, a swim, a hike, sniff skin with Hillbrane. Her skin was as creamy-smooth as the plump waxy surface of the orchids in the shower, and the little pink crease at the back of her knee maddened him—it was so soft, so tender, so ticklish. Always. Ever since he could remember starting to notice—

He had to concentrate.

He was just tired.

Pushing himself away from the table restlessly, Raleigh called the floor matron for a jug of cold black tea with mint and sugar and hibiscus blossom to sharpen his powers of concentration. He had to make this look good, so good that his own case would seem flawless by mere comparison. His tea came, and he stood out on the lanai for the few moments that it took to drink the first glassful, resting his eyes on the late-night mist that rose off the canal.

All of the lights in the long dormitory were on.

Everybody here was wrestling with their evaluation cases; had anybody else made his bold daring choice for the solution to the problem that underlay them all?

Where was the room in which his own case lay open for evaluation, and to whom had it fallen to do the analysis, and would they realize what he had done?

The puckery astringency of the hibiscus blossom married with the tannins in the tea, and with assistance from the sweet smoothing influence of the sugar they begat a mind-tonic together.

Clarity.

Raleigh turned off all the lights except the one blue-white narrow-beam lamp above the desk, opened the stiff pasteboard cover of the evaluation packet, and started to read.

The same case as that he had been given, well, that wasn't much of a surprise. It would make a better test if everyone performed to the same specification. The same case, and Raleigh knew the solution to it now, but this solution did not seem to conform—so what was going on here?

Someone else had made the choice he had?

That wasn't it.

The solution was not orthodox. At first review it seemed a little questionable in more than one of its aspects. But what was different about it was not different in the same sense as what Raleigh had done. It was original. Original, creative, someone had put real thought into the case beyond the application of schooling and technical analysis protocols.

Raleigh read on with a deepening sense of uneasiness and tension. It was good. It was very good; it gave point after point in logical progression, but every one of them marshaled in so novel an order of battle as to be both wonderful and strange. Why hadn't he thought to approach the case that way?

What was he going to do?

The case was brilliant.

Brilliance disturbed Raleigh as deeply as it did any decent Jneer. Brilliance was nonconformal behavior. Nonconformance destabilized the status quo, and put unacceptable pressure on the terms and conditions of the social contract—

Oh, as though what he had done was any different?

But it was different, because this was his opponent. Therefore this case would have to fail. His opponent had to lose. The Jneer who could write such a case had every right to expect to prevail, and that was what made Raleigh as unhappy as he was about the fact that the case was beautifully done.

Even its flaws—and there had to be flaws, it was unthinkable that there not be flaws, the failure in the case was too obvious to overlook—even its flaws were beautifully done. Elegant. Almost insultingly so, an aesthetic of brilliantly understated oversight, a qualification in the test thrown out as obviously as if a demand for attention.

Look at me. I'm a lacuna. I'm much too obvious to have been a real mistake. I just was tucked in here to make sure that you were paying attention. It goes without saying that nobody would be thick-headed enough to honestly neglect to account for the failure of the human body to manufacture ascorbic acid in sufficient amounts to maintain the health of the population while alternative natural sources are being cultivated.

Wasn't that just a little bit more obvious than it needed to be?

Suddenly Raleigh realized that he was angry, frowning at the text, chewing his lip. His body was tense with it.

Too obvious: his antagonist was making fun of him, and by extension the entire process. And everyone who was a part of it. This was not the work of a sincere mind, this was the product of an intelligence with rather more appreciation of itself than respect for others. Making fun of the Comparisons in theory and in practice. Making a mockery of it all.

All right.

He knew what he had to do now.

He was going to take this case apart.

By the time he was finished with his analysis it would be clear to all concerned that arrogance and insincerity were not traits to be rewarded in Jneers.

Podile knocked at the thin rattan lattice of a door. "Aitch Harkover. Breakfast, Aitch, are you awake?"

She'd delivered all the other breakfasts; this was the last.

There had been no answer from Harkover the first two times she'd knocked today. After three delivery attempts she was not obliged to worry the issue any further. Harkover could just let her know when she was hungry. Harkover would anyway, so it wasn't as though Podile could be said to be shirking her responsibilities in any way.

That was the critical thing to remember, always.

It didn't matter what you actually did, so long as no Jneer could accuse you of slacking and make it stick.

She was ready to turn away and push her service cart down to the end of the hall, where her apartment was. There were signs of life within, though, rustling noises, and Podile decided to indulge her curiosity.

Maybe Harkover had actually been asleep. That was always funny; the Jneers would work themselves into a frenzy, staying up all night, and then when they collapsed they overslept and woke to panic and hysteria with their work still uncompleted and far fewer hours left to get it done.

Fun to watch.

A bit of petty revenge on the entire class, perhaps, but revenge nonetheless, and an Oway had to find gratification where she could find it.

She knocked again. "Aitch Harkover. It's your breakfast, Aitch. Are you going to want to eat? Lunch won't be up till twelve." Though she was expected to provide food on demand. There was little anyone could do about the quality of food that she provided in response to demand, and between-meal snacks were very seldom the least bit appetizing. Unless the Jneer was polite, or attractive. Raleigh Marquette, now, that was one toothsome bit of sculpture. Oh, yes. Indeed.

Fumbling sounds at the door, and then it opened.

"Already?" Harkover asked, and she looked genuinely surprised—not as though she was playing the absent-minded genius. That was so old it always amused Podile that anybody could be gauche enough to try it on. There was no accounting for taste, and especially no accounting for the execrable taste of the Jneers.

"Yes, Aitch. Last call. Another five minutes and your coffee will be stone cold." Was already merely warm. But that was just what Harkover got for not paying attention. Podile decided that she might, *might*, go for hot coffee if Harkover asked . . . but only if Harkover asked nicely. Otherwise she'd go for coffee, right enough, but what with one thing and another it was just bound to get cold again before it found its way to Harkover's room at last.

"M'sorry. This case has got me all tied up in knots." Harkover stood aside, holding the door for Podile to move through with her cart. Harkover looked tied up in knots, for a fact. It inspired a sudden charitable disposition of mind, in Podile.

"You and everybody else, Aitch." That was only fair. "There's more rice here if you'd like it, so-and-so down the hall doesn't eat rice. Anything in particular about this case?"

She was just making conversation as she unloaded the meal onto the work-table. Jneers liked Oways to take a respectful interest. Not too detailed an interest, no—of course Oways couldn't be expected to get too close to the technical engineering process. Podile thought of her daughter, her beautiful baby eight-year-old daughter, who everybody said had such an unusual flair for problem-solving; and swallowed back her bitterness. It was no more Aitch Harkover's fault than her own.

"Hard to explain," Harkover said, chewing on the corner of her lower lip. Her response seemed genuine, untainted by any false sense of superiority. Podile found herself warming to this young woman—not so much younger than she was, not really, but Jneers didn't grow up as quickly as Oways had to. Privilege delayed the maturation process. "It's a really solid case. Textbook, almost. There's got to be a flaw in there somewhere, I just know it, I sense it. And I can't find it. It's stressing my structurals all out of tolerance."

Of course there was a flaw in the case somewhere. No case was perfect; no case could be perfect—there was always going to be something. The measure of the Jneer's technical skill was more in coverage of mission-critical elements than in comprehensive coverage. She knew that; she ran the recorder in the evaluation sessions and Unresolved Issues. She knew how to listen. She had learned.

"If it's anything like the case you prepared, it's that much harder to read your evaluation case fresh." And the cases were all the same. Made it much easier for the proctors to do their piece of the job. "That's part of your challenge, if you don't mind me saying so. You just spent two days figuring out how you would solve a problem. Now you have to forget you ever saw anything like it before, and evaluate someone else's approach with fresh eyes."

Harkover was staring at the covered meal tray, her arms folded tensely across her modestly rounded breasts. Still frowning. "Yes, of course. It's just that I feel so inadequate. I thought I'd done a good job. I can think of so many things I missed, or got wrong, and I can't find anything in this case. Anything at all."

You are not alone, Podile wanted to say. *Nine out of ten Jneers go through their lives secretly convinced that they're frauds at heart, who are only avoiding detection and disgrace by luck. And every tenth Jneer is fooling herself.*

But she settled for pushing her cart to the door instead; she had no interest in offering anything like advice to this young woman. "You'll do just fine, Aitch, trust me on this. Everyone has nerves. It's a sign that your brain is working, nothing more."

Reassuring Remarks section four, title two, subhead seven. Harkover smiled, weakly it was true but with apparently genuine appreciation of the fact that Podile was trying to make her feel better. "Thanks for the rice, Podile. See you later."

So she would, indeed. At Unresolved Issues, among other places.

"Study well, Aitch Harkover."

Now that she'd offloaded all her breakfasts she could get back to her stores-and-receipts reconciliation.

If nobody bothered her for something to drink or rope to hang themselves, she might even be finished by lunchtime.

TWO

COMPARISONS

Hillbrane crossed the threshold of the assembly hall with a sense of relief that had more to do with sheer fatigue than a sense of having done well at her task. The case she had been given to analyze still upset her: it was quite other than she had expected, and the thoroughness with which it had been prepared called her entire understanding of the way in which one was expected to complete one's Comparisons into question.

She knew that she had done the right thing.

She could not have been mistaken.

It was beyond imagining to suppose that she had so utterly, so disastrously misinterpreted all that she had heard over the years.

And yet—

The case she had prepared had been presented with an obvious flaw, one she admired for its elegance. The case she had been given to analyze had had no such flaw. She could hardly convince herself that the deficiencies she had eventually unearthed were there by design, because by their nature they were minor and speculative.

There was no reason in the case to assume that the atmosphere at Waystation One would not successfully screen an adequate amount of ultraviolet radiation. Could she be sure that the failure she had cited to account for increased risk of skin cancer was an actual fault on the part of the Jneer who had prepared the case?

Before an actual analysis could be performed on site there was no reason to suspect a deficiency in trace minerals in the soil at Waystation One, so was the failure to account for the impact of a potential magnesium deficiency on the viability of sperm and ova really a mistake?

The assembly hall was full, they were all here. All of her class of Comparisons, and one of them was either far more intelligent than she, or she had become unaccountably stupid since her arrival.

Maybe there was something in the water, this water, the water in Stiknals. Maybe that was it. Hillbrane waved back in response to a cheerful salute from Raleigh, and found a place near the back to sit down and wait. It was over now. She'd done the best she could, not that it really meant so very much—no Jneer had ever been actually reclassified after Comparisons. Well, not in decades, if not longer.

It was over, it was done, and inside of a very few minutes it would all be academic. With luck she would be called early, and then she could get back to quarters early, to prepare for her evening of celebration. The moon was to be full over Stiknals tonight in celebration of the end of Comparisons. She was looking forward to counting Raleigh's ribs by the blue moonlight reflected off the water of the canal into the interior of the flower-boat she'd hired.

They were expensive, the flower-boats—flowers themselves being a luxury item, a resource-intensive drain on the soil and other systems for as little return to the ecosystem as they provided. Their hire had cost a not inconsiderable portion of the death benefit she had from her parents, but Hillbrane didn't care. This was her Comparisons. She would be a woman, tonight, and Raleigh would be with her.

Tomorrow night—Selchow.

She hadn't seen Axel, but she had the boat for three nights; who could say who would be her partner for the last night she would spend at Stiknals?

There were Oways coming into the assembly hall. Oways with red portfolios; as Hillbrane watched one of them went up to Raleigh where he sat talking to Minner, twirling the stem of his palm-leaf fan between the palms of his hands. It had begun. Unresolved Issues was formally under way.

Closing her eyes, she willed herself calm and wished herself confident—in her stomach she felt neither calm nor confident. She just didn't understand. She would soon, and it would all be all right. She just had to wait it out, then talk it out, and then walk out. That was all she had to do.

Someone coughed politely near her left shoulder and Hillbrane straightened up with a start, opening her eyes. An Oway. With a red portfolio.

"Aitch Harkover?" the Oway asked, glancing from her to the portfolio as if making a comparison. He had a picture of her there as well as her name, Hillbrane guessed. "If you'll come with me, Aitch."

Well.

It would be good to go in the first series and get it over with. It was silly of her to wish for five more minutes of preparation time. She'd wanted to get it over with, so she had no right to feel it was unfair of her to have to go first.

"Coming immediately." Ten of them all told would go to begin; there were five evaluation panels, and each would accommodate the presence of two Jneers. Ten at once. The assembly hall looked emptier already. Hillbrane followed her Oway guide into a windowless, airless corridor leading away from the hall, feeling nervous and fatalistically resigned at once.

This was it.

The Oway stopped in front of a numbered door and checked his portfolio; closed its cover with a muffled snap, and passed it to her. "Here you are, Aitch Harkover. They're waiting for you. Good luck."

Luck was not an issue.

She was a Jneer.

After a moment the Oway seemed to remember that he

should get the door for her. Bowing her head with a stubborn sort of nervous resolution Hillbrane went through.

The door closed behind her.

It was a fair-sized room; there was a chair for her, and across from her in front of another now-closed door from what Hillbrane guessed was a near-identical corridor sat another like chair for her antagonist. There was a long table at the front of the room, three proctor-evaluators already seated, and an Oway—Hillbrane thought she recognized her, was it Podile? The woman who brought meals to their rooms, at any rate.

All of these things Hillbrane noted as if automatically, while her attention returned to her antagonist even as she looked around her.

Raleigh.

The person on the other side of the room facing the panel, the person for whom the antagonist's chair had been provided, was Raleigh, on his feet and staring at her with an expression on his face that she could not quite interpret—horror? Distress? Disbelief?

She sat down, because it seemed the thing to do. There was a chair provided for her. Her knees felt wobbly.

How could it be that Raleigh had prepared that case?

She'd never realized that he had an intellect of such stature as to make his tie-flaw so hard to detect.

But why had he made his flaw so hard to find?

She was going to have to interrogate him in depth about the choice he'd made . . . and suddenly she wondered whether she wanted to play fingers-and-toes with him, at least until he'd set her mind at rest.

Her feeling of uneasiness had not abated. It had only gotten worse.

"Please be seated, Ar Marquette." The middle person on the panel—a nameplate identified her as Phipps—spoke a little sharply. Out of the corner of her eye Hillbrane saw Raleigh stumble backwards clumsily and sit down more as though he had suddenly felt a great pain in his belly than like a man merely taking a load off his feet. "We have some unresolved issues with your analysis of this case. Perhaps you'd be so good as to satisfy Aitch Harkover on the question of why you failed to take the potential for accelerated soil depletion into account when you built your stores-and-resources table for Schedule Six."

It was the most obvious error in the case, if there was any that could be said to be obvious. But Hillbrane was watching Raleigh now, and what she saw in his face only deepened her sense of confused unease into something that was all too much like panic. Because Raleigh was surprised.

He shouldn't be surprised.

He was supposed to present the appearance of being surprised—in order to preserve the polite fiction that he hadn't gamed the system by conspiring by common understanding to force a tie. A draw. Raleigh was doing a good job of looking surprised, but she knew Raleigh—knew him, and until two minutes ago had been looking forward to engaging in energetic and prolonged sex with him. She knew. She could tell.

Raleigh wasn't playing at being surprised.

The potential for accelerated soil depletion resulting from the resource-intensive crop rotation plan upon which he had based his stores-and-resources schedule had not been part of Raleigh's analysis.

And if that wasn't part of his analysis, then neither were the other things she'd found. Because they were even more technical than the potential in Raleigh's plan for exhausting the soil before the colony had fully developed more growth-base to replace spent fields with fertile ones.

"Well. Aitch Harkover." Raleigh spoke slowly. Hillbrane suspected that he was taking advantage of the almost lazy accent he'd inherited from his Tropical mother to cover the fact that he was thinking as quickly as he could. "I haven't provided a subsidiary schedule for soil depletion in my analysis because I believed the Agronomic Indices to be included in my case by reference. Since the scenarios are repeated there—and since the corrective actions are neither resource nor time intensive—I felt it went without saying that the Colony would monitor nitrogen and other trace metals in the soil. And inoculate accordingly, by organic or inorganic means, depending upon the severity of the situation and the time available before each plot came up seeded."

Yes, that was what she would have said, and she had struggled long and hard with herself before she'd reported it as a failure in the analysis at all. That wasn't the problem. The problem was that Raleigh was making it all up as he went along. She knew. She'd known Raleigh for most of her life. He hadn't thought about it. He was surprised to hear of the unresolved issue she had found in his analysis.

By inference that meant—

He hadn't done it on purpose.

But there hadn't been anything else, and so . . . and so he hadn't put any tie-generating flaw in his case on purpose.

Raleigh had meant to win, not to break even.

And when there was a tie, both parties left Comparisons as mediocre Jneers perhaps, but Jneers still. If there were no winners, there were no losers. Raleigh had meant to win, and had done his best to take advantage of tradition to do so—at her expense.

Because if he won, she lost; what happened then?

"Accepted?" the man marked Verdis asked, and Phipps and the third panel member—Aarons—nodded their heads in agreement. "So note in file, please, Podile. Aitch Hillbrane. Ar Marquette has questioned an apparent failure to take certain potentially lethal dietary deficiencies into account in your analysis. Explain to us please if you will why you made no allowance for the prevention, early detection, and treatment of ascorbic acid deficiency in the diet as you have established it in your Resources."

Hillbrane sat paralyzed, unable to respond.

This wasn't the way it was supposed to be. Raleigh was to have made an obvious error, a self-evident error, a clear and unambiguous oversight; and claim that he had simply not considered the alternatives. She was to make a similar statement, having also made a cringingly obvious error.

They both would have accepted a half-hearted rebuke from the panel, and they would both have gone forth as comrades, having stood the test of live fire together and demonstrated their willingness to put the aggregate good over individual glory.

Raleigh had upset all that.

Raleigh had betrayed her.

She would be damned before she would pretend to have forgotten, given this unprecedented development.

And yet if she said nothing—

"Baseline nutritional requirements are embedded in the Supplemental Provisions. That's what *he's* saying, isn't it?" No, this was no good. She could hear the childish spite too clearly in her own voice; and he had hit upon the strategy by luck. She had her pride. She would not stoop to subterfuge.

She, not Raleigh, was the betrayed party. She would maintain her honor, and she would be adult about it. "But that isn't why I made no such allowance. Nor can I believe that I must be any more explicit in front of a panel of Jneers."

Because everybody knew, and everybody maintained the tradition, or else it was not tradition after all. They would see through Raleigh. They had to.

What, oh what would happen if they didn't?

Raleigh sat stiff as a whittled post in his chair, listening to Hillbrane speak without quite making sense of the words.

Baseline nutritional requirements . . . isn't it?

Of all the misfortunes he had had to bear during his life— his flawed personal genetics, the failure of his parents to conform, the great unfairness visited upon him by nature and nurture alike when they had sent him forth into the competitive world of the Jneers with barely enough brain to get by—this was beyond imagining.

How could he have guessed it would be Hillbrane? Could anyone in the entire history of the entire Colony Fleet have had worse cursed luck?

The panel expected something more out of Hillbrane; she hadn't begun to answer the question. She had to know that. It had to be as obvious to her as it was to him. Hillbrane.

But it would be all right then, wouldn't it?

Because it was Hillbrane.

No such allowance. Hillbrane had the sharp edge that he lacked, the depth and breadth of intellect that he could only envy. She didn't even so much as notice, either. Hillbrane would be all right.

He was going to have to defend himself.

With Hillbrane as his opponent it was suddenly almost impossible that the panel would believe a genuine error had been made. Unless he could create at least a reasonable doubt in the proctors' minds, he would be left to himself in isolation, shunned as a man who had tried to take advantage of the system and had failed.

Jneers were expected to take advantage where they found it.

They were not expected to fail, because success was its own justification: failure by implication was an indictment written as well as signed in one's own hand.

Hillbrane had as much as told the panel that she'd only left the baseline nutritional requirements qualifications out in order to prove herself a willing coconspirator in the centuries-old plot to keep Jneers as Jneers from generation to generation.

He would have to convince them otherwise. Fortunately for him, her analysis of his case—the criticisms she had presented—gave him a clue, a hint, reminded him of details of her solution to the case.

"Ar Marquette?" Phipps asked, sounding a little dubious. Uncertain. Raleigh wondered, suddenly, what must be going on in the minds of the panel. Had something like this ever happened before? "Your reaction, please."

Very well. It was Hillbrane. By a miserable stroke of hateful luck she had been assigned as his antagonist. The unfortunate Jneer betrayed by trust into complacency, whose observance of the traditional mores of Comparisons Raleigh had intended to use to his own benefit, was the last person he would want made less accessible. At the same time, however, if there was anybody who could survive under any circumstances, it was Hillbrane. It was a fight to the death for him, and an inconvenience for her.

He had started this.

He would not back down. Not even if it was Hillbrane who opposed him.

"Aitch Harkover's defense does not convince. How are we to believe that so critical an issue was not merely passed over with insufficient thought, but ignored altogether? This is not the action of a careful planner. Whether there were other reasons for the failure or not, I would ask the panel if we can afford such niceties in the middle of a colonization effort."

He waited, trying not to pay attention to the furious tension in Hillbrane's body language, clearly perceptible even at some lengths' remove. He would prove he was a Jneer by main force of pressing the advantage at the expense of personal relationships, if not by virtue of superior analytical skills. Hillbrane's evident sense of personal betrayal must be turned to his advantage in the judge's minds, and he could best do that by maintaining his poise and pressing his advantage.

The panel was skeptical.

After a moment one of them spoke.

"How does Harkover's response differ materially from yours, Ar Marquette? She's right about the supplemental provisions, you know."

He knew. And the confusion had given him just enough time to come up with an answer. "The supplemental provisions as defined account for general nutritional maintenance under stress situations rather than a catastrophic failure in a major supplemental element. Reliance on supplemental provisions to avoid the development of ascorbic acid deficiency and other related diseases is only possible when excess quantities are available and consumed. At the same time—"

He was warming to this; he was good at thinking as he spoke.

The panel was relaxing before his very eyes, perhaps not obviously, but it was clear enough to a man whose future depended upon being duly convincing. He wouldn't think of Hillbrane. He couldn't afford to, he'd lose his train of thought.

"—at the same time, the consumption of the quantities of supplemental provisions necessary to obtain a therapeutic rather than prophylactic dose will create in itself a correspondingly severe hypervitaminosis condition as a result of taking in excess B-complex vitamins, with a corresponding danger of vitamin A overdose in extreme cases. Nor does the case so much as allow for sufficient excess supplemental provision to be carried with the party to serve as medication against ascorbic acid deficiency disease—scurvy—in the first place."

There was no reason for the case to have done so. Nobody would seriously interpret Hillbrane's case as complete; it would never have been implemented as written. The more convincing his argument, however, the more sharp the suspicion he could create on conscious and subconscious levels that Hillbrane's failure to account for protection against selected nutritional deficiencies had been an actual lapse of competence, rather than the bow to the demands of tradition that it had unquestionably been.

If she had meant to make the error for tradition's sake, would not her pride have demanded she make her incomplete solution at least viable?

This was good.

He had almost even convinced himself.

"To summarize. The supplemental provisions can't be responsibly used to cover for ascorbic acid deficiency disease because increasing the dose to a therapeutic level creates the conditions of B-complex vitamin toxicity. Nor does Aitch Harkover's case include provision for a sufficient quantity of the supplemental provisions to be used for such a purpose, if we assume some unknown solution to the toxicity issue for the sake of erring on the side of liberality in the analysis. One concludes therefore that Aitch Harkover neglected to account for these conditions because she failed to include the potential liabilities in her risk assessment."

That was good, "one concludes." It was nothing personal—and indeed it had been nothing personal, when he'd been reviewing the case. What would he have done had he suspected that it might be Hillbrane?

Nothing personal. Phipps raised one eyebrow at him, nodding approvingly. "Rebuttal, Aitch Harkover?"

He had not been offered the chance to argue back. The panel had accepted his explanation for the error that Hillbrane had found, as he had accepted Hillbrane's identification of what seemed to be an error. It was all but won. And he could explain everything; Hillbrane was sure to understand once he explained. She'd be impressed by his logic, even. Maybe. Surely. Maybe.

What difference did it make?

"Can't you see what's going on here? He's manipulating you!" Hillbrane's voice was resonant with outrage and disbelief. "Yes, I left it out. I meant to leave it out. Jneers have always left something out of Comparisons. It's part of our tradition. Can anybody believe a Jneer would be so stupid as to genuinely have forgotten to account for critical nutritional requirements?"

She shouldn't have said that.

Raleigh froze, in order to prevent himself from wincing at the tactical error she had made. If it had been anybody else he wouldn't have cared. But Brane—treasure of his heart, or of his loins anyway—he would have wished, he did wish, that somehow this Comparisons might be declared a draw after all. Almost. Almost he wished it.

It was impractical to wish that.

Hillbrane herself sat staring at the panel, breathing heavily; Raleigh knew she had realized her mistake. Prudently she declined to risk compounding it, and after a moment's silence, Phipps spoke.

"We will go into conference now, young people. It will be a few moments before we can release a resolution statement."

And leave him here alone to face Hillbrane, without even the Oway's presence to temper the full and flamboyant expression of Hillbrane's wrath? Because Podile had risen when the panel members had, and was following them out of the room.

This was good, Raleigh told himself firmly. He could talk it out with her. He could explain. She would have to accept his reasoning.

Yes, and a man could breathe without a tank in deep space's oxygen-rich atmosphere.

Doomed.

Raleigh heard the door close behind the Oway, Podile, with an emphatic crack of the latch, and braced himself to stand against the inevitable onslaught of Hillbrane's righteous fury.

Podile closed the door behind her, then leaned up against it, folding her arms defensively as she did so. There really wasn't a conference area per se on this side of the wall; it was a storage area—and not much used, to judge by the dust. But who could have predicted the need to confer? And there was no place to send Harkover and Marquette, unless they sent them into the halls on either side. There was traffic in the halls. It would make things awkward for them. Other Jneers would be curious and want explanations, and until the panel decided how to react to this situation, nobody really had one to offer.

The panel leader, Gresne Phipps, perched herself on the edge of a storage case and looked from face to face quizzically. "Well. What are we going to do? Podile, we'll be grateful for your input, but officially you just lost the power of hearing, right?"

Fair was fair. "Thank you, Gee Phipps. There must be something about this room that deprives people selectively of the power of speech as well. Or is it my imagination that I've never heard of anything like this happening before?"

Phipps shook her head. "Not in my experience. What about it, Jule?"

The others looked as blank as Phipps. "Never," Jay Verdis agreed. "We'd have heard. Unless it had been hushed up. No, we'd still have *heard.*"

"They couldn't have kept it a secret. I can't imagine," Tee Aarons admitted, with a shrug of his shoulders. "So what do we do with Marquette?"

This was wonderful fun. She could be grateful to that lovely young Marquette for making these people squirm; except that she had felt that Harkover was sincere, and Marquette was duplicitous. Still, Jneers didn't see duplicity as a problem, so long as it could be excused as operant behavior.

"Rehearse. Cases. You reviewed their cases. Tell me what you think," Phipps demanded. Verdis looked uncomfortable; Aarons spoke right out, though.

"It was a beautiful case. I don't believe I've ever seen one so well done. I'd be embarrassed to set my own Comparisons against it. And his analysis was masterful. Restrained, thoughtful, complete. Most people stop as soon as they hit an obvious error."

That was all it took, the one obvious error. Find that, and leave one for the other candidate to find, and you both went home Jneers, and your children—whether or not they had the analytical ability of an enzyme—would sit in the chair in school that could have been her daughter's, rejoice in the enriched learning experience that could have been her daughter's, grow up to perpetuate the trick and maintain the Jneer monopoly on the good life—which could have been her daughter's.

If it wasn't for the polite fiction. If the Jneers still cared, after all these years, about the guidance of the Fleet rather than ensuring that their own kind would be comfortable and secure in privilege while others could only dream of the life of a Jneer.

She had to stop thinking so loudly. Somebody would notice. They might even remember that she had a daughter; because the official attitude was to maintain a polite pretense that if she tested well, she might be rapt up into the ranks of the

Most High. It was just a pretense, like Comparisons, and everybody knew that—or everybody, everybody, everybody knew that no Jneer would ever dare actually try to do his best, because it might show a fellow Jneer at a disadvantage.

Now she was liking Marquette over Harkover again. But it was Verdis' turn to talk.

"I'm not completely clear on the details." They had each been responsible for reading multiple cases, after all. There was a point to be made there, though: Aarons remembered Marquette; Verdis had a hard time calling Harkover to mind.

Therefore Marquette actually was out of the ordinary, quite apart from the issue of the hole that wasn't there.

Hadn't Harkover herself indicated as much?

Not to put too much weight on what had been a casual exchange of commonplace expressions, but still . . .

Verdis went on. "If it's the one I'm thinking about, it was a very solid case. Thorough. She made unusual choices, now that I think about it, quite different actually from what one usually sees. But still. There was the problem with the nutritional profiles. It *could* have been an oversight."

It didn't do to get creative in Comparisons. There was a very fine line between deviance perceived as the sign of an independent mind and that perceived as evidence of a failure of method. If the fault in Harkover's case was determined to have been left deliberately, she might get away with independence of mind; but if she had given the impression of an undisciplined thinker, it was going to be all too easy to attribute the failure to lack of comprehensive scope and adequate grasp on her part.

"He was making that up about the Agronomic Indices, you know," Phipps said suddenly. "At least I'd bet on it. He didn't write that into the case on inclusions. He forgot. He left it out."

"It was a good save, though." Aaron's response held the hint of indulgence, of warm affection. This was not a good sign. Aarons should be on Harkover's side by rights. If he preferred Marquette over Harkover, she didn't have much chance of carrying her argument. "And he was right, the Agronomic Indices are included by reference. So if his case was implemented, the fault would be immaterial to the success of the mission."

"While Harkover's explanation really won't do." It was looking worse and worse for Harkover, because it was Phipps—senior member and swing vote—who was arguing against her now. "The mission commander can't afford to rely on baseline provisions. By the time she knows she's got a problem there's been progressive physical and mental deterioration going on for weeks, and that means higher potential for accidents and lower productivity across the board. Worst case, your whole staff is invalided out, and by that time everyone's too fogbrained to figure it out. No. If she meant to fall back on the baseline provisions she's miscalculated."

Harkover had lost.

So what?

So what if Harkover had lost?

All that they'd proved so far was that the Comparisons showed Marquette to be the better engineer.

There were plenty of worse engineers in the inventory, so what difference did it make?

Then Aarons said something odd, and Podile thought again.

"What do we do with Jneers who fail in Comparisons?"

She should remember, Podile admonished herself. These were Jneers she was listening to. She had been thinking of the situation as one in which Mechs had won in Comparisons. They were trying to decide how to handle a Jneer who had lost: quite a different matter.

"Three things could happen." From the sound of Phipps' voice she was thinking out loud. She was making this up as she went along, like Marquette a few minutes earlier. "One. We say this is a tie, setting aside any questions we might have about Harkover. No perturbation in the system. But Marquette's blown her out of the water, and he knows it, so it'll come out sooner or later."

Interesting that nobody seemed to have noticed the extra

dimension to the problem, the violation of the social contract. But maybe it was just that they were still trying to decide if such a violation had in fact occurred. She would fix the answer in her mind and wait.

"Two, we say that he's done a better case, he's a better Jneer. But if he did a better case than her, how do they rate against the others? What happens if somebody else gets a placement she wanted? What happens if she gets a placement, and somebody says, 'Well, I'm as good as Marquette, and Marquette's better than Harkover, so I should have Harkover's job if I want it?' A nightmare. We'd have to rank everybody. And there were reasons why we grew away from internal status-rankings over time."

Most of those reasons having to do with the unfortunate fact that bright parents did not unfailingly have bright children. Well-educated parents could almost always count on having well-educated children, but that was as far as it went, and that wasn't far enough for any parent. Parents naturally wanted their children to enjoy the same quality of life as they did. So the sons and daughters of strategy engineers had to be guaranteed the baseline status of a Jneer at the very least; and it all went downhill from there.

"Three," Podile said. They all stared at her; involved in their problem, they seemed to have forgotten she was there. But she knew where they were going, now. It would be better if the distasteful suggestion came from her, and they could get this over with. She had no intention of working overtime. She had an appointment with her daughter's mathematics teacher to discuss the steps she needed to take to get her baby into Enrichment.

"Three, you make up your minds that Marquette did a better case than Harkover because he's a Jneer and Harkover did an inferior case because she's not. You find a comfortable Oway staff position for her so she can't really complain, and after all it was her choice to try to game the system." Yes, that was just about what they had been thinking about. The relaxation and relief were almost tangible.

"An interesting approach, Podile." Phipps was the senior person here. Verdis and Aarons would take their cues from her. "It seems a somewhat drastic solution, though. Harkover built a good case, didn't she? Do we really have no use whatever for a Jneer with her level of ability?"

They had already downgraded Harkover's level of ability in their minds. Suddenly Podile was sorry that she was here. Not because of what she had said, but because these Jneers—these three Jneers, who were going to have to decide Harkover's fate among them—would not be so rude as to suggest that there was anything undesirable about being an Oway.   Not to her face. And that would mean less emphasis on the emotional impact, the punitive effect of plucking Harkover out of the midst of Jneers and sending her into the support ranks instead.

Verdis coughed. "Well. In practical terms. We don't have the resources to reconstruct the system right this minute, and Marquette's won. I think we all know that whatever the motives might have been, his case is more complete than hers is."

That much was true. Safe to agree upon. Aarons seemed reluctant—perhaps sensitive to the injustice of Harkover's now all but certain fate. But the line of argument was simple and persuasive, and once you got Jneers focused on a line of reasoning it was frequently all but impossible to perturb their course—so straight and true it was. Rigid, and unbending. It was not their fault. It was the way they had been raised, and that meant she was complicit by implication, because Oways raised Jneers.

"She only did what we all did." Aaron managed a mild protest at last. "Does she deserve to be labeled a loser for conforming to the norm?"

But it was a weak protest, and already half-hearted. The system had been put in place to avoid ranking Jneers against one another. If Harkover's case was acknowledged to be adequate, just not as complete as that which Marquette had provided, then the specter of exhaustive rank-ordering exercises was raised just at a time when the Fleet could least afford to divert any of its energy from the task that faced it—the antic-ipated arrival at Waystation One, the constitution of the first colony, and the arrangements to be made to ensure that the colony would survive.

Because once the Colony Fleet passed Waystation One there would be no further physical contact with the colony. Only limited communication would be possible, and messages could provide no comfort when there was no chance of turning the Fleet back to rescue the colonists if something went wrong without abandoning the entire mission—an unthinkable be-trayal of the world that had sent them out, then fallen silent.

There was not enough motive power available to brake the Fleet and then restart it, whether forward or back. They could not betray the Founders. They were the last, the best, the only hope. There had been no contact of any kind with the system of origin that had sent them for more than three hundred years.

Harkover would be sacrificed.

Fleet couldn't afford to reevaluate its Comparisons at this crucial juncture. Therefore Harkover was not to have submit-ted a case that was merely less complete than that of Mar-quette. Harkover was to have submitted a case that had actually failed. She was not to be allowed to continue as a Jneer. She would be an Oway, now, and it was hard and unfair, but life was hard and unfair for Oways.

"It's too big a hole." Phipps' voice was resonant with de-termination and finality. "The risks to success of the case mis-sion with that left out are too great. It isn't a mistake. It's a failure. Hard to accept, I know. But there it is. If a colony went out on her case it would fail, and if a colony went out on his case it would at least have a very good chance of catch-ing the problems she identified in time to make an adequate correction."

Podile supposed there was a certain amount of justice to that, after all.

It was still unfair.

But knowing the ways Jneers interpreted events, Podile

knew that Harkover had no future left among them regardless of the proctors' actual decision; so it was better this way, in the end.

The door closed behind the Oway secretary—Podile—and Hillbrane twisted herself where she sat to glare at Raleigh with as much venom as she could manage.

"What do you think you're *doing*?"

His nerve seemed to have deserted him with the panel. He was pale, and fearfully defensive.

"Brane. Come on. I didn't know. How could I know? If I'd only known. It's not my fault."

Not his fault? How in the name of the Mission could he sit there and say that it wasn't his fault, with a straight face?

"You cheated, Raleigh, I never would have guessed. You cheated. How could you? Can't you see what you've done?"

It had been unpleasant to discover that Raleigh had been her antagonist in the first place. It had been horrifying to realize what he'd done, terrifying to perceive that the panel didn't seem to grasp the depth of his treachery. All of that emotion demanded an outlet. Raleigh clearly deserved to be the target of her fury now—anger sharpened with terror that she dared not acknowledge to herself.

Raleigh had stiffened in his chair, clearly affronted. The skin over his cheekbones blotched a dull red sun-burnt color when he got mad. "I'm not the one who cheated, Brane. I did my case. I did the best case I knew how, and you're telling me that *I* cheated?"

Oh, he infuriated her. "Cheated. Common understanding, you knew what was expected, Raleigh. What were you trying to do? What did you think you were going to accomplish?"

What could be worth the public scorn that would be his once this came out?

She knew.

He'd always been insecure about his position.

"It's not like *you're* in any danger." Raleigh's resentful response was indirect but conclusive. He would know she knew. "You're right up there, Brane, you always have been. But me—they're not suggesting all the Jneers in the right age group join First Colony, Brane, only most of us. Do you know what's going to happen to the ones who stay with Fleet? You'd have done the same in my place. Admit it. Be fair."

Oddly enough she could see his point. Waystation One was an achievable goal, one they would reach in a matter of some months now. The founders of the Fleet had mandated the composition of the First Colony, true enough, but the population of the Colony Fleet had not grown as much as the Founders had predicted. The entire issue of the First Colony had to be revisited in light of the current realities.

Nobody with an ounce of self-interest would willingly forgo the immediate opportunity presented by Waystation One in favor of the chance their descendents would be alive to colonize Waystations Two, and Three, and Four.

Most of the Mechs would have to, but that was not a Jneer's problem. Somebody did have to continue to the other colony worlds; with the survival of the species at stake, it would be madness to risk the entire population on one uncertain colonization attempt. It was a terrible choice to have to make. Could she blame Raleigh for wanting the same chance that she confidently assumed for herself?

"I didn't have to cheat to pass Comparisons." None of it changed the emotional impact of the betrayal, though. And the cold tone of voice in which he had made his rebuttal, that couldn't have been just gamesmanship. "You shouldn't have to. If you really felt you had to cheat to pass—maybe you're right, Raleigh. Maybe cheating is the only way you could pass."

No, he'd meant to press the advantage. Even knowing that his duplicity would be obvious, Raleigh had willingly done his best to make himself look good at her expense. The choice he'd made to cheat on Comparisons was one thing; she could almost understand that, and to understand was to forgive for a Jneer.

But the choice he'd made just now to cut her down, herself, personally and individually, Hillbrane Harkover, simply in order to secure his position—that was incomprehensible. And therefore necessarily unforgivable.

"It's easy for you to be superior, Harkover." Raleigh's own frustration—evident in the sneer he put into her last name, he almost never called her that, and only when he was really angry—seemed to have the effect of making him sullen. He was staring at the far wall as he spoke now, refusing to so much as look at her. "You'll do all right any way it goes. You always do all right. You have no idea what it feels like. It's a failure in empathy on your part."

It was almost more than she could endure.

He had cheated and he had lied, he had taken advantage of the dutiful observance of every other Jneer of the centuries-old communal expectations, he had done his best to pull her down even knowing finally that it was a friend he had betrayed—and her righteous indignation was a failure on *her* part?

A sound at the far end of the room broke the waiting stillness as Hillbrane struggled for what she could possibly say to that.

The panel was returning.

The Oway Podile opened the door and held it open, and the three Jneer judges on whom her fate depended filed back into the room.

They sat down. The middle panel member, Phipps, the speaker, folded her hands and looked from Hillbrane to Raleigh, and then back again.

"Ar Marquette," she said. "Aitch Harkover. You present us with an anomaly situation, one for which there is little precedent. I'd like you both to know that we have been struggling with this."

But not for very long. What was there to struggle with? She'd done what she'd been expected to. Raleigh had not. He was in the wrong. There was no question about it.

"Aitch Harkover. We fully sympathize with your feeling

that the failure in your case is a matter of administration only, and value-neutral over the critical term. We can't see it your way. The failure is not value-neutral, the failure is critical, and therefore we have reluctantly concluded that your case fails to stand up in comparison. Ar Marquette."

Hillbrane stared, while the ground dropped into the maintenance tunnels and took her stomach with it.

Failure. Critical. Reluctantly concluded. The words caught against sharp protests in Hillbrane's mind and hung there, resonating. What had Phipps said? How could she have said such a thing?

What did it mean?

"Ar Marquette, we find that your case is superior in comparison to that prepared by Aitch Harkover. We counsel you to note carefully the issues Aitch Harkover has raised and take appropriate measures to guarantee against a possible recurrence of similar oversights in future. We recommend you review the index cases on file in common library systems for that purpose."

And for a moment Hillbrane relaxed, her relief more huge and tremendous than she ever could have believed. It was all right. This was the way it was supposed to be, this was the way it was supposed to work out. Counsel. Avoid future repetitions. Review the index cases, and go forth an Engineer.

But they hadn't said anything like that to her.

"Thank you," Raleigh said, and he sounded rattled. Why should he sound upset? She was the one who had been betrayed. "I deeply appreciate your flexibility. If I may be excused I'll go now, and—"

The frustration and the fury built past the point of prudent suppression. This could not be allowed to happen. Raleigh was not going to walk out of here as though nothing had happened. She owed it to herself not to let him get away with this.

"You can't mean to tell me that I'm wrong."

Her interruption cut Raleigh off in mid-movement as he started to stand up. He froze, then slowly subsided into his chair again as Hillbrane loosed her wrath.

"With all due respect. You're charged with evaluating Comparisons. You must see what he's done. Do you really mean to endorse this underhanded behavior on Marquette's part? If he'd done his case like an honest Jneer, it sure as entropy wouldn't be better than mine. If I'd done what he did, you should all be able to tell that it would still be better than Marquette's. How can you send him out a Jneer, and not me?"

Was that what they were going to do?

Really?

What else was she to make of what she'd heard?

Nobody spoke.

The stillness wore on Hillbrane like an ever-increasing weight that demanded words to lift its awful bulk away from off her chest so she could breathe. Nobody spoke; until in desperation Hillbrane asked the question that lay at the heart of the matter.

"What do you propose to do with me?"

She could hear sobs and anguish in her voice, and clenched her fists until her hands whitened. Being very angry made her cry. It was humiliating. If it was possible to hate Raleigh even more than she already had begun to, she hated him more right now for causing her the added loss of face inevitably associated with involuntary displays of emotion in public.

"Well. Aitch Harkover." Phipps rubbed at the fingers of one hand with a gesture seemingly expressive of discomfort before raising her eyes to look at Hillbrane again. Who was Phipps to sit in judgment, anyway? Hillbrane meant to find out. She would be lodging a very strongly worded protest with the highest possible authority, and she would have names and specifics when she did so—so that the administration would not be able to protect itself beneath a veil of anonymity. Podile was there. Podile would tell her everything she needed to know.

"A suitable position will be identified for you in a related field of endeavor. We will make every effort to see you well placed out of respect for your unusual situation. The Oways are as mission-critical as Jneers, after all. You won't suffer for your move into a parallel career path."

An Oway.

They meant to deny her her heritage and her place in the forefront of her Fleet. An Oway. They meant to deprive her of her birthright as a Jneer, for no better cause than that Raleigh had cheated.

"I can't believe this." There was no sense in even trying to conceal her contempt. Let the panel squirm. If her language made them uncomfortable, fine, they should be uncomfortable. What they proposed to do violated all the laws of justice and common sense, never mind common decency. Raleigh had cheated. How could they suggest for one moment that she be the one to suffer for it?

No, she wasn't going to let this pass. "Marquette commits a blatant act of nonconformancy, and based on his deviance to norms you deny my abilities as a Jneer? Let's analyze this a little more thoroughly than you seem to have done. In what way does disregard for our tradition bear upon *his* ability, *his* qualifications as a Jneer?"

One of the other panel members raised a dismissive hand, scowling angrily. "One might as well ask the obverse question. What does Ar Marquette's observance or disregard have to do with your qualifications? You're angry and you're upset, we can understand that. Sympathize. But there's no excuse for irrational argument, Harkover."

This wasn't going the way it was supposed to. The air around her seemed to have thickened up, somehow; she could hardly breathe, and the sound of her own voice was garbled and muffled in her ears. "Irrational, is it? Well. If it's true, that my case fails. If my reaction to being told so is to propose an irrational argument, then it does a disservice to the Fleet to buy me off with a sinecure as an Oway. Are you sure the Mechs isn't the correct choice?"

There. That would do it, if nothing would. No Oway could approach her case treatment, let alone a Mech. By reducing their analysis to its absurd conclusion she would be able to show them the flaw in their premise. They would realize that if the Mechs was not the right answer then neither was the Oways, and proceed from there to the understanding that they had no choice but to declare her Jneer after all. She would have vindication.

The panel members exchanged glances, clearly stunned by the persuasive force of her argument. Out of the corner of her eye Hillbrane could see Raleigh slumping where he sat, evidently in fearful anticipation of what would become of him when his behavior became common knowledge. There was no way for him to stop her from publishing what he had done. What he had tried to do. He would be forced off the Noun Ships entirely, a traveling Ponics engineer for the rest of his life.

"Good point," Phipps said, and brought all of Hillbrane's fantasies of vengeance to an unpleasantly abrupt halt. "The case demonstrates very strong mechanical skills and considerations. We wouldn't have suggested it, Harkover, but I'm glad you're able to see it so clearly. You could certainly make an invaluable contribution as a Mech, in savings to demands on engineering resources alone."

No, she had to laugh. This had become absurd, surreal. "Yes. Of course. My Jneer education, after all. Think of all the minor problems I'll be able to handle without calling any real Jneers into it. Unless it's really technical, of course, beyond my capability, then we'll still need outside help. Maybe Raleigh and I will be able to work together."

She hadn't heard anything so completely ludicrous for as long as she could remember. Unfortunately nobody else was laughing.

"I'm surprised you're willing to consider such a thing, Harkover. But it does you a great deal of credit. Very well, it's agreed, you'll transfer to the Mechs as soon as we can arrange transport. There isn't any family? Well. Less complicated, then, all to the good."

Phipps pushed herself away from the table as she spoke, angling herself up from her chair with both hands on the arm rests. This could not be happening, Hillbrane told herself. No. She was having a nightmare. This was a stress-dream.

She could not believe she could have imagined so bizarre a series of bad turns, not even in the worst conceivable nightmares.

The panel filed up the center of the room and turned behind Hillbrane to leave by the door she'd used to come in. Podile opened the door to give them passage, and then she spoke.

"I'd suggest you return to quarters, Aitch Harkover. You'll want to pack. Excuse me."

Then Podile went away as well, and Hillbrane was alone again with Raleigh.

What had Podile just said? She'd want to pack? Jneers never packed. Oways did that for them. Jneers had more valuable things to do with their time, that was why there were Oways in the first place.

But she, she was to be sent to the Mechs, and why would an Oway stoop to packing for a Mech—even a Mech who had been a Jneer until just now?

Raleigh cleared his throat.

Hillbrane turned her head slowly to look at him. It was an enormous effort to move a muscle. The weight of her head upon her shoulders was astonishing. What had happened here?

What was to become of her?

"I'm supposing this means our date is cancelled?" Raleigh asked, with a feeble grin.

He was trying to lighten the atmosphere. She knew it. Still she could only stare. She could not even speak, made dumb by shock.

"Brane—"

But it was no good, and Raleigh appeared to realize that at last. He quit the room by the door opposite hers, leaving her alone. Hillbrane sat frozen in her place and trembled uncontrollably with the awful accumulation of words both unspoken and unspeakable until the next Jneer came under escort to stand Comparisons, and needed the chair.

THREE
TRANSIT

When Hillbrane next took thought for where she was, it was sunset on the Grand Canal of Stiknals, and the flower-boats were leaving. How she had come to be where she was she could not call to mind; all she could guess was that the primitive portion of her brain had driven her to the one place of sure refuge for her on all of Subtropical: the flower-boat she had hired for her private celebration of the end of Comparisons.

Comparisons were ended, right enough. Herself with them.

How could she begin to understand the enormity of the disaster which had befallen her?

Looking around her with a stunned sort of amazement, slowly reawakening to a sense of time and place, Hillbrane took stock.

She was sitting cross-legged on the reedmat platform of the guest salon on a flower-boat. The bamboo shutters that shielded the gauze wall panels from the heat of the midday sun had been tied up on two sides; someone was out there now raising the panels at the front of the salon.

Hillbrane could see out over the stern of the boat, but nobody would be able to see in unless the lights inside the salon were brightly lit. They were not lit at all now, unneeded during the daytime, and at night would normally be only bright enough to permit those inside sufficient light to appreciate what they saw and did without fear of betraying those same sights and activities to the outside world.

Evening.

There was a freshening breeze on the canal, and the voice of happy revelers mingled with the almost metallic report of bamboo cleats clattering upon themselves, flower-boats putting away from the docks, loading ramps being taken up. The boat rocked gently, very gently, beneath her where she sat; the parade of the flower-boats had begun, then, and soon the rising moon would reveal a caravan of lights and music on the Grand Canal making its serpentine way into the labyrinthine reserve of Stiknals' renowned aquatic gardens.

Hillbrane remembered the gardens.

The entire fleet of flower-boats could get lost in it; a large part of the allure of the experience was the sense of being alone, all alone, for though one might vaguely hear a voice raised in laughter in the night the heavy growth of vegetation muffled even nearby words till they seemed far, far away. The staff and crew on the flower-boats made a point of furthering the illusion; the servers who came in to set and take away food wore dark gray clothing, never made a sound, and only made eye contact by occasional accident unless spoken to directly. The music never became loud enough to intrude itself upon one's consciousness unless one paused to listen for it. For all intents and purposes she was alone, and maybe—she thought, dully—maybe that was the best choice she could have made. Quiet time. Time to herself, to think.

Her boat slipped cable and swung slowly out into mid-canal, joining the train. As it pulled away Hillbrane could see by the red-tinged rays of the fading sun that most of the flower boats were still delayed at the docks; she was among the first of the boats to get away. They'd get a good place, deep within the gardens.

She had intended to share this with Raleigh—

But when she examined that thought she found a leaden emptiness in her heart, rather than a sharp pang. Yes, she had planned to spend the time with Raleigh. That had been before.

Things were too different now. Should she not turn the boat back to the docks, pay the cancellation fee, go back to her room at the academy?

She had to pack, after all.

Yet why should she deny herself this treat, this last excursion, and hasten into exile? It was expensive, yes, but what good would credit do her among the Mechs? What was there to spend it on once one left the Noun Ships? Produce from the Noun Ships was exported, true enough, but as luxury goods at luxury prices. It would be better to drink ersatz coffee than pay inflated prices for the tea she'd had for the asking every day of her life. Saving up her credits so that she could afford tea would only be a constant reminder of her reduced condition.

No, she would take her cruise alone. The administration would probably have her out of here within the day; it was certainly how she would have suggested managing it, if she had been asked.

Presented with the case.

The warm breeze of evening filtered through the gauze walls of the guest salon, bringing a fragrance of lotus and sandalwood with it. The mesh on the gauze was just tight enough to cut the force of any wind to a gentle caress, and there were smokepots on the foredeck—behind the solid wall at her back—to mask the unpleasant stench of rotting vegetation. One of the crew had come in with warm scented towels and hot tea, seven different kinds of cold pickles in seven differently sized and shaped ceramic dishes. She had barely noticed, until the steamy fragrance of the jasmine that scented the towels caught her attention.

Slowly she unfolded her legs, leaning forward to pick up a hot rolled scented towel. Slowly she pressed the yielding texture of the toweling to her face, willing the unpleasant stress of the long day out of her pores to be wiped away from her skin.

The music had begun to play. Night came down suddenly in Stiknals, in order to preserve the effect of life near the equator of a given world; it was gray and purple upon the water, and the flower-boats that passed them and they passed were ghostly and ethereally beautiful with white blossoms in the deepening dusk. Hillbrane watched the traffic on the river float by, slow and silent, mesmerized.

She drank some tea.

Someone had opened the roof up now; she could see the sky. The moon would be rising soon.

Why had she insisted she be a Jneer or nothing?

Oways at least could live in Stiknals, work in Stiknals, even afford a flower-boat for very special occasions.

Was that so bad?

She hadn't been thinking.

The masseuse would be coming in; Hillbrane felt sure that the captain of the flower-boat would have cancelled the extra masseuse when only one passenger came on board, regardless of previous expectations. She needed to get washed before the masseuse came: it was an important part of the relaxation process.

Headroom on the flower-boats being at a premium, Hillbrane sat on her heels beneath the low showerhead to soap and rinse her skin; not before time, either, because the masseuse knocked on the decking outside the gauze wall and came through the screen-door not five minutes after Hillbrane came out of the small bath to stretch at length upon the futon and wait for her.

What would she have done differently, after all, had she been—who was it—Phipps?

Raleigh had violated the social contract. If it came out, it would mean the destabilization of an entire culture. Society was under enough stress already as Waystation One loomed ever larger in peoples' thoughts. In order to avoid depriving Jneers and Oways of certainties developed over centuries about what their roles were, what people could expect in return for what personal sacrifices, the establishment was all but forced to behave as though Raleigh had not cheated—as though she had genuinely failed, instead.

The masseuse's strong warm hands worked the long muscles in her back again, and again, and again before coaxing the tension out of her neck and shoulders. Hillbrane welcomed the crackling feeling in her neck as muscles gave up their fierce clenched energies and relaxed. She had let herself get angry because she'd been taken by surprise. There had been no reason for her to reject the panel's offer of Oway status out of hand, as she had done.

She should go back to the panel and apologize. It would be humiliating, but they would understand. She would ask to be allowed to accept an Oway slot rather than go down among the Mechs, and they would almost certainly be more than willing to oblige. Nobody really wanted to send her to the Mechs, Raleigh himself least of all.

Then once the Comparisons were over and the Fleet's attention focused entirely upon Waystation One, she could approach the panel for reconsideration. She had an advantage; she would offer to prepare a plausible cover story for why she had failed, truly failed, her Comparisons, only to show herself a qualified Jneer after all in some subsequent test.

The masseuse left. Hillbrane lay in the shadowy luxury of the guest cabin enjoying the euphoria a massage always brought, feelings sharpened and intensified by her relief in realizing that she didn't have to lose this privileged life after all.

She had merely overreacted, and let emotion cloud her judgment and dictate her words. If that wasn't Mech behavior—she told herself, with a wry grin at her own earlier emotional extravagance—what was?

Now that she'd settled her mind, she could relax and enjoy the pleasures of a flower-boat under a full moon, and if she was by herself—well, solitude was salutary, after a day of such emotional upsets as she'd had. She ate her dinner with a good appetite, then lay back on the padded sleeping-bench to drink warm fragrant rice wine and watch the moon through the lush vegetation, listening to music, at peace with herself. Calm. In control once again.

It would be all right.

And—once it had all been sorted out—wouldn't she make Raleigh pay, for what he'd put her through?

The sound of half-wild monkeys screaming in the trees woke Hillbrane before the flower-boat had left its overnight mooring. The sun had risen, the sky was clear and bright, but it was too early yet to have warmed up to the point at which the heat would be unpleasant. The cabin attendant brought breakfast in; Hillbrane drank her morning tea with tamarind and turbinado sugar, alone in the world. Alone in an uninhabited Eden of warm slow-moving rivers, luxuriant foliage, the cries of unseen birds declaring their dominion over an Earth yet untouched by hominid hands. Waystation One.

Waystation One might offer such luxury, in fact, as Stiknals preserved the illusion of a semitropical river delta. It was foolish of her to reject her chance at Waystation One, but she had come to her senses in time. She would go straight to the administration from the docks and explain herself to them.

The flower-boat started to move as she finished her pastry, gliding almost noiselessly out of whatever backwater or lagoon they'd spent the night in to join the parade back to Stiknals docks. The party hadn't stopped on more than one of them. Was it not being seen that made people think they could not be heard? Having no conversational partner to distract her, Hillbrane listened to the people around her with wry amusement.

The boat that she was on passed one in which people were still drunk, and clearly had not slept; they were utterly incoherent under the combined influence of liquor and lack of sleep. Then they passed one silent but for snoring; in another a couple were apparently engaged in a subdued sort of a food fight. Finding a place in line, her boat swung in behind one of the larger party boats; the people on that one were playing a game of one-upsmanship, very traditional for Jneers, and Hillbrane soaked it all in with keen amusement.

No, I'll be your boss. And—and Mansin will be, yes, rolls-keeper—

She was conscious of a guilty sense of eavesdropping. It didn't make the listening less pleasant, though; rather the more so.

Well, Barcol, I'd rather be rolls-keeper than Structures. And you're going to Structures. You know you are.

Maybe she should make a sound, Hillbrane thought. Maybe she would cough, or start singing. Still, what harm did it do for her to overhear them? It wasn't as if secrets were being shared. It wasn't as if everyone on the canal couldn't hear everything they said in the early morning atmosphere.

There's nothing wrong with Structures. Yes, you. My mother was in Structures. It's a clear sight better than going down to the Mechs.

A momentary silence; Hillbrane froze, though nobody could see her. Going down to the Mechs? What kind of a remark was that to make? She couldn't pick up an explanation out of the confused babble of voices that came up, after the shock had apparently worn off. Then someone raised her voice, and it was all too clear.

Lived as Jneer all her life, can you believe it? I heard she was well thought of. Cheating, no doubt, it's the only explanation. You can't cheat in Comparisons, though. She failed. She's gone. First time it's happened in nearly a hundred years, from what I heard.

They were talking about her.

Hillbrane knew it, and yet could hardly believe that it was true, the way in which the facts were being interpreted was so different than the truth of the matter.

There was a reply from the other ship, but it was muffled and indistinct—as though the man who spoke had his back to Hillbrane's boat. It was easy enough to guess the comment from the response. It was too easy.

Someone from Temperate. Harkover. Berand? No. Hillbrane. Hillbrane Harkover, that's the name. Would you believe she tried to issue an ultimatum? Mech, all right.

It was so frustrating, hearing only parts of the conversation. Hillbrane could catch a few phrases out of what was spoken next, but only a few.

Mistake. All her life. Likely. Way she was raised, what's the difference?

There was that one clear voice again, though, and while Hillbrane didn't recognize the speaker by sound alone, she was rapidly developing a very strong feeling about the woman. Not a friendly feeling, either.

Sidle, you can't make a salad out of sawdust. It's not just education that makes the difference between Mechs and Oways and Jneers. This is just proof. All of the advantages, and a Mech after all. Imagine. We might have ended up working with her, and not being able to figure out what was wrong.

And another boat pulled in between Hillbrane's boat and the party boat they had been following. It was too late. The damage had been done. Hillbrane's plans for staying on as an Oway and leveraging herself back into the Jneers from that advantageous position crumbled like the flakes of crisp butter-pastry in her hand. She didn't have a chance. The story was already out; the Oway—Podile—must have gossiped about it.

Scandal traveled faster than any known force in the universe.

Why hadn't she guessed how it was going to be?

A Jneer had failed Comparisons. A Jneer was to be cast out, deprived of status. It was a personal disaster for Hillbrane, but for other Jneers it was an unsettling event. Could they have failed Comparisons? Were they at risk? Might they wake up one morning and find themselves imprisoned within the stark walls and narrow corridors of a Mech ship?

Only if it had really been a Jneer, a genuine Jneer, who had failed.

If the person who had failed had been a Mech all along, there was much less of a problem. It wasn't necessary for Hillbrane to be a literal Mech; no, simply never really up to baseline Jneer standards would do. People would defend themselves against their own uncertainty, their own fears of inadequacy by rationalizing the situation. The only rational explanation was that she had well and truly failed, because she simply didn't have the intellectual capabilities necessary to compete.

It was clearly impossible to expect to be quietly readmitted to her proper place until the fear had died down.

She would have to go down among the Mechs, and she would have to stay there for longer than she liked to think, because winning back was going to be much more difficult once she had left the Noun Ships. Mere presence was seven points of entitlement, after all.

Oddly enough she was not so terrified as she had been yesterday of that prospect. She had a plan, now, general though it was.

She would go down amongst the Mechs.

But she'd be back.

It had been the worst night of Raleigh's life, so he was glad when the Oway came to call him before the dean. He'd been expecting trouble, and he didn't care. It didn't matter. Nothing mattered. He had won. His position was secure.

What good was a secure position without Hillbrane?

It had been because of her all along. Because he had been desperate to be sure that he would be there with her. Because he knew that she was the one he wanted to share his life with—Brane—he hadn't even realized it until now, but it had all been for Brane. And by the bitter irony of cruel Fate only now that it was too late did he understand.

There was nothing that he could have done differently, though, even had he known. The loads had been stacked against him from the start. For all his life, really; this was no different than the unkind tricks that life had been playing on him ever since he had been old enough to realize that he was being duped and manipulated and done out of what was his by right by people who thought they were smarter than he was.

Hillbrane . . .

If Brane wasn't his by right, who had a better claim to her? And now Hillbrane was gone. Her room was empty. The color had gone out of his life, and the Oway who stood in the doorway waiting for him was not Podile and had no sensitivity. No empathy. No heart.

"The dean would like to see you," the Oway said again. "Quite urgent, Ar Marquette. I wouldn't want to keep the dean waiting, shall we go?"

Disagreeable fellow. Oways should always be women. The men never seemed to quite understand how important it was to provide proper support. Raleigh ignored him, standing in front of the bathroom mirror combing his hair and examining his image critically. He looked awful: pasty face, gray lips, rings beneath his eyes. Anyone could tell by looking at him how serious a shock he had sustained.

"Ar *Marquette*."

Raleigh was ready, now. He ambled to the doorway, and his weary stumble was unfeigned. "All right, all right. We can go now." Sometimes you just had to remind Oways, that was all. Sometimes they forgot that the only reason they enjoyed the privileges of the Noun Ships was because they were useful to Jneers. Nor was any Oway—attempting to abrogate the dean's authority or not—ever to tell a Jneer, any Jneer, what to do.

It was early, Raleigh noticed. No one seemed to be up and about in the dormitory. Many of his classmates had gone out for parties, true, and probably just weren't back yet. He'd gone out himself and partied. No, he hadn't partied; he'd drunk, but he hadn't seemed to be able to get drunk, and so he had come back. Hillbrane's room had been empty. All of her things were gone.

It was all so unbelievably unfair.

The dean was eating breakfast at her desk, wearing purple flowers in her hair this time. She beckoned him in—her mouth being full of scrambled egg—and the Oway closed the door; they were alone.

She drank some tea, as if to clear her throat.

"So. Ar Marquette. May I congratulate you on a superb case."

If she insisted. Raleigh raised his eyebrows and wondered if he looked as dull-spirited as he felt. "Thank you. Very kind." There was a hint of a slurring sound there, and Raleigh frowned to hear it. He would have to enunciate carefully. He wasn't drunk; he didn't want anyone getting the mistaken impression that he was.

The dean daubed at her mouth quickly with a cloth napkin before pushing herself away from her desk and standing up. "At the same time, you must know that the story is all over Stiknals this morning. It'll be all over the Noun Ships in five days." That was how long it took to get from Subtropical to the furthest of the other Noun Ships. Raleigh understood.

"I'm sorry it had to be that way." And he meant it. How many of the Jneers here in Comparisons would think things through and come to a conclusion? Would any of them not? He hadn't taken gossip into account in his planning; he'd assumed that the administration would keep the incident close as a matter of principle. He'd known that he might well suffer reprisals for his daring act of independence, but had not guessed that the administration might let the secret slip, in order to effect them.

The dean waved off his expression of regret. "Well. People will talk. There was an Oway present. There's the fact of it to be considered, still, and so I'm going to ask for your cooperation."

To do what?

He waited, trying to look respectful—devastated at the unexpected failure of a friend—and dignified by intellect, all at once. He didn't think she needed any help from him. She knew where she was going.

"The job does need doing. Also, if we can get you away for a few months people will forget how interested they were in the story, and all you're likely to get will be the occasional, 'Hey, aren't you the one . . . ' "? She'd picked up a portfolio

from the corner of her desk and leafed through it absentmindedly as she spoke. She somehow hadn't quite yet come out
and actually said what she had in mind. Raleigh was too genuinely tired to feel like playing guessing games with his own
immediate future.

"I'm sorry, I don't understand. What are you talking about?"

Closing the portfolio with an emphatic snap, the dean tossed
it at Raleigh, who only barely caught it. His reflexes were
slow. Lack of sleep would do it every time.

"Inventory," she said, as if it explained everything. Unfortunately it did. "There's always been a discrepancy between
the Mech resource reports and what they ought to be. This
close to Waystation One we can't take any chances on resources, we need to know what the Fleet really has available
rather than what the Mechs will admit to. I want you to head
up an inventory team, Ar Marquette. Go find out what we've
actually got out there, and by the time you get back, this whole
unfortunate affair will all be superceded draft."

Punishment.

They weren't going to reclassify him from Jneer; they
couldn't. He'd made that impossible for them. They would
punish him one way or another, though, and sending him out
to spend weeks in inventory on Mech ships certainly seemed
an effective punishment to Raleigh.

"Thank you, Dean," Raleigh said, and thought that he'd
caught the balance he'd been aiming for between sarcastic
knowledge and ignorant gratitude rather well. For a man who
had had his life, over these past few days. "An opportunity to
really contribute materially to the future success of the Waystation One colony. When can I start?"

If she appreciated the subtleties of his tone of voice and
turn of phrase, though, she gave no sign. Nor any sign of
having even noticed. "Return to quarters, but keep to yourself,
all right? You have three days to generate your inventory grids
before the freighter's due. You'll ship out on the *Zebulon* for
the afterfleet, to start with. Your first target is a sweeps station
named *Hyrcos*."

Oh, good. It would take days just to get to the afterfleet, the ships that trailed the rest of the Colony Fleet to ensure that stragglers could be intercepted and rescued. Days on board of an outbound freighter heavy with surplus produce to be doled out amongst the Mechs, its storage rooms stacked with manufactured items of one sort or another. Cotton cloth. Wooden artifacts hand-carved by Oways. Standard pharmaceuticals, from Jneer laboratories. Yes, it was a wonderful opportunity, all right.

"I'll be ready. Shall I excuse myself now?" Because she'd said quite enough. He wasn't interested in hearing any more of it. Inventory, indeed.

Were they already planning on letting him fall out of the planning process, out of sight, out of mind?

Had they decided to shut him out of the future?

The dean nodded and made an inappropriately kittenish gesture with her hands, as if shooing him out the door.

If they thought they were going to be rid of him that easily, they were mistaken.

Raleigh took leave with a nod of his head. He had work to do.

There was no rest for winners.

He hadn't come this far just to be passed over in selection for any reason the administration could invent.

Hillbrane was half expecting to be met at the docks, so seeing Podile standing there waiting with a packing case beside her was no particular surprise. She recognized the packing case as her own. They'd had Podile pack for her after all; one last service the Oway performed for a Jneer who was no longer a Jneer. It meant nothing. It signified only that they had wanted her out of the way as quickly as possible, and weren't willing to wait for her to come pack up herself.

Hillbrane crossed the gangplank with a sense of bridging the chasm between Jneer and Mech, but going in the wrong direction. It disheartened her, even though she knew she would be back. She didn't know how she was going to make it work, and that introduced an element of uncertainty into the equation.

"Good morning, Podile." There was no reason why she should make things awkward for the Oway. Good manners knew no caste. "Have you got something for me? My case, thank you."

Podile forestalled Hillbrane's attempt to grasp the carry handle of the case. "Yes, Aitch, I'm to escort you. You have an appointment in Dispatch, but there's no need for you to carry that, we'll get a trans."

Aitch. Podile knew she was just Hillbrane Harkover, now, but still called her Aitch—and not out of habit, either. The name had been too deliberately spoken for that. Hillbrane felt a surge of irrational gratitude that threatened to bring tears to her eyes, and controlled herself with a stern effort. She could best demonstrate her appreciation of Podile's courtesy by taking it in stride.

She nodded, and followed Podile's lead to the trans waiting for them at the edge of the pavement that fronted the docks.

They left the city of Stiknals and rode over well-paved roads for nearly an hour before the characteristic dome of a hardened bunker came into view. There had never been an accident in the delivery corridors, not that Hillbrane had ever heard of, but the system itself remained carefully protected against an uncontrolled event.

If something breached the series of airlocks between the loading docks far beneath Stiknals and cold empty space beyond, an entire system of pressure barriers and vacuum locks would stem the loss of precious atmosphere. The system worked very well; the atmosphere that escaped with every launch was so minimal that most of the stockpile of bottled atmosphere that had been issued as a part of Subtropical's initial resource allocation still lay untapped. After nearly four hundred years.

Into the building, then, through the massive corridors of concrete and steel and through set upon set of blast doors to a small passenger lift. The medical evacuation lift. Hillbrane knew of its existence—Mechs with certain medical conditions came to the Noun Ships for treatment as vacancies were available in hospital—but she'd never seen one. It was hard to imagine being able to fit a litter into so small a space. It smelled like hot metal, dirty lubrication fluid.

A relatively short walk from the evac lift brought Hillbrane and Podile into an administrative office area, and Hillbrane found herself relaxing. This was at least familiar in concept. Offices she understood. This was not as nicely appointed an office suite as those with which she was familiar, perhaps, but what good did comparisons do her?

She was here now, and her goal should be to make the best of her time here. Constant recollection of how she had been wronged and what she had left behind were wastes of energy.

There were people waiting in the antechambers; two people only, one older, one not so old, sitting together. Mechs. Hillbrane politely declined to notice them, and Podile led her through to the office of the resources dispatch manager.

Had she become a resource to dispatch? Hillbrane wondered suddenly. It was an amusing conceit, one which the officer herself did nothing to dispel. The officer stood up as they came in and offered her hand to Podile, then to Hillbrane.

"Good morning, Podile. Aitch Harkover, I understand. Shan Muriff."

Her name. The officer's name was Shan Muriff. Hillbrane took a moment longer than she would have liked to realize that that was what the officer was telling her.

Shan sat back down. Hillbrane looked around her for a place to seat herself; there were some chairs against the wall, but otherwise nothing. One was not expected to stay very long, apparently. Still it was a new experience for Hillbrane.

"Well, ladies. Hillbrane. I understand you've been made available to address our chronic problems with the rest of the Fleet." That was delicately stated; and yet Shan did not hesitate to use Hillbrane's first name, as though they were on terms of intimacy. Or she was Hillbrane's superior. "We'd like to start you out in the forefront area. There are apparently some issues with the Forenet, generating concerns amongst the people working there. We could use your evaluation and analysis of the situation."

This sounded encouraging. True, it might simply be a diplomatic way of saying "Go down among the Mechs and stay there." Still, an assignment to evaluate and analyze Mech concerns about the Forenet clearly required her to report—to Jneers. She had her access lines opened for her already.

"It sounds like a good opportunity, Shan." On multiple levels. "What information is available to help me get started?"

Shan looked a little surprised; what, had she expected Hillbrane to object? To kick up a fuss? Throw a tantrum? Or was Shan simply not accustomed to people using *her* first name, as she had used Hillbrane's?

"I've got a delegation waiting for me outside, Hillbrane. Mir Tobias and Cawdor Warrine from the forefront ship *Deecee*. You'll be traveling with them once I give them their briefing, and believe me, they've got plenty of complaints for you to review."

Well, Shan might be calling her Hillbrane by assumption of superiority, or Shan might be calling her Hillbrane by mere force of habit. Or Shan might be speaking to her as a still-valuable member of a partnership whose goal was to ensure the success of the mission, despite the best efforts of the notoriously short-sighted Mech community, if need be.

Nodding, Hillbrane turned to go so that Shan could get on with the Mech interview yet to come.

The forefront ship *Deecee*.

She was almost grateful to be away so quickly.

Time wasted waiting for transport out was just that much more time before she could return.

The dock officer looked up as Cago—who had only ever been called "Cawdor" by people who didn't know him—walked in with Mir. From the look of mild surprise on Shan

Muriff's face, Cago told himself, she might have been completely unaware of the fact that he and Mir had been sitting outside of her office waiting for more than an hour.

The surface women had passed them as though they hadn't been there at all, so maybe—Cago admitted to himself, grudgingly, but willing to be fair—maybe it was his mistake, and he and Mir had only just now arrived. He could have imagined the wait time. Muriff had certainly not kept the surface people waiting, and there was no reason to suspect her of being gratuitously rude, was there?

Double standards were rude by definition.

"Gentlemen," Muriff said, folding her hands in front of her on the desktop. "I know you're in a hurry to get back to your jobs, so I'll make this quick."

See? Cago scolded himself. *She values our time. You only imagined that you sat there for this long, with not even as much as the offer of a cup of tea for breakfast. We get to breathe this good rich air, so why should we complain?*

"The technical council is concerned by the reports that have been coming in about the condition of the Forenet. We've assigned an engineer to the problem, you saw her outside just now. Hillbrane Harkover. Now, she's an engineer, true enough, but I think you'll find she'll be most comfortable on the *Deecee* if you treat her just like one of your own."

Oh, yeah. Right. That's what the occasional visiting Jneers always said: no special treatment, just one of the work crew. Jneers' entire lives were special treatment. When you actually treated them as you treated everybody else, they got all offended on you.

"What's her background?" Mir sounded skeptical, as well he should. The whole thing was more than just a little suspicious; they'd been complaining about the Forenet for years, trying to get someone's attention before a disaster did it for them. Why was an engineer assigned, so suddenly? And why only one of them? She didn't look old enough to have any significant expertise in the field of plasma interrupt field generation and maintenance. She looked young. She looked very young. In fact—

Muriff's hesitation was merely fractional, but it was there. "Well. Harkover's a wide-spectrum analyst. The technical council felt that a generalist was our best bet at this point. No previous bias, open mind, you know. The problem is that when you're a recycle specialist—"

"—everything looks like a systems backlog," Mir and Cago chorused, completing the old saw, exchanging glances as they did so. In fact, what Hillbrane Harkover actually was, was clearly an engineer fresh out of Comparisons. If they were lucky.

Otherwise she had failed Comparisons and was being sent away as unfit for the challenging intellectual world of the Noun Ships. Mir wouldn't suggest that, though. It had been years, but Cago remained sensitive—some had told him a little too sensitive—about his own grandfather, who had failed his Comparisons and spent the rest of his life struggling to reclaim his lost status.

Cago in turn had spent most of his life enduring the misplaced humor of people who couldn't resist pretending he shared his grandfather's aspirations and class identification, so Mir would just keep his mouth shut. Cago was a Mech, and proud to be one.

Muriff smiled weakly. "Ah. Yes. Exactly. Well. Let me introduce you, and you can all be on your way home. Maybe there will be better news for us at the next Allmeet about the state of the Forenet. Wouldn't that be a change?"

What would be a change would be if Jneers and Oways ever started taking Mech warnings seriously instead of ignoring their warnings until deciding to shut the Mechs up by throwing some token resources at the problem. That would be a change. No other action would be taken, however, because every time a Jneer came in with a report that supported Mech complaints, the evidence was promptly dismissed as tainted by association—with Mechs.

Just as long as they all understood.

"We'd welcome it." Mir somehow managed to keep a straight face. "Let's go. Soonest started, after all."

Hillbrane shipped out for her new life on board of a freighter that was laden to its maximum capacity with surplus from Noun Ships stores to be divided out among the Mechs. It wasn't really set up for passengers; the crew had turned one of the two tiny private berths over to her, but there was hardly room to so much as breathe in so small a space. Hillbrane appreciated the delicacy of feeling which had led the two Mechs to give a Jneer her own space. There was too little else to appreciate here for that to make a real difference, though.

She spent her waking hours in the cupola, watching. Three days' travel from the Noun Ships to the forefront gave her plenty of time for contemplation. The Noun Ships she already knew. They looked like rounded asteroids from the outside, because that was exactly what they were: selected pieces of space rock, excavated, reinforced, sealed, pressurized, terraformed, injected with atmosphere, and fitted with nuclear plasma core rocket engines that provided the Noun Ships with electricity and heat when they weren't being used for motive power.

They were only very seldom used for motive power.

Once the Noun Ships had been set in motion, they required very little by way of encouragement to supplement the forces of inertia. Conversely it would take every fraction of power that could be wrung out of the engines to stop the Noun Ships: and if that ever happened short of their final goal at Waystation Five, it was anybody's guess as to whether there was enough juice left in the plasma cores to ever bring the ships back up to speed again.

So the Noun Ships held interest, but not as much as the Forenet.

Once upon a time the entire Fleet population had rotated through the Noun Ships, and every Jneer had had a chance to examine the Forenet for herself. Exactly when—and exactly why—things had changed had never been convincingly explained to Hillbrane, but change they had. Mechs came to the Noun Ships, but most Jneers did not travel except between Noun Ships. Hillbrane had never seen the Forenet before in her life.

The Forenet was a plasma mantle that all but surrounded the entire Fleet like the near-invisible membrane hood of a gigantic aquatic man-of-war, shielding the loose collection of ships within its gauzy embrace as a jellyfish guarded its internal organs. It was mere molecules thick, held in place by the pressure of minuscule space dust bombarding it from the outside balanced in careful equilibrium against the low-level particle leakage from the propulsion systems of freighters and the small but inevitable presence of escaped atmosphere.

It was also—Hillbrane discovered—very slightly luminescent, a chemical reaction of some sort storing as light the kinetic energy generated when the plasma mantle absorbed the strike of a particle of space debris. The Forenet glowed, very faintly it was true, but perceptibly so. She could see its presence as a vague fuzzy halo in the dark space against which the ships still before them were silhouetted. Nimbus. Aurora. She wasn't sure exactly what to call it, but she knew it was fascinating.

For the past centuries the Colony Fleet had followed the course chartered for it four hundred years ago through the emptiest space available—or the space that had looked emptiest from that centuries-old vantage point, anyway. The nearer they got to Waystation One, the less empty they found space before, above, and beneath the Fleet's thin plasma bubble.

Demands on the Forenet were growing week by week. The closer they got to Waystation One, the more difficult it became for the forefront ships to scour the space ahead of the Colony Fleet and intercept everything that exceeded the Forenet's tolerance.

The Forenet itself was mesmerizing in its ghostly beauty. Hillbrane spent hours in the cupola, staring. The issue she'd been asked to look into—the adjustments that the plasma intercept fields required to account for their entry into less empty space—was neither complex nor worrisome.

Of course the generation parameters should be changed.

That would be a simple matter of resetting the defaults from the last time the Forenet's characteristics were changed; it didn't really need a Jneer to do that, but who was she to argue? People who didn't really understand what they were doing frequently demanded that an expert do it for them. Unnecessary perhaps, but it was human nature.

After two or three days had passed the Forenet disappeared, and Hillbrane knew by that token they were too near to be able to see as faint and dispersed an outline as that of the Forenet. She could see a glowing object out ahead, however, one that resolved itself into a maintenance ship as they got closer. A forefront ship, with its own plasma intercept field to protect it out beyond the Forenet. The *Deecee*. She watched its approach with dread and anticipation: anxious to get to work, fearful of the new environment in which she would find herself.

Too soon.

Too soon, and the freighter met the *Deecee* at the Forenet out in the middle of nowhere with the Colony Fleet behind them and nothing but a little local red-white star ahead. Hillbrane delayed her descent from the cupola until the last minute. They didn't need her to offload cargo. But they were Mechs, would they remember to take her bags with them? She could not afford to take the chance.

One last hungry look at the Noun Ships and Hillbrane climbed down out of the observation cupola, sliding the connect-door at the bottom of the ladder open to reveal an unexpected scene of chaos. Noise. Confusion. People were moving cargo in the old-fashioned way, from hand to hand; where were their autocarts?

Or were they too cheap to spend energy on automated tools, preferring physical labor on demand to resource planning?

Mechs.

Best if she got out of the way.

It was awkward squeezing her way through the corridors, but no one seemed to be paying any attention to her. All to the good. Her quarters stood open, but no packing had been done; Hillbrane didn't understand that. If they hadn't meant to pack, why had they opened her quarters? And if they had meant to pack, why were her things still disposed as completely as they could be under such straitened circumstances?

There was no understanding the mind of a Mech. Hillbrane simply set herself to the task of packing, determined not to create any unpleasantness over the issue. When she had finished she sat down to wait, leaving the door open, and before too long she saw Cago and Mir in the corridor, on their way— she presumed—to quarters of their own.

Was it her imagination, or did Cago look a little startled to see her?

Within moments he was back. "Hillbrane. Hey. Where've you been?"

Where did he think? And what was it to him? Hillbrane looked around her pointedly. Wasn't it obvious? "I needed to get packed." Since it wasn't being done for her. And—to be fair—why should it be? She knew she was true Jneer, but these Mechs didn't. And even if they had, would a Mech even know how to support a Jneer to maximize her contribution?

The way Cago quirked his eyebrows, though, one would think that the need to pack had yet to occur to him. Was she missing something? "Oh. Yeah. Well, we'll be ready to turn the f-boat back on auto and get home. You just sit right where you are, we'll come get you."

F-boat. That was what Cago called the freighter. "Sitting," Hillbrane replied, with as much dry humor as she could muster. What had she been doing up till now?

That wasn't the problem, was it?

Had Cawdor and Mir expected her to help move freight?

It was hard to credit. Yet perhaps she'd nailed it. Where had Mir and Cawdor been, if they hadn't been moving freight themselves?

Did Mech folkways require people to finish a communal task before seeing to their personal effects?

That made no sense. There were no Oways to see to the administrative details. She must have misinterpreted.

Sighing in resignation, Hillbrane settled down to wait.

The corridors of the freighter were narrow and low-ceilinged, and the air was stale. She'd had a headache since the day she'd left the Nouns. Hillbrane could only hope that the dilapidation was specific to the freighter. People could be relied upon to take better care of their own living quarters than of mere goods-movers. Even Oways could be guilty of that brand of carelessness.

Cawdor and Mir came across Hillbrane's field of vision through the open door to the cabin that had been hers. Standing up, Hillbrane lifted her satchel, gazing pointedly at her personals-trunk, but the Mechs had already gone, and for all she knew they wouldn't bother to come back. She took up the strap to the personals-trunk and touched its trundler, setting her disgust at their behavior firmly aside in favor of making sure she could negotiate the narrow cabin doorway without damaging the finish on her trunk.

The Mechs were ahead of her, well down the corridor, but as she started after them they did have the basic courtesy to pause and wait for her. Neither of them had more than one satchel, but no. She was going to get along. She was not going to let carrying her own luggage become an issue with her.

As she came up behind them, they turned to walk on, continuing their conversation without a break.

". . . so anyway, she says the fabric's gone on that filter. We're going to have to go with the ceramics for a while."

What were they talking about?

Ventilation? Reclamation? Recirc? What?

Did it occur to either of them that she was totally excluded from this conversation?

"Could see about doubling the fabric we do have," Mir suggested. "Of course that might degrade performance on oh-two scrub. Okay, ceramics, then."

"No, wait." Cawdor stopped, half-turning in the narrow corridor to look at Mir and Hillbrane both. "Why should we go to ceramics if two-ply will work? We can ask Hillbrane." He gestured toward her, two hands palms-up, fingers flat and pointing in her direction. As if she were a dish of soup on an Oway meal-line, and he was offering Mir lunch. "She's a Jneer. She'll be able to tell us. What do you say, Hillbrane?"

Finally now Cawdor looked at her, looking for all the world as if he expected thanks and admiration from her. What was so brilliant about his proposal that she should respond favorably to it? She shrugged. "I'd be glad to examine the problem, Mir. After I've found a fix for the Forenet—"

There was a lot of alliteration in that phrase. For whatever reason Hillbrane wished she'd thought far enough ahead to rephrase herself: it might sound flippant. But it was too late now, and she had to finish, they were waiting. "—of course. If that will do."

For some reason this seemed to disappoint Cawdor. But he nodded at Mir. "There. Problem solved. Come on, we're out of here."

What had she said wrong?

Hillbrane followed the Mechs, feeling sheepish now and irate at herself for feeling uncomfortable without good reason. Without knowing why. They were heading for the bottom of the loading area, by the looks of things; the decking was even more worn and uneven, if that was possible. Just to the other side of an airlock corridor the Mechs stopped, turning to watch back down the length of the short passageway.

The airlock door slid across the rear end of the passageway, right behind Hillbrane. Through the small scratched viewport she could see the corresponding door at the other end, and realized to her dismay that she was already on the *Deecee*, after all.

It was dingier and more dreary than the freighter had been. Clean, perhaps, but so worn and so used; how long would it be before she could once again breathe air scented with flowers, not smelling of ionization? It was hard to inhale deeply enough to get enough air, the atmosphere was that foul in her nostrils. Not as if the Mechs even noticed, and why should they?

She could hear the pumps working, recovering air from the airlock.

The outer skin sealed, the gate port closed, and the tell-tales cycled through their procedure. Pressure check. Cross-check between motive systems, both ships. Separation. Disengage.

She was stuck, and went after Cawdor and Mir, looking around with a morbid sort of interest now that she knew she was to be living here for the near future. Gray. Scratched. Dented, faded, old. It was probably good enough for these Mechs, for people who had never lived any other way, but how was she to survive here?

It was a long walk, and it ended in a common room where people were assembled. There was no beverage service, though, and not a snack in sight.

Mir set his satchel on the nearest table and sat down on its surface. "Listen and learn, people. We have a treat. All of these years trying to get help from the Nouns. Well, I'd like you to meet Hillbrane. Aitch Harkover, here to give us what we've needed for so long. She's a Jneer fresh from Comparisons, and we all know that the *Deecee* isn't exactly Seaboard, so let's all try to help her feel welcome. Aitch Harkover?"

Cawdor took her satchel and the pullstrap of her personalstrunk; Mir held out his hand. Hillbrane swallowed hard, then used Mir's shoulder to lever herself up to sit on the table's surface beside him.

"Hello." Twenty, perhaps thirty people, all looking at her. Most of them with some version or another on their faces of Cawdor's reserved, neutral, somewhat skeptical expression. "My name's Hillbrane Harkover." *But you can call me—Aitch.* It was an old Jneer joke, and traditional between Jneers and Oways; still, she was alone here, and during her time in transit with Mir and Cawdor she had realized early on that Mechs used each others' first names by default.

It would just cause unnecessary confusion and conflict if she tried to insist on being treated differently. "My mother called me Hillbie, but my friends call me Brane. The issue of the Forenet is critical to the entire Colony Fleet, and I'm honored to have been chosen—" that was stretching it, but why humiliate herself in front of these Mechs by revealing the truth of the matter? And she *had* been selected, in a sense—"to be part of the solution. Thank you."

Now would be a good time for polite applause, people, Hillbrane thought. It didn't happen. Instead she heard a smattering of "Well said," "Good to have you, "Welcome to *Deecee*, Hillbrane."

It wasn't what she'd wanted, but it would do.

Cawdor held out his hand to help her to her feet. His skin was dirty. It was a fine strong hand, for a Mech hand, the wrist white at the joint where the skin stretched taut, the fingers square-tipped and steely-hard. It did its job admirably well; oddly heartening, in this alien place.

"Come on," Cawdor said. "I'll show you a place you can leave your things and we can get something to eat. I bet you could use some settling-in time, am I right?"

It might have been well-intentioned, but it was patronizing nonetheless. Hillbrane suppressed a grimace of distaste. "Stowage, good. Lunch, dinner, whatever—yes, I'm hungry. But after that I'd like to get straight to work, if you'll show me where the generation station is."

There it was again, a fractional hesitation on the part of the Mech, an equally subtle impression of shrugging off an irritating or distasteful sensation of some sort. She wasn't accustomed to people who were so easy to read. Didn't these Mechs care if everybody knew how they felt? How could they ever hope to negotiate to advantage without the truth of their agenda in reserve?

And—most disturbingly, coming as it seemed out of nowhere to strike Hillbrane in the stomach—if the Mechs were not arguing like Jneers, if they were telling only the flat un-varnished truth when they brought their complaints to the tech-nical councils, did that meant that everything the technical councils thought they knew about the condition of the Fleet was dangerously overcorrected to too optimistic an evaluation, based as such evaluations were on the presumption that the Mechs were exaggerating the problems that they faced?

She shook herself. Cawdor was looking at her with a quiz-zical expression in his sharp black eyes. Raleigh's eyes had been beautiful and—she supposed—beloved, but they were unquestionably narrower than Cawdor's.

As if that had anything to do with anything.

"Nothing like jumping right in, I guess," Cawdor said. "Right."

Right.

The room was emptying rapidly; people smiled and nodded at her on the way out, but nobody stopped to talk. There would be plenty of time for talk later.

Cawdor picked up her satchel, Hillbrane the pullstrap of her personals-trunk, and out of the room together they went to see what her new quarters were like.

Stores were stowed, reports were logged, inventory rec-ords were signed over to the inventory people. Cago Warrine was at the end of a very long day and ready to rest his weary headbone; and yet a nagging concern drove him to the control room where the ship's plasma net generation status display was to be found. That young Jneer, Hillbrane. She was so focused. Or was she just afraid? Afraid, they didn't need. Afraid was good for nobody. Afraid was no way for anyone to have to be, ever.

The control room was a long narrow corridor between a ventshaft and a stores area. It was normally staffed four at a time by the control jocks on shift, and one of them would be checking periodically on the plasma shield—spooling the rate of feed, watching the per-square particle yield, making the assessment sensor sweeps of the Forenet itself to ensure that no accidental tear in the fabric of the Forenet would go undetected for long lest it threaten the Fleet.

It was true that the Noun Ships could take more than a few hits before their atmosphere-shells would be compromised, but as true that it didn't take many hits at near light speed to make a serious impact. It had been four hundred years. It was supposed to be another eight hundred years before the last crew of the Colony Fleet reached its final destination at Waystation Five. The Noun Ships had to last another eight hundred years, and even one hit a century added up over time.

Today there was an extra person there, but she wasn't spooling rate of feed or checking particle yield or doing mass calibrations or any of that sort of thing. Cago stood for a moment and watched before intruding himself; he didn't want to startle her.

She was a nice-looking piece of work.

He'd noticed the strong tight line of her flanks the first he'd seen her.

At that time he had told himself that it was just her unusual clothing that made her so eye-filling and attractive; he didn't usually see his crewmates in golden yellow silk sarongs with a perfectly tanned midriff between the braided band riding below a supple waist and a ribbon-tied bodice sheltering a creamy golden blossom in its cleavage.

That's what he'd told himself then.

Since, he'd noticed that whatever it was, it was as magnetic when she was wearing a standard pair of workslacks and the classic short-sleeved cottonesque shirt of the Mech crews. He hadn't figured out exactly what it was, but he was not minding the figuring out of it.

Just now there was more to worry about than where it was that this Jneer was keeping her charisma. She hadn't moved the while he'd been watching her, except to raise a hand toward one meter readout and drop it again without invoking any feedout.

It was too obvious.

She didn't have a clue.

The longer she sat here, the more obvious it was going to get, and before long she was going to realize that. It wouldn't help. He had to do something. His crewmates would naturally look to him, because of his personal background. It was not something he was looking forward to, but he was the best man for the job.

"Hey, Rena." Calling out a greeting to the nearest netjock, Cago made his entrance at last, carefully not noticing the Jneer's startled jump. "Allie. Good to be back, thanks. Shapmell, finish that crostic yet? Hello, Hillbrane."

The stations in the control area hadn't had extra chairs since Cago had gotten here, and that had been seven years ago now. He'd been in a hurry to leave his home ship, not because there was anything wrong with it, but because it was his home ship. *Deecee* hadn't been much different, but it hadn't been his home ship. Different enough.

Cago squatted down on his heels beside Hillbrane. He liked the *Deecee*. He liked the people here. He hoped to be offered a berth-right here, to grow old with these people. What might be behind the strange sense of restlessness that had crept up on him over the past few days he couldn't begin to guess. Whatever it was would doubtless resolve itself in its own good time; in the meantime, here was this problem with Hillbrane.

"Hi, Cawdor. I thought you were going off shift."

Yes, that was right. That was what he'd told her hours ago, at dinner. That was what he'd meant to do, just as soon as he'd finished up on one or two details.

"I'm on my way. Just thought I'd stop by." She sounded timid and anxious beneath her superior Jneer façade. He couldn't afford to even think about smiling. "So how's it going?"

He couldn't do anything for her without her help. If she was going to try to keep up appearances—

But Hillbrane Harkover took a deep breath and laid her hands flat on the surface of the console, looking almost relieved. "Cawdor. I said I didn't need any orientation time. I thought I knew exactly what this was going to look like and what I needed to do to get started. And I was wrong. Start over?"

Cago knew that the relief he felt for his own part wanted to express itself, but he didn't dare. It was a move in a good direction on Hillbrane's part. It was maybe a good sign. "Me, you don't have to ask. Nobody wants you to burn out, though you will if you try to get it all done too quickly."

It was a terrible strain on a Jneer to admit that she could have miscalculated her own ability. It would embarrass her if she showed too much emotion in front of people she didn't know. Well, she was a Jneer, it would embarrass her to show much emotion in front of people she did know, when they were just Mechs. He knew. He had a grandfather to prove it by.

He had to get her out of here.

Cago stood up. "These corridors were charted by a maniac. Come on, I'll find you back to your slot." That was good. It was casual, reasonable. Logical. They could save face for everybody.

Hillbrane creaked slowly to her feet, and followed Cago out. He tried to decide how to say what he wanted to say, and didn't get very far before Hillbrane spoke in a voice that was small but determined. "How old is that system, anyway? Hasn't it ever been upgraded? This is the Forenet we're talking about. What could you people be thinking of?"

It could have been confrontational Jneer talk, but no, she was sincere—and open-hearted. A question, with honest outrage and wonder behind it.

"If you don't like the looks of our netgen station there's a lot that's going to make you unhappy, Hillbrane. It's been four hundred years. And, nothing personal, but since they stopped rotating engineers as well as mechanics and technicians through the entire Fleet and shut them up on the Nouns to do smart things and think smart thoughts, we just haven't been able to get support."

Was this the time to tell her?

Would it make it any easier for her to be here? Or was there some other reason why he wanted her to know?

Why not take the chance, for whatever reason?

"If my grandfather hadn't had some influence, it might be even worse than it is. But he came down from Jneers. Some problem with his Comparisons, I never got the full story. He had contacts, though, and they never forgot him. Nobody knew what kind of hold he had. Guilty consciences, maybe."

She stopped cold in the corridor with her head bent forward.

He'd gone too far.

It was just what she'd pick up from common gossip soon enough, but had he been too obvious?

"Well. If he had influence, and they had guilty consciences, why didn't he go back? It's nicer on the Noun Ships, you know?"

She was handling it well, keeping her tears to herself. Cago didn't feel any better to have his suspicions about her, or more correctly about what she was doing here, confirmed. It didn't have to matter. His grandfather had proved to everyone's satisfaction that it was the education and the contacts that made a Jneer useful to have around. Comparisons were irrelevant.

"I never quite figured that out myself. Maybe his influence was only good so long as he stayed away. Maybe even he decided that he liked it here."

And it didn't matter. It was only to give Hillbrane some food for thought—and give her the news that whatever had happened to her in Comparisons, she wasn't the first Jneer to find herself alone and out of place on a Mech ship. Maybe even start her toward understanding how much her help could mean for them all. Maybe.

"There's no forecast possible. For personal preference," Hillbrane said. Her voice wasn't wobbling so much any more. Cago had heard that line before, but in a slightly different form. "Thanks for helping me find my room, Cawdor. This is it, isn't it?"

There's no accounting for taste. It was what his grandmother used to say when they asked her about her choice of breeding partners. "Oh. Yes. As a matter of fact. Sorry. I must be sleepier than I'd thought." She was right. She had a better head for navigation than he did. "Tell you what, why don't I come get you for breakfast."

Hillbrane actually smiled. "I've got a lot of studying to do, but—thanks. Sure. See you later, then."

Because he definitely was double-shifting. And that was not good for long-term productivity. "Later, Hillbrane. And welcome to the *Deecee*."

He was glad she was here.

But he wasn't going to think any more deeply about that until he'd had some serious down time.

FOUR

DEECEE

Comparisons had been over for two months now, and all those young Jneers had dispersed back to their points of origin. The dean had given Podile an appointment at last. It was in the final time slot of the day, and just before a recess period; so the dean's mind would hardly be on business. But an Oway took what she could get, especially when she had a personal agenda to put forward. Podile had a daughter to see to. Daughters were serious business.

The dean's name was Gadje Ankara, and it was always a bit awkward to decide how to handle a name like that—the consonant was hard, not soft, which would normally make the initial sound a bit like retching, but convention dictated the use of the letter title rather than the actual initial sound.

Gee Ankara it was.

Podile waited quietly until just before the mark to rap at the door for entry. "Podile Tarcutt, Gee Ankara. I have an appointment to see you."

The dean's desk was stacked high with data-tapes and storage boxes, mini-cubes and keepers. Preparation for Allmeet, most likely. Jneer representatives were due to start out on their prenegotiation visits to the Mech ships within the month, and Podile was going to be one of them—in masquerade, as it were. From what Podile had gathered, the Jneer proposals were likely to be controversial.

"Of course, Podile," Dean Ankara said. "I was reviewing your memorandum earlier today, as a matter of fact." Then she went shuffling through her documents in an unconvincing show of concern, of having things right at her fingertips. Jneers rarely had anything right at their fingertips—except their manicures. That was what Oways were for. "Let's see. It was your nephew, wasn't it? Child Byrnie."

Well, yes, it was child Byrnie; the dean had at least that much right. Podile supposed she shouldn't be too hard on the dean. The Jneer response to potentially controversial items of business was to document so thoroughly that no angle could come as a surprise. As a result, they typically spent a good deal of time on hammering down loose edges that really had no bearing on the case one way or the other. Self-protection. Jneer defense.

"My *daughter*, Gee Ankara. Placed first in her analysis skills assessments from the day she started her course of academics." And had such joy in the work that Podile had come to understand that she had to have that exact sort of work for her daughter forever.

Byrnie had been born to be an engineer.

She loved analysis, and she was good at it, and Podile was in a position to know—she who sat quietly with her recorder as the Jneer academicians discussed case after case in Comparisons. Every year, for the past eight years. "Her advisor tells me that she might qualify for Enrichment. I need a senior academic's recommendation to take her petition forward, Gee Ankara, and I was hoping that I could prevail upon you to oblige."

Now the dean pushed herself away from the desk, leaning back in her chair. "Enrichment." *Here it comes*, Podile told herself, and did her best to resign herself to it. *Hypocritical speech number twenty-six: you don't really want to be a Jneer.* "Well. Congratulations, Podile. You understand of course that Enrichment is highly competitive, even among Jneers. And that there's no connection between it and any potential for a status change."

You don't really want a status change anyway. Why would you want a status change? Being a Jneer was nothing special; it was a lot of hard work for far fewer rewards than people realized. Yes, she knew the speech, she'd heard it. The song-text convinced nobody that Podile knew of.

If being a Jneer was not better than being an Oway, then Jneers would not take such care to ensure that Oways were not permitted to contaminate the ranks of Jneers. If nobody would want to be a Jneer once they knew what it was like, there would be Jneers stepping down to be Oways at regular intervals, and there would be no need for barriers.

As it was, Jneers protected their own and their privileges with a fierceness that belied the official story, no matter how many times it was repeated.

"Of course, Gee Ankara. Naturally. Pushing my daughter into an area of endeavor for which she is unsuited is the last thing I would do." Code for *Yes, Dean, we know our place. We'd never dare to suggest we could do your job as well as you can do it, let alone perhaps better.*

"It's just that it's genuinely the thing she loves more than anything else in the world. Analysis. She's ahead of all the others in her class. I'm confident that she could be a valuable resource to the Fleet's mission in a support role, if I can get her the education she needs to be of service."

And the cold hard facts of the matter were that the only way to make a status change from Oway to Jneer was through an Enrichment program of some sort. Jneers could swear that there was no connection between Enrichment and a status change till the Colony Fleet reached Waystation Five. Enrichment was the link; and if it was true that doing Enrichment didn't mean you'd get a status change, it was equally true that there was no possibility of a status change without the academic background you could only get in Enrichment.

Gee Ankara nodded with an approving expression on her face. "Good. Good. That's the right motive, Podile, welfare of the child. And who knows? We're going to be short of Jneers after the colony leaves, after all."

Podile had heard the rumors. She kept her expression calm. "I'm not sure I understand, Gee Ankara." There was no reason for the dean to confide in her. On the other hand, it was late, Ankara was probably tired, and it wasn't as if it was a big secret—was it? Just not public knowledge. Not yet.

"Well." The dean spread her arms wide and shrugged dismissively. "It's not important. And there will be some discussion at the Allmeet, of course." And she could not confide in Podile, because Podile was an Oway, and the official Jneer story was that it had been an Oway—not any of the Jneers— who had let the news out about that Jneer who had failed in Comparisons and been sent out to the Mechs. It hadn't been Podile. The dean knew it. And if the dean didn't know it she should.

"Naturally." But there was face to maintain. Oways were expected to take the blame for such incidents. They were expected to do so without complaint, as well, because it didn't reflect poorly on them, after all—did it? Nobody expected better of Oways. "If I could have your endorsement, Gee Ankara. This is more important to me than I can say."

Her baby wasn't like the others in her peer-group. She lacked any basic sense of practicality. But she thought about things, turning them over in her little baby brain until the oddest questions rattled out of her at the oddest times. Her baby was an engineer bred and born. Byrnie deserved Enrichment if anybody ever had.

The dean beckoned Podile up to the desk with a wave of her hand. "As long as you keep in mind that it doesn't guarantee anything, Podile."

Podile knew she should say nothing; she should smile and wait until the dean had endorsed the documents she needed and then she should leave. The last thing she could afford to do was anything that might jeopardize her daughter's chances at Enrichment. She stood quietly and controlled herself until Ankara handed the documents back to her; and then she could no longer resist the temptation to take advantage.

"We'll be needing Jneers, Gee Ankara, you said." She had

her daughter's place here, in her hands. And what was the worst that could happen? The dean could throw her out, but was unlikely to rescind her signature just because Podile had asked an indiscreet question. "Do you think that there might be some chance for my daughter? Perhaps if she does really well in Enrichment."

The dean didn't do the normal Jneer thing, though, she didn't roll her eyes in frustration and repeat the no-status-change mantra in a pained tone of voice. She winked instead. The gesture caught Podile entirely off her guard.

"Well," the dean said, with an inflection in her voice that seemed to imply that she was making an admission of some sort. "There's no getting around the fact that it's a good time to be in Enrichment, Podile. I'll let you in on a little secret. There will be vacancies. We don't have enough Jneers to ensure the survival of the Waystation One colony and remain as resource-rich as we've grown accustomed to being. Something's got to give, and we can't take any chances with the colony. You can figure it out. But keep it to yourself until the Allmeet, and—"

Gee Ankara held out her hand, her intention too obvious to be mistaken. "—Best of luck to you and your daughter, Podile."

Rumors were one thing. This was more definite and more extreme. The Jneers meant to monopolize the Waystation One colony, contrary to the principles laid down at the time of the launch of the Colony Fleet.

Byrnie could be an engineer when she grew up.

But what would mass exodus of engineers do to the rest of them, on their way to Waystation Two?

Or did she want Byrnie to be part of the Waystation One colony?

Status—or survival?

Podile knew the dean's words had upset and unsettled her. She was going to have to think about this.

Bowing her head with the proper degree of deferential submission Podile shook the dean's offered hand, and went away.

* * *

"**C**helbie. Hey. Chelbie."

Chelbie was for Aitch Ell Bee, for Hillbrane.

Hillbrane heard Galen calling her outside the dining room, and set her spoon down with a species of frustrated resignation. Not again. People had been at her for days now, two, three times a day, constantly challenging. There wasn't the first hint of meanness to the genial competition—quite a change from home, where no competition escaped inevitable overtones of power play and position jockeying. This was more along the lines of play, pure and simple; but still a person could get tired of it.

"I'm in *here*." She raised her voice, and let a little of the frustration she felt escape along its upper register. "I'm eating my *oatmeal*."

As if that would stop anybody. Shifts were loosely defined here on *Deecee*, Hillbrane had noticed; people got a shift's work done, either more quickly or more slowly than the actual span of the shift, and then they simply set their work aside till the next day. It was an adjustment for Hillbrane; with nobody in a leadership position defining a day's work, it was left up to her to decide how much effort she was going to give back to her crew in return for her rations on a given day.

Stressful, if liberating in a sense, but there was a corollary. Since people did their work on their own schedule there didn't seem to be much of a taboo against accosting other people for help during their off times. But there really wasn't anywhere else on board to get a meal, so Hillbrane was stuck, and Galen came piling through the door with a small gray metallic something in both hands and a gleeful expression on her face.

"Here's one, Chelbie. This time we've got you. What does it do? What is it for? What is it made of, and how would you fix it?"

It was hazing, but in so mild a form as to be hardly worthy of the name. Jneer hazing focused on figuring out where a newcomer fit in to the existing social structure, the extant hierarchy. This Mech hazing seemed designed as much to give Hillbrane face in front of the new crew as to help *Deecee*'s crew figure Hillbrane out. Or maybe that was just a side effect.

Like not getting to her oatmeal before it was cold.

Hillbrane reconsidered her evaluation of the Mech hazing, turning the object over and over in her hands. To the extent that it meant that her breakfast got cold it was punitive, at least in a sense. A very tenuous sense.

She found the seam in the device and pried it open. They played fair, if too frequently; they only brought things she had some chance of figuring out. Membrane and meter. Nozzle and valves. Ceramic disk filter. What was this gasket doing where it was?

"Scrubber." Hillbrane announced her decision. "Organic molecules, I think. So I'd guess it's a Berenice cycler, recovery systems, intake." Galen wasn't giving her any obvious cues, so Hillbrane plunged on. "Aluminum-six-forty shell with a ceramic lining, epoxy fill. But I don't see what's wrong with it. So I can't guess how to fix it."

She'd made Galen happy—Galen, and the other crew members who had gathered to watch. Wyatt. Neyrem. Ivery. Rena. Cawdor. People Hillbrane had known for a mere handful of days; but they'd behaved well toward her. Good-hearted people.

"You're right, you're right, you're wrong, you're right and you're wrong. Okay. That was a tough one. I don't know, maybe it's a cheat." Even though Galen was having fun at Hillbrane's expense, there wasn't the least bit of an edge to her crowing. Oh, maybe a thin edge. The thinnest of edges. Good-hearted did not have to mean saint. "It's a capacitor circuit on the plasma flow generator. And it needs new ceramics. The disk's been eroded, but it takes a scope to see it, unless you notice the copper stain on the core edge there."

Raising her eyes from the object in her hands, Hillbrane stared. "You're joking. Capacitor circuit? What kind of a capacitor circuit do you make out of an organic scrubber? Come on. You're making a joke."

Galen seemed clearly to take no offense. "Nope, nope, nope. Fair on the level. This one's been doing plasma flow generator duty for two hundred years. No wonder the disk's eroded. How would you fix it, now that you know?"

Hillbrane examined the little valve with new interest. A scrubber, as a capacitor. Why not? There was no reason, no engineering reason, why the one should not serve as the other, though surely no Jneer would ever think of such a thing. Scrubbers weren't built for capacitors. But if the *Deecee* had needed a capacitor, and had a spare scrubber, why not?

She was gaining an appreciation for the genius of the Mechs, and it lay in making do with ingenious approaches to running vital systems in an environment where resources were scarce. The Mech solution was not the optimal solution: it was merely the expedient one.

That gave Hillbrane her clue. "A Jneer would fix it with a replacement disk, and since I'd have to order the disk from the Nouns where the labs are, I'd just order a new capacitor and junk this altogether. But if that would work, you'd have done it by now. A Mech would fix it by . . . let me think. Oh. Okay. If this is a capacitor, the filters in the capacitor loop are redundant. I can cannibalize the ceramic replacement filters to replace this disk."

It was a stupid solution, an ugly solution, but it would work and the materials should be on hand. "How'd I do?"

"The caploop filters are redundant?" Galen asked Wyatt, sounding a little dubious. "Maybe I'd better swap out the back-ups and use them instead, just in case."

Wait a minute, Hillbrane thought to herself. Did this mean that Galen hadn't had the answer? And if so—was Hillbrane herself certain that it was a good answer?

"Run parallel," Wyatt told Galen, with a shrug. "Conceptually it works for me. Hillbrane, are you sure?"

"No! I'm not sure!" Hillbrane felt near-panicked, and yet still not threatened. How did that work? "I was guessing, Galen. I thought you already knew. But a ceramic mesh filter should do the job of a ceramic disk filter on this scale so long as the plies are correctly offset. We could test."

"Of course it will work. Now that you mention it. But yes, we'll test." It had only been partly a joke, only mostly in fun. Hillbrane felt suddenly terrified at how ready they seemed to take what she said and go off and implement it. What if she'd been wrong?

She wasn't wrong.

But testing was good.

And she'd found a solution that Galen hadn't tried.

Well, maybe it had been half-serious, or maybe they had wanted to see what her solution would look like. She didn't think she'd failed the test, whichever it turned out to be. The ingenuity and resourcefulness of the Mechs was a constant wonder to her—but a Jneer could contribute as well.

Demonstrably.

Hillbrane applied herself to her only-just-warm oatmeal with a happy heart and a better appetite than she would have imagined.

She'd get back to the Jneers when the time came, but it was good to feel like a contributor in the meantime.

Cago Warrine was in a hurry and didn't care who knew. Where had Aitchel got herself to this time? Not in her quarters, not on the propulsion line, not down in forward scans. Not having supper. He needed to find her; the meeting was about to start.

"Rena, have you seen Chelbie?"

Rena looked up from her registration run with an expression of mild surprise on her face. She didn't answer; had she heard the question?

"Help me out here, Rena. Mir's asked me to make sure she's at Allmeet. It's her first one. Do you know where I can find her?"

Still Rena stared, for just long enough to make her point. Cago felt his skin prickling with embarrassment and annoyance: what was so interesting to everybody about the time he spent with Aitchel? It was his time, wasn't it? Nobody had heard her object, had they?

"There's a set of stores down next to Sandy's. Virgin territory, untouched for years. You might try the out-corridors."

Oh, fine. The out-corridors. Aitchel had no business out there; she was young. Not as if he could say a word in front of Rena, not if he didn't want more misplaced humor from her. And the rest of the crew. What business it was of theirs he couldn't guess.

"Thanks, Rena. Later." The out-corridors were where the older people lived, people with berth-rights on *Deecee*. They had more room there because there was empty space out by the hull, but younger people were supposed to limit the time they spent in those areas. The shielding was good, but not so good that mutagenic energy never got through it.

Only people who could afford to sustain damage to their genetic material were safe in out-corridors—people who had had their children or who weren't having children. But Aitchel couldn't get enough of old stores areas.

Cago supposed it was just as well that the thrill hadn't worn off yet; what was depressingly second-rate and antiquated to Mechs who lived with it was still new and fresh and exciting—quaint and exotic—to Hillbrane Harkover, Jneer.

Once he knew where to look it didn't take too long before he found her, because she didn't know how to close doors and was always letting all the light out into dim corridors. In the out-corridors, all right. Rustling about in stores areas no one had so much as glanced at for decades, making her little Chelbie sounds to herself. Cago slid one shoulder into the far edge of the doorway to brake his momentum and called out for her.

"Say, Hillbrane. There's a meeting you don't want to miss. Come on, we'll be late."

Poking up her smooth-combed head with that great bunch of tight-kinked hair crimped off at the back of her neck. Stylus between her teeth. Dust all over her clothes. These ships had all been spotless on commissioning way back when, but dust was as much a part of life as breathing, and they had honest dust aplenty now. She sneezed, and rubbed her nose with a wadded ball of dust-streaked tissue.

"Hi, Cago. Right. Okay."

She had finally stopped calling him Cawdor when people had started calling her Chelbie, even though it hadn't been his idea to call her Chelbie. Anything was better than "Cawdor." Chelbie sounded like a cook, but Cawdor sounded like—like what?

"Look at you," Cago remonstrated, in tones of patient wonder. "Dust all over." Aitchel was on her feet now, gazing up at him with an expectant sort of an expression on her face. Cago started to dust her shoulders off, but abandoned the effort as soon as it was well begun—the territory got too dangerous too quickly. "What are you doing down here, anyway?"

She was waiting for him to move so that she could leave, among other things. "I'm having fun. This is great, Cago. Some of this hasn't been touched since the day it was loaded."

That was a bit of an exaggeration, maybe. But not too much of one. "And it's all useless, or else it would have been stock-cycled by now. Team meeting. You want to be there. Everybody on board needs to hear and speak, let's go."

Now that he had stepped aside she was out into the corridor in a brisk bouncing trot, glancing back at him over her shoulder with an impish grin on her face. "Well, come on, Cago. It's a meeting. We'll be late." She dusted off her backside with the palms of her hands as she spoke. He wished she wouldn't do that. She had a nice round little backside that raised all kinds of premature thoughts in his mind.

The room was full when they got there, so they squeezed into the back. Mir was there with Hagen and Nolte at the front of the room; Nolte had been elected Speaker for the *Deecee* for this round of talks, and had just come from meeting with the Nouns. The woman that Nolte had up there with her was someone Cago thought he'd seen before, Aitchel apparently recognized her as well, elbowing Cago in the side.

"Hst. Cago. It's Podile. But she's an Oway, not a Jneer."

Interesting. In other years they'd always gotten a Jneer representative . . . or had they? Would any of them have known any different about Podile without Aitchel here?

Since Nolte was talking, though, any private discussion of that would have to wait. "We've all had a chance to review the proposals of the Nouns regarding the makeup and conduct of First Colony. I've got the message you want to go forward, basically that we don't like the composition ratio and we don't think the scope is realistic in light of how Fleet has changed over the years. Our Noun representative Podile has heard it all. This is her time to share how she'll be responding to our position in Preliminaries."

When Fleet had first been chartered Allmeet had been conducted by means of intership communications. It had been a tedious and time-consuming process, but worse than that, during one especially contentious meeting an entire contingent of forefront ships had been dropped out of the net altogether— only to find out later that the meeting had gone ahead over Mech protests to carry the issue that the forefront ships had been arguing against.

The forefront ships' take hadn't been something that the rest of the Mechs had supported, and it wasn't likely that the forefront ships would have prevailed, but that had all been clearly beside the point. They had never come so close to mutiny before or since, if mutiny was a meaningful concept in what was technically a cooperative venture like the Colony Fleet.

Allmeet took longer to accomplish with actual representation and it was resource-expensive to conduct, but at least everybody either had a voice or knew the reason why.

Podile stepped forward and raised her head, clearly intent on being heard at the back of the room. "There's been a lot of concern expressed about the composition of First Colony. I know it may seem that we're trying to change the rules and hope nobody notices."

She smiled, but nobody laughed. She straightened her face and continued. "The misunderstanding that lies at the heart of the matter is simple to explain. The founders of the Fleet didn't set numbers based on the ratio of engineers to technical people. The founders of the Fleet made an independent evaluation of what skill codes and job competencies would be required to make First Colony work. That hasn't changed, even if the Founders were mistaken about what Fleet would look like when we got to Waystation One."

Yes, that was the Nouns' line, all right. The original colonization plan had called for a basic ratio of one to four to five, engineers to administration to technicians. That had been before the engineers had absorbed administrative functions as well as clinical medical skills such as surgery and pharmacology, true.

It had also been when the Fleet had still been confidently expected to be one-fourth again as large as it was by the time it reached its first colony. The argument that there should be a relative increase in the number of Jneers could be understood in light of the fact that the Jneers had absorbed high-end administrative job skills over the years, leaving the Oways to perform what amounted to fetch and carry over a wide range of technical complexity and sophistication.

But the argument that the absolute number of Jneers used as the base figure should remain at the level predicated by the founders for First Colony, even in light of the changes in ratio representation within the Colony Fleet—that made much less sense, unless one allowed self-interest into the equation.

"Now, you have among you on *Deecee* Hillbrane—Aitch Harkover. She's an engineer."

Was she indeed? The bald assertion seemed to surprise Aitchel; Cago could sense her body stiffening. They'd never really talked about it since she'd come here, but it had certainly been Cago's understanding that she'd failed Comparisons and been booted out, as his grandfather had been.

"And she has every expectation of being in the colonization party when it's finally on its way. But more than that, she's just come from reviewing the Waystation One scenario, and she can tell you why the party's composition should be the one we propose. Am I right, Aitch Harkover?"

This was revelation. Why did it feel wrong? Cago snuck a

hand around behind Aitchel's back to steady her. No, this was blackmail, that was why she had gone pale. He saw it in an instant. The others would see it, too. The Nouns had kicked her out, but now that they needed her help they'd make all kinds of promises—calling her an engineer, telling her she'd be in the colony party. Blackmail. And the question was, how would Aitchel react?

She didn't seem to know herself. Cago willed supportive energy to her, hoping she'd come through. She swallowed hard; Cago could see the muscles in her throat working.

"I'm sorry, Podile, but I can't answer that question. My analysis was not based on a descoped colonization party."

Good for you, Aitchel, Cago thought. *Don't be fooled by their promises.* Podile herself, predictably, seemed less pleased.

"And since we are not proposing a descoped party, I can take your answer as in the affirmative. So. You can see that our position is supported by—"

"You may not assume that my answer supports your concept," Hillbrane interrupted, loud and clear and firm. "I said I hadn't considered a descope. And we all know that the colony party has to be descoped. Without accepting that you can use no part of my case in your argument."

Fight fair. Cago could almost hear her say it before she continued. "As Speaker Nolte will state, Descope is required, and that means reevaluating the colony's composition. You're not using me to undermine the Speaker."

You're not using me to undermine *my* Speaker. Cago wished she'd said it: it would have made her position clear, sent a message to the Nouns that Hillbrane Harkover could be neither bribed nor bought.

"Very well." Podile's voice expressed obvious frustration. "And still that issue of descope is not decided. Perhaps it will only be after we are agreed on the size of the First Colony that we will be able to come together on the issue of its composition ratio. Till then you know what I will be saying, on behalf of the Colony Fleet's engineers and administrative staff.

The colony should go forward at the originally proposed *number* of engineers and administrative staff. We do not agree that any proposed descope is necessary, or that any such descope should necessarily impact the number of engineers and administrative staff required to ensure the long-term viability of the Waystation One colony."

No change.

That was what was most discouraging to Cago: they tried to understand, they tried to be flexible, they tried to give quid pro quo. But at the end it was always the same. The Jneers never changed. And the Oways followed the Jneers.

Mir gave them all the wave. "Thanks, people. It'll be another three weeks before Nolte gets back. Till then there's maintenance waiting, let's get to it."

Another three weeks and nothing would change. Three months, and nothing would change. Three years and nothing would change.

Three hundred years and—

"Hey. Cago. Can I get the scenario? I wonder what the answer really is, now."

Aitchel's voice called him up out of his morose loop. The scenario. Waystation One. She wanted to see for herself.

So was she a Jneer?

Or was she a Mech?

"Sure, Aitchel. But you'll need the pink monster in Control to run the sims, if that's what you want."

There was one way to find out.

Let her at the common Waystation One model, let her do her analysis on what changes should be made in the Nouns' proposal. If she came up without any, she was a Jneer. But if she thought for herself—she would still be a Jneer by birth and by breeding, but Cago would be forced to ask her to marry him.

That was all there was to it.

* * *

Raleigh Marquette laid his arm around his guide's shoulder wearily, half-stumbling down the hall. "That's it for stores, then," he announced with satisfaction. "Alys. I'll be going in the morning, there's the freighter on rounds."

Three months and more on inventory, working his way from ship to ship. Three months: but he was finished with the afterguard at last, and he anticipated a much easier time of it on the Ponics ships. They were substantially larger, but there were fewer of them. And the diet was necessarily fresher: he'd not been feeling himself since he'd left the Noun Ships.

"And you've seen for yourself." Alys didn't shrug his arm away, but she didn't lean into him either. She simply continued down the hall as if there was no contact between them. "The inventory is exactly what we've been reporting. I don't know why they make you do this."

That was a sore subject. But his conclusions were changing. The inventories were in fact exactly as reported, or as close as reasonable variance would allow. And they couldn't be. There was no way they could be what the Mechs reported, what the Mechs showed him. Too little of the original inventory had survived. It was counterintuitive.

"Oh, I agree." That much he could commit to, with a whole heart. "The inventory is perfect. I can tell the resource planners on the technical council that everything adds up." He could also tell them that he thought the entire Mech fleet was hiding something.

The demands on stores were constant, and still the stores inventories were outdated and useless: why had they even hung on to some of that garbage, if not to fake accountability? Where had the resources absorbed over the centuries gone to? Something was rotten in the Mech portion of the Colony Fleet.

"It seems to me that you were expecting something different," Alys—his liaison on this particular vessel—observed. She made no attempt to mute the skepticism in her voice. "In fact, you came on like an auditor. There's wrongdoing, before Heaven, and you were determined to uncover it."

Well, perhaps he had been a little heavy-handed. He'd been

frustrated. It hadn't seemed possible that a conspiracy on this scale actually existed, but there really was no other explanation for it. Once he'd made up his mind to just walking through the appropriate motions—and to stop wasting energy looking for hidden stores to which he was not to be allowed access in any case—he'd felt much more relaxed about things. Rested. Refreshed.

Ready to offer his services to people in a position to benefit from them, but even there he'd met with disappointment.

"I uncovered it, all right." *And I'd like to uncover you, with your permission, of course.* But the women weren't interested. Raleigh didn't understand it; folklore insisted that Mech women were sexually insatiable, and that bagging a Jneer was the height of their ambition.

There was the superior genetic package a Jneer had to offer any potentially resultant children, after all, and the superior vigor of healthy young Jneer males as compared to the relatively weak and feeble Mech men—at least that was the theory. Raleigh knew it couldn't be him, and he wasn't about to get back to the Nouns and tell the truth. He'd kept careful records of the ladies' names, with a cryptic code of his own devising that could very easily be misinterpreted by a casual reviewer.

Alys was looking at him, waiting. Patiently. Clearly not about to let him go with that statement unexplained. "What I mean is that I convinced myself. Your stores finally convinced me. I admit I thought there might be a little natural exaggeration occurring in reports to the technical council."

That was what he would do in their place, at any rate. With the competition for resources the way it was, everybody tended to make out as if things were just a little bit worse than they actually were. That was why the technical council made a practice of cutting the allocation by ten to twenty percent across the board, and the Fleet hadn't fallen apart for lack of resources yet, so it was obviously the right thing to do.

She didn't look convinced, but they were at the end of the corridor. She stepped out and away from underneath his arm, politely not noticing that it was even there. "I'm glad we've given satisfaction on that point. You know that we get underfunded constantly, maybe we'll be made whole on your report. Well, good-bye, Marquette. Have a good trip to Ponics."

And she was gone with a nod of her head and a brisk step backwards, pivoting on her heel and away down the hall. Raleigh watched after her, bemused. She was not convinced by his story; why should she be? Nevertheless she hoped that they'd be "made whole," on his report. Not likely, when what he had to report was that there was consistently no sign of the resources distributed by the Noun Ships through the technical councils.

The Mech story was that such resources were fully consumed as issued, but they could hardly be that fully consumed. No. The Mechs were either resource-starved or they were hiding something, and they were all without exception in better shape than he was. Robust. Fit. Able to lift and carry loads which left him gasping.

Maybe it wasn't that surprising that nobody wanted to have sex with him; they probably figured he'd collapse halfway to heaven and leave the crucial piece of business undone.

Now, as often these days, Raleigh's thoughts turned to Hillbrane. What must it be like for her, cast out into this environment? Had she been let in on the secret of the stores? Was she getting any sex, or did the Mech men despise her as weak, as the Mech women apparently despised him?

He had to get her back. She didn't belong here, in these cramped quarters, in these narrow halls, living in community with Mechs and breathing their stale air. Hillbrane deserved Waystation One. He deserved Waystation One. And he was going to figure out a way for both of them to get what they deserved.

As soon as he got back to the Noun Ships.

As soon as he told the technical council what they needed to know about the Mech reports.

That would serve them right for scorning his public-spirited offers of Jneer babies, wouldn't it?

And he and Hillbrane could live happily ever after.

Smiling, Raleigh sauntered off down the low-ceilinged corridor to seek his dim and distant quarters, and get packed.

It was her day off. Hillbrane sat in the closet they'd cleared out for her to use as a laboratory, humming happily to herself as she ran a set of calculations on viscosity of field. Her own little closet, her own little lab, and while such things were more or less taken for granted where she'd come from, on the *Deecee* space was at a premium and this was a luxury.

Space they would let her use was at a premium, at any rate.

Space out toward the hull there was in plenty, but people under post-reproductive age were subject to strict internal restrictions as to how long they were allowed to spend out there, how often.

She'd come to the *Deecee* in the first place to work a problem on the Forenet as the Fleet traveled into less and less empty space after so many years. Some time ago an engineering directive had instructed the reduction of the Forenet's thickness and rate of capture; that had been in a deeper void, and had been mandated to conserve energy resources.

At least that was the only reason Hillbrane had unearthed for the original reduction.

And now—after so many years—enough of the nozzling had been replaced with fixtures that had only needed to accommodate a lower rate of flow that simply restoring the original system defaults caused problems of its own.

The technical council had ordered an emergency survey of the fixtures in place to assess the magnitude of the problem, though Hillbrane didn't quite understand that. Surely a documents search of maintenance records would yield the needed information?

But it wasn't her call. The survey was under way, the *Deecee* doing its part with the rest of the Forefront ships. The technical council wanted assurance from her that the problem could only be solved with new fixtures, and Hillbrane was close to finishing her proof. Only fixtures that conformed to original specifications could be required to perform to original specifications.

It wasn't always the case, but true enough on the Forenet, and the Forenet was—Hillbrane confidently expected—self-evidently more important to the Colony Fleet than the uses in climate control aboard the Noun Ships to which the original complement of replacement parts had been gradually diverted over time.

There was a tone at the door, and Hillbrane reached over for the admit without taking her eyes off her simulation as the calculations ran. She had a model plasma generator all her own; Rena and Ivery had built it for her out of scrap and surplus, pancakes and piecrust and piezo resistors. It was a piece of work that only increased her admiration for the Mechs' apparent abilities to improvise; could a Jneer have done that?

Would a Jneer even have thought to use a pulse laser on a plasma fabric generator model?

"You. Hillbrane."

It was Cago at the door; Hillbrane smiled at her model. "You too, Cawdor, what brings you to my cell? Welcome." The others tried to leave her alone, when she was in her lab. She didn't mind the occasional interruption. She especially didn't mind Cago.

"There's a work crew going out to the forward station, Aitchel. Maintenance on the shipnet generators twice a year, whether it needs it or not. I thought you might like to come. It's not usually open out there. You like storage areas. They'll all be empty, but that's never stopped you."

He was absolutely right. Hillbrane watched her model spool for a moment, then put down her protective goggles. The model would run without her. If it snagged—well, she'd have to do some recovery, but the data would still be there. "Great. I'm with you. What can I do to help?"

Standing aside to let her into the corridor, Cago smiled at her. He did that a lot. Most of it was a sort of a suffused grin that softened his whole face and elicited an involuntary smile of delight from her in response. "You can come help calibrate. I wouldn't ask you on your off-day, but you've never been out there. It's clearing the airlock that takes the most time, really. An hour. Maybe an hour and a half, but we all have to come and go together. It's a really conservative airlock."

This was more interesting than just getting access to a new storeroom. She'd never seen the shipnet generator stations except on remote; since airlocks were opened as seldom as possible, nobody had offered to take her out there just to gratify her natural curiosity. It was nice of Cago to think about her. She wouldn't mind spending the day in recalibration; she and Cago worked well together—or at least she enjoyed working with him.

Six others were waiting forward when she and Cago arrived. They'd hurried, but she'd kept up and she wasn't out of breath; she was proud of herself. She'd been so weak and miserable her first few weeks here that she was very glad indeed to finally be acclimatizing to whatever it was that had debilitated her so. These people she knew, but not too well; they were on crews that were on countershifts from hers—Delacourt, Sanders, Ivery, Farsi, Wyatt, and Neyrem.

Once she and Cago were within speaking distance, Delacourt waved them into the airlock, stepping across the pressure threshold into the airlock chamber. "Cago. Chelbie. Good of you to give us a hand. Let's go."

It was a large airlock as airlocks went, but still and close as all airlocks were. Hillbrane felt a little uneasy about the fact that she'd only come to look at storerooms, but they needed her to help calibrate—that was her excuse. Cago and the others had apparently accepted her fascination with storage areas as an obscure sort of antiquarianism, harmless if in rather bad taste. Sooner or later she'd find where they were *really* keeping things, though; and what then?

Would she feel vindicated to have uncovered the secret she knew must exist, or unhappy to have validated every Jneer suspicion about the baseline duplicity of the Mechs?

More than that, how would she feel about herself, to have taken advantage of their trust and confidence only in order to prove them all liars? What did that say about her own integrity?

There was little conversation during the wait for the airlock to complete its cycle; people took naps. Mech airlocks were so slow, especially ones out near the skin of the ship. She was glad to get out. Once the airlock cleared, the others went ahead to start their work; the calibration was the last step, she wasn't needed till later. She could explore.

She had storerooms to look at.

Most of the storage areas out here were shallow door panels wedged into odd angles and marked with glyphs identifying what had once been behind them: tools, replacement parts, maintenance equipment. Hillbrane opened them one by one, taking her time so as to draw out the anticipation and the suspense for as long as possible.

No luck.

She got a brief burst of air from compartments left sealed for years and years and years, but there was nothing left inside any of them but odds and ends, scraps and rubbish. Packing cases. Old dilapidated wheelers. Frayed strap-ends of containment nets. Nothing.

It was a long walk from the airlock out along the great curve of the hull of the *Deecee* to where the plasma generation station was, and though there were storage niches all along the way, they did not provide much distraction or amusement.

They were all empty.

Where were the stores that had to be here?

She couldn't ask, not in so many words; because the Mechs had been claiming for years that there were no such stores. That the original loads had been depleted over time until there was nothing usable left, since the Noun Ships had not stepped up to their expected place in the supply chain. That the Founders had always intended for stores to be replenished constantly from goods produced on the Noun Ships, and shipped out—rather than absorbed by the privileged lifestyle the Jneers had carved out for themselves, with the Oways' complicity.

Even the emergency oxygen sets were long gone, waiting at some Noun or another for recharge. That had been a point of contention for years; Hillbrane didn't even need to ask to know.

Even the Mechs knew better than to cannibalize the oxygen sets in the lifeboats for onboard use. As sets were discharged over time due to emergency or leakage they tended to accumulate with the Nouns, who were in no particular hurry to send them back. The Mechs made do in the meantime, which was why the corridors were lined with greenstrips, banks of ponics scrubbing the air and producing oxygen.

As far as Hillbrane could tell they didn't do either very effectively and contributed only to the general sense of claustrophobia that had weighed upon her from her arrival. She tried not to think about it.

She had been here for five months now.

These people weren't liars.

There was still room for so profound a difference of perception that the effect was the same, but Hillbrane was beginning to doubt it, and it introduced an element of reluctance into her expectations of returning to the Jneers. She would have to speak out. She would have to explain. She would not be popular.

She wasn't looking forward to it. Nor had she much more time to solve the problem; Podile's speech had made it clear that the Jneers knew quite well she was rightfully one of them, and as one of the group of Jneers at the beginning of her reproductive life she could confidently expect to be placed in the colonization party, which was to consist of as many people with breeding potential as possible.

Some older people would have to be part of the colony for their skills and authority, that was true; and some children would be included as well, when they were part of a young healthy family. But First Colony, Waystation One, would be mostly young people. The success of the colony would depend

upon solid population growth, especially in its early years—
when developing and replacing labor resources would be critical.

So she could be sure that she would be there.

But what about these Mechs?

How was it going to feel to leave them behind?

She could hope that her new friends would be selected, she
could even take steps to see that they were, but what kind of
influence would she really have if she brought back a message
as unpopular as "the Mechs have been telling the truth all
along"?

The whole thing gave her a headache.

She went to find Cago at the worksite and talk, so that she
wouldn't have to think about things.

Out on the site at last, Hillbrane joined Cago quietly at the
first calibration station and had a look at what was there. She
could see from the ship's diagnostics how the plasma generation stations overlapped their fields to set a protective barrier
far enough out from the ship's skin itself to safely absorb the
ferocious impact of particles, howsoever minute, traveling at
near light speed, and fully attenuate the energy before the particle could impact on the hull.

Plasma shields were only organic in the strictest sense of
the term; they could not be said to be sentient in any sense.
And yet through a trick of physics and mechanics, the plasma
shields behaved as though they possessed a primitive level of
consciousness, pooling at points of impact, passing the energy
out and away in great billowing waves.

Gazing through the specfinder out into black Space through
the thin filmy barrier of the plasma net, Hillbrane had a vision
of sorts, a thought about her model.

The plasma net behaved like a sentient being, evening itself
out after a particle strike. It sought and maintained equilibrium
thickness.

If she pulsed the feed from the largest nozzles and the small-
est nozzles to complement each other, if she timed the pulse
waves correctly, could she achieve the effect of a constant rate

of spool from a standard nozzle? Or would the smaller nozzles overheat and plug up under the strain of forcing a pulse through?

It was worth investigating. She could see the coding in her mind, wave forms overlapping with musical harmony. It would be an interim fix, if nothing else, but it was going to be a few hours before she could get to it. Clearing the airlock alone took more than an hour, and the job that Delacourt and Wyatt were on was not one that could be rushed.

Cago was sitting with his back to the wall and his hands clasped over his templed knees, watching her. Plopping down to the floor by his side, Hillbrane put her concerns about storerooms and colonies to the back of her mind. Cago was a nice guy. She liked him. It was hard to stay worried about things with Cago around.

And there was no time like the present to ask him a few questions about life, the universe, and everything.

FIVE

FORWARD STATIONS

"**W**hat do you mean, you don't have First Sex?" Hillbrane demanded, astonished and outraged and half-convinced that Cago was feeding her a line. Taking advantage of her ignorance. "How do you learn how to do it?"

Three hours, sitting and watching Wyatt and Delacourt work.

It wasn't something she could really help with; plasma generation station maintenance was strictly a two-person job, and reserved for people who had been doing it for long enough that their efficiency as a team was maximized.

She couldn't even watch, because she got in the light, and the others were generally doing what they could to stay out of the way until the time came for the final calibrations to be run.

Exactly how the subject had gotten around to First Sex Hillbrane was not sure, but Cago wasn't backing down in discomfort. No, he was arguing back.

"You learn with the person you've decided on. You learn with your partner. It's a collective effort. Or at least there's another word we use when it's not."

What was he talking about? One person? Decided on? "This makes no sense, Cago. Since when is there some kind of a connection between life partners and sex partners? Everybody knows that doesn't work. What if my mother had been stuck with nobody but my father to have sex with? Can you imagine? What a bore."

She didn't remember all of that much about the private lives of her parents. She did remember that it had frequently been up to her father to help her Oway nurse with the domestic details, because her mother seemed to have frequent sex appointments. And her parents had loved each other; too much— the only reason they had died together was that her father had gone back into the fire after he'd got Hillbrane out.

She'd always resented that about her father. If he had had a little more self-preservation in his blood, she need not have been an orphan.

"Now, Aitchel." Cago's voice was warm and rich with affection, fraternal and admonitory. Well. Maybe not fraternal. How would she know? She'd been an only child, like most of the rest of the Jneers that she knew. "It's not quite as bad as all that. My parents are happy with each other, and they keep having sex. At least they keep having children. That's why I had to leave: we were running out of room."

This insistence of his that happiness and a monogamous sex life were not self-contradictory confused her. People simply didn't thrive on the same food every day, day in, day out, week after month after year. It was unnatural.

In the quiet of the corridor the metallic sounds that came from Station Four as Wyatt and Delacourt worked resounded clearly, even though the air was less than fresh. Watching them work from where she sat beside Cago, Hillbrane caught Delacourt's eye; Delacourt was smiling. For whatever reason. Frowning at the open doorgate to Station Four's generator as if the answer could be read in the grate that fronted it, Hillbrane struggled with the alien concepts Cago seemed intent on inculcating.

"I can't imagine going for three years without . . ." she began.

Station Four exploded in a sudden roar of black smoke and pellets of insulation, knocking Wyatt and Delacourt clear to the opposite wall.

Cago grabbed her, fierce and sudden, and rolled with her over the bruisingly hard decking down-corridor, away from the station.

Fire, Hillbrane thought, and panic seized her. Fire. The fire suppression systems were heavy gas, they'd suffocate—

She couldn't see what was going on; Cago had her wrapped in a protective embrace, his body a shield between her and the station. She was frantic to find out what had happened, and struggled to free herself, but even as she fought against Cago's arms around her, he let go and rolled away again with a desperate sort of energy. Turning back to the fire. Turning back to the explosion. He couldn't go back there—the fire—he would be burned—

But once he no longer held her, she was free to move, and found her footing, supporting herself against the corridor wall as she struggled to her feet. No fire. Debris, and there was blood on Delacourt's face, but whatever had exploded had not sparked.

The plasma net generator.

Wyatt and Delacourt were back on station, and there was a new sort of urgency in the grim tension of their bodies as they worked. Hillbrane understood as clearly as if she had been told. The plasma net generator on Station Four had failed at the point of contact and fused down, sending a plume of pulsating energy erupting into the ship's corridor; that had been the explosion.

So there was no fire, but the plasma net generator had failed, an entire segment of the ship's net was gone, the hull was unprotected. They had to get the replacement put in and on-line. Every moment counted, and Wyatt worked with Delacourt in grim and focused silence to bring the net on-line and shield the ship.

Minutes passed.

No one spoke, and in the listening silence tense breathing was all too eloquently descriptive of the pressure Delacourt and Wyatt were under, the urgency of the task.

Long minutes, slow minutes, minutes as full of time as

hours, minutes that seemed to stretch for days—

Then Delacourt snapped the net-cage shut, first one latch, then the other, and clamped the hinged hatch cover door across the access portal with trembling but determined hands. The access portal, the maintenance gate, the netstation's monitor shields in turn; Hillbrane herself was feeling the tension, breathing deep and trembling in mute fear.

Wyatt set the defaults and switched on.

The lights dimmed as power drained into the ship's net: and the alarms went off, the klaxon shrieking as the emergency floodlights strobed.

Hull breach in segment three two four one eight stroke six. Hull breach. Hull breach. Evacuate at once, evacuate, evacuate. Repressurization cannot occur until repair has been completed. Evacuate.

The speaker's voice was calm and clear, the accent the old-fashioned standard common to all such prerecorded announcements in the Colony Fleet. If it had not been an emergency it would be funny, the stark contrast between the calm considered tone of the warning and the urgency of the situation.

There was no time to be amused.

Cago grabbed her by one arm and pulled her with him. Station One. Recalibration had to be completed before they could afford to leave. A hull breach had been announced, they had to evacuate, but they had to bring the ship's net back on-line first, or risk additional damage to other portions of the ship: and recalibration could not be rushed.

"Station. Number one relay. Spool is seventeen, viscosity twelve, vector six. Mark. Two. Three. Report."

One relay down. "Number one relay, spool seventeen, vee-twelve, vector six, check."

Only twenty to go.

Taking a deep breath to center her energies Hillbrane concentrated on the here and now, and tried not to think about the fact that they were losing atmosphere moment by moment as they worked.

* * *

By the time the last relays were brought on-line Hillbrane had a headache, equal parts stress and her own imagination—she hoped. It was a long walk back to the airlock. There was no supplemental oxygen between here and the portal, and the airlock itself would take more than an hour to complete its cycle.

There was no time to lose, but the others weren't setting out for the airlock. No, the others were gathered around Wyatt instead, and as much as Hillbrane wanted to get out of this compromised corridor—as panicked as she felt, her heart pounding, her breath coming in short sharp shallow panting gulps—she didn't want to go first. What was the matter with Wyatt?

The air.

Wyatt was bent near double in the corridor with his hands braced on his thighs, gasping for air as though he was suffocating, his face gone white and bloodless. There had been a hull breach. They were losing atmosphere. And Wyatt was a blue bloater, a man suffering from a genetic disease that made him less tolerant of low oxygen than normal healthy people were supposed to be. Wyatt was dying.

The realization hit Hillbrane in the pit of her stomach and paralyzed her for long moments. How could it be that Wyatt was going to die? She'd never known anyone who'd died—except for her own parents, and that had been different, unique. Polite people didn't die in public. She liked Wyatt.

But they had to get to the airlock. Wyatt might be more susceptible to the thinning air than the rest of them, but none of them were going to survive unless they got back into a fully-pressurized environment. The autolock had been set as a matter of procedure: nobody could come through from the ship until they cleared the threshold—one door would not open until the other door was closed. They had to get to the airlock. They had to get started.

Still the others were frozen in their places around Wyatt, and could she blame them? If it was terrible to her to realize that she was going to have to abandon Wyatt to save herself, if it was horrible to realize that she had to leave Wyatt to die, how much more awful must it be for the people who knew him better than she did, people who had known him all their lives?

And still they were all Mechs. Accidents happened. Wyatt understood. It had to be.

Why weren't they saying good-bye?

Cago moved on Wyatt with Delacourt beside him, and took Wyatt's left arm, pulling it over his shoulder as Delacourt repeated the gesture on Wyatt's other side.

Hillbrane stared.

They weren't going to leave him.

The hull was breached and they were losing atmosphere, and these idiots were going to try to drag Wyatt all the long way back to the airlock with them—Wyatt, who was as good as dead already?

She couldn't believe it.

Yet that was what was happening.

Cago and Delacourt started down the corridor with Wyatt between them, grim determination clear on their faces. Hillbrane backed up in front of them, unable to stop staring, incapable of fully grasping the magnitude of this idiocy.

Wyatt was a dead man. As short of breath as he was already, he could never make it to the airlock before he had suffered irreparable brain damage. What good did it do anybody to drag a corpse to an airlock, at grave risk to themselves? Because carrying, half-dragging, Wyatt was going to be hard work, as well as slowing the whole party down.

Hillbrane could hear Cago's gasping breath. It made no sense. The stupidity of this failure to think straight made her furious.

Worse than that, the others were not moving ahead, the others were not making the rational choice and saving themselves, no, the others walked behind Cago and Delacourt. *Behind.* They weren't carrying anything, and yet they stayed?

Speechless and appalled, Hillbrane stared, till Cago glanced up and caught her eye. She couldn't quite interpret the expression on his face, but it wasn't something she liked.

Disappointed, somehow.

But why would that be?

"You go on, Aitchel," Cago said, or wheezed. "No need for you to do this. Mech thing. Go on."

Well, that was the first sensible suggestion she'd heard since the alarms had gone off. Of course there was no reason for her to stay. There was no reason for anybody to stay. There was no reason for them to endanger themselves to carry a dying man back to an airlock that they would never reach in time.

She turned to go—and somehow couldn't leave.

These weren't stupid people; there had to be a reason for their irrational behavior.

She had to go, she had to run, she had to get to the airlock. If she collapsed there at least she would be closer to rescue than she could hope to get if she followed these idiots carrying their almost-corpse. Wyatt had panted himself into near-collapse. The strain of carrying him forward was all too evident on Cago's face. Why didn't they realize that heavy physical labor was the last thing a person should do in a situation where oxygen was thinning?

One step, two steps, three steps, then Hillbrane stopped and looked over her shoulder at Cago in an agony of confusion. Cago wasn't looking at her. Head down, shoulders straining, Cago was struggling under Wyatt's all-but-dead weight to move forward. This was insanity. They would all die, instead of just Wyatt. There was no way they could get to the airlock in time to save even themselves at this rate.

What kind of people made so self-destructive a decision as that, let alone without discussion or argument? It was as though they hadn't even thought twice about it.

"Shake a leg, Chelbie," Ivery called from the back. "There's no time to waste, go on." No hint of mockery or scorn in her voice, none. Clear certainty of possible death. Clear acceptance of that possibility.

Ivery was right, of course.

There was no time to waste, no margin for error, none. Her chest already ached, her lungs were sore with fruitless effort to pull more oxygen out of an atmosphere that contained too little. Her head throbbed, as if a sharp oppressive weight lay close upon her skull, making it difficult to think.

Let these misguided Mechs martyr themselves for no good cause or valid reason. She knew what she had to do. And she knew that she had to hurry.

She wasn't dying for anybody if she could help it.

Cago watched Hillbrane go with mixed emotions at war within his heart and mind. He had been wretched with misery from the moment the explosion had occurred; he never would have brought her down here if he'd been thinking. And he should have been thinking. There was always the chance of a disaster, and the crew knew it and accepted it as part of life. But Hillbrane? How could she have known? And since she could not be expected to know what every Mech knew, how could she have accepted the risk in any meaningful sense?

It was his fault for bringing her down here, his fault for not thinking. She would go ahead. She would be waiting at the airlock, though it was unthinkable that she might engage the airlock with the rest of her team still in the halls behind her. Hillbrane would be all right. Wyatt was dead, or as good as, because there was no way to get him through the airlock in time.

He'd always been one of those unfortunates hypersensitive to reduced oxygen. Something to do with the genetics that had shaped his lungs and compounded his blood. Something like that.

And still it was so hard that Hillbrane had fled. She was a Jneer. She was practical. She thought things through on a clear track to a logical conclusion. It was nothing personal. Hillbrane had not abandoned her crew to save herself. She'd merely evaluated the circumstances and made the sensible choice.

Cago struggled on with Wyatt and Delacourt, feeling the strain in his lungs as he worked to keep Wyatt on his feet and moving. Maybe if he concentrated on practicalities it would be easier. There were five pieces to the journey back to the airlock; three of them long, two of them short. This was one of the short pieces, from the stations to the first turning, the turning Hillbrane had cleared and disappeared around.

There was no telling how long he was going to last before some of the others would have to take over. He had to make it as long as possible. Wyatt would be much heavier by then: the dead weight of an unconscious man was that much different from the weight of a man even semiconscious. Cago knew that he was one of the strongest people with this crew, right here, right now—he and Delacourt. He had to get Wyatt as far as he could. It was going to be difficult. Already the effort made his pulse pound.

Cago focused his eyes stubbornly on the decking a few feet ahead of them and moved forward. Here. They were at the first turning. They'd finished the first short leg. Three long legs, one short leg, and they were home free. Surely he could carry Wyatt at least as far as the next turning; that wasn't even half the total distance. Surely he could make it that far.

Delacourt was breathing hard.

This was going to get a lot worse before it got any better.

They fought on. Wyatt was having trouble keeping to his feet, even supported on two sides. Cago dreaded the time to come when Wyatt would lose consciousness. They were less than halfway down the first long corridor to the turning; and he already noticed himself missing a step here and there. He fought to keep from staggering.

The physical effort was stressing the limits of what he could do, all too quickly. His body was on fire with the stress of anaerobic effort, muscles worked too hard with too little oxygen. And yet he couldn't give up, he hated to give up, he knew too well that the others would tire even more quickly.

Couldn't he at least reach the turn in the corridor before he had to surrender Wyatt to another of the crew? That wasn't even halfway, it was barely a third of the way, couldn't he at least make it that far? It was only another few dozen yards, now, he could see the turning—

No, Cago realized, with the bitter taste of frustration and defeat sharp in his mouth. No. He wasn't even going to make it to the bend in the corridor. There was a rumbling sound, a roaring sound in his ears that meant that he was going to drop within moments.

He was going to have to stop and hand his task over to one of the others, before he fell—and pulled both Wyatt and Delacourt down with him. As much as he hated it, he had no margin for stubbornly pushing himself when it was the progress of the group that he had to think about.

The roaring in his ears was growing louder moment by moment, a clattering rush like an empty draycart out of control. No good. Cago staggered to a standstill in the corridor, Wyatt half-conscious and swaying on his feet between Cago and Delacourt.

Delacourt was looking up ahead of them in the corridor with a confused expression on her face. What, she heard it too? They were both spent, then. Or maybe she was just astonished at how little of the distance that they had to cover had been put behind them, how much further they had to go.

Ivery came up beside Cago, and he wanted to see who would spell Delacourt before he relinquished his hold on Wyatt's arm. Ivery was short, it would be awkward. But Ivery wasn't trying to slip between him and Wyatt. Ivery was pressing past, turning herself sideways in the corridor to get by, hurrying out ahead.

Cago stood and stared. His brain was not working. He felt as stupid and as slow as a man on the wrong end of three shifts back to back. What was going on? What was happening?

Ivery came back around the bend in the corridor.

She had Hillbrane with her.

And Hillbrane had—a wheeler.

White in the face and pale-lipped, gasping with the effort it took to pull enough air into her lungs, narrow-eyed with desperate determination, and she had a box on wheels with her, a box big enough to hold the body of a helpless man and move it forward as swiftly as it could be pushed.

Sanders and Farsi came around from behind as Cago stared, and with Ivery's help they got Wyatt into the box. Cago still stood and stared, till Farsi came back to him and took him by the arm to move him along. Right. They moved as a group. Nobody left behind. Neyrem helped Hillbrane, Sanders helped Delacourt, Farsi helped him, and Cago guessed by the strain that he felt in his lungs even at rest that the atmosphere was thinning perceptibly and dangerously moment by moment.

There was no time to wonder at Hillbrane.

She was a Jneer, but she had thought of a solution and she had come back to them to share it, and if Wyatt had any hope at all it was because of Hillbrane's wheeler—

They had to get to the airlock.

Then he could ask her to marry him.

As soon as he caught his breath . . . if he ever did.

She couldn't breathe. The air grew dark around her as the long seconds passed, and a sort of snow of white burning particles perpetually adrift in her field of vision gave Hillbrane a headache and annoyed her at one and the same time. It was an annoyance all out of proportion with its relative importance, because who needed to see when they were dying?

That was perhaps the answer, Hillbrane realized, to the extent that it was possible to suffer so vigorous a thing as a realization while her head ached fit to split like a ripe melon.

She was going to die. If she stopped to think about that she would be frightened, angry, paralyzed with confusion. As it was she found herself in a towering rage at the white sparks that danced in her field of vision.

There was no air.

The sound of the wheels on the decking was drowned by the rushing sound of her blood in her ears. The wheels were loud enough for all of that. It was much easier to move a weight in a wheeler than drag it, as she had hoped it might be. That had been a good guess. She should probably thank whomever had thought of it. Cago, probably.

Hillbrane clung to the lip of the cart as it traveled through rapidly chilling corridors, pushing out from time to time when she found the strength to move her feet. She had to concentrate on holding on. Nobody would have time to come back and get her if she fell by the wayside.

They stopped moving.

Gasping for breath, Hillbrane sank to the decking and sat there with her back against the wall. The airlock. Yes. They were at the airlock. They had to wait, though, for everybody to get here before they could engage. Was everybody here?

Now that she wasn't working so hard to hang on to the cart, her breath came a little more easily. The white spots in front of her eyes that had bedeviled her had grown transparent; it was almost as though they weren't there at all. Hillbrane could count. She couldn't match feet to faces, on the floor, but she could count feet. One. Two. No, she had to count pairs of feet, two feet to a person. Right. One pair of feet. Two pair. Three. Four. Five, six.

Hillbrane frowned.

There had to be eight.

She counted again, one pair, five pair, six pair; and then she remembered that Wyatt was in the wheeler. That was all right, then, wasn't it? The airlock door was almost closed; they would have air soon. If only she could be sure about her numbers. Wyatt was one pair. Three, four, six, seven.

No. There were still too few feet. Someone was out there. Someone had fallen behind. There was someone stuck out there in the corridor, abandoned, marooned, dying—once the airlock door closed there would be no possible chance of rescue and survival—

The others had all sat down now. They had given up, or else they hadn't realized. There was no sense trying to speak: she knew she couldn't get the wind for it, not and hope to move. And she had to move. She had to stop the airlock door somehow. She could not bear the thought of someone left behind, not after they had all worked so hard to bring Wyatt back.

It was more effort than she had ever dreamed possible just to crawl. She wasted long moments trying to catch her breath once she'd rolled over onto her hands and knees, and she had no time to waste. There was no time. The airlock doors were closing. She had to get to the airlock doors, if she could but put her body in their track the doors would halt and reset, lock themselves off for fifteen minutes. It would give her time to explain.

Struggling toward the airlock, Hillbrane ran into an object that she hadn't realized was in the way. She'd thought the path between her and the airlock doors was clear; what was happening to her? Had the wheeler rolled across the doorway by accident? She could use it, if it was the wheeler, she could push it on ahead of her. Into the gap between the airlock doors. There were only six pairs of feet, and Wyatt. Someone was still out there.

She couldn't get past the obstruction in her path. She pushed with all her might; it didn't move. What was the matter with her?

Then she realized that it was Cago, and he was holding her, keeping her from the door. Talking to her. She could make no sense whatever out of what Cago was saying, but the meaning behind his words was clear enough. It was too late. The person they had left behind back in the corridors was doomed. Even if she could stop the airlock doors in time, they had no strength—no strength left, and no air. They could not go out and rescue their fallen comrade. Their only chance to survive at all was to let the door close and let their partner die.

Half-sitting, half-lying on the floor in Cago's arms, Hillbrane stared at the airlock doors as they came together. Locked, and sealed. Now it really was too late. She had no air with which to weep; she could only stare in mute misery. Somebody was on the other side of that door. Somebody had watched it close and seal, sealing their death warrant with it. Somebody . . .

Her body had grown as heavy as lead weight. Now that she no longer struggled toward the airlock, Cago's embrace relaxed, and Hillbrane pushed herself away to lie on her back on the decking and gaze up at the ceiling with unblinking eyes.

Someone left to die.

Six pairs of feet; and Wyatt.

Silence fell in the airlock. There was only the hissing sound of air being drawn into the chamber from the interior of the ship. There was no need for there to be a sound at all. Air only hissed in airlocks for the psychological effect it had, the role of the noise in fooling people into thinking that they could breath more easily even while the atmosphere itself was still substandard.

Lying on her back on the decking Hillbrane was glad of the sound, whether artificially produced or not. It might have been just a simple psychological trick. But it was working. She felt better moment by moment.

Who had been left behind?

After a while she dragged herself over to the wall to sit up once more, beside Cago this time. Glancing around her she took inventory, not wanting to seem too obvious. There were Farsi and Neyrem to her right and Delacourt between them; Cago to her left. The wheeler in the corner, empty now, because next to it Ivery and Sanders sat to either side of Wyatt to make sure he stayed seated in an upright position.

Who was missing?

She couldn't make sense of it, and counted again, using calibration posts this time to try to find the hole in ranks. Delacourt and Wyatt on four, Sanders and Neyrem on two, and Ivery and Farsi had covered three. She and Cago had been on station one. So who was missing?

Oxygen kept hissing into the airlock. Wyatt was ashen-faced and blue-lipped, but Hillbrane could see him breathing, and it looked almost normal from where she sat. She knew she had counted. She had. It was almost worse than having left someone out to die in the first place, this not knowing who it was that they had left—that they had given up.

She tried again.

Cago, that was one pair.

Farsi, Delacourt, Neyrem; Ivery; Wyatt, and she could count him without qualification now, because he was sitting with the rest of them. He was six, which made Sanders seven, and she was eight; so where—

Hillbrane stared at her own two feet stretched out in front of her, aghast.

It couldn't be.

She counted again.

It was.

They were all here, all safe, all alive, all whole.

She had counted wrong. She had forgotten to add herself. They had not made a terrible mistake. They had not left one of their own to die.

She had so nearly killed them all for so stupid a miscalculation—if she had stopped the airlock, they might all have died, for who knew what damage the extra minutes would have done them?

Seven pairs of feet. And Hillbrane.

It was too much.

She tucked herself against Cago's side and wept until the world went dark and quiet for her at last.

Cago sat on the floor with an arm around the sleeping Hillbrane, waiting for the airlock to finish its repressurization. It seemed to take forever, and he knew it was only about an hour. It had taken less time on the way in, but that had been before they'd put a hole in the ship's skin.

Ivery and Sanders sat on either side of Wyatt, who was breathing more easily moment by moment. Farsi and Neyrem sat with Delacourt, because she'd hit her head and there was no sense in taking any chances. He was alone with Aitchel, and she was asleep.

He was so proud.

Nobody would have thought about looking in a storeroom for a cart. Nobody had thought about those storerooms forever. Who knew? And if Hillbrane hadn't made the right choice, done the right thing, used her knowledge to save Wyatt instead of herself, who would ever have known? No, she had shown her true mettle today. She was no Jneer. She was a Mech, but a Mech with a Jneer's education, a Jneer's background . . . and that would make her dangerous.

The repressurization sequence was nearing completion; he knew it from the program displays. Hillbrane was going to want to wake up, so that she could go to her quarters and go back to sleep. He gave her a little shake; and then a larger one.

"Come on, Aitchel. Back to the world. Wake up."

She awoke with a start, and put her hands to her head, pressing against her eyebrows with the heels of each palm. Yes, she probably had a horrible headache. All of them had headaches, it was the inevitable result of low oxygen. There would be a medical team waiting. She could take a powder.

"What." Her eyes were much less red than they had been, and her nose was also back to a near-normal color. There would be no obvious signs of crying to embarrass her. "Oh. Okay. Are we there yet?"

Perfect timing. There was the tone. The doors started to open up on freedom and safety and the comforting familiarity of the *Deecee*'s corridors. Full of people, but that was standard operating procedure. The hull breach alert would have been referred to the central coordination post, and there had been the alarms that went off when the available oxygen and atmospheric pressure fell below parameters.

The officers of the watch would be there with the emergency response team, and usually anybody else who didn't have anything in particular to do would tag along. Just in case an extra pair of hands was needed.

As soon as there was room to move a body through, Ivery and Sanders urged Wyatt out into the corridor so that the medical people could put him on precious supplemental oxygen. They had more trouble getting supplemental oxygen out of the Nouns; it was as if the Jneers in Fleet suspected they were misappropriating the gas to use for some contraband purpose, somehow. As if you could do anything more important with oxygen than breathe it. As if anyone would waste it.

Wyatt through, Delacourt was next, and by now the door was open wide enough to let people in to escort the rest of them out one by one. Mir was there; Cago sent Hillbrane on ahead and waited inside the airlock while Mir took it all in. The telltales on the wall. The atmosphere registers revealing the increasingly hostile environment on the other side—the wrong side—of the airlock wall. The cart, the cargo bin on wheels that had saved Wyatt's life—and maybe the rest of their lives along with it.

"Where did *that* come from?" Mir didn't need to be told what it was doing here. They all knew that Wyatt was vulnerable to low atmosphere. In a perfect world Wyatt would carry supplemental oxygen, prescribed by Jneer physicians if need be. "I haven't seen one of these old things since I can't remember."

They were inefficient and awkward as cargo movers—they were old. That was why this one had been abandoned in some storeroom in the first place. "Chelbie remembered seeing it on our way in. Come on. We should let her tell it, this is a good one." And Aitchel, *his* Aitchel, was a hero. She had done valiantly and well. "His" Aitchel? Who said? And yet she had done well.

Out in the corridor the medteam had Wyatt on a mask, but he was sitting up and looking well. Delacourt's eyes didn't seem to be looking in precisely the same directions, but it was hard to tell—who watched other peoples' eyes closely enough to tell a difference, before and after a whack on the head? For all he knew she could always have been a bit cross-eyed. With luck she was just concussed, nothing more serious.

Everybody else was standing around Hillbrane, who had her arms crossed and hugged to herself and a frown of concentra-

tion on her face. Maybe of pain; she had a headache. One way
or the other Aitchel did not look comfortable, and Cago wondered what was going on with her.

Mir went forward to where Hillbrane stood, intercepting the
medic's headache potion on his way to deliver it personally.
"Chelbie. Drink this, you'll feel better. What's the story with
the cart?"

It seemed that everyone started talking at once, then as
abruptly shut up, looking expectantly at Hillbrane. Hillbrane
kept shut, though, so Ivery started off again.

"Wyatt went down at the station," Ivery said. "You know
how far that is. Cago and Delacourt started walking him, but
it was slow going. Chelbie, here, she went ahead—"

They had all thought she had fled to ensure her own survival, that she hadn't realized she couldn't engage the airlock
prematurely without dooming some of them to death. Nobody
had thought that Hillbrane meant to engage the airlock and
abandon them. Cago was sure of that.

The emotion of past hours had caught up with Ivery, though,
it seemed. She let her voice trail off, and Sanders picked up
the narrative.

"She came back with the cart. Blue in the face with it. Once
we got Wyatt into the cart, we could all move much more
quickly. We made it. If we hadn't had the cart, we might not
have."

They wouldn't have. Cago didn't need to insist on the point.
They all knew what their margin had been, and that the only
reason there had been a margin at all was because Hillbrane
had come back with the cart. Covering the same distance as
the rest of them three times, and her a Jneer and tenderly
raised. It was the sort of thing that took genuine courage, or
a fine fierce determination at the very least. So why was Hillbrane frowning? She had proven herself. She was never going
to be teased for her Jneer background ever again.

"Aitchel." Cago called her name, speaking past the bodies
that stood between them. "You did a great thing, Aitchel, you
saved our lives. What's the problem?"

She looked straight at him, standing up on her toes just a bit to see. People got the idea and let him through to her. There was something going on here that Cago couldn't figure out, not readily.

"I'll tell you," Aitchel said, with an air of stubborn determination. "I'm lucky I remembered. I'm glad it worked. But I only knew the cart was there in the first place because I've been spying since I got here."

That shut people up. Aitchel looked like she was sorry she'd ever been born, but she didn't back down from whatever it was she'd decided she had to say. That was his Aitchel. Stubborn. He loved her for it.

"Everybody knows the Mechs aren't as poorly off as they claim. Everybody knows. All of those supplies must be going somewhere, it's just not possible to actually use things up that quickly. I could understand putting on a show, you don't expect me to stay. I don't expect to stay. I've been trying to figure it out."

She wasn't making perfect sense, but it was enough, and Cago felt his heart ache near to breaking for her. The pain was very unexpected, and surprising. Poor Aitchel. Poor self-deluded little Chelbie, facing her moment of truth, and in front of all these people.

"But there's nothing here. And you aren't pretending. You wouldn't risk Wyatt's life on it. And I'm not going back if they won't have me. Why should they have me? I've got to tell them the truth, and they won't like it, and that means I'll never go home."

Something had happened while she spoke.

Something had changed.

Cago stared, wondering, trying to understand, while Mir filled the silence that seemed to demand an answer to the question Hillbrane Harkover wasn't asking.

"You've seen for yourself, that's good, Chelbie. It doesn't change what you did for us. We owe you for seven lives, that's a lot. So far as we're concerned, you've got a place on the *Deecee* as long as you live, if you want it."

Berth-right.

And Aitchel didn't even know what it meant to be taken in to a ship as permanent complement. Many of them—himself included—were still finding their places in the Fleet, unsure of where they would find a home. Aitchel had a berth with her name on it now. She didn't have to wonder who would take care of her when she was old.

"All right." Hillbrane nodded, with dignified humility. "If you say so. Thank you. I want to speak at Allmeet, Mir. Because the Nouns don't know. I mean that they really believe it."

That was it, Cago realized. What had changed. She had been near-hysterical, vulnerable. And just in the course of a sentence she'd straightened up inside, in some way. Poor little Aitchel, he'd been thinking. She wasn't poor and she wasn't little, she was a grown person with more status now than he had—whether she realized it or not. So he felt protective, that was just the way he was. She could take care of herself. Because she had just taken responsibility for herself.

"We'll see about that." Cago knew that there was a procedure, and Chelbie had certainly earned the right to be heard on *Deecee*'s behalf. "But later. We need to get you all to quarters. Get some rest. Get some food. You need recovery time, you all do."

Come to think of it. Yes.

The medical people took Wyatt and Delacourt away, and the rest of them moved out to the mealroom with the crowd for escort, just to make sure they would all make it there safely.

It had been a long shift.

He was ready to call it a day.

If he'd known this would all happen, would he have called on Aitchel to come with them?

Sure he would. She was a hero. It didn't matter why she'd known the cart was there. If she'd elected not to remember it, or if she'd forgotten it under the stress of the event, at least one of the crew of the *Deecee* would be dead right now. Permanently.

It was just going to be a lot more complicated now to court her, now that she had her own berth-right—

And he'd worry about it after he'd slept.

For now it was enough to breathe the air; and maybe get some dinner.

Hillbrane couldn't sleep.

Every time she closed her eyes she was running down the corridor again, and again, and again, and never getting to where she needed to be in time. Not even knowing where she needed to be, but knowing that something horrible beyond imagining was going to happen if she didn't get there. Running. Not being able to breathe. Knowing something horrible was going to happen if she couldn't get to where she had to go . . .

Finally Hillbrane sat up in her bed in her little room deep in the heart of the *Deecee*. This was getting her nowhere, and she had a notion she was going to need her wits about her in the morning. What was she going to do?

Drawing her legs up to her chest and wrapping her arms around them, Hillbrane put her head down, resting her forehead on top of her bent knees. There was too much to think about. She couldn't possibly be expected to think it all through and get any sleep, not on the same night. She had to get to sleep. She was exhausted. Her whole body ached, her legs from the lactic acid residue of anaerobic muscle respiration, her ribs from fighting to draw enough of the increasingly thin air into her lungs to lift the weight of slow incremental suffocation off her diaphragm.

And every time she closed her eyes—

She'd never been at risk for her own life before, except for the fire. And that had been different. Her father had helped her out, and she had fled with the strength and fleetness only panic could grant. Today she had panicked, and she'd been afraid, but she had had to fight her own fear every step, tiring herself that much more dangerously.

She hadn't been so much afraid for herself as for Wyatt and the others, because they were clearly going to stay with Wyatt, which meant they all would probably die.

Had that been the difference?

It seemed rational.

Survival response would naturally favor flight, not return to a dangerous environment. It stood to reason that violating her own sense of self-preservation would require reserves of strength she almost didn't have.

What was she to make of the others, then?

She'd heard no discussion, sensed no hesitation. So far as she could recall there had been no thinking twice on anybody's part but hers. They had simply, naturally, automatically assumed the risk in common, merely to provide Wyatt a chance.

Risking themselves. Risking her. The lives of seven people for the life of one, and not even the life but the mere chance of life. If it had gone wrong, eight people might have died, and she might have been one of them.

What sort of a survival strategy was that?

It didn't matter. She didn't have to think about it. She couldn't think about it, it was too near and too threatening. And what was she to make of what she'd done? It had all come out right; she had won praise. Why did she feel so guilty?

Was it just because she was one of the Jneers who was responsible for the lack of emergency oxygen in the out-corridors to begin with?

Think, Hillbrane admonished herself, fiercely. There had to be a way around the mess her mind was in. What had it been that had worked for her that night on the flower-boats? Positive action. She had to find some plan of action she could take that would respond to what had happened today. If she could just decide what she could do to make a difference, surely she could turn the loop off in her mind and go to sleep.

She would go to Allmeet and tell the Jneers there that they were mistaken about Mechs and resources. She owed it to the *Deecee* to do that much at least. It would not be a popular message, but they would have to believe it coming from her—they knew she was as good a Jneer as the next, Comparisons notwithstanding.

Didn't they?

Or would they discount her words as evidence rather of her revealed Mech basic nature, and not evidence of having been mistaken all these years at all?

The colony was going to need flexible people. The colony could not afford to be directed by people who would rather deny a woman her birthright than acknowledge that wrong had been done. Hillbrane felt a sickening sense of certainty that the Jneers at Allmeet would do just that, however, and reject solid testimony as contrary to their preconceptions. Hadn't she watched it happen, and to her, before her very eyes?

Then she was simply going to have to make herself heard, one way or another. The colony was too important to risk it to Jneers. She had thought that it should be mostly Jneers, when she had lived on the Noun Ships; now she knew differently.

She would not be part of First Colony; she could accept that, because if she brought the truth about the Mechs home to the Noun Ships, she was unlikely ever to be welcomed back as one of them. All right. She would not be part of the First Colony. If only the Jneers would listen to her, she could have an important role to play in the survival and prosperity of the colony, whether physically part of it or not.

Which led her right back to the Mechs in the out-corridors today, Cago and Delacourt taking the burden of Wyatt's increasingly helpless body on their shoulders without a moment's hesitation or a second thought.

Wyatt was the best plasma field generation station repairman on the *Deecee*, and his skills went beyond that narrow field. What if it had all happened in the colony, in some sense?

What if the choice had been to let Wyatt die and try to save themselves, or risk themselves to survive as a group, and Wyatt had been the lead biogeneticist? Without a lead biogeneticist, less knowledgeable people would have to step up and make the decisions about soil amendment and crop rotation, expected yields, efficient rate of irrigation or minimax temperature ranges.

And maybe they would do as well.

Or maybe the loss of the lead biogeneticist would endanger the entire colony at a critical point in its establishment.

If there were one man and one woman in the world and only one survived, for all intents and purposes they had both failed. So it made sense to save each other, even risking both, because to save oneself at the expense of the other meant the same as if both had died.

Was it truly the survival-oriented instinct to take the chance on saving all the group's resources, when to lose any given resource might well doom the entire enterprise?

Hillbrane raised her head and stared at the wall at the foot of her cot, startled out of her self-reproachful mood by this novel idea.

It was not the Jneers' way.

But the colony had to be more truly cooperative a venture than the Jneers perhaps had stopped to realize. And she was in a position to say so. Because she was a Jneer.

She knew what she had to do now, and it was more than just using the venue of Allmeet to shame the Jneers into admitting that the Mechs were starved for resources while Jneers lived in comfort and security. She had to explain about what had happened today in the out-corridors. She had to find a way to communicate somehow what was important about what had happened, and what the implications were for the makeup of First Colony.

She was definitely going to have to sleep on it, and for that—obviously enough—she had to sleep.

She knew what to do.

Swinging her legs to the floor, Hillbrane found her footfloppies and slipped them on. There was an overshirt hanging across the chair attached to her readstation, and she shrugged her shoulders into its commodious folds, buttoning even as she went for the door. People were about *Deecee*'s corridors in various states of undress all the time. There was no reason for anyone to look twice at her.

She knew where Cago lived. She'd been by his room from time to time over the past months. Knocking on the door with great determination, she waited—not very patiently—for him to answer the summons and let her in.

She'd woken him up. Good. That meant his room was full of sleep. She wanted some. He stood in the doorway puffy-faced and with his hair sticking up every which way, and Hillbrane sailed in past him with a sense of great relief and satisfaction. Yes. This was right. This was good. She sat down on the edge of the bed and unbuttoned her work shirt, pushing her footfloppies out of the way. The bed was warm, and smelled like Cago. It was a comforting smell. She hurt less badly already.

She lay down with her back to the room, and after a moment the lights went off and Cago came to bed with her. He slid one arm under her neck and tucked her to him with his other arm, drawing the covers up over them both, made a place for his chin in the pillow behind her head and relaxed there. Holding her in his arms, and nothing between them but underwear.

She'd cried herself out earlier today. Now she simply lay in Cago's arms, and let the fear and tension, anxiety and uncertainty evaporate from her body in the comforting warmth of his embrace. Now she could sleep.

And, smiling, she did.

SIX
ALLMEET

Slowly Cago Warrine awoke in a great roseate glow of blessedness full of the voices of angels and the soft warm perfumed breezes of Paradise. That the angels sounded like the groaning and perpetually cross whispering of the *Deecee*'s ventilators, that the perfumed breezes of Paradise were borne aloft on a strong undercurrent of day-old laundry detracted not a single tessera from the picture of his bliss: he was in bed with Hillbrane Harkover, alone in his room with sweet Chelbie, and she slept with her cheek pillowed on the inside of his arm, snoring softly with the innocence of a cherub.

Of course she was snoring.

She was probably still processing fluid from her lungs, subclinical edema brought on by yesterday's strain. His arm was asleep, and he was going to need that hand to get dressed, because every bone in his body still ached.

And yet.

He'd thought he'd been dreaming, but here it was hours into the day after yesterday, and she was still here.

What was she doing here?

Well, sleeping. That much was obvious, wasn't it? No. In the larger sense. Had they been intimate?

What did he mean, asking himself that? How much more intimate could two people get than sleeping together in one single bed, and unmade since yesterday, as near to being nude as never mind asking?

They couldn't have been.

He would have remembered.

Surely he would have.

And they were both tired, and they were both sore. The signs weren't right.

Did he mean to suggest to himself that a young woman had come to his bed in the middle of the night and they'd both gone to sleep? Not just any young woman, but Aitchel the Jneer with her nice round flanks and her softly ripened thighs, that neck like the stalk of an exotic water flower and lips that looked as soft as petal-velvet, Hillbrane Harkover had come to bed, and all he had done about it was to sleep?

Lazily she stirred against him, stretching her back. Rounding her spine against his bare belly, tucking her sweetly curved backside into his lap. Or where his lap would be, if he'd been sitting down. The sensation that overwhelmed him was proof enough of the dire truth of the matter: because what he felt was a surge of affection, protective, half-fearful, fierce and too clear for there to be a mistake.

Well, of course he wanted to have sex with her. A man would have to be crazy insane not to want into that beautiful body.

But it was too clearly so much more than just that. Cago could only sigh in resignation, putting his free hand to her shoulder. They had to get up. She had to wake up, he needed his arm back. And he was more than merely infatuated with his Chelbie; he wanted to marry her for ever and always, and there was no telling whether Jneers even did that—let alone whether she'd marry him.

Still.

She had come to his room, hadn't she?

That had to mean something.

"Aitchel. Wake up." He didn't want her to wake up. He wanted to be here with her, just like this, forever. Well, all right, maybe a slight modification in position . . . no, they had to get up. But he didn't want to whisper in her ear, either. He'd had spiced meatballs for dinner last night. It had been Lowell's night to cook. Lowell had a wonderfully liberal hand with the onions.

"Come on, Aitchel, they'll be closing down the meal line." You could get something to eat any time, of course. But the pickings between mealtimes could get pretty thin. On the other hand, maybe it would be better if they missed the meal period—people would talk. Hell. There wasn't going to be any graceful way around this. Why didn't he just make up his mind to enjoy the false suppositions people were going to make?

"Sleeping beauty. It's laundry day. They'll be coming for the sheets." He was saying anything that came into his head, no matter how nonsensical. It seemed to work at last: she stretched again—while he thought resolutely of integral calculus, and mostly succeeded—and rolled over.

He rolled out of her way, hastily, and fell off the edge of the bed onto the floor. It wasn't a long fall. It was more embarrassing than anything else. He swore at the impact of the unforgiving floor against his own utterly inadequately padded rump, and Hillbrane was—wouldn't you know it—wide awake at once.

"Cago! Cago. Are you all right? What are you doing in my—oh."

No, she had come into his room, not the other way around. Cago struggled to his feet with as much grace as he could muster, grabbing his robe on his way up. He was still sore. They had worked hard, yesterday, and it hadn't been just the thinness of the atmosphere.

"Up and at 'em, Aitchel, it's time we were doing. You want to borrow a shirt?"

As he asked it he found one that wasn't his, and picked it up off the floor to hand to her. She stared at the garment in his hand with a species of confused horror: this was not going well. "So, you were maybe walking in your sleep last night, or something?"

He offered the polite explanation in as casual a manner as

he could muster, on his way into the lavatory. He remembered at the last minute to close the door. He half-expected her to bolt from the sheer awkwardness of it all while he was closeted away; but when he came out she was still there. Sitting on the edge of the bed in her footfloppies with her shirt on. Staring at her feet.

"I couldn't sleep." Okay, so the walking-in-your-sleep gag was out. "I knew I would be able to relax if I came here. I would be able to be comfortable. No. I would feel safe."

She raised her head as she said it, looking him in the eye with an expression of dawning comprehension and bemused joy on her face. It was practically more than he could deal with, first thing in the morning.

His throat was sore from the work of breathing, yesterday. Just now there was a lump in it. Most inconvenient. "Let me be your safe place, Aitchel," Cago said. "I can't think of anything I'd rather be." Well, king of the Colony Fleet, maybe. Maybe.

No.

She was smiling—half in apparent disbelief, half in what seemed to be appreciation of the humor of the situation. "I'm not going to be a Jneer, Cago. They're not going to want me back, not ever, not after what I have to say to the Allmeet. We'll be stuck with each other and *Deecee*, I'm afraid."

That was right. She didn't understand. She was tenured to *Deecee* now. He was marrying into property, Jneer or no Jneer.

"Can we please talk about it over breakfast?" Because he was hungry. And if they didn't get dressed and get out of here soon it was going to be hours before they had another chance.

Oddly enough it seemed she realized that. She grabbed a pair of his workpants and got them fastened around her lucious hips somehow. Let people talk. So long as he and Aitchel were clear on things.

"You said it, Cago. I'm starved."

It would take a few days to recover from the stress they'd subjected themselves to in yesterday's near-tragedy. Near-disaster. Yesterday's misadventure.

Just as well if they were both too tired to really have much spare physical energy.

He was going to want to think things through very carefully before he made another move, because what had begun to happen—what had happened, what was happening—between him and his Aitchel was too important and incredible for him to be able to afford a single misstep.

She was the most important thing in the world, was Hillbrane.

He wasn't sure exactly how it had happened, but he was happier than he'd ever thought he could be that it had.

The setup for Allmeet was on Subarctic, not any of the Noun Ships that Raleigh had visited before, but it still felt like homecoming. He could feel relief and familiarity—a sense of rightness and proportion—come flooding into his heart and mind from the moment he set foot on the surface, like a great weight lifting from off of his chest. It was—he told himself, tasting the delicately scented fragrance in the cold crisp air— as though he could breathe again, for the first time in months.

Five months.

Five months in exile from the Noun Ships, traveling from ship to ship to ship, taking inventory. He didn't regret the time, how could he? He had seen more of the Fleet in five months than eleven out of twelve of his peers would see in their entire lives.

That gave him an edge.

He intended to use it.

Allmeet was to be held in the city of Winter Quarters—the only permanent facility on Subarctic, named for its function rather than its paradigm, as would have been more traditional. Winter Quarters was built of stone and sod, its few wooden structures made of now-ancient timber that had been treated to reduce fire hazard. There on the gravel apron in front of the receiving station was a wheeled cart with six shaggy ponies, waiting to carry him to the city. Who was that Oway sitting in the cart? She looked familiar.

The woman from Stiknals, the floor monitor from the Academy.

What was she doing in Winter Quarters?

"What a nice surprise," Raleigh said in greeting, stowing his personals case on the floor of the cart as the Oway porter settled his trunk behind. "Podile, I think. How nice of you to come and greet me. How have you been these months gone past?"

The cart's driver shook the reins, and the little ponies started off with a will. Podile unfolded a heavy woolen wrap and laid it across Raleigh's knees; now that they were moving the chill in the air did feel a little sharp. It was bracing. But a wrap was a welcome idea.

"I've been tasked to support the Allmeet, Ar Marquette. In fact I've been asked to escort you directly to the Speaker as soon as you've arrived. Your reports have been received with very keen interest, you should know."

As he had anticipated. Expected. Hoped. And still he was impressed with himself: he hadn't thought to go directly to the Speaker, the senior member of the joint delegation of engineers and administrative support staff.

Once upon a time there had been three Speakers, but the engineers and the administrative support staff had banded together to balance out the numerically superior Mechs, and the Mechs had never dissuaded the administrative support staff from consulting their best interest and following the Jneer lead since then.

So for all intents and purposes the Speaker for the Jneers was the single most powerful person in the Colony Fleet. The Speaker for the Mechs was second. There were more Mechs, but the Jneers were right, and with his reports as ammunition the Speaker was going to be able to force them to admit it once and for all. After all of these years.

Winter Quarters lay to one side of a deep lake that was part of the Fleet's reservoir system, put in place to guard against a time when water captured from asteroids as the Fleet traveled might no longer suffice to serve the replacement needs that existed. So prudently had the Founders planned, so fortunate had Fleet been that Lake Subarctic had been untouched for centuries, and its massive sturgeon grew to immense proportions unmolested.

Podile brought Raleigh to the Speaker on the upper floor of a wooden kremlin overlooking the lake. Speaker Girosse stood with her back to the room, her eyes apparently fixed on the snow-covered tops of the hills that lay miles distant on the other side of the water.

"Excuse me, Speaker," Podile said, by way of announcing him. "I've brought Ar Marquette direct, as you instructed. He's brought his final report with him. Shall I call your advisors?"

The Speaker turned away from the window, lifting the long sleeves of her winter kimono to pivot with effortless grace in her spotless tabi. "Not necessary, Podile. Thank you. Have you had rice, Marquette?"

She was stunningly beautiful, dark-complected, her skin a luminous black; and yet she spoke with the soft self-effacing diction of Winter Quarters as if Subarctic—and not Desert—was her native dialect. She was also twice or three times his age, but Raleigh felt the force of her personal charisma as he'd felt nothing since he'd last seen Hillbrane. He put the thought behind him for the moment. All in good time.

"Not yet, thank you, Speaker. We came direct, to be at your disposal absolutely."

Her accent threw him back into his own after months with the flat uniformity characteristic of the Mechs. It was a positive pleasure to hear her speak, her quiet voice like welcome rain in the parched landscape of his mind.

"I won't keep you, then. Podile, you'll see he's taken care of? Oh, one or two quick questions, Marquette, and I'll let you go."

She was welcome to keep him. He was anxious to oblige her; she was the one who held the key to the next stage in his plan. The colonization party. She would have final say on its exact composition, and she would review selected portions of it by name; so that if she was favorably disposed when she saw "Marquette" on the list, so much the better.

"At your disposal, Speaker. With a whole heart."

And she knew it. She was still gracious enough to smile and incline her head, as if in gratitude for what they both knew was simple acknowledgment of the power relationship between them. "Your reports confirm long-standing suspicions that our colleagues not on the Noun Ships are over-extreme when they call for more resources. And yet you have no positive evidence. How confident are you of our ability to bring this truth home to our counterparts in negotiation? If we insist on such a thing, we must have a persuasive argument."

He'd wondered himself. But after a while he'd realized what the answer was, so obvious as to be all but self-evident. "Very confident, Speaker. It proceeds by logical inference. If the resources were as scarce as claimed, the failure rate of all systems would be much higher due to lack of replacement materials, to generalize across examples."

And there hadn't been a catastrophic failure on a critical system within Fleet resources for thirty years. The Speaker would know that. He didn't have to make it explicit for her to follow the rest of the argument.

"The rate of live births is consistent with that for people on the Noun Ships, and the accidental death rate is no higher than normal attrition in a challenging environment serves to explain. The evidence may be negative, but it is there."

From the smooth unfurrowed serenity of her expression she was pleased, though she did not smile to show it. "Are we calling the Mechs liars, then, Marquette?"

He'd thought about that too. She didn't need to know that.

He took a moment to collect his thoughts, staring past her out of the window over the lake to the hills beyond. The brilliance of the light on the snow was indescribable.

"Not liars, Speaker, with respect. But set on something we can't provide and that they don't need. It's been part of our

If Byrnie got into Enrichment she would be kept too busy to remember that she even had a mother. . . .

"I'm sorry, Speaker. There. In the green cap."

Byrnie, with her fists full of snow, and the strings of her green woolen cap flying as she ran. It almost broke Podile's heart to see her. For Byrnie she could do anything—and yet she needed the Speaker's endorsement before they would grant her child what should have been her natural right.

Speaker Girosse smiled. Was it her imagination—Podile asked herself—or was it a little sad, that smile? "My son is there in the checked pants. Look at that. His mittens are gone. Again."

One of the nursery-minders had noticed that, as well, and came running from the warming booth with a replacement for the misplaced mittens. The boy was a little bigger than Byrnie was, well fed, but seemed happy enough to stamp a little transit in the snow for himself, fully occupied in some imaginary task that involved making a circuit in the snow.

"Handsome child." It was hard to know exactly what to say. The child was simply not engaged in play like the others were. Wasn't that a sign of sorts about where his interests lay? It didn't do to put too much emphasis on small, and most likely transient, things. And the son of the Speaker for the Jneers and Oways would get Enrichment whether he was apt for it or not.

"As a species we find intelligence to be attractive. It's the expression in the eyes. Peculiar, but in my experience there's no mistaking it."

The Speaker was watching Byrnie, and the tone of her voice was sorrowful. There was no other word Podile could think of to describe it.

So Speaker Girosse had decided.

She had weighed Byrnie's test scores, and Byrnie's aptitude profiles, and all of the measures that the Jneers used to keep a careful distance between privilege and the others, and had found Byrnie wanting. Not by reason of intelligence or aptitude. By reason of caste.

"Well. Of course every mother sees only the best in her own child." Podile had to say something before she let her rage get the better of her. It would be so good to tell Speaker Girosse what Podile thought of her and her precious system. But she had to work with these people if she didn't want to end up like Hillbrane Harkover; she had to avoid that at all costs. For her daughter's sake.

"It's only too true. And appearances are deceiving. Especially appearances colored by maternal instinct, but doesn't each one of us believe that she's just a little bit better than the average Jneer? Or Oway. Or Mech, I suppose."

Byrnie was better than the average Oway. Byrnie was better than the average Jneer. Podile knew it. How could the Speaker not see it, just by looking at her? Podile watched her beautiful baby playing, and her heart burned within her. Her child. They were denying her child what was only her due, and only because Byrnie's mother was not a Jneer.

Speaker Girosse continued, her voice meditative. Heavy with grief and resignation. "But there comes a time when even a fond parent has to face facts. A child isn't best served by being placed in an environment where the odds are against attainment. Doesn't every child have a right to be placed where she can do her best, and be recognized for doing well?"

Why grief?

Why resignation?

Now the Speaker sighed, and folded her long slim hands within her heavy sleeves. "There is only one chair empty at Enrichment that hasn't been filled for your daughter's age class, Podile. And my son has no place yet. I had hoped that he could take that chair and get the very best education, whether or not his intellect is of the first caliber. But it isn't, Podile. I can't help that. I've denied it to myself for as long as I could. I can't make it work any more."

Suddenly Podile understood.

Speaker Girosse was not merely the single most powerful Jneer in the Colony Fleet.

Speaker Girosse was somebody's mother; a loving mother,

who had weighed her own child and found him wanting on the only scale of values Speaker Girosse really understood.

"He'll be happier." Podile could promise that honestly, knowing it to be true. "In the long term." It sounded so inadequate, as comfort. Yet how could she, an Oway, reach out to this Jneer, even as mother to mother?

Speaker Girosse drew a deep breath, and then nodded. "Yes. Thank you." And then she smiled, a queer expression of pain and promise. "And so will Byrnie, Podile, she will be happy. Or at least she will have all the chances she deserves to be happy. I have countersigned the documents. She is to go to Enrichment with a status code of Jneer, and have her chance to compete with her peers. It is for the best, for all of us."

Podile was stunned.

Yes, it was only what Byrnie deserved, not by virtue of birth, but by right of ability.

Still, she had been fighting for recognition for her daughter for so long that it was only at this moment that Podile realized she had always secretly believed that it would never happen.

"Thank you, Speaker Girosse."

No, the words were no match for her feeling. But Speaker Girosse smiled again, a fine open smile of genuine pleasure and good will this time. Mother to mother. Heart to heart.

"No thanks are called for, it is only the right thing to do and I am happy to do it. But you're welcome. It's time for cocoa, would you like to come? I've been told that adults are allowed to put some brandy in their mugs, if they're inclined."

Brandy might not be a bad idea.

"I don't mind if I do."

And then she was going to hug her baby till Byrnie squirmed and complained and ran away.

Byrnie would be Jneer. Byrnie was a Jneer, from this time forward.

It was a miracle, and it was only right.

*　　*　　*

"Here are your credentials, this is your meal ticket, this is your room code. Service map available in room. Welcome to Allmeet. Next."

Sometimes it seemed to Podile that she had spent her entire adult life processing people one way or the other. Into Comparisons. Out of Comparisons. In for Guest Weeks. Out for school holidays. She handed a packet to the next Mech delegate, looking off past the man's shoulder to the timepiece on the dormitory foyer wall.

"Sif Brandner, yes, please sign here. Thank you. Here are your credentials."

Someone was talking, and she realized with a bit of a start that it was her. She lost the thread of her recitation and met the Mech's eyes, confused and embarrassed; he gazed back at her expectantly, looking a little tired. Looking an entire volume on the relations between Oways and Mechs, and how Mechs expected to be treated.

Hastily, Podile caught up her thread and shuttled it across the warp of what she needed to say. "Yes. Your credentials. This is your meal ticket."

She'd been in this receiving queue for ten hours, and it felt far longer. It was just two days before Allmeet was due to convene; Winter Quarters—which offered the only sizeable concentration of workspace on Subarctic—was filled to capacity. Many more Mechs and they would have to start putting them up in the fishing village across the lake, either that or build snow-houses. That would hardly do. She could just imagine the Mech reaction to being lodged in structures made of frozen water; it would seem the height of Jneer extravagance.

". . . welcome to Allmeet. Next."

They had to be careful enough to avoid the appearance of ostentation as it was. Allmeet might be a holiday for Mechs, but it was nothing but a tiresome chore as far as Podile was concerned. She wanted to spend all of her time with her daughter, rejoicing in the miracle that Byrnie was too young to understand.

". . . sign here. Thank you. Here are your credentials."

Byrnie had a full Oway staff to support her and the other children in Enrichment, though. And now that she was going to grow up to be a Jneer, she needed to develop self-sufficiency as well as the habit of delegating most of life's unnecessary little chores to Oways. It was best for Byrnie. But Podile had no intention of letting Byrnie grow up without a mother, as so many Jneers did.

". . . You'll find a site map in your area."

If that meant doing what it took to win continued cooperation from her management she would do it, even if travel took her away more than she would like. She could be strong, for Byrnie's sake. Once the First Colony was away, she would be able to spend as much time with her daughter as she liked. She would make it happen, one way or the other.

"Welcome to Allmeet. Next. Hillbrane—"

She'd been reciting by rote memory, lost in her own thoughts. The name on the list in front of her startled Podile out of her abstraction. Harkover was gazing at her with open delight.

"Call me Chelbie, that's my new name. My Mech name. Podile. How nice to see you."

Apparently genuinely so. Podile rose to her feet in numb astonishment to return Harkover's enthusiastic hug across the table. Well. This was awkward. She hadn't seen Harkover since she'd spoken on the *Deecee*, and that had been nearly three months ago now. She hadn't thought Harkover had been particularly happy with her then.

"Aitch Harkover. Well." Funny. She hadn't anticipated meeting Harkover in the Mech line. Shouldn't she have? She'd noticed Harkover's name on the delegate list, now that she thought about it. Harkover looked so different from the girl Podile remembered from Comparisons. She'd gained a pound or two, maybe. "It's good to see you back on the Nouns. I saw your name down for Presentations, didn't I? You're looking well."

More than just the gain or loss of the stray ounce of flesh.

There was a lot more person behind Harkover's face than Podile had seen there before. Grown up. Matured. Self-confident.

Weren't those Jneer traits?

What was different about this in Harkover?

"Thanks, Podile." Harkover took up her packet and marked her name on the list as Podile sat back down slowly, confused by the change she sensed in Harkover. "Right. There are my credentials. Meal ticket. Site map in quarters, welcome to All-meet. Nice to see you, Podile, talk to you later.—Parity! Wait up!"

Youthful exuberance, unfettered and unrestrained. Podile stared after Harkover for a long moment. Jneers didn't bounce that way, not young adults, not in public—there was always the risk of being made to look frivolous. Light-headed, insincere.

Didn't Harkover care?

Was that what had happened to her? Was it just that she didn't care any more if her peers made fun of her?

No.

That wasn't it.

Harkover was simply secure where she was, that was all. Secure and happy. *Imagine*, Podile thought, with wonder. *Imagine being happy as a Mech.*

"Excuse me, where do you want me to sign?"

The next in line had waited patiently for long enough, and called her back to her duties with no trace of a rebuke in his voice.

Podile gave herself a little shake.

"No, please, excuse me. I'm sorry. Temporary code slip. Ciller Marneff, yes. Here you are, please sign."

Well, then maybe Harkover had really been a Mech all along after all. It was the only explanation Podile could come up with in a hurry to explain Harkover's serene self-confidence: she'd found her level. A Mech. Think of it.

And still Podile couldn't help but feel a twinge of wistful jealousy that distracted her well past the last of the Mechs to check in for Allmeet, and kept her company as she went to sleep that night.

Allmeet convened in the open courtyard of the kremlin at the water's edge, and Raleigh Marquette stood at the window on the third story of the watchtower taking it all in. Speaker Girosse had offered him a delegate's ticket to admit him to the ranks of Jneers gathered in the courtyard; he appreciated the offer, but had declined. It was much nicer watching from the kremlin's watchtower. It was warmer inside, for one, and hot tea was no further than three steps' distance across the floor.

"Good morning, ladies and gentlemen. Today I wish to speak to you of the reasons why you should reject the objections Speaker Nolte has made to the colonization plan I have proposed on behalf of my constituency. I do not object to characterizing this plan as the 'lifeboat' plan, for want of a better reference."

He could hear Speaker Girosse just as well from here, too. The tower rose above the speaker's platform, and the sound carried up through the old treated wood. Well, that and the public address system, of course. He couldn't see Speaker Girosse, but he could watch the crowd, Mechs to the left as he faced them, Jneers—and Oways, of course—to the right.

"Speaker Nolte has said that to alter the plans of the Fleet's Founders is to act rashly, without adequate necessity for change. But Speaker Nolte has also claimed that we cannot successfully ferry the full complement envisioned by the Founders to Waystation One. We do not have the hull capacity. His projections speak of a colony three-quarters the size of that originally planned."

Where was his Brane, down there in that crowd? Sipping hot tea to help him concentrate, Raleigh scanned the Mechs row by row. They all looked alike to him. They were all dressed alike, heavy fabric workpants, sturdy black boots for footgear, shirts and overshirts and jackets padded with a double thickness. No gloves. He didn't know how they managed here in Winter Quarters dressed like that. It made him cold just looking at them.

"Speaker Nolte observes that our proposal to use one of the Noun Ships for transport and place it in permanent orbit around Waystation One as a lifeboat innovates dramatically. Coupled with what Speaker Nolte has been pleased to characterize as a break in the social contract between parties comprising the Colony Fleet—that is to say our proposal for the nominal makeup of the colonization party—he warns against social unrest, to the detriment of the Fleet's continuing mission as well as to the detriment of First Colony's survival chances. We find his reasoning faulty."

This was his stroke of genius. Raleigh paused to savor it, distracted from his search for his Hillbrane.

Moving a Noun Ship had never been part of the plan. A gradual move from the ships to the Nouns over time had been envisioned, the Noun Ships taking up the slack as the more vulnerable smaller ships gradually fell out of service.

But if they used a Noun Ship itself for transport . . . the Noun Ships would support a population of up to thirty thousand people; they had been designed with such a density in mind. If they used a Noun Ship for transport, they simply gathered on the ship and drove it into orbit around Waystation One, free to colonize at leisure. Gradually. Carefully. With minimal call on existing resources for ferry service, since the Noun Ship's lifeboats could be used.

The rest and ease of comforting familiarity would be available to the colony party during its most stressful, early years, and if the proposal took a Noun Ship away from the Fleet— what if it did?

Would the Colony Fleet really forget what waterlilies looked like, in the space of a mere four hundred years?

The argument was as persuasive as it was unexpected. This was a genuine innovation, but more was yet to come. Raleigh set his tea glass down and braced his arms on the deep wooden sill of the watchtower's window. He knew what came next. He was looking forward to this.

"We are prepared to offer significant arguments in favor of this 'lifeboat proposal' not yet set before you. The primary point of contention between us has been the absolute numbers and percent representation of our various job families within our First Colony party. We have not yet made explicit the corollary to the lifeboat proposal, which is that the colony party go forward as proposed by the Founders—"

There, that caused a stir. As much of consternation among the Jneers as sheer astonishment on the part of the Mechs. The Speaker had held the vital detail in reserve throughout opening arguments deliberately: the Jneers were surprised, the Jneers were visibly taken aback, and that would give the proposal credibility with the Mechs that it could not have hoped to gain otherwise.

Not that Raleigh was worried, any more than the Speaker was.

His peers would realize soon enough that the advantages inherent in having extra hands to labor more than outweighed any potential aggravation in having to manage them.

And the Mechs would be too surprised to realize that they were wanted for laborers. Then again, what if they did realize that? Mechs were laborers. Mechs had always been laborers. That was what Mechs did. Where was the downside in being given the chance to come to First Colony to provide manual labor, when that was all one would be doing if one stayed with the Colony Fleet?

"Two thousand engineers, man, woman, and child. Three thousand administrative support staff. Five thousand technicians. Approve the lifeboat proposal and we will have room to accommodate fully one quarter of the entire population of the Colony Fleet without endangering the survivability predictions. This is the best proposal. This is the strongest protection we can offer the First Colony. This is what both parties, engineers and technicians, want. This we propose, and I respectfully invite your very careful consideration of the same."

A silent still figure among the excited crowd below caught Raleigh's eye, and he couldn't help but smile.

Hillbrane.

Sitting with her arms crossed, slumped in her chair, and though he couldn't see her face from his vantage point, he knew her body language, and her glorious halo of thick wheat-colored hair.

She would be suspicious of what motives might lie behind Speaker Girosse's unexpected concession to the opposing party. But she would not betray her kind to the Mechs when she had come to her conclusions. And soon—sooner than she could possibly guess—they would be together again, Raleigh and Hillbrane, as they should always have been.

To build the future together on Waystation One.

He could wait, because he knew it was not for long.

The night before Hillbrane's presentation she could not sleep, but paced back and forth in her quarters restlessly. Her speech was written, copied out, ready, waiting; her argument was sound.

She couldn't relax.

Days of argument and counterargument had passed. Opening statements. Arguments for. Arguments against. Rebuttals of arguments for and against, rebuttals of rebuttals of arguments.

Final statements, changing nothing, convincing no one.

She had to convince them.

She had to change their minds.

Yet how could she hope for a hearing? Peoples' convictions were fixed, and had been since the first day. Less than six months ago she would have been confident that it was because the Jneers were right and the Mechs mistaken, and subterfuge if necessary was allowable in order to carry the Jneer point of view, because it was the correct point of view. Now she knew what the Mechs were saying, and she believed them, and she was desperate to communicate to her former peers that if they did not listen to what the Mechs had to say, a disaster was going to come down upon the First Colony and destroy it.

But did she believe it because it was true?

Or because she was still thinking like a Jneer, and took it for granted that her perspective was the only correct one? Had her convictions—but not her basic paradigm—changed simply as a function of which side was willing to claim her? Were the Mechs right when they claimed that the ferrying capacity did not exist? Or was she simply taking it as given that whatever she thought at any given time was the one real answer, and it just happened to be the Mech line for now?

She welcomed the signal at the door, the promise of distraction.

"Aitch Harkover. Are you in, please?"

Podile. Come for the copy of Hillbrane's speech that was to be provided to Speaker Girosse as a courtesy. Tomorrow was the last day of deliberation, and Speaker Girosse would deliver her final remarks. Hillbrane wondered why Podile went through the motions of collecting the papers when nothing any of them could say would change the Speaker's mind.

Hillbrane opened the door.

"On the table. There," Hillbrane said, and stepped aside to let Podile into the room. "For what it's worth. I'm discouraged, Podile."

She didn't care if Podile knew. She felt comfortable with Podile, and Cago wasn't here to complain to. Podile had been charitable toward her. Talking to Podile was maybe a mistake, because Podile was an Oway and Oways sided with Jneers. That made her the enemy. No, it made her the antagonist, but it was precisely the tendency to think in terms of antagonist and protagonist that had polarized the Allmeet. It was a critical point in the Fleet's mission. They couldn't afford to be divided. How were they ever going to resolve the differences that had grown up between them, Jneer and Oway and Mech?

"Discouraged, Aitch." Nodding in acknowledgment, Podile crossed the threshold to go to the table where the copy of Hillbrane's remarks for Speaker Girosse was waiting, wrapped up in a stiff piece of red-dyed paper, tied with a thin twine of twisted grass. Hillbrane noticed that Podile's heavy cloth overcoat had a fur lining to its hood. Doing well, was Podile. "In what way discouraged? If I may ask."

Well, if Hillbrane hadn't been willing to talk about it she'd hardly have raised the issue in the first place. Would she have? "We don't seem to be making any progress, that's all. Has anybody changed their minds about anything since we got here? On any important issue, I mean."

Podile hesitated, her back to Hillbrane. She seemed to be weighing her comments carefully. "You don't need to be as discouraged as all that, Aitch. I can't share any specifics, you know that, but I don't mind telling you. You might be surprised at how carefully the Speaker is listening to everything that's being said. I've seen adjustments."

Adjustments were all very well. But what was needed was change. Change. Not adjustments to a preformed, predetermined argument simply in order to make them seem responsive to the concerns of one's opponent.

Yet Podile wasn't stupid, and it would be very arrogant of her—Hillbrane reminded herself—if she failed to take into consideration the fact that Podile knew the difference between a real adjustment and a cosmetic one as well as the next person. Jneer, Mech, whatever. Hillbrane sighed.

"Well, all right. I guess we'll all hear about it tomorrow. Wish me luck, Podile, I'm pretty nervous about this."

Podile had the packet, and turned around to face Hillbrane on her way out. The expression on her face was unexpectedly open, candid, even supportive. "You've got to speak your piece, though," Podile said firmly. "Stand up for what you see as the right thing. You'll do just fine. Ar Marquette will be cheering you on, from the observation deck."

Raleigh?

"Oops." Podile reacted to Hillbrane's surprise with a girlish shrug and an almost-giggle. "You weren't supposed to know that. Were you? Shame on me, and Marquette waiting with the Speaker right now to review the remarks. Well. You know

Oways, we can never keep a secret. That young man has been having it a little too much his way lately, if you ask me. Good night."

Winking broadly at Hillbrane on her way out, Podile closed the door behind her. Leaving Hillbrane standing by herself in the middle of the room, stunned.

Raleigh.

Could it really have been weeks since she'd even stopped to think about him?

Raleigh. Waiting with the Speaker. And had been having things his own way lately? Raleigh, who had betrayed her, cheated to ensure his own position. Cheering her on, was he? He probably felt he could make it all right with her, with a joke and a smile. That would be just like him.

He did get away with too much. But he wasn't getting away with what he'd done to her.

He had yet to begin to pay for that.

Tension ran out of her like cold tea down a slopsink drain. Hillbrane stretched herself as tall as she could manage and held the pose for a long moment before she relaxed, smiling.

She knew something they didn't know.

She felt irrationally better about things.

There was nothing like a bit of petty personal spite to put the life and death of the First Colony into proportion. Now she could get to sleep.

Hillbrane Harkover stood at the speaker's place facing the seated Allmeet assembly, Jneers and Oways to her right, Mechs to her left. It was cool in the enclosure, and she was glad of that, because she was prickly and uncomfortable with apprehension.

She was back on the Nouns, but not as she had anticipated when she'd left Stiknals. She had come to make her speech, and her speech didn't even matter, because the Jneers had offered to take enough Mechs to make the colony go in return for agreement that one of the Noun Ships accompany the colony to Waystation One. There were problems with that suggestion, but they were not the problems Hillbrane had come prepared to argue.

To make short work of a long proof, she stood in front of the Jneers and Mechs ready to declare herself intransigent, gone native, Mech by allegiance and no Jneer pretensions about it, to throw away any last chance of working her way back into her birth-culture. That was all right. She had made up her mind to that weeks ago. She had not expected to make the sacrifice for nothing, though. The argument was no longer at issue. There would be a full complement of Mechs in the Waystation One colonization party.

It had to be said, regardless.

Whether or not Speaker Girosse had co-opted her argument by formulating the lifeboat proposal, what Hillbrane had to say to Jneers about Mechs was a word that needed to be heard.

She'd had her chance to waive her speaking time, she'd had ample time to change her pitch. She felt as passionate about it as she had the morning after Wyatt had almost died. She had the final speaking slot; after she was done, Speaker Girosse would take the platform and restate the Jneers' proposal in whatever final, adjusted format it was to take. That meant everybody was here, whether or not they were particularly interested in listening to her.

If it worked, it would be worth trading her birthright for fifteen or twenty minutes on the platform.

If it didn't work, she would still always know in years to come that she had done her best, and had resisted the temptation to compromise between the welfare of the Fleet and her personal comfort and prestige as a Jneer.

"Engineers and mechanics, administrators and technicians." When she'd been little they used to play at Allmeet. They'd taken turns being Speaker and mocking Mech attempts to shape the consensus in directions contrary to that in which good Jneers knew it had to go. She remembered the formula. She also remembered the sense of self-importance, the play-acting. This was the real thing.

"We have behind us centuries of history traveling as a Fleet, and in those years we've grown accustomed to certain roles relative to one another. We've all gotten comfortable with sets of assumptions that have been useful to a greater or lesser degree in regulating the flow of communications, specifically between those of us living on the Noun Ships and the rest of the Fleet."

Us and them. Who was to say that prejudice was not a useful element in the social interaction of groups whose intermediate goals could conflict while the shared final goal remained unchallenged? Prejudice was shorthand, and provided a ready framework within which to relate. So long as it didn't become a barrier to important messages, was harm done overall?

Yes.

Because sooner or later the habit of supposing that the other, Jneer or Mech, was one way or the other did inevitably color and occlude the transfer of the information that meant success or failure for them all.

"Our approaching rendezvous with Waystation One and the impending departure of the First Colony party has surfaced aspects of our habits of communication which may have become counterproductive. I would like to share two pieces of information that I have gained recently as a member of the crew of the forefront ship *Deecee*. I believe both pieces of information to be pertinent to the long-term survival of the Fleet and the best outcome for First Colony."

She didn't have to argue the representation issue, that was moot. It simplified her message. All she had to do was make her pitch without being preachy. It was quite possibly arrogant of her to even presume to make her points as if everyone did not in fact understand them perfectly well already. She had been raised Jneer. She had a natural right to arrogance.

"You may have seen the bio in the schedule. I was educated Jneer until Comparisons. At which time I left the Noun Ships for a posting on *Deecee*."

She had been perversely gratified to discover that it was still a scandal. One muted in light of the greater problems that faced them all, yes, but the Jneers and Oways here on Subarctic knew exactly who she was and what had happened to her. She beguiled herself with the fond hope that public opinion would turn against Raleigh soon, if it had not done so already. He had committed an act of shocking betrayal. He should pay.

He was here, somewhere, watching? In the kremlin's watchtower, perhaps?

"The issue of resource allocation that has come up during the past days of this Allmeet was familiar to me. I made it my business to find out where those Mechs were hiding all the goods they consistently claimed weren't there. Speaker Girosse has suggested that resources being allocated from the Noun Ships must necessarily be perfectly adequate, because the failure rate within the rest of the Fleet is not higher than it is."

As an argument from lack of evidence it was ingenious, but flawed. She did not have Speaker Girosse's credibility, either as a Jneer or as a Speaker. What she did have was positive evidence. There was no telling whether the fact that she had once been a Jneer would be credibility enough; she could only do her best.

"I have spent the past five months with the *Deecee*. I spent a good portion of my time opening every locked door I could find, looking for stores, hidden rooms, stockpiled surplus. I can be very obnoxious when I put my mind to it—"

This frank acknowledgment earned her a modest laugh from the audience, the first reaction they'd shared with her. It was a mark of goodwill. They were at least listening to her.

"And I found nothing. I found less than nothing. More than that, I found a consistent pattern of ingenious accommodations in response to a dearth of resources. You wouldn't believe some of the things these Mechs got up to. Ponics in the corridors for atmosphere. Siphon nozzles for hydraulics. Berenice cyclers for capacitor circuits on the plasma flow generators. Our aggressive conservation of Fleet resources has created a genuine deficit situation—genuine, engineers and mechanics, administrators and technicians—sometimes in critical areas."

And Jneers conserved resources to maintain the comforts of life on the Noun Ships. But she didn't need to make that point. She didn't want to push it. She only wanted them to listen to what she had to say, and really hear it.

"I found something else on *Deecee* that I wanted to share with you. We have evolved distinct cultural styles over the years, as well as coming to share a set of opinions about each other. Here on the Nouns we value technical excellence, we seek it out, we nurture it, we reward it. We use it to measure ourselves against each other to decide precedence and access to the best jobs and lodgings."

If she hadn't found the Jneers familiar with her story, she might not have had the face to make this part of her argument. It was risky. But all that she had heard, by oblique reference and indirection, pointed to a public perception that something had gone wrong in Comparisons at Stiknals this year. Not that she had failed due to incompetence. Something quite different than that was widely assumed to have happened.

"Our teamwork is hierarchic and defined by a single point of direction, delegation of authority from a single leader. On *Deecee* teams are comprised of peers whose authority is equal while individual skills may differ. The implications of this different paradigm in a high-stress environment like a colonization party are obvious enough without my insisting on them. One point I'd like to make in particular, though."

She had to maintain her momentum, she had to finish before she bored people. There was so much that she wanted to tell them all about what she'd learned on the *Deecee*. If she tried to tell them everything, they would stop listening and hear nothing.

"When a team's hanging on a single leader, if you lose the leader, the entire effort collapses. We've all seen it happen. If the team runs on the Mech model, there is no single leader. Lose one team member, the team may stagger a bit, but it keeps going. This is a potentially invaluable lesson for us to take with us on our way to Waystation One."

Someone in the middle ranks of seated Jneers started to applaud, to Hillbrane's consternation. She wasn't done. She hadn't finished. She hadn't made her recapitulation and conclusion, her argument was technically incomplete, rhetorically unbalanced, oratorically flawed. But once one Jneer started to applaud a Mech followed suit to as not to be undone and it gathered its own momentum.

Hillbrane stood for a moment on the platform facing the applause of the Allmeet, frustrated and relieved at once.

It was out of her hands. She had done what she could to publish her findings. She would simply have to do her best to follow up in private as it became possible.

Nodding her thanks, Hillbrane yielded the platform to Speaker Girosse, who was waiting her turn.

All to the best, perhaps.

Maybe three more words would have been three words too many. Allmeet was comprised of intelligent people. They would not need to have all of the implications spelled out for them. Maybe she would have antagonized them if she'd gone a single step further.

Encouraged by the applause, relieved that her ordeal was over, anxious about how well she had been heard, Hillbrane sat down in the front ranks of the Mech representatives to listen to what Speaker Girosse would have to say.

Speaker Girosse took the platform and folded her hands in front of her so that the drape of her heavy sleeves, meeting in front of her at a crisp and precise geometrical angle, seemed to meld into a single visual element having more to do with stonework than clothing. It distanced the Speaker from the crowded courtyard, in a sense; as if she was speaking from within the fortress of her garments, broadcasting a message to Allmeet across the battlements of her lapels.

"We can all thank Aitch Harkover for her open and insightful remarks. No less than those contributed by the others who have spoken these days past."

Hillbrane relaxed into her chair, to the extent that it was possible to do so. They weren't very comfortable chairs: light, folding, portable. It helped keep everyone awake, she supposed.

"Debate clearly must continue on several unresolved issues. We have neither the time nor the information available on which to base a rational decision on the lifeboat proposal."

This argument was disingenuous. The Mech delegation at Allmeet was perfectly willing to agree here and now that the lifeboat proposal was a rash innovation, and that it was too late to seriously consider reworking the entire structure of the First Colony proposal. That was certainly what Speaker Girosse would say on behalf of the Nouns . . . if it had been a Mech proposal.

But if the Jneers insisted, the Mechs would go along with the pretense that it was a serious question. It was this practical streak that formed the backbone of the Colony Fleet, and had kept the Noun Ships secure and privileged for so long. The lifeboat proposal was a new idea. There was no particular reason to presuppose it to be a bad one. If the Jneers insisted, the Mechs would go along. The lifeboat proposal at least allowed for the originally planned numbers of Mechs.

"Before an informed final decision can be reached, more information is required. It is also time to send a forerunner to Waystation One, this cannot be delayed much longer."

A forerunner? Yes. The scout party. That was true. Hillbrane hadn't thought about it recently; it was to be a Jneer thing, after all. And what information it would bring back would be sure to support the Jneers, as well, so the forerunner was fundamentally irrelevant to Mech interests.

"And although it is something we have long discussed as a concern, Aitch Harkover very properly calls our attention to the crucial need for mutual trust and the fullest sincere cooperation across all elements of our Fleet. Therefore, speaking together as your authorized representatives, Speaker Nolte and

I have agreed that the forerunner ship to be dispatched in five days' time shall carry a Mech crew."

Hillbrane blinked. This was going in an unexpected direction. She knew better than to believe her speech had really convinced the Speaker; on the other hand, she didn't need to believe so much in order to hope that her words had made it more imperative that the Jneers at least seem to include the Mechs in all aspects of the Waystation One colony plan.

"Aitch Harkover is in a unique position to evaluate not only the quality of crew function but the objective value of the information the scout ship will obtain, and therefore Speaker Nolte and I feel it best that the Mech crew be drawn from the forefront ship *Deecee*."

Now Hillbrane sat stunned. This was not something she had imagined happening. Her first reaction was panic: what had she done? Her friends, the crew of the *Deecee*—because of her they were to go forth on a scout ship to face the dangers of the unknown. Waystation One. Because of her . . . and she as well, and who knew what perils they faced, what they would discover?

Applause greeted Speaker Girosse's proposal: tentative at first, sparked to a general expression of approval as the Mech delegation picked it up. The noise filled Hillbrane's ears and toppled her reservations, neatly transmuting apprehension into anticipation.

She would go to Waystation One after all. She would go to Waystation One with Cago and the rest, the first people to touch the ground on the long-anticipated First Colony world, and who knew exactly what they were going to find?

She didn't know if she should join the applause or not. Was it presumptuous of her to clap for the announcement of her own preferment?

And yet she was delighted at the prospect that Speaker Girosse had just opened for her.

The feeling overwhelmed her. She started to clap, and with her whole heart.

Perhaps she had given up her chances of being one of the

First Colony party by insisting that her Jneer peers acknowledge the truth about their treatment of the Mechs. But she
would see Waystation One; she would set foot to the long-
awaited world and breathe air never tasted by a human until
that moment. She would taste water virgin from the bosom of
its earth. She would lift up her eyes and see a genuine sun in
the sky for the first time since the Fleet had left its system of
origin, nearly four hundred years ago.

She would be there.

And she could hardly wait.

SEVEN
GOFORTH

The scoutship *Goforth* was the single most beautiful piece of machinery that Cago Warrine had seen in his entire life. Cargo forward design, power amidships, the quarters in one long four-part line down the central rib of the ship, and as perfect—virgin, absolutely untouched—as the day she had been loaded into long-term storage, part of the ballast below the living surfaces of the Noun Ship Altitude.

Ivery called out sharply from her clamshell on course station. "Watch it, Cago, you're drifting on inhibitor thrust—help!"

Part of being virgin meant she hadn't been tested in nearly four hundred years. Cago blipped his gas mix, and inhibitor thrust steadied. That had been a good call on Ivery's part. If inhibitor thrust got out of hand, it put excess pressure on navigation paddlejets, and any excess of anything was not the Mech way. With exceptions.

"Thanks, Ivery. Sanson, would you choke on the inhibitor jet nozzles for me again, please. Let's try fifteen for a while."

Excess in most areas was a waste of energy, but he couldn't get enough of sweet Hillbrane. Okay, so it wasn't like he'd never, ever, ever had experimental sex before in his life, even if Mechs didn't institutionalize it like Jneers with their First Sex. It was still almost more different than he could believe. She was—

170

"I'm going to give you fifteen points, Cago, I'm worried about emergency response. Agreed?"

Sanson's clamshell was right next to where Cago reclined against the scooped back of his station: power flux regulation. Cago nodded; Sanson turned back to his own panels—fuel systems—apparently satisfied. But with something on his mind.

"And take that smirk off your face." It was spoken low enough that no one else need hear it, though there were fully eight people in the *Goforth*'s quiet softly lit Direction room. "You're as bad as Chelbie. Come on. Have some consideration. We haven't had your party yet."

She was so sweet, so soft, so one hundred and five percent Aitchel Hillbrane Harkover that he could hardly stop thinking about her. He knew one thing for certain. He'd never felt anything like this before. Something similar enough to enable him to identify the fact of the matter, and he'd been fond of people before.

Never anything like this.

"First things first." Although he directed his mock-stern retort at Sanson, it was as much for himself, and Cago realized that as he said it. First things first. Aitchel was the most wonderful thing he had ever imagined happening to him. Which didn't change the facts. "We have to get to Waystation One and back again before we can have any parties."

Then he raised his voice, determined to concentrate on his immediate task and ignore the fact that Aitchel was here. On navstation. Working the calibration of the ship's forward proprioceptors.

"Rena. What do you say? What's the harvest profile look like? Will we be able to sustain the idle on core?"

Eight people here in *Goforth*'s Direction room. Twelve people all told from *Deecee* on *Goforth*'s trouble-shooting status check cruise; now all they had to do was rendezvous at Subarctic, pick up some Jneers, and get on with their mission.

Aitchel was holding up magnificently. It was poor taste of the Jneers to send that Marquette to Waystation One with the woman he'd wronged, but it was probably some kind of an obscure joke. Marquette didn't even matter any more; Aitchel was a Mech, with a berthright on *Deecee*, and as far as Cago could tell, she was proud and satisfied to be one.

Unless it was just a personal thing.

Personal between the two of them, that was.

"We're starving where we are," Rena admitted. "But we've been back under the plasma brollie for two days. We'll be just fine once we head out. Plenty of fissionables."

Good point. The room was quiet again, its eight stations glowing gently in the cool blue-carpeted dimness. Aitchel's navstation would double for the long-range navigator when he came on board; the Jneers were holding the precise track to Waystation One close—as though they were concerned that the Mechs might take *Goforth* and set out on their own, if they could do it without bothering with Jneers.

And whoever the suspicious Jneer was, he was probably right. This time.

"Let's get to the docks, then," Aitchel suggested. "The sooner we get past the Forenet the sooner we'll be full up on fissionables. Too bad we have to stop at all."

Right. Subarctic was in view, and Aitchel as short-range navigator had a right to their fullest attention. The status check started at the back of the opposite side of the room, Mir's station.

"This is mission coordination. Docking phase initiate, prestate. We rendezvous with the docking station beneath Subarctic, and we do it perfectly. Next."

"We're talking to the dockmaster, all conjoined systems are in sync. Smooth as coverwax. Next."

That was Orly on sensors and communication. This close to Subarctic there wasn't much maneuvering to do on *Goforth* itself; the ship was computer-slaved. They could dock on manual if they had do, Cago was sure of it—though they'd never tried. But so long as the ship was slaved, the Jneers felt so much more secure about the whole thing. Jneers understood hard coding. Manual maneuvering made them nervous.

Reserves and resources, ship's life support, Aitchel for the navigation station; no anomalies. No discrepancies. *Goforth* could fly itself, and would, given half a chance and a good navigation code set. Of course having a good navigation code set was crucial.

"Nothing to tell you," Farsi on rates and vectors admitted. "Sanson, come on. Anything?"

"Fifteen points makes me happy if it makes Cago happy. No dents, Cago, we just got this boat. I don't want to be the one to put the first scratch on it."

Nor did he. "Power flux stable. Smooth as silk." Even Ivery should be pleased, not that she would feel it necessary to say it in so many words.

Aitchel didn't wait. "Moving in, then. Twenty minutes to umbelicus docking station. You all mind what I told you about my sweetheart Marquette, now."

Cago didn't think there would be a problem with that. Aitchel's residual outrage was still strong enough to be persuasive, and he thought about the implications as he watched the *Goforth* close on Subarctic on his visual screen.

All the way to Waystation One and back with a crew half Mech, half Jneer, one half doing all the work and the other half giving all the orders as usual. All the way to Waystation One and back with Hillbrane Harkover and Raleigh Marquette on one ship, and not a very big ship either.

It would make a good test of group function in stress situations, right enough.

"Ten minutes to docking station."

Since the Mech crew had done the test cruise, they had managed the cabin assignments their way, Mechs on one side of the ship's spine, Jneers on the other. Well, Jneers and Oways. There were to be two or three of them traveling with the Jneer contingent. He'd seen to it that Aitchel's room was as hard to get to from Marquette's as any on board, just to minimize any chances of accidental contact. Then he'd put himself next door to Aitchel for no better reason than to just be there.

"Five minutes. Seamless. Perfect. No possible grounds for nit-picking," Aitchel warned and prayed at one and the same time. Cago didn't mind. They all had the exact same thing in mind, after all.

"Four minutes." The gray-pocked underbelly of Subarctic grew larger and larger on his screen until he could no longer see anything else.

"Three minutes. Umbilicus on visual."

When they had gone to Altitude to take possession of *Goforth*, the existing atmosphere had been carefully evacuated prior to opening an actual bay door to permit *Goforth* to drop down into free space. That had been a one-time-only event, though. From now on *Goforth* would board like any other boat, passenger or otherwise: through an umbilicus that led from an airlock set. It was much more efficient, and safer, to pressurize an umbilicus than an entire docking bay.

"Thirty seconds. Umbilicus on orientation cycle. Target sites confirmed."

Goforth came to a stop gently, delicately, daintily. No contact. No stray scrape from a wild sweep as the umbilicus sought its orifice. Perfect.

"Pressurizing." Sanson took up the narrative; this was his piece. "Umbilicus atmosphere is positive pressure. Safe signal has been transmitted. Opening port."

On screen now Cago could see the umbilicus corridor, empty at first. Then a single Jneer came strolling down the articulated tube toward the terminus, where Delacourt and Neyrem would be waiting to welcome the Jneers as they came on board.

"Taking on passengers. Stand by."

The first Jneer passed the focal lens of the vee-cam and disappeared into *Goforth*. Then another one showed up, and another. Young people. Nice clothes. No hurry. No luggage to speak of; did Jneers travel light? Or did they simply expect *Goforth* to be like a Noun Ship, only smaller and faster?

One Jneer in particular caught Cago's eye, because of the almost studied casualness of his ambling stride. Thin. Blond—

more or less. Face as sharp and angular as a carved rock, cheekbones, narrow chin; Cago couldn't tell whether both of his eyes were the same color, but something told him that this was—

"Raleigh Marquette."

He couldn't quite decipher the emotion in Aitchel's voice. He wondered if it might not be better for the both of them if he didn't think too much about it. Aitchel and Marquette had grown up together, after all. There was no getting around the depth of some emotional bonds.

Nor was there to be any getting around the fact that they had a long trip ahead on a small craft.

He had his work cut out for him, because—for whatever irrational reason it might be—he wanted to kill that smirking Jneer the moment he first laid eyes on him.

Interesting.

Marquette cleared the terminus, and the next Jneer came onscreen, and Cago pushed his feelings about Marquette into a box and clamped the lid down firmly until he could examine them in private.

"The umbilicus is clear. We are receiving the disconnect pulse from Subarctic. Remote scan initiate."

No, there was nobody left in the umbilicus. The terminus could disconnect: but not before Subarctic had sealed itself off once more, protecting its atmosphere from catastrophic loss.

Then the umbilicus started to retract, slow, staid, and decorous. Cago watched it go with a bit of hunger, eager to be on the way to Waystation One.

"Separation complete," Mir announced finally. "We're full complement. Let's get out of here."

Waystation One, the goal of four centuries. Waystation One at last.

Killing Marquette would wait till they got back.

For now there was work and a mission, and he was eager for both.

*　　*　　*

Goforth was small and cramped, and Raleigh found himself sleeping four to a room for the first time in his adult life. It was primitive. It was disgusting. But at least it was clean, and he did have other Jneers for company who could empathize with him and share his dismay at being so close to Mechs; and there was one factor that overshadowed all others, to make a pleasure garden of this little craft.

Hillbrane was here.

He'd held himself carefully aloof at Allmeet, not wanting his behind-the-scenes machinations to become too obvious by revealing himself. He had been waiting for this opportunity to speak to her, but he had no fear. By the time they set foot on Waystation One, Hillbrane would be his own sweet Brane once again, forever and always.

Once *Goforth* cleared the Forenet, Raleigh took the all-important navigation course correction module from his satchel and carried the little disk with him back to the Direction room to start in on Hillbrane. Small room, quiet, intimate, and fragrant with the smell of freshly brewed coffee since it was the beginning of a shift; the room was also full of Mechs, but Raleigh had eyes only for Hillbrane, standing by her post—the navstation, his navstation, their navstation—in the middle of the room.

She was talking to some Mech who stood too close to her with his thumbs in pockets; solid and compact, dark-eyed, thick dark hair brushed back off his forehead. Raleigh thought he might vaguely recognize the man from Allmeet—Warrine. That was the man. Her honey-colored hair looked dark in the dim light, as if still damp from her morning wash; Raleigh felt his desire for her surge up and fatten on that thought.

Hillbrane in the shower.

Warm water falling on bare skin, slim fingers bejeweled with soap suds probing into intimate places.

He gave a cough to announce himself and clear his mind.

Focus. One thing at a time. She would be angry at him about Comparisons. He would overcome her pique by presenting evidence of his contrition, everything he had done to win her back, and nobody here on board was in a position to contradict his claims, so he was golden.

"Good-morning, Aitch Harkover. I've brought the course update."

Formally, but with the playful intonation that had always served as pet language between them. Hillbrane looked back over her shoulder at him as he spoke; her expression gave no hints that she might be ready to forgive and forget. It was the fault of the Mech beside her, no doubt. Distracting her with some trivial technical issue.

"Raleigh. They gave the course to *you*? Well."

She hadn't known he was to have charge of the long-range navigation portion of the mission. She hadn't secretly found out everything she could about his presence here, not even with Podile on board to provide information. For a moment Raleigh knew disappointment, but it passed. It was very early in their cruise still. The Mechs must have kept her much busier than he had anticipated.

"I must say it's nice to see you again too, Aitch." He could tease her a bit about her cool reaction; they'd been friends since childhood, after all. It had only been a bit of abysmally bad luck that had come between them, no malice on his part.

If she hadn't been his opponent—if she hadn't lost her temper, and issued what had been more or less an ultimatum—she would have been admiring his ingenuity and ability to see through the layers of accumulated administrative cotton wool to a solution to his problem, as Speaker Girosse had. "You're on the navstation, I see. Well. Perhaps we could have a little talk while we're working."

Including her by reference, as the Jneer that she was. Reminding her that she was in fact different from the rest of the crew here, reminding her that he was much closer to her than anyone else, at the same time.

She didn't seem to have noticed.

"No, you do your thing, Raleigh." She turned away from the navstation as she spoke. That Mech wasn't going anywhere, hadn't melted back into the background the moment it became clear that Raleigh wanted to speak to Hillbrane; very bad manners. There was something in his body language that Raleigh didn't like. "Cago and I were just discussing a problem on power flux. We'll go work on that, if Ivery can cover."

Not what Raleigh had in mind at all. "Oh, if you're busy, Hillbrane, I'll come back to do this when we can share a talk together." When he could have her undivided attention. When he could make her understand how much he loved her, and how much he'd done for her, and that she shouldn't be angry at him just because things had worked out the way they had by accident. If she hadn't gotten angry at him, it didn't need to have happened that way. She shouldn't have gotten angry at him.

She was staring at him with a look in her eyes that seemed two shades more to the "hostile amusement" side of neutral than Raleigh liked. "No, Raleigh, we need that course correction. And we have nothing to talk about. Cago and I have a pressure station we want to go check on anyway."

And she actually stepped back, stepped away from the nav-station, reaching for the hand of the Mech beside her as if automatically. Without conscious thought. Raleigh stared, dumbstruck with horror: had his beautiful Hillbrane so far lowered herself as to take a lover from among the Mechs?

Or worse—could it be that she had become fond of one of these people, so that she preferred his company to that of a man from her own caste? Because mere sex was bad enough, when it was Hillbrane but not with him. But finding companionship, affection, he could not force himself to imagine love in the arms of some disgusting Mech male—

"You guys," one of the other Mechs said. A female Mech, and not half bad-looking, but she wasn't looking at him. She wasn't even looking at Hillbrane and the Mech. "It had better be a *big* party."

"And it had better be soon, too," someone else added. The slightly embarrassed grin on Hillbrane's face was too spontaneous, too genuine. Hillbrane and the Mech had become lovers. Everybody knew it, and she didn't care.

Had she no shame?

"Don't hurry yourself on my account," Raleigh said to no one in particular, and sat down at the navstation that Hillbrane had just vacated. The seat was still warm from the sweet press of Hillbrane's body, but the thought was suddenly almost intolerable to Raleigh. Some Mech. Some dirty Mech, to savor Hillbrane's sweetness, to taste her berry mouth and kiss her honey-dusted skin. Some Mech to press his lips against her eyelids, to press the palms of his dirty Mech hands against the luscious ripeness of his Hillbrane's exquisite backside . . .

It was disgusting.

It nauseated him.

Half-blind with jealous rage and shocked affront, Raleigh broke the seal on the course correction module and keyed the navstation editor to reset. Perhaps it would be better to forget all about Hillbrane. Any Jneer who could stoop so low could not be worthy of the name. He couldn't afford to be distracted; he had work to do.

The course update.

Nothing was happening on the navstation's diagnostic screen; Raleigh hit the engage twice, three times, and something finally moved.

Hillbrane.

He loved her.

How could she betray him?

And with a Mech.

Set course to baseline, the diagnostic screen suggested. Well, of course he wanted to set course to baseline. Wasn't that what he was here for? Raleigh keyed the execute with an impatient frown. *Goforth* had been provided with a course instruction when Fleet had been commissioned, but that course had been based on a set of assumptions about what space held between the point of origin and Waystation One, and those assumptions were out of date.

Recalibrate? the diagnostic screen asked. Raleigh sighed. It was a good application, but it was so simple-minded. The computing systems he had worked with all his life had been somewhat more powerful than this one apparently was. He wasn't used to having to separately approve each minute step of the process.

Recalibration complete. Rationalize index points?

Of course. Raleigh hit the execute another two or three times, hoping the authorization strokes would persist in buffer and spare him quite so many inanely obvious questions. The course needn't have changed all that much over four hundred years—a functional equivalent of nearly twice as long, when one considered that the source information had already been four hundred years old when it had been received at their system of origin. But even a minor change could set *Goforth* off just far enough that its transmissions back to Fleet would go too far wide of the target to be captured, or make finding Waystation One much more difficult than it needed to be.

Hillbrane. And some Mech.

If he had ever guessed such a thing might happen—could he have ever loved her, if he'd known how little discrimination she could show, if he had realized that she could share the most precious and private pleasures her body could afford with a mere Mech? A dirty, uncouth, undereducated, ignorant, unlettered, unlearned, gauche—

The diagnostic screen was chattering at him, the speed with which its silent screen was scrolling with text almost as shocking as if it had come accompanied by actual sound.

Baseline calibration replaced, ok.
Source configuration alpha . . . cleared.
Source configuration beta . . . cleared.
Source configuration gamma . . .

What?

This wasn't what he was supposed to be seeing. What was going on?

Source configuration omega . . . cleared.
Source configuration alpha sub alpha . . . cleared.

No. This wasn't right. The damned thing wasn't updating *Goforth*'s nav preloads with delta information. The navstation was trying to set a new course instead, one that replaced the original code with information from the course correction module interpreted as if *Goforth* had launched for Waystation One four hundred years ago and from the source planet rather than four days ago and from the Colony Fleet.

This was completely wrong.

Abort.

Raleigh gave the order, but the navstation did not seem to be listening.

Source configuration mu sub epsilon . . . cleared.

Source configuration mu sub . . .

Abort, Raleigh insisted, keying the codes with increasing vehemence as his panic mounted. *Abort. Abort. Abort.*

Discard all changes, reset to default? the station asked; *Yes*, Raleigh agreed, with a sigh of relief that he swallowed back only just in time.

But what the navstation read back was *Abort.*

He'd overloaded the buffer.

Now what?

His fingers were sweating, but he kept his breathing calm. The last thing he wanted was for someone to notice what a stupid mistake he'd made.

Save over default?

No.

If the navstation saved over default, the *Goforth*'s present course would be physically overwritten, and the only good information left on board would be the little course correction module that Raleigh had brought with him.

Yes, the screen read, echoing an answer Raleigh had previously provided and applying it to the wrong question.

Reset complete; defaults reset. Course information has been changed. Changes saved. Old data purged. Proceed on course, yes/no.

But he did have the correct course on the course correction module. The navigation standard called for triple redundancy, and though he had inadvertently invalidated *Goforth*'s default and its recovery module alike, it wasn't as if it was a fatal error. He had the correct course. It was just a question of reloading it, some shift when he could have some time to himself to be sure of what he was doing.

He was too upset to be able to deal with this now.

Hillbrane's treachery had shocked him beyond measure. He needed some time to himself for meditation before he could trust himself with so important a task as long-range navigation, especially with this mess to clean up.

Fine.

Set location to scan. Goforth would figure out exactly where it was by comparing indices from the course update to local factors. And once that happened it would know what to do—*Increment course from location, execute.*

Nobody needed to know.

And it was all Hillbrane's fault.

Taking up the course correction module, Raleigh tucked it carefully away into his shirt pocket.

He'd get it all fixed before anyone knew there was a problem.

Yes.

Once he had recovered from the shock of Hillbrane's betrayal and self-abasement, he would make everything right again.

On a scoutship the size of the *Goforth* space was at a premium, and there was no common-room in which to eat. The galley was nothing more than a small prep room off the main corridor leading from the front of the craft back toward Direction. Four times a day the service window opened to serve food, and the people would take their trays away to wherever they could find to sit down.

Galley chores were shared on the duty roster, and the non-Mech crew on board—Podile included—didn't have too much to do. The Jneers were always the first in line when the window opened, not because of greed, but because of boredom.

This was the first time Podile had been teamed with Raleigh Marquette. He didn't take direction well, even when politely phrased in words suitably submissive, as appropriate from an Oway to a Jneer. It wouldn't have been a problem under normal circumstances: the Oway who had grown to adulthood without learning how to let Jneer arrogance roll right over her did not exist.

But they were on the *Goforth* now, and the Mechs were running the ship. They were much more self-assertive in groups than she had ever expected.

"Almost out of that ragout," she noted to Marquette in as neutral a warning tone as she could manage. "We're going to have some disappointed customers at the end of the line."

"So?" Marquette shrugged, and served the next person in line with an over-generous scoop of the spicy vegetable stew across too large a mound of steamed rice. "First come, first served. Don't worry, I set ours aside already."

"Here." She'd tried to take over the dishing-out duty before, and it hadn't worked. "Let me spell you, there's the cake to section. It's okay. I'll take the ladle."

But dishing-out was a novelty to Marquette, and he was having fun. "I'm fine, Podile. Really." It just wasn't going to work. "We're almost done anyway. Hello, Brane."

Next in line, appearing at the window, was Hillbrane Harkover, with a guarded and suspicious expression on her face. Oh, good. Exactly what Podile needed right here, right now, to thoroughly destabilize the situation. Marquette and Harkover, of all people.

"Ragout day," Harkover caroled, just in case people didn't already know. "I like ragout. Especially the eggplant part."

Such exotic vegetables were delicacies on Mech ships. Podile had discovered that on her mission to *Deecee*. Marquette wouldn't understand Harkover's point, though—Jneers ate eggplant anytime they had a taste for it.

Marquette shook his head, obviously genuinely regretful—and as obviously oblivious to what was going on. "Sorry, Brane. Fisch got the last of it. There's plenty of loaf on the side, you want a double slice of loaf?"

The vegetable-protein loaf was in plentiful supply because Marquette had served as much rice and ragout as people wanted, and if you could have your bellyful of rice and ragout, you couldn't be bothered with loaf. Podile had tried to encourage the Jneers to take loaf; it was part of the careful balance of nutrients for this meal, and the idea was to take the right portions of everything. She hadn't been persuasive enough. Why take loaf when you could have a double portion of rice and ragout instead, just for asking?

"I don't want two slices of loaf. No." Harkover sounded perfectly reasonable. Still. "I want a slice of loaf and a portion of rice with ragout. You can't be out already. There are six people in the line behind me. Counting you and Podile that makes eight people. You've only served two-thirds of the crew so far."

Podile didn't need to be able to look out and see for herself to know that those six people were all Mechs. People who had been on shift in Direction. People who were looking forward to rice and ragout.

"I'll be glad to share some of mine, Brane. Only for you." Marquette started to reach behind him, to open the warming slot where he had apparently stashed the plates he'd dished up for the two of them. Podile froze in mid-slice, her eyes fixed on the glistening sugary surface of the sheet-cake.

He had told her he'd set food aside, but it violated all of the unwritten rules of fairness. The person who controlled the portions fed everybody before he fed himself. That was so obvious. How could Marquette not see it?"

"Raleigh! You didn't!"

Podile heard honest shock in Harkover's voice, honest horror. Harkover's voice was a near-whisper: she wouldn't want to let this secret out. It would only cause trouble.

It seemed to Podile that Marquette was getting a little frustrated. "Well, then, I'll just make more. Kind of a waste, though. If you ask me." And one angry voice from the corridor outside, beyond Podile's narrow line of sight, resounded through the little galley. A man's voice. Cago, Podile thought. Harkover's Mech sweetheart.

"If you paid any attention to what you were doing in the first place you wouldn't run out. But give the Jneers everything they want, and let the Mechs go hungry. It's a pattern."

This was it. It had been building for as long as they'd been on board together.

"Hey, what is this?" Marquette was getting angry. Why should he take any criticism from Cago? The two of them had a rivalry going, all the more intense for the fact that neither of them would acknowledge the existence of a possible threat in the other. "If you have something to say to me about how I do my job, you look me in the face when you say it."

Cago was halfway through the galley window in an instant, grabbing Marquette's apron-smock in both hands, hanging awkwardly across the sill. "Fair enough. How's this, Marquette? You're loading your Jneer friends up with the good stuff and leaving us dry loaf, and not enough of it. Where we come from, the last person in line gets the same meal as—"

Backwards through the galley window Cago went, and it was as much of a surprise to him as to Podile, to go by the expression on his face. Things were sounding ugly out in the corridor. Marquette had backed away from the window to lean his back against the warming slots. He looked pale. Physical confrontation was not part of Marquette's skill-set, from what Podile knew about him.

It certainly seemed as though they were headed for a fistfight. Podile could hear curses and challenges, and there was nowhere she and Marquette could go to get away from this—

She thought about the connecting door an instant too late, and had only started toward the door to lock it when it slid violently across its track and slammed against the hollow side of the jamb with so much force she almost thought the door would jump its track. Harkover. Harkover, and she shoved the door back closed as firmly as she had opened it—and locked it down.

All right, Harkover had the door, and in order to make way

for her, Podile backed up beside the service line in front of the open window. Voices were raised in earnest anger in the corridor, and the timbre of those voices was rough with the constriction that tightened the throat when shoulders were tensed for a fight. The window. Oh. Yes.

Podile reached out and let the gate drop and locked it off, while Harkover stood glaring at Marquette in an obvious attempt to gather her thoughts.

"We have a situation here," Harkover said. She sounded very calm and reasonable, actually. Surely her earlier emotion hadn't been an act to bring a problem to a head?

"What is the matter with these Mechs?" Marquette demanded, with as much bewilderment as resentment in his voice. "You'd think nobody ever ran short on a meal line before."

Harkover took a step forward, and Podile was amused to see that Marquette seemed to plaster himself just that bit more firmly against the bank of warming slots. But Harkover wasn't coming for Marquette, Harkover was pacing, and the pent up energy she radiated made the galley feel even smaller than it had before. Podile wouldn't have thought that to be possible.

"There isn't anything the matter with the Mechs. I'm not a Mech, and I'm mad at you. Every time a Jneer serves, the line runs out of food. You haven't noticed because you're always the first in line."

Maybe she had a point, Podile thought. Maybe the Jneers really hadn't thought about that. Since they were always at the front of the line at mealtimes, none of them had had the experience of having the desirable entrée run out before they got a portion.

"There isn't enough in the ration to feed everyone," Marquette protested. "Hey. Somebody's just got to eat loaf. That's all."

"The rations are supposed to feed everybody." Harkover was talking to Marquette, Podile knew she was. But she was projecting her voice forcefully in the direction of the now-closed galley window. They would be able to hear every word she said, in the corridor. They might even quiet down in order to be sure they didn't miss any of the overheard chewing-out. "If you served the right portions, the ragout would last all the way through to the final tray. Then you get your share. After. Never before. It's only fair."

"So? It's not like it's a conspiracy thing, *Harkover*." Marquette was unquestionably angry now. But Harkover only *sounded* angry. She didn't look the least bit ruffled to Podile. "You want ragout, fine. We just make extra. What's the problem?"

"It's unfair to the people at the end of the line. Enough is enough. Breaking into rations for the next meal is not an option."

What was she getting at? Marquette had folded his arms, clearly about ready to stop listening. But since it was Harkover he was talking to, Marquette did not seem to have totally discounted what she had to say. Not yet, anyway. "All right, let's hear your solution."

"I don't have a solution," Harkover snarled. "I didn't make the problem, I don't know how to fix it. But I'm telling you. Either we all learn to serve up consistent portions, so the last gets as much as the first, or we're going to have to feed the Mechs on shift first and let people off-shift wait their turn. Excuse me. I have to go knock some heads together."

And with that Harkover unlocked the galley door and stormed out of the room. Turning, once she got out into the corridor, to express the frustration she clearly wished to communicate by kicking the door.

Podile cracked the galley service window, cautiously.

It had gotten quiet outside.

"Okay," Harkover said. "That's enough. We're all grown-ups, here, right? We all had to learn, didn't we? Well. Ah. You all had to learn. But I'm getting the knack of it. Really."

The shuffling sounds were changing out there, somehow. Podile eased the window grate up just a fraction higher. She didn't want to draw any attention to herself, but she had to figure out what Harkover was up to.

"You want ragout," someone said. One of the women. That was a good sign. Women could negotiate. It was not a fair thing to think, perhaps, but it was true. "I want ragout. They want ragout. And we know what we'll see when we clean plates in an hour or so. Someone's scraps. Ragout. You know it."

"You're right, Dela. I want ragout. But hey, I'm a big girl. I have to give these people time to learn rationing. We all know how easily rationing comes to Jneers, don't we?"

Laughter. Reluctant, but resigned. "Ah," someone said, with humor evident in his voice. "You're just covering for your friends. All right, Chelbie, we'll try not to get personal. I can tell you one thing, though. I'm getting in line as early as I can for supper."

Podile stood with her hand to the galley window grate for several moments, listening as the corridor quieted.

Harkover had done it.

She'd set the explosion off before it had gained enough strength to cause real damage, and she'd defused the resulting conflagration with a little playacting and some self-deprecating humor. And some leadership.

She never would have guessed that Harkover had it in her.

But she couldn't afford to stand back and marvel at Harkover's crowd management, not if she wanted to do her part. Doing her part meant not giving anyone too much time to notice that something actually quite unusual had happened, so she opened up the galley service window to face an expectant Mech with an empty tray. Delacourt. The woman Harkover had called Dela.

"Well, how about some of that loaf, then," Delacourt suggested.

Podile nodded. "Can do. Two slices?"

But before she had made the delivery, in the moment between the lift with the tongs and the drop to the tray, Marquette shouldered his way past her with a dish in one hand and a spoon in the other.

"Here, have some of this ragout with your loaf."

Marquette had the dish he'd reserved for himself and Podile and set aside in the warming slot. There was easily enough for three or four people there. Delacourt was looking at Marquette a little skeptically; Marquette insisted.

"Really. It'll make me feel better. I don't get my rear end chewed off whole every day. I'm not doing that again. Ragout?"

This time Delacourt smiled and accepted with good grace, and Podile knew that Harkover had succeeded.

She wouldn't have missed it.

They might be able to learn to work together after all.

Raleigh Marquette was lying on his bunk in quarters when the allship spoke his name.

"Raleigh. We need you in Direction, bring the course correction unit. Cross-check on some nav stats."

Hillbrane's voice. Raleigh yawned. He could continue to lie here and dream of how it was going to be on Waystation One: just he and Hillbrane. Oh, there would be other people there too, of course, but once he'd gotten Cago out of the way Hillbrane would come back to him. There would have to be a probationary period while the Mech wore off her, of course, and she would have to prove her remorse and loyalty before he—

Nonsense, Raleigh told himself firmly, and sat up to leave his bunk. No such thing. He would take Hillbrane back in a minute and he knew it. He would open his arms to her without reservation. He was willing to fantasize about causing bodily harm to another human being to get her back. He would do anything. And he knew it.

"Coming directly," he commed back on allship. The course correction unit he had with him day and night; it was in his pocket. It was only a palm-sized data store, no more than an ounce or two in weight; sometimes he almost forgot it was there, but so long as he had it with him he knew that it was safe.

Hillbrane was seated at the navstation when Raleigh arrived, and Cago Warrine standing there with her. Always. It was disgusting. Raleigh wouldn't have liked the man even if he hadn't been Hillbrane's love toy. To accord a Mech the status of her lover—rather than a biological masturbatory implement—was unthinkable. It was almost bestiality. But Cago had Hillbrane, and he didn't—

"Raleigh." Mechs usually kept their distance and used the more polite form, Ar Marquette. Raleigh hoped Hillbrane's direct address would not set precedent. "We should be on forward scan for the first checkpoint. Guidepost Alpha. A cloud nebula. There's something out there at 275 degrees—west of heading—that might be the cloud nebula we want. Are you sure about those nav stats?"

Of course he was sure.

They were exactly where they were supposed to be.

He'd spent hours in here while Hillbrane had been offshift, carefully, laboriously loading *Goforth*'s data store with the information from the course correction module. Piece by piece. A little bit at a time. He couldn't afford any more global dumps after the potentially disastrous mistake he'd made the first time around, but that hadn't been his fault. That was Brane's fault. Hillbrane's fault, for consorting with a Mech and flaunting her degraded behavior in his face.

"Let's have a look, Brane. If I could have the station. Can you give me that cloud nebula on maximum discrimination, please."

He was going to have to plug in his index information and have a look. "Correct for angle of approach to zero deviation. Yes. Thank you." It wasn't a very good picture, but the correction gave him a look as if from head-on. It should be enough. He had index fields.

"What I want to do is find the reference frame—good. Here. Now if we proof these two approaches . . ."

Side-by-side, and then superimposed. The navigation information he carried was his only really reliable reference; it could not be overwritten on board. So he knew that if there was a variance between ship's nav and his course update, it meant that they were off course.

Raleigh swore.

"I don't understand it. Something in the course update must have failed." What had gone wrong here? He couldn't afford to let the course update he'd been doing come under examination. If someone who really understood the process had a look, they'd be able to see that the log had been tampered with and the chronometer that registered the inputs had been forced to reset, and guess from those facts that he'd not only made some really stupid mistakes but had tried to cover it by destroying the ship's baseline course.

There would be no possible recovery for him from an error of that magnitude, if it ever came out. "It'll take me a bit to see where I went wrong, Brane."

He didn't want her here. She knew too much. His admission of the lesser error in loading the course correction would not stand beneath her scrutiny; he was willing to pretend to the smaller stupid mistake only to cover for the potentially much more deadly one that he had actually made.

But only he knew that.

He had to keep it that way.

"Oh, I'm going off shift," Hillbrane said. And tucked her hand into one of Cago's back pockets just as easily and unself-consciously as Raleigh could imagine. "It's been a long day. Mir will be here, you know Mir, don't you? He'll take over from there."

Because she was going to bed, to bed with Cago. She had just said so, as clearly as if she'd used the words themselves. She wasn't even doing it to annoy or upset him; it was something so natural and comfortable with her that she wasn't even thinking about what she was revealing. That settled things for Raleigh. He hadn't been sure how personally he took all this before. But now he knew he hated Cago Warrine.

"Over to Mir. Got it. Good night, Brane."

She was already on her way out, and Cago close behind.

Raleigh took a deep breath to calm his emotions, scowling at the navigation stats.

Who would have ever guessed that he would have to stoop to contesting with some unschooled Mech for his Hillbrane's attention?

How could he be expected to concentrate on his task, under so much personal pressure?

He'd destroyed the ship's baseline navigational set, by accident. And he'd done a physical data override of the restore banks, so he'd destroyed that too. He'd thought he'd got it all fixed, restored from the course correction he had, and there was no reason for anyone to ever find out so long as there were no further problems with Goforth's navigation.

He had to get it right this time. There was no alternative.

What he had already done could potentially mean the destruction of the ship and everyone on board. As much as Raleigh hated Cago he saw no reason for suicide, not even one that would take Cago with him.

He could fix it.

It would take time, but he could fix it.

And once he had rewritten ship's default, and overwritten the restore banks, and changed the log to hide his tracks no one would ever know how close to calamity he had brought them.

Cago's fault.

It was all Cago's fault.

Wasn't that just like a Mech, to let personal issues interfere with the vital programming of the ship's nav?

"Someone's got to tell her," Delacourt insisted. Cago was glad to note that she kept her voice low, because even though the people on galley shift probably couldn't hear them and there were only Mechs waiting in line there was no telling when someone would join them in the corridor. "It's not fair to hide the news. She has a right to know. And we have a right for her to know, so she can tell us if we have a problem."

Cago moved a step forward in the meal line, scowling. "I don't see why it has to be me, Dela. She and Marquette have a history. I don't know how much. Why me?"

But he thought he knew. Exactly because of history. If any Mech on board was going to attack Chelbie's ex-boyfriend and possible ex-lover to Chelbie's face it was almost going to have to be him.

So Dela didn't bother to answer that question. "He's been on the navstation two out of three shifts, Cago. It doesn't take that long to load a course correction, or even to reset one. Something's gone wrong with the process, and it's too important to leave in a Jneer's hands. Or too important to let just one person handle it, Jneer or no."

Cago nodded. He'd heard it the first time someone had approached him yesterday. He knew what the assignment was, he just wasn't particularly interested in the task.

But it was Chelbie. His Aitchel. And he did have a responsibility to her. The rest of the crew had kept clear of confronting Marquette thus far, out of respect for their crewmate. Now that it had gotten to where people were starting to really worry, he couldn't argue that it wasn't his job. It was his job. He was her partner. If he wanted to be her partner, he had to accept it.

"After we eat," he promised Delacourt, who was at the galley window waiting for her food now. "Before shift change. It'll be done."

He wasn't looking forward to it.

But now he had signed up, and that was that.

Pulling off her other sock, Hillbrane massaged the pale toes of her right foot, sitting cross-legged on her bunk in the cabin that she shared with Delacourt and Ivery and Podile. Her feet hurt.

It was coming up on that time of month.

Delacourt had just wandered in from some errand or another and sat down, but rose to her feet once more almost as soon as she had settled back. "Podile," Delacourt said. "Hey. Let's go make sure the mover's still in good kit. What do you say?"

There was someone outside, visible to Dela through the open door—so much was obvious. Podile looked a little startled at first, but went along. "Good idea. I've been a little concerned about that, myself. I'm with you. Later, Chelbie."

Chelbie. Hillbrane grinned at them, feeling no need to make a comment. She knew what was going on, now. It tickled her to hear Podile use her Mech name, though.

Now that she was alone in the cabin, Cago Warrine's dark solid figure appeared at the threshold. "Say, Chelbie. Can I come in?"

What would he say if she said no?

As if she would. Privacy was precious on this ship, and it was nice of Dela and Podile to make way for her to have a few moments alone with Cago. "Be my guest. What's on your mind, then?"

He closed the door behind him before joining her on her bunk. He reached out for her foot and started to rub her toes, while the moment stretched.

Something *was* on his mind.

She could wait, and let him speak in his own time; he was good at foot massage. "I'll give you exactly three and a half hours to stop that."

Cago grinned, but didn't shift his concentration. His frown was back almost as soon as it had lifted. "Chelbie. No, Aitch Harkover. I've come to speak on behalf of your crew."

Oh, formality. All right. What could be the problem?

How could anything be a problem, when it came with foot massage?

"There are two parts to this, now, Aitch. There's the Aitch Harkover part and the Chelbie part. Which do you want to hear first?"

"The Chelbie part." No question. That was where her heart lay. Aitch Harkover was of no interest to Hillbrane any more. "Of course."

Cago frowned a little more deeply. "The Chelbie part isn't

from the crew, it's from me. This Marquette. He could get you back into the Jneers, Aitchel, I bet he could. If you gave him half a chance, and a good reason to."

"Maybe." From what Podile had told her Marquette was certainly moving in influential circles. On the other hand, the common understanding among the Jneers had seemed to be that she did belong on the Nouns by right, for all the anomalous position Raleigh's treachery had put her in. She just didn't care any more. "But for that I'd have to want to be a Jneer. And I'd have to make nice with Raleigh. And I don't want to do either of those things."

He had her little toe between his thumb and forefinger. It made her tingle all over. "It's none of my business, Chelbie. But you can see my position. I'm a Mech. You were a Jneer. He is a Jneer. He's good-looking. You grew up together. All of these things. I don't know where things stand."

Oh.

Was that it?

This was odd.

It hadn't occurred to her that Cago might think twice about Raleigh.

"Doesn't amount to squat." Her right foot was blissed out. She offered him her left foot, shifting on the bunk so that her right foot could lie against the wall and glow. "I'm sorry if I didn't say so before, Cago. But I want to be here, and with you. Even if there wasn't you, I think I might prefer to be here rather than go back." Well, prefer to be a Mech, she meant. "I never felt part of a community like I do on *Deecee*. I never felt like I was a contributor. And since there is you, I'm dead certain of it. I'm not going back there. Raleigh's history."

She pushed her foot flat to Cago's chest, so as to communicate directly between her heart and his heart by physical contact. "History," she repeated. "You're where I want to be. Now and forever. Us."

No, she wasn't being grammatical, and she wasn't being very coherent either. But she didn't need logic or rhetoric to communicate with Cago. All she needed was to speak her mind in honest sincerity. There was no more powerful message than that.

Cago sat quiet for a moment or two while his heart listened to her heart. Through the underside of her left foot, but whatever worked. Then he nodded.

"All right," he agreed. "I'm glad to hear it. It won't come up again. Now. The Aitch Harkover bit, though. It's also about Marquette. There are feelings that there may be something wrong with the nav data. I was asked to put the question before you, since you're our other primary navstation expert."

She tensed involuntarily. The nav data? Had she done something wrong? Made a mistake? "Tell me about it."

"We haven't seen it ourselves, the other Mechs I mean. But I hear he's been coming on shift every time you're not. Nobody thinks it takes that long to run a course update, not even with diagnostics and backups, not even with the old interface. Conclusion? Something's wrong. And he's trying to fix it without having to come out and say so."

Not something she had done. Not unless it was her error Raleigh was trying to fix, and she didn't think that was likely. Cago was right. It didn't take two shifts out of three to run the navstation properly. Not unless there was a problem somewhere.

"We're off course." Once the suggestion had been made things fell into place a little too decisively for them to be entirely coincidental. "And we haven't heard back from Fleet on status report. It could be because we haven't asked them for positive read, and we haven't, we don't have any emergencies to report. Or it could be because our sends aren't getting through. Being off course."

Misdirected signals ran a very small chance of being intercepted by accident. If *Goforth* was no longer where it was expected to be, the messages it was sending to Fleet were vanishing into the deeps of space, and Fleet wasn't getting through to them because they were not listening in the correct direction. That would explain a lot. "But Raleigh's got the course correction. The update. And ship's computers have the initial load baseline. So what could have gone wrong?"

"We want you to find out. As a navigator. Just to set our minds at rest."

Raleigh showed no signs of doubting his ability to get *Goforth* back on course for Waystation One.

But the potential for disaster could not be ignored. If something had gone wrong with the nav data, it might challenge their ability to get from Waystation One back to Fleet with data Fleet would need to ensure that the First Colony was correctly outfitted to face the environment they would find there.

"Okay." Fair enough. "I'll check into it. I'll give the whole system the once-over. Starting next shift. Cago, you're at the wrong end of the bed. Let's work on *your* navigation skills a bit."

If they'd thought there was an immediate problem they wouldn't have sent an embassy through to her via Cago. So it could wait another hour or so.

She knew how to take advantage of an hour or so, she did.

She meant to use this time to ensure that Cago surfaced at the far end of it with fewer insecurities on the issue of exactly how important he was to her than he apparently had harbored in silence up till now.

Raleigh had tried to vary his visits to Direction to make them look more casual than they were, but tonight he was almost too eager to get to his task to force himself to wait the extra hour or so after the end of Hillbrane's shift before he went to use the navstation. He was close. He was so close. One more night and he would have made it, they would have been within scanning distance of Waystation One and nobody need ever be the wiser.

One more night.

Raleigh loped casually into Direction with an easy confidence in his stride. It had been hard. But he had done it. One more set, only one more set of calculations to be laid in as if called up from the ship's navs. He could get some sleep. He hadn't had much rest over the past days—more than a week since they'd first run into a course problem, but it was just that hair short of academic now.

He put out his hand to the edge of the clamshell to turn it toward him, so he could sit down.

The clamshell didn't spin like it should.

There was a weight that was not supposed to be there, and it was far too late for him to turn around and make a quiet retreat. He hadn't seen her. She wasn't tall enough to be seen from behind when she was at her station. Hillbrane. White in the face, and glaring at him with a cold fury in her eyes that made him feel as though he had done something wrong.

And he hadn't done anything wrong.

But he knew she would blame him for what she thought he had done wrong—

"Ah. Good evening, Brane." He was trapped without possibility of escape; so there was nothing to do but try to put the best face on things. "You're keeping late hours. What's the occasion?"

A good offense was a strong defense, and so forth and so on from the great books of tactics and negotiation.

"I thought I saw something in the nav log I couldn't figure out." She wasn't playing along. She'd read the same books. That was awkward. "So I thought I'd see what was giving a false reading. Only the more I looked the worse it got. Raleigh. What have you done to the ship's navs?"

Predictable, her "What have *you* done?" It wasn't anything he'd done. He'd been upset, and there had been a mishap. He'd been working to make it right ever since. "I had a little trouble with the interface early on. I'm working with it. There's no particular cause for alarm, Brane, what are you so worked up about?"

She'd know he had a perfectly good set of course data with the course correction module. She'd know that. How could she not know that? And once they got to Waystation One they'd know exactly how to get off again. He had been a little worried about getting to Waystation One, what with the difficulties he was having with the ship's course.

But the course update module knew how to get from Fleet to Waystation One and how to get from Waystation One to where Fleet would be by the time they were scheduled to leave. So as soon as they got to Waystation One he could plug the course correction module into ship's nav systems and leave it there to do its thing. Then he could catch up on his beauty rest.

But Brane seemed determined to be petty—her revenge, indirect but venomous, for the unfortunate coincidence that had pitted them against each other at Comparisons. It was too bad of her to be vindictive. He expected better of her.

"Worked up," she said. She stood up from the navstation to get as nose-to-nose with him as she could. Under less tense circumstances he might have found her proximity hopeful, but it seemed too clear that she simply didn't want to raise her voice and disturb the others who were working in the room. "You destroyed the ship's default navs, Raleigh, you overwrote the data with null fields. Twice. And then you loaded a course correction on top of an arbitrary index, a random index so there's no hope of recovering the original data load."

Yes. He knew that. Why did she think he'd been there all those long nights, trying to get back on some kind of a course? "It was an accident, Brane, it could have happened to anybody. The nav system is original issue. I had no way of knowing it was going to overwrite."

She wasn't even listening to him. So much seemed clear from the way she picked right up on her rant again. "You left this ship with one, count them, one master course. One. But you didn't think it was important enough to tell anyone. Raleigh. Have you no imagination at all?"

What did she mean by that?

Of course he had an imagination.

He couldn't have thought of himself as creative otherwise. All intelligent people had imaginations. That didn't mean she should overreact to a situation that was history anyway. Raleigh opened his mouth to tell her so, but one of the Mechs in the room interrupted.

"We have Waystation One. Forward scans. Index target confirmed, Waystation One—"

Everyone in Direction stopped what they were doing to gather around the forward visual screens and stare. Even Hillbrane seemed to forget what she'd been saying to him.

This was it, then.

Waystation One, a tiny little dot in the black starfield, with its sun somewhat off to one side. A little pearly white sort of a world, reflecting the light of its star—and something else?

"What's that?" one of the Mechs asked, and pointed. The others had apparently noticed something too, because one of the Mechs was working on a forward scan. Orly. The Mech's name was Orly, that was right. Raleigh was proud of himself for remembering it.

Orly pushed back in his clamshell and stared straight at Hillbrane and Raleigh. "Moons," Orly said. "Two moons. That's not in the data set."

Silence.

After a moment Hillbrane shrugged, as if uncomfortabe. "Moons could have gone undetected. It's hard to catch something that small at a distance."

But none of the scenarios took such a contingency into account; it called all the speculation about using a Noun Ship for a lifeboat into serious question. How could a body the size of a Noun Ship be successfully orbited around a world with two unexpected moons, without obviously perturbing the existing satellites' orbits?

Those moons were either new, or had somehow gone undetected when the planet had been identified as a refuge world four hundred years ago. If they had gone undetected, well, that was one issue. But if the moons were new—and a mere four hundred years was the blink of an eye in the life history of planets—their orbits would be intrinsically unstable.

Would Waystation One have to be foregone, because the

risk of a new moon's orbit decaying was too great?

Would they be able to haul those moons into a safer orbit around another world within the same system? Would they be able to calculate a stable orbit, and defuse the danger that way?

The Mechs were apparently focused on a slightly different question, however. "Is it Waystation One for sure with those moons, Chelbie? Are we still on course?"

She hadn't raised her voice to confront him, but she hadn't kept her accusations to herself, either. And this was what came of it: she had created uncertainty and anxiety among the crew. It was all so unnecessary.

"Well. Why don't I just confirm," Raleigh answered for her, easing past Brane where she stood, to settle himself at the navstation. "Cross-check against the course correction . . ."

He slid the module out of his shirt pocket and into the station scan smoothly. He knew what the cross-check would show. There was no doubt whatever in his mind.

"Waystation One," Hillbrane confirmed, but she had gone over to sensors and communication and was reading the screen over the shoulder of the Mech who was stationed there. "Those atmosphere composition stats conform to the index, Orly. There couldn't be two worlds so much alike so near each other, that's counterintuitive. So it's Waystation One. But those moons—"

"Moons or no moons, that's our course destination." Raleigh made the statement with as much finality in his voice as he could muster. He was a little provoked at Hillbrane walking all over his input like that, as though she felt his word wasn't going to be good enough for her Mech friends. "And Brane's right. The moons are not in the prediction set. We'll have to recalculate our approach."

He caught Hillbrane in the act, glancing quickly over to the station that Warrine usually manned. Warrine wasn't here. She would have to deal with him for a change, Raleigh thought uncharitably. It served her right for being so missish about things.

"All right," Hillbrane said. "You take the nav stats, Raleigh.

I'll do the vectors on Farsi's station. Sanson, run the power flux model for us. And we need to be sure about this. So we'd better get started."

That was his girl.

And she would be again, too, just as soon as he could get her away from her Mech entourage for long enough to awaken her to a sense of what she stood to lose by turning her back on her Jneer heritage.

Raleigh shunted the course correction module back into its case and put it away. They didn't need the module to recalculate the approach; everything they needed was in the ship's resident memory. There had been just enough room, but it was there. Manual reentry was a fearfully inefficient means of program storage, but it had been all he had.

Waystation One.

Who knew what changes in a person's life would come about in the new world, once they made planetfall?

"**F**ifteen minutes to orbit," Hillbrane said, keying the allship to global transmit. "All hands on deck. Er. As it were."

She'd always wanted to say that. And she was a little punchy. They didn't need everyone to come to Direction, but everyone was going to want to be here to look. That could be a problem if there was an unexpected course correction, true enough. But no one was going to want to miss the first real-image, close-orbit visuals of the world they'd been looking to reach for four hundred years.

"On auto, Chelbie," Mir—on mission coordination— warned. "Mark seven. Six. Five. Four. Three. Two. On auto."

It had been an intense few hours, but the course was good for approach on two moons. Waystation One's surprise satellites weren't in what a person would call a regular orbit, since their planes of transit were at an odd angle to each other, but the smaller moon was further out, so the odds of a collision were probably minimal. For now, at least.

On auto.

Hillbrane waited, but nothing blew up, and nothing bumped, and all of the readers she could see were reflecting data apparently more or less unperturbed by the shift from onboard guidance to control based on his course correction module.

Raleigh stood up from the navstation and stretched, yawning—as much in nervousness as weariness, Hillbrane guessed. He had been just coming on when they'd found Waystation One. She had already pulled a full shift, and that had been more than ten hours ago. "That was intense, Brane."

So it had been. They had only just gotten the calculations checked and loaded in the nick of time. Raleigh was talking and yawning at the same time, which made it difficult to understand what he was saying. "And we're going to have to do it all over again to get off." He patted his shirt pocket with a curious gesture. "It's a good thing we've got backup."

What was he talking about?

She was too tired to think about it.

Goforth closed on Waystation One moment by moment, and while Hillbrane knew abstractly that the ship was slowing down, the increasing nearness of the world and its orbital companions gave her a dizzying sensation of vertigo.

Ten minutes to orbit.

There was the outer moon, dimly glimpsed at the lightcusp of the planet's dawnline. Direction was getting crowded: only twice as many people as usual, though, really.

Waystation One rose on the ship's horizon blue and white with the colors of water, the colors of home.

Five minutes to orbit.

Goforth passed beneath the planet's inner moon, and the visual was startling, even though the data had been coming through on monitor for hours. There were patterns in the color of the world they were approaching; was it clouds they were seeing? Hillbrane wondered. Or was it the dim outline of land masses?

"We have orbit stabilization," Mir announced. He sounded choked; Hillbrane realized with startled appreciation that the contours of Waystation One were as indistinct as they were at least partially because she was crying. Her vision was blurred with tears of joy and wonder that she had not even noticed.

This was it.

Home.

"We can start registration runs on next shift." Her voice was so strained with emotion that it came out a feeble croak. She cleared her throat. "We'd better get a break, people, we've been up all night. Come on. We can all be back before we start descent."

And since she was the short-range navigator she would be responsible for that. The next shift got to pick the place, lining *Goforth* up with the location that best met the parameters set for a secure foothold on an alien world. Once they were on the ground she could have it out with Raleigh over his irresponsibility. Who knew whether they could not have found a way to fix the damage he had done, if only he had let somebody know that he had a problem?

She could afford to put it off until she had had some sleep.

She could hardly think straight.

Now that they were here the rest could wait.

EIGHT

WAYSTATION ONE

Goforth thundered through atmosphere thicker than any Hillbrane had ever experienced in her life, and the ship pitched and yawed as the atmospheric pressure changed abruptly between areas of cloud and areas without. Clinging to the arms of the station, glad she was strapped in, Hillbrane looked around her frantically; would *Goforth* shake itself to pieces?

Nobody spoke.

Ship's guidance systems made another correction on the fly and the *Goforth* dropped several thousand feet before self-arresting with a none-too-gradual resist rocket firing sequence that rattled Hillbrane's teeth in her head and sent Raleigh Marquette—standing behind her station—stumbling helplessly across the room in an uncontrolled stagger, colliding with a sickening thud against the far wall.

He'd be picking pieces of his palmtop out of his shirt pocket for a day or two, she thought with grim amusement. It was Raleigh's own fault for being too stubborn to go strap in, in quarters like the rest of the crew.

The pressure sensors warned of an approaching trough in the atmosphere, but she was watching for it this time. She wasn't about to take another hit like that if she could help it.

This time the overrides were smoother, and the impact of the adjustment on the order of a much smaller shock. Raleigh had gathered himself up and come back to stand behind her once again, tucking things away. "Brane. Pay attention. I think I chipped a tooth."

It was just the sort of comment that would have passed for banter between them, just one year ago. Hillbrane ignored him. She had work to do; she eased the adjusting power back as *Goforth* plowed into a higher-pressure area.

Waystation One was larger on the visuals screen moment by moment. Oceans. Lakes. Rivers. Mountains. Brown sere spaces and great green steppes, and the spectronomy confirmed that the plant life was chlorophyllic.

Home.

She could no longer see past the planet's horizon out to space beyond; they were close to the surface now, in a rapidly decaying orbit. She was supposed to be controlling the rate of decay. It was an optical illusion, she knew it was, but the ground looked so close—why hadn't the glide wings deployed? Was there something wrong with ship's guidance systems? She could issue an override, but if she moved too soon the wind shear would tear the glide wings off and the ship's computers would lose control of their descent entirely.

Twice she reached out with a hesitant hand, and twice withdrew. The mountains were close beneath them now, the plains still far below. There were clouds at the same level as the *Goforth*. They were sinking too fast. She had to do something.

Hillbrane reached for the override on the glide wing deploy, and just then the tell-tale blinked, the lights changed, the ship's computers deployed the glide wings and cut the rockets back.

It seemed so quiet.

Goforth dropped low across the green plains; they could see land features now—a gentle contour, a river, a sea or great lake beyond. They had analyzed those features from the registration scans, they knew what was there, and still they were actually seeing them now. It was different. Hillbrane wasn't sure she understood why, but the impact was unmistakable.

Out to sea now, and the sun glittered on gray water as the *Goforth* turned, losing altitude all the time. Turning back to approach the selected site from the water, so that they could judge its nearness to the mountains. They were slow enough now that they could look at the mountains without needing to take emergency action to avoid crashing into them, but the visual image from the surface below—the vision of the ground rushing by, beneath them—made it seem that they were moving much more quickly than before.

Goforth wheeled again, a three-quarter turn this time, taking its ground and field from a different approach angle.

The mountains had gotten much further off, pink and white in the distance. They were so close to the ground now that Hillbrane could see scrub vegetation below, rocks, bushes, green groundcover. *Goforth* dropped its autolaunch platform package and picked up speed while Hillbrane watched the sensors anxiously to see whether the base would deploy correctly. It seemed to take so long, the big gray aero-cement blocks swelling in the open air, unfolding block by block to form a platform, hardening as it went.

Now all they had to do was hit the mark.

"Air's clear," Rena—on circulation and pumps—announced. "Dust, pollen. Microbial forms are nonreactive. We can breathe this stuff."

They had to get down to it, first.

"Maybe I'll just get back and get strapped in—" Raleigh suggested. He sounded shaken, but she didn't have time to respond to that. They were out of time.

"Hang on, Marquette," she warned, with grim amusement. *Goforth* was so close to the hard ground that one miscalculated move could end it all. It was terrifying to be here, to see the ground rushing away from them; even more terrifying to look to the horizon and know that there was an autolaunch platform that they had to find before they stopped. Tiny. Big enough for the *Goforth*, but one single autolaunch platform, in all of this new territory . . .

She saw the autolaunch platform, its gray color almost shockingly alien in this green-and-brown landscape. She saw its lights, watched it communicate onscreen with *Goforth*'s autonavs.

They were so close to the ground.

What if there should be a little rise, between them and the autolaunch?

They were going more and more slowly, so slow—what if they fell to earth before they reached the landing platform?

They were on their final approach run now, and the autolaunch platform on-screen was at near eye level. She hadn't realized it was as high as it was, as large. *Goforth* dipped its nose toward the earth and slid into the autolaunch platform, scraping its belly as its hooks deployed.

And then it stopped.

The moments ticked away as the heat radiating from the hull soaked into the aero-concrete of the autolaunch platform, cooling the ship's hull as the concrete cured and hardened. Second-stage deployment. The autolaunch platform needed that heat to stabilize itself, to finish its transformation from its compact cargo form to a launch base. While it absorbed the heat from the hull and the ship's engines to harden itself, it was pulling that thermal energy deep into its heart to guard it there.

The airlock alert sounded: *You may now exit the vehicle safely.*

Hillbrane reached across herself for the master release on her safety webbing. Her hand was trembling.

"Well," Mir said from his post at Mission Control. "Let's go have a look."

She wanted to cry. They were here. They were really here. Waystation One, after all these centuries.

But she wanted to see, to smell, to feel the air, and she couldn't do that if she sat and wept.

Cago came into the room as the others were leaving. He held out his hand, and Hillbrane took it, noticing only as an afterthought the fact that Raleigh still clung to the back of her station. Rattled, maybe. If he needed help he could just ask for it. It would do him good.

She couldn't be bothered to think about Raleigh.

Hand in hand, she and Cago went out of Direction for the

airlock, to see what manner of world it was that they had come to.

At the bottom of the offload ramp Cago turned to make sure that Aitchel was steady on her feet. He knew that this was just the same as going from the *Deecee* to one of the Nouns—the absence of vibration underfoot, the different way the flooring gave when there was solid ground beneath the deck instead of the ceiling of a cargo hold. He knew that. Abstractly and objectively he knew it.

But subjectively he was weak in the knees and wobbly. This was solid ground. Even the Noun Ships were only solid for so far; and then they were space.

Ground.

Earth.

A world, the world, *terra firma* if not Terra, Waystation One.

There were steps in the autolaunch platform that led from the level where the *Goforth* rested down to the dirt. It was hard to mind his step, because he couldn't stop looking around him. Nobody noticed him staggering like a drunken man; they were all in a daze.

The ground stretched away forever and ever, further than his mind could quite grasp. It was so open, and there were mountains far away to the—what? The east? The south? He knew the words for direction, but what did they really mean?

It didn't matter. There were mountains. He had seen them on flyover; he knew how big they were, and now they were so small.

The immensity of the sky overhead was terrifying. Cago found Aitchel at his side and put his arms around her, seeking stability as much as comfort. It was so high overhead, and there was nothing there above them but atmosphere, and nothing holding it to the earth but the gravitational pull of the planet itself. Gravitational fields were expensive and hard to maintain, and what would happen when the inevitable power fluctuation set in?

This power would not fluctuate.

The dynamo that ran this gravity plant was within the molten core of the planet itself, and there was no stopping a rotation of this magnitude, not for too many years to imagine.

Someone turned the cycler fans on, but there was no need of cycler fans, nor was there any ducting or ventwork. It wasn't cycler fans. It was a breeze, coming off the water miles away to the opposite side from the mountains. North, Cago decided. He would call the mountains north, until someone came up with a better idea. They'd know where west was when the sun went down—

The breeze carried the warmth of the sun away; suddenly he was cold. He wasn't wearing a jacket. It was a useful reminder: the sun would go down, there would be breezes, and they needed to have quarters prepared by the time it got dark. That, or sleep in the *Goforth*. He didn't want to go back into the scoutship, not even for a minute. He couldn't get enough of the huge empty borderless immensity of the sky, and himself beneath it.

"So." His voice was too choked and strangled; there was no sense to it. Cago coughed and tried again. The atmosphere on *Goforth* had been oxygen-rich; he'd gotten spoiled. "So. Aitchel. Mir. Where were we going to make camp?"

He had to raise his voice to be heard from where he stood with Aitchel; Mir stood several paces off, weeping without shame. Cago wished he hadn't noticed that. It made it all the more difficult to keep his own voice steady, and there was work to do.

Mir wiped his eyes with the back of his hand. "We should be not too far from running water. That direction. I was watching for the river as we came in." Mir gestured out ahead of them, off at an angle to the line of the ship and the autolaunch platform. "The ground feels solid, and it scanned solid, but let's be careful. Scouting parties, by fours, constant comm contact. Carry the surface probes out front. Eight stay behind to unship the mover and check the loads, we'll need to deploy the ramp to clear the ship. Let's go."

Raleigh Marquette had sat down on the ground with his back to the autobase, staring out over the prairie flats with their scrubby covering of alien vegetation. Lichens. Mosses. Creeping groundcovers, crabbed little shrubs. Well, that was what they looked like, anyway; no trees in sight. It was a young world yet.

"Two Mechs, two Jneers on each team." Aitchel startled Cago by speaking out; and her tone was very strong and determined. "Oways counted with Jneers. Dibs on Tyler and Podile. Hey. First to find the river gets to name it."

Marquette had been limping, Cago had seen him. In Direction with no station to strap into, probably. Hadn't he stopped to think about how irresponsible it was to risk an injury just as they were landing? It would be a month before they left again, thirty days of intensive information gathering. They couldn't afford any invalids. Marquette would just have to stay behind and help unship the mover, and miss his chance to name the river after himself.

He'd miss *his* chance, if he didn't get started. Ivery had a team set up already. If the mountains were north and the ship was aligned on a north–south axis, Ivery's team was headed north by northeast. Fine. He would go due east. Unless Aitchel started out east by northeast.

It was good to have a task that required his attention.

The wonder of Waystation One could all too easily overwhelm a man.

"Here's the comm unit, Cawdor." Aitchel was teasing him. She only ever used his actual name when she was making fun. "I'd like to find the river before sunset. If you think we could get a move on."

And there were Tyler and Podile, waiting. Cago gave himself a mental shake. "Way ahead of you, Hillbrane."

There was so much to marvel at.

But marveling was doubtless best done from a shelter, with a meal under one's belt.

* * *

The mess dome was brightly lit, warm and noisy, full of the fragrance of hot cooked food. Hillbrane sat on one of the benches that ran around the room's perimeter with Cago beside her, taking it all in, almost too tired to move.

They'd found the river—well, Delacourt had found the river, and had named it Deecee. The ground was uneven but stable, there had been no problems with the tracked-mover even with the extra load of Raleigh's weight on it. He'd wrenched his leg, his knee, or his ankle or something, during their descent to planet surface. She didn't know exactly. She didn't exactly care, either. She was worn out and ready to sleep.

The Jneers were making too much noise.

The temporary shelters had not been successfully raised by sundown, and they'd had to finish the job by artificial light—a regrettable drain on power, but she supposed it didn't make any difference in the long run. In the long run they were leaving shortly. She wasn't sure that made sense, but she could be comfortable with the rationalization.

It had taken them longer than expected to get the shelters up even after sundown. It got cold in a hurry. But there were stars, and the moons were magical. She had caught herself frozen in place, staring at the sky; and her teammates waiting for her to complete her piece of the task, so that they could start on theirs. Time and again. The moons were almost physically magnetic; it was hard to take her eyes off them.

So they were all cold and hungry and exhausted by the time the skeleton of the mess dome had been raised. They'd overcompensated a little. They'd overcompensated a lot. It was almost too hot in the mess dome, and someone had figured that it had been more than two mealtimes since anyone had eaten and put three meals' worth of food out all at once. Wasteful and improvident, but Hillbrane was too tired to care.

Let them party.

The work could start again once everyone had rested, and

work there was in plenty. Finishing the mess dome. Raising the dormitory building and the growhouses. Bringing the ponics unit on line. The range of tests and samples that Fleet was going to need to have in order to ensure that the colony party was as well prepared as possible.

Fleet and the colony party reminded her.

Where was Raleigh?

She wanted to have it out with him about something.

She was going to have to stand up to do it, and she really didn't want to. Her arms and legs felt heavier than they had ever felt in her life. Someone had snuck lead weights around her wrists and ankles whilst she'd not been looking. She was so comfortable here with her Cago, who had fallen asleep. She loved him asleep in a different way than she loved him awake, because his sharp intent dark-eyed face looked so different when his eyes were closed.

No. She had to concentrate. There was something she was supposed to say to Raleigh.

What would it matter if she let it wait?

This was the promised land, Waystation One. This was the goal toward which the Fleet had struggled for nearly four hundred years, the first of the hoped-for colony worlds. It was real. They could breathe the air. They were safe and warm and sheltered and she had Cago beside her. Why shouldn't she heed the fatigue of her body and lapse into a well-deserved and restorative sleep?

Because there was something she had left unresolved between herself and Raleigh, and it had something to do with the ship.

That was why. And every time she closed her eyes and rested her cheek against Cago's strong warm shoulder, she stirred again and roused again.

She had to know.

After a while Hillbrane found the strength to stand up, knowing that it would be easier to do her errand the more steps she could put between herself and dreams of rest. The mess dome was large enough for all of them and could handle a group twice the size of the *Goforth*'s crew at once; it was filled with cased supplies being used as furniture, but they would get it all stowed properly before they left. Part of their mission was to ready quarters for an advance party, and ar-rrange the first few days' worth of food and supplies where they could be got at easily.

The present confusion of crates and portalumes made it more difficult for Hillbrane to make sense of the room, the people asleep across boxes, other people still sitting up over yet another packet of half-eaten food. Chaos. Well, chaos was probably unavoidable, a healthy outlet for the fierce excite-ment of the past day and a half.

There, in the middle of the room—of course, always in the middle of things. Raleigh. Podile beside him had put her head down on the portable worktable and gone to sleep, and Raleigh was making a card-castle of ration crackers. Singing to him-self. Something about jelly. Leaning against boxes and bodies as she went, Hillbrane worked her way laboriously around to where Raleigh sat; the weight of her own arms and legs was astonishing.

"You. Marquette. Raleigh."

He was in even more trouble with her than he had been before. About something. There was no reason for him to look up at her with such an owlishly hopeful expression on his face. Maybe it didn't matter all that much after all that he had be-trayed her, that he was responsible for her exile to *Deecee*; maybe she had gained more from the experience than she ever could have imagined possible. Maybe. But he was still a du-plicitous rounder, and until he at least acknowledged the fact of his treachery, there would be no reconciliation between them.

"Why. Brane. How nice."

He sounded drunk; Hillbrane wondered about that. Oh. Punch-drunk. Of course. So were they all. She leaned forward with her arms braced to the table for balance. She felt so tired. She could hardly keep her head straight on her shoulders.

"It is nice. Yes." Here on Waystation One. But that wasn't

what she needed to speak to him about. "Raleigh, we need to tell Fleet about the moons. First thing in the morning you've got to get the message out; I want to see the confirmation."

Because there was no way to be sure the message had been received without a readback. Transmission was a matter of narrow focus. If it wasn't aimed correctly it could easily go astray, and a confirmation from Fleet would go far to reassure her that Raleigh's return course was true.

Raleigh frowned. "Excuse me, Brane, have you seen my tablets? I need my tablets. Headache. Tablets please."

More than drunk, he sounded childishly petulant. He'd taken a bad spill on their descent; she'd seen him limping, and he hadn't been able to pull his weight on the work party. There was a good chance he was mildly concussed, and working as long and as hard as they had done had left everybody a little over-fatigued.

She had a headache herself, now that she thought about it. She'd gotten used to headaches during her first two or three weeks on the *Deecee*, though she hadn't noticed any such chronic problems since. Stress would do that.

"I'll get your tablets, Raleigh. You talk to Fleet in the morning."

"Can't sleep," Raleigh moaned, rubbing one eye with the heel of his hand like a five-year-old. "Maybe three tablets, Brane, you're a real friend. My head hurts. It's bad."

Okay, so he wasn't drunk and he wasn't concussed, he was just exhausted. Overtired. Unable to sleep because of an excess of excitement. She wanted to have assurance that he'd heard what she had said to him, but she could tell she wasn't going to get anything like a coherent response out of Raleigh tonight.

It would have to wait.

She felt like she was walking underwater, it was so difficult to move. It took forever to find the medical kit, and not because it was buried or concealed, simply because it took so long to walk over to the box marked "Medical" and open the crate. Headache tablets. Three, for Raleigh. Three for Hillbrane. Six for her pocket, in case she wanted them in the morning, in case Cago woke up with a headache.

It seemed almost more effort than it was worth, just taking tablets to Raleigh. She swallowed the medicine herself almost mechanically, drifting as if asleep on her feet over to where Cago slept slumped against the wall.

He should lie down.

He'd be sore in the morning.

He grumbled a little in his sleep as she got him laid sideways, but he didn't wake; and Hillbrane curled up next to him and closed her eyes.

Raleigh Marquette woke to a dull ache that seemed to consume his entire body. The pain in his head seemed to double and redouble with every tentative move he made to straighten a cramped arm or move a badly angled leg; only the bitter knowledge that he couldn't get an anodyne without physical movement kept him from freezing in his place, enduring the pain, and hoping someone would come to his aid by magic.

No sense looking for help.

Everybody was asleep. Worn out. Exhausted. There was no sound at all in the mess dome except for the noises people made in their sleep, and they weren't particularly restful noises, either. Breathing too hard. As though they were all running in their dreams and panting with the imagined effort.

He had to get up.

He nudged Podile, who still slept with her head down on the table by his side.

"Podile. Podile, honey, wake up, I need your help."

She roused slowly, but she didn't seem to have quite the headache he had. At least not to look at her. "Sore," she murmured, half-asleep; Raleigh nodded encouragingly, but carefully. He wanted to move as little as possible.

"There's medicine in the kit. You could get some for both of us." He'd seen Hillbrane find it yesterday, or at least before he'd gone to sleep. She'd apparently bought his addle-pate act.

It hadn't been all an act, either, but he was lucky it had worked.

And lucky to have Podile to help him. Oways knew what their mission was, it was to help Jneers, and he was a Jneer. She pushed herself away from the table slowly and with apparent difficulty, but gave no sign of thinking twice about complying with his request.

That was why he had wanted Oways on *Goforth*.

He'd explained it to Speaker Girosse in terms of representation, skilled technical support, any number of reasonable and logical reasons why at least one Oway should be among the scout party, but the fact of the matter was that he knew he could rely on Podile to take care of little chores like this.

Podile brought his medicine and a sipperpak of water to wash it down with. He took four tablets, and carefully shared out as many into her hand before he put the packet of tablets away in his shirt. She had not been knocked from one side of Direction to the other during *Goforth*'s less than silken-smooth descent through the atmosphere. But any appearance of stinginess was abhorrent to him.

He started to feel better soon.

It took him a while, and not a little courage on his part, but Raleigh stood up, and—holding out his hand for Podile—wove his way quietly through the crowded mess dome with its litter of crates and sleeping crew toward the antechamber.

It was light outside, almost painfully bright. They hadn't had much time to stand and wonder when they had arrived; now was his chance.

He opened up the door and slipped outside, and Podile came with him.

It was a bit chilly outside.

He put his arms around her for the warmth and gazed out across the low flat prairie to where *Goforth*'s autolaunch platform could be dimly glimpsed beyond the gentle rise of a small hillock.

The contour was deceiving.

There wasn't much of it, but what there was made transport complicated and judging distance impossible.

"Isn't she beautiful?" Podile asked, in tones of hushed and near-religious wonder; after a moment Raleigh realized that Podile was talking about this earth. About the view. About the world, Waystation One.

"Beautiful." Cool, but what was a little chill compared to the privilege of being the First Colony's first representatives in their new home? There was something Hillbrane didn't know, and he hadn't told her either. Something none of them knew, except for him. At least for now. He wondered how long he could keep it a secret and how best to let the news out. Carefully.

"Wouldn't it be something. To never have to leave," Podile said.

Raleigh had to smile.

"It would be something, all right. To be part of the First Colony. Imagine being a part of that."

And she would be, although she couldn't know that now. She still only hoped to be selected for First Colony. She had no way of realizing the truth.

The course correction module had still been in his shirt pocket when he'd come to Direction to watch Brane land the ship.

It had been between him and the sharp edge of something when he'd gone crashing across the room. It was destroyed. Unsalvageable. Irreparable. He would have thrown it away into the river last night, but he thought he might need it for evidence.

They couldn't leave.

The information *Goforth* needed to find the Fleet, the only record they had left after his difficulties with the outbound course, their only backup information on Fleet's vector of travel and intercept options—all of that had been safely stored on the course correction module.

Of course some of the data was also stored in ship's resources, and of course he shouldn't have been carrying the course correction module around with him in his shirt pocket so casually. But since he had been, there was no changing things now. There wasn't enough of the data in ship's stores to make a significant difference.

This was home.

They would all grow old and die here. It was just that he was the only one who knew that, here and now.

And maybe it would be just as well if he kept the information to himself until he had a chance to convince people that they wanted to stay. Timing was everything.

His headache wasn't gone, but it was better.

"I need to go send a transmit to Fleet, Podile." He needed to be away from camp before Hillbrane got up and remembered what she'd been asking him to do last night. "So I've got to get the solar panels deployed on *Goforth*. Will you drive me out? They're going to need the transport back here; you can leave me."

He'd get the solar panels for the commstation deployed, yes, and from the relative comfort of the empty ship. Vacant of people who might ask embarrassing questions. He could yet think of some way in which to use the awkward situation he was in to his advantage.

Of one thing he was certain.

All he needed was a little time to shape people's perceptions and reactions, and he would come out on top of this. Unscathed. A hero. The man who had guaranteed them all their place in the First Colony, without the dread uncertainty of waiting for Colony Fleet to make the choices.

Yes.

A hero.

So long as he just managed things correctly, he'd be golden.

Cago could feel a breeze against his face, and the sensation was so odd it nearly distracted him from what Mir was saying.

"Thirty days, then we leave. We're a little behind because we all slept in—"

People laughed, sheepishly. This was a breeze he felt, not ventilation. It was cooler against his temples and the exposed portion of his neck because he hadn't shaved; the stubble on his cheek kept his face warmer in some places than in others. It was so new. It was so wonderful. It was home—or at least it was to be home for the people who would be the lucky ones.

"So. We'll get started. We need one work team of eight to seal out the mess building. The rest of us need to get water in place first thing, six people to set up the treatment plant, four people to get the hoses in, and that leaves six people to rough out the foundation for the dormitory—where's Marquette?"

Aitchel stood with her arms around him, leaning her head up against his shoulder. Taking it all in. She started a bit when she heard Mir say Marquette's name, but it didn't last. Or else she was distracted. She probably figured she knew where Marquette had gone, and she was probably right, too, being Aitchel. Not that that meant she was right all of the time. Just that she'd known Marquette—and preferred Cago.

"I drove him out to *Goforth* earlier, Mir," the Oway woman Podile called from the other side of the group. "He said that he needed to get the solar panels deployed. To send some information back to Fleet."

Aitchel nodded to herself, but Cago felt her do it. Right down to his toes. She hadn't said anything to him about the results of her promised confrontation with Marquette; he wasn't surprised. They'd been busy. And it didn't seem to be so important to him any more now that they were here on Waystation One; their safe arrival proved the course was good.

Would he be selected for First Colony?

What if he was, and Hillbrane wasn't?

What if she was, and he wasn't?

Giving himself a little mental shake, Cago concentrated on Mir's instructions.

If he was chosen and not Aitchel, he wouldn't go.

If she was chosen and not him, he'd. . . .

"So, Cago—" Mir's voice called Cago's mind back from wandering yet again "—why don't you grab some people and form a crew to work in the mess building. You'll need three Mechs, the rest can be Jneers. Dela. If you could start roughing in the dormitory's foundation, please."

One way or the other that decision was in the future.

He could have Hillbrane on his work crew here and now, and save worrying about being separated by First Colony until he knew whether or not there was anything to worry about.

Three days, Raleigh thought, leaning wearily on the wide end of the piece of prefab structural construction material he held in place for the foundation of the first growhouse. Three nights, at least, so it was sometime on toward the end of the fourth day they'd been here, and he was almost beginning to wonder if it had been such a wonderfully clever idea of his to come.

It was cold. The moment a man stopped working the little breeze cut through exposed flesh to the bone and made him shiver. He knew all of the reasons for it, the unaccustomed work, the relative thinness of the air, the fact that Waystation One's gravity exceeded that standard to the Noun Ships by just enough to put every muscle under constant strain.

He didn't care.

All Raleigh cared about right now was getting through to the end of the day. They would all gather in the mess building after sunset, because the dormitories were still under construction.

He would be warm even if he would still be hungry, no matter how many bits and pieces of other peoples' rations he could manage to cadge.

"Raleigh. Raleigh!"

He roused himself with a start, having fallen into a sort of daze while he waited for the others to be ready for his piece of prefab. Hillbrane Harkover's voice. Hillbrane, and he'd successfully avoided any missteps for three days. Four days. However long it had been.

"Over here, Brane."

He didn't have the energy to shout. He didn't care enough. He was tired. She wanted to talk, she could come talk to him, but there was no sense in her expecting him to jump to her command. He didn't have it in him. He wasn't a Mech.

He kept his face carefully half turned away as she approached, his attention divided between the foundation work and watching her come. It wasn't an easy approach. There were pieces of equipment and building materials piled everywhere, and nothing getting done as quickly as they wanted it to happen. Tired. There were two and a half shifts between sunrise and sunset on Waystation One, at least right here, right now. They had to take advantage of each moment of daylight, but there was no question that efficiency was suffering.

"Raleigh. The comm station. Mir's been back to *Goforth*, and the panels aren't deployed, there's no setup. What's going on?" What kind of an idiot did she think he was? Of course the solar panels weren't deployed. If he got the comm station up, next thing you know they'd be expecting him to log the stats to find the Fleet and report safe arrival at Waystation One. And that would blow his cover.

"I ran into some minor technical problems the first day, Brane. Just haven't been back since, that's all. Busy, you know." He rocked the prefab panel under his care back and forth by way of explanation. "Why, is there an emergency?"

The work crew was comprised of Mechs and Jneers, but there were more Jneers than Mechs on this one. Raleigh had been studying the Mechs. He thought he knew how to dodge any accusations from Hillbrane, and come out looking like the more reasonable of the two. He had the benefit of the majority, after all.

"Raleigh." Hillbrane was playing right into his hands, too. Exasperation made her sound petulant. "I can't believe you came back from the ship and didn't say anything to anybody.

Here I thought we were just waiting for a readback. Does Fleet even know we're here?"

It was an encouragingly short space between petulant and petty. With any luck he'd have her over the edge in no time.

He kept his tone mild and reasonable. "Why Brane. I'm sure they realize we must be here by now. We lost some time on inbound, but it wasn't that long. And we've needed all available hands to get the base up. Here."

It was just the sort of obtuse refusal to acknowledge a perfectly reasonable concern that would drive her into a rage with very little effort on his part. "We have to communicate with Fleet. We have a responsibility. There are things Fleet needs to know. The moons. This atmosphere. Gravity."

"All in good time—"

"Hey." Tyler, one of the Jneers on the work crew, earned Raleigh's sincere gratitude with a timely interruption. "We need that prefab, Raleigh, come on. You can talk later."

Or not.

Raleigh ducked his head apologetically, smiling sheepishly at Hillbrane. He'd love to stay and chat. Really he would. But he was needed by his work crew. How could she hope to argue with that?

"Damn it, Raleigh, we're not on a field trip here, we need to report to Fleet!"

By losing her temper. He couldn't have asked for a more perfect line. Shouldering the prefab onto the base course, taking care to struggle visibly with the clumsy thing, Raleigh raised his voice to show a little temper of his own.

"*We* have to get these growhouses up and running, Brane, we're running behind, remember? I can't afford to waste a day fooling with a solar panel. And *you* should be with your crew. We've got work to do, okay?"

Perfect.

He had them right where he needed them to be: sympathetic, resentful of Hillbrane's irrational demands. It helped that everyone was tired and aggravated by the day's inevitable frustrations. Yes. It was going very well indeed.

"Let me give you a hand with that," Sanson—a Mech—suggested. His voice was full of supportive camaraderie, and Hillbrane just stood and stared at them. Helplessly. There wasn't a soul on the work crew just now who hadn't taken Raleigh's cause over Hillbrane's, accepting the proposal that the work that they were doing should take precedence over everything else.

At least until they were caught up.

The work was important. Vital. And so were they, for doing the work, and Hillbrane was odd man out.

Had she learned nothing about losing her temper, even after it had cost her a comfortable sinecure as an Oway?

"The minute we have a chance, then." She could make no demands. She could issue no ultimatums. She could not even demand the data and go do it herself, because she was needed on work crew as well as everybody else. "They need the advance information. It's for the First Colony."

"Three days either way isn't going to mean the failure of First Colony." Humorous belittlement. The perfect finishing touch. "Let's just keep our sense of proportion here, Hillbrane. I think I hear Cago calling you."

For a moment he thought he had overplayed his hand; Hillbrane's confused hurt was too genuine.

But they were all tired enough to be uncharitable, under cover of a joke.

Tyler laughed.

Tyler laughed and one of the Mechs snorted, and Hillbrane's face set into a mask of curious contempt.

Good.

She wouldn't want to open this conversation again any time soon.

"You're derelict in your duty, Raleigh," Hillbrane said. Raleigh made a funny face, secure that Hillbrane couldn't see him mocking her from where she stood. "I'll take it up with you again, for certain. Shame on you for letting us all down."

She didn't know the half of it.

And the stronger her language became, the more it secured his position among his peers, who would close ranks around him to make common cause as Jneers against the contempt of a Mech who had once been one of them.

Raleigh composed his face and concentrated on fitting the prefab into its slot.

Hillbrane went away.

With luck her disgust would silence the questions she might have until he had discovered a way out of his predicament.

Miracles could happen.

Podile hurried toward the shell of the first growhouse with her tabulation in hand, a feeling of trepidation in her heart. She was going to have to tell Mir immediately, and it wasn't as though Mir didn't have plenty of other problems to concern him. But it couldn't be helped. The implications were too critical for her to be able to hold the information back and live with herself.

She already knew Mir wasn't working with the dormitory squad today, she'd checked there first; everybody else was at the growhouses, now that the water treatment plant was finally in working order—after only eight days.

It was taking them all much longer than they had expected.

The work was harder than anybody had anticipated. The sun was bright, the breeze was fitful, the air was clear and so pure that it seemed a person couldn't get enough of it—but it was cold; the sky impossibly high, the mountains so terribly far.

Psychologically and physiologically sapping.

The sun reflected off the solar panels of the growhouse's sides and roof and blinded her. She couldn't see a thing, but she could hear voices, so she went in.

There was a full work crew there: ten people, four Mechs, six Jneers. Another crew was getting the foundations in for the second and third planned growhouses. The rest of the crew of the *Goforth* were with Mir or doing the administrative chores, as she was.

All present or accounted for, and now that the first structure was roughed in they were getting the beds ready for first crops and setting up the irrigation system. The watercourse had been the first element of the growhouse complex to go in. They could pump out of the river, and once the water had run through the filtration system they could drink it.

Real water.

Never been recycled.

Water from heaven, rainwater and snowmelt and icemelt, water that was worth so much more than merely its weight in gold. . . .

"Ar Marquette."

He and his crew were filling in a bed with growing medium, sterile soil that *Goforth* had brought with them. Breaking open the packed cakes, breaking the compressed mass up with blows from a stick, raking the medium out to fill the bed. They all looked sweaty, but not uncomfortable. It was warmer in here. And there were four walls and a semiopaque ceiling high above; so the immensity of the world around them could be more easily ignored.

"Podile. What news?" Marquette pulled his rake up and set the butt end to the floor, resting his forearms across the tooth-edge. Podile showed him the tabulation.

"Stores inventory, Ar Marquette. I need to find Mir, it's important. There's bad news—"

"Now, Podile, there's no such thing as bad news, just new opportunities," Marquette interrupted with an impish grin. He did impish grin very well; she'd noticed that about him from the beginning. How long had that been? Comparisons, at Stik-nals. So long. Almost a year, surely.

"Right, Ar Marquette. The opportunity." And she should be careful about using language that might be construed as un-necessarily alarmist. "The opportunity is that we're going through rations at almost twice the scheduled rate."

She showed him the tab summary, but he made no comment. Didn't he understand? One way or the other, now that she'd voiced the issue, she should probably explain why she thought it was an urgent issue. Minimizing uncertainty by sharing information was important when people were under stress.

"We've been drawing rations for eight days now. The days are longer, that could contribute, but we're down nearly twice as many days' issue. At this rate we're going to have to go on short rations."

Marquette sucked in his cheeks, puckering up his mouth in a droll gesture. Waggling the rake back and forth gently.

"Well. We'd better be sure these ponics are up and running in double-quick time, then, hadn't we? Podile. I'll tell you a secret."

Not lowering his voice, not making the slightest attempt to prevent being overheard. The people nearest to them had already stopped to listen. As Marquette spoke the others on the crew gradually stopped working too, clearly keen on hearing what Marquette had to say.

"I don't want to leave, Podile. I like it here. If I return to Colony Fleet as scheduled, who knows if I'll get to come back? But I'm already here. All I have to do is stay here, and I've got my place, guaranteed. We're not going to run out of food. These growhouses will be up and producing before the rations run out, and there's plenty to tide us over if we have to break into advance party stores."

How could he say such a thing? The stores for the advance party were critical. Podile did not try to conceal her confusion, and Marquette responded with quick reassurance.

"We can be more careful, you're right, we're still adjusting, that's all. But don't worry about the food. I am absolutely certain that we won't run out."

Podile didn't know how to react.

Did Mir know how Marquette's mind was operating?

"Well. Whatever." She could think of nothing particularly intelligent to say. Marquette's casual assumption that the stores for the advance party were his to dispose of was deeply shocking. "I've got to go find Mir with this report. Excuse me, Ar Marquette—"

"Call me Raleigh." This time his interruption was low-voiced, seductive, petitioning. Flirtatious. "We could be part of a wonderful new chapter in the history of the human race, Podile, you and I. We shouldn't be bound by caste restrictions any longer. Call me Raleigh. Call Aitch Harkover Hillbrane, or Chelbie, or whatever it is she thinks her name is these days."

Oh, this was too much. He was perfectly within his rights to flirt with her, it was just the Jneer in him. And that first-name business had been part of Jneer flirting since there had been Jneers. But Harkover? He had absolutely no right to suggest she use Aitch Harkover's first name. Only Aitch Harkover—Chelbie—could do that.

"I'll let you get back to what you were doing." She used as firm a tone of voice as she could muster. "Thank you for your time."

Mir was not going to share Marquette's relaxed response to the rations issue.

She couldn't imagine what she was supposed to do about Marquette's startling suggestion.

And whether or not she only imagined that Marquette was hinting at something, she was profoundly disquieted by something in his manner that she did not understand.

Was this something she needed to share with others not present? Or could she leave that to these people who had also heard Marquette, Jneers and Mechs alike?

Was it her responsibility, or theirs?

She needed some time alone to think about this.

"Lumber load," Cago called out, and the man on the drag line let the slack out carefully, watching the bundle of prefab construction beams start its descent from the top of the riverbank as he did so. Raleigh Marquette was the anchor-man, and Marquette wasn't usually part of Cago's work group; Hillbrane said Marquette was avoiding her. But belaying the lumber loads was the easiest job on station today, and Marquette claimed that he was still suffering from injuries he'd sustained during *Goforth*'s landing. Ivery had gone to work the growhouse rakes, and they were stuck with Marquette.

Marquette was good at getting himself into the easiest jobs—but Cago couldn't be bothered to care about Marquette. Not really.

"Coming at you," Marquette called back. Cago tracked the bundle of prefab structurals as it slid down the transit line from up top, judging his moment. If he reached too soon he would just set the balance off, and run the risk of spinning a package of beams against the embankment.

If he waited too long to take control of placement the load would touch down before he had it where he wanted it, and that meant extra effort to reposition the raw material before he could unship the load.

"Slide her on over, Cago." Aitchel was braced on the platform, ready to lend a hand. One of the final tasks on their list was to build a pumphouse at water level and slave a pressure system to the machines that ran the growhouse sprinklers, so that the plantings they'd be starting would continue to grow between their departure and the arrival of the First Colony's advance party.

They'd thrown the pump hoses into the river when they'd got here, pulling the water on a suction pump to fill the growhouse cisterns and give them drinking water.

It had been three weeks.

They would be leaving soon.

The river was a good twenty-five feet below the surface, its channel carved down into the subsoil. Efficient movement of water required a pump at water level and an assist pump on the pipeline at the top of the riverbank. A pump at water level called for a pumphouse. A platform. Somewhere they could anchor waterlines and site the pump, a working platform where hoses could be purged of accumulated silt or debris, and maintenance could be performed on a more reliable surface than the friable clay that formed the river's steep high embankment.

One hand on the end of the load of structurals, Cago walked with the prefab, following it for its last few feet of drop to the platform. The riverbank was too steep and the water was too swift and deep for them to be able to risk pitching materials over the side; besides which, that could damage the structurals. The pulley system they had rigged moved material much more slowly, perhaps, but at least it was safe.

"How are we doing?" Cago asked, just to make conversation. Aitchel looked tired. They were all tired; this was work, and he was hungry. He thought he'd been hungry since he got here, the result of working too hard on an inadequate ration. Their rations would have been fully adequate to support physical labor on one of the Nouns or a forefront ship, but Waystation One was different.

Everything was just that little bit heavier.

First Colony was going to need a lot more fat in its diet for its first years' supply, and bone density was going to be a real issue.

"One or two more loads and we'll be forced to take a break while the framing crew catches up." Aitchel made no secret of how distressing she found the prospect of a rest, either.

Tired, but in good spirits.

He had to smile at her; he couldn't help it. Purely out of affection, needless to say, because with the work that they were doing and the hours they were putting in nobody had the energy for anything more strenuous than affection. Or at least he didn't. And it wasn't for lack of interest, either.

"Swing a load, Cago?" Mir called down to him from above. Cago beckoned with an exaggerated swooping gesture of his hand. Maybe he didn't have the energy for frisky behavior, but thinking about it made him feel less weary. Damnedest thing.

"Come on down, Mir."

He could use a break.

He could use it to flop down in the short wiry scrubby

vegetation up top and stare at the sky and catch his breath. He was getting more accustomed to the atmosphere, but physical exertion made it plain that the available oxygen was not what he was used to. It was worse for the Jneers. The environment on the Noun Ships was more oxygen-rich than the Mech ships, so they had further to go to get acclimatized, in a manner of speaking.

And speaking of Jneers—

"Travel down." The call from up top was Marquette's cue to lean out against the brake line and be ready for the weight of the load to stress the slider. Sitting down on the job was the largest part of the task; Marquette was collecting his coils, ready to receive.

"On belay. Go ahead."

On Marquette's signal the work crew up top swung the load up and away from the riverbank, hanging in midair on the slider cable. Ready for descent.

Fine. Cago turned around to say something to Aitchel. And then Marquette yelled.

"No, wait—"

Cago spun around, crouching instinctively.

As he turned he saw Marquette fall back against the embankment, as if his foot had slipped. There was a splash. Marquette had lost the brake line in his fall, the load of prefab structural came screaming down the slider, and it was heading straight for him.

He jumped out of the way, flattening himself as he went, throwing himself to the ground to try to escape the killing blow of the square end of a prefab structural.

Aitchel.

The load's gather-rope broke as it hit the platform, the prefab structural beams scattering like matchsticks across a table. Cago stumbled to his feet, unmindful of the wild vibration of the slider cable. Aitchel. Aitchel had gone down, and the prefab structural beams rattled up against one another and hid her from his sight.

Scrambling like a madman, Cago clawed his way across the

jumbled pile of prefab to find Aitchel. She hadn't gone into the river, that was good. But when he turned her limp body over there was blood on her face. Her eyes were open but staring, without focus; if Marquette had hurt her, Cago was going to carve his guts out with a dull spoon. . . .

"Why, I don't know how it happened, I had the rope, I lost my balance, is Brane hurt? It's not my fault—"

Marquette was behind him, spewing a spate of excuses and idiocy.

Cago turned around and hit the bastard as hard as he could. Caught him in the pit of the stomach. Good. Marquette went over backwards, tripping over the pile of prefab structural beams, and fell down out of Cago's line of sight.

It was a start.

But he couldn't spare more than a thought for Marquette. By now some of the others on the work crew, with Mir in the lead, had slid down the steep bank to see what had happened and to give them a hand. Mir was shouting up for a stack of floor facings to use as a makeshift litter, so they could get Chelbie up to the surface.

Delacourt stood with him while Mir checked Aitchel's unresponsive body over quickly, and then Aitchel twitched.

Cago was on his knees again in an instant.

Her mouth was working, but no sound came out, and yet her hand was making a good grip as she clasped and reclasped her hand in Mir's.

Maybe just stunned?

The breath knocked out of her?

Marquette had called belay. If he hadn't been in position, he'd be an idiot to call it; letting a load slide like that could get somebody killed.

Like him, for instance?

Could he be sure he'd seen Marquette slip back? Or had the belay rope been out of Marquette's hands when Cago had turned around to see why he had shouted?

Maybe Aitchel was right about Jneers, Cago told himself as

he helped Mir slide Aitchel's still-helpless body onto the ad hoc litter they'd prepared.

Maybe Jneers were not lower forms of life. Some of the Jneers on this mission seemed to be okay.

But Raleigh Marquette might have just tried to kill him.

And Marquette had been willing to put Hillbrane in harm's way to do it.

There could be no tolerance for either of those facts. There would be a reckoning.

As reality began to jell once again around her, Hillbrane found herself lying on the long table in the mess area, surrounded by Jneers. And Cago, whose voice was so cold and savage that she only knew it was him because she could see that he was talking.

"Don't play innocent. You gave the call. You couldn't actually be that clumsy. You tried to kill me."

Even then she could hardly recognize her lover behind the furious expression that transformed his face. And Raleigh was ugly. There was no other word that could describe it, Raleigh was *ugly*, and if she hadn't known him for all of her life, she would be afraid to be in the same room with him.

"I'd be careful how I threw accusations around, Warrine. You don't know a thing about the facts here. It was an accident. Nobody would believe for a moment that I'd do anything that might harm Hillbrane."

She was starting to remember what had happened. The load of material coming down the long cable; Cago ducking, just in time. Impact.

"You weren't trying to hurt Aitchel, you were trying to get rid of me, you stinking—"

"Tch," Raleigh said. "Jealousy. Who do you think's going to believe you? A Mech, making such outrageous claims. You're just lucky I'm not a vengeful man, or I could take exception to your tone of voice."

Silence.

This was bad.

Because the Jneers in the room seemed to be buying it.

Cago stood silent, as if measuring up the situation, weighing his opponent's strengths and weaknesses before he made his next move. Hillbrane looked around her frantically. Where were the Mechs? Where was Mir?

She had to do something before Cago's righteous fury created a polarized situation. It was bad enough that the certainty existed in Cago's mind. If there was to be violence . . .

Trying to stir, Hillbrane felt an involuntary grunt of protest coming on, and gave it full permission. "Uh . . ."

Cago turned to her in an instant.

Raleigh was a little bit more slow.

"Cago." She found her voice oddly wobbly. Cago raised her up to a seated position carefully; nothing was broken, then. "Cago, what hit me?"

She knew well enough. But she needed time to figure out how to keep Raleigh from using Cago's own passion to create the appearance of an us-versus-them sort of situation, or to give the Mechs time to get here. Whichever came first.

"No permanent damage, Aitchel," Cago assured her. There were depths of tenderness in his voice that she found astounding, even after all this time. "Took the breath out of you good and proper. How come you never look that way when I kiss you? The magic is gone."

She had to put a stop to this line of nonsense at once. Sooner. The touch of Cago's hand against her face was as tender as though she had been made of the thinnest-walled glass in the Colony Fleet. She had not really understood until now how inestimably precious she was to him.

Which apparently maddened Raleigh beyond all sense of proportion. "You heard him?" Raleigh demanded of the Jneers. "He says I did it on purpose. Hillbrane, I've had about as much abuse from this low-life as I'm prepared to take. This is the last straw."

And he could have the Jneers seeing it his way all too easily. Hillbrane knew the truth of that. Who would believe a mere

Mech, when a Jneer swore to the contrary? Here and now on Waystation One there was a balance of power of a sort. But when they returned to the Fleet . . .

"Raleigh, you're overreacting," she protested. Because he was. He was deliberately setting Jneers against Mechs with the words he chose; she'd seen him do it before. "Calm down. I'm the one got knocked over. Come on."

They couldn't afford internal dissent, not as stressed as they all were. They had just had one accident. That they hadn't had more was more luck than care, since care could not stand against the cumulative effects of fatigue and hunger.

"I won't be accused of such contemptible behavior," Raleigh said; oddly enough his voice sounded genuinely aggrieved. And "genuine" and "Raleigh" just didn't go together. "What would you think of me?"

Cago met her eyes, and Hillbrane read Cago's answer there as clearly as if he'd spoken it aloud.

Nitrogen-rich fertilizer.

The door at the far end of the mess building opened; Hillbrane could feel the cool air rushing in.

"Marquette, Chelbie. Good to see you both here. There's a problem."

It was Mir.

He had some Mechs with him, and as the Jneers broke ranks to let him come through, Hillbrane thought she saw something in his hand.

"Mir." Her voice sounded much more her own to her, now. The shock was wearing off, or maybe just going under. There was so much else to worry about. "What's the news?"

Mir and the Mechs stopped a pace or two short of the table, keeping the table itself—with Hillbrane on it—between them and Raleigh. "Look what we found at the river," Mir said, and held something up.

Something small and clearly broken, its casing compromised, covered in dirt and sand. What was it?

"Warrine. You ignorant brute." Raleigh clearly recognized it right away, and that gave Hillbrane her clue. "Look what you've done. Mir. Can it be salvaged, can it be fixed at all?"

It was the course correction module.

The course correction module, with the only information they had left on where to find the Fleet and how to get there. Raleigh had never been back to *Goforth* to uplink. She'd gotten tired of nagging him about it; he made things ugly for a person.

But if the course correction module was damaged—how were they ever going to get back to the Fleet?

Cago looked stunned and confused. Hillbrane noted unhappily that the Jneers had all collected around Raleigh, but Mir spoke before Cago could respond to Raleigh's implicit accusation.

"Ask us where we found it, Marquette. Dela was trying to figure out how you could have slipped, with no skid marks in the riverbank."

Raleigh hadn't slipped?

It hadn't been an accident?

Mir was still talking. "That's where we found the course correction module. Not where you and Cago here came to blows. It must have dropped out of your clothing when you fell down, however it is that that happened. And I'd like an explanation as to the condition of this piece of equipment."

Hillbrane held out her hand, and Mir gave her the unit. Raleigh stepped forward as if he meant to take it, but Cago was between Hillbrane and Raleigh, and Hillbrane happened to know that Cago was not in a good mood.

"Oh, this is fine," Raleigh spat, bitterly. "I'm the one who was attacked, can we please just keep that little fact in mind? And now the course correction module is destroyed, and you blame me. It was all Mechs who found it, of course. My. How convenient."

Raleigh was lying.

Raleigh was lying through his teeth like the contemptible sneak that he was. If the course correction module had just dropped out of his pocket, just now, why had he blamed Cago for destroying it? *Look what you've done*, Raleigh had said. Too far from Mir to be able to see exactly what condition the course correction module was in.

"This has been broken for a while." She held the unit up to get a better light on it. "Look. Some of these shards are actually worn down around the edges."

The case had been shattered on impact against something very hard and very sharp; she could see particulate matter inside the case, scoring the surface of the all-important record media. If it had been in Raleigh's pocket and just now fallen, it would not have had time to collect dust, dirt, grit, pieces of what seemed to be lint. No.

Was that why Raleigh had avoided calling Fleet?

Had their lifeline been severed for all of this time?

"I never thought I'd live to see the day." Raleigh sounded grief-stricken, with an element of righteous indignation to give his words a little edge. "Brane. You know better than that. And to try to twist the truth, just to protect your Mech lover. I never would have dreamed it."

She wasn't fooled.

Raleigh was lying now, and had been lying for weeks, and would be lying all the way back to Colony Fleet where he would face an accounting—

"Cut it out." Mir's firm order stopped the recriminations in Hillbrane's throat. "At this point I don't really even care how it got damaged. First things first. Can it be salvaged? Can we recover information? Do we have a way to contact Fleet? Anybody. Jump right in."

Hillbrane knew the answer.

She waited.

Raleigh would be forced to admit . . .

"No. I never contacted Fleet, I thought it was more important to get the base ready before we left. And now I'm sorry, believe you me."

She shot Raleigh a glance that was admiring despite herself. Even now. Even here. He would continue to lie; but what good could it do him now?

She knew he hadn't contacted Fleet because he couldn't. He

had no data. The course correction module was trashed and it had been trashed for a while. It had probably been in Raleigh's pocket all along, carried with him every moment out of fear someone would discover it moving his kit into the dormitory or something of the sort. And yet he would continue to pretend.

"And how are we going to find the Fleet without a course?" Mir insisted on the single pertinent question, leaving all of its implications and background for later analysis.

"No way," said Raleigh.

Suddenly Hillbrane understood Raleigh's lies.

He had never meant to leave once they got here.

But since they were all stranded, if he was to be discovered as the man who was to blame for it, he would not be able to manage things to his liking while they waited for the First Colony's advance party. Since they were all stranded, he had no choice but to lie flamboyantly and outrageously and with as much determination as he could muster, if he was to hope to be part of First Colony as a brave pioneer rather than a contemptible self-serving malefactor.

Hadn't that been behind the cheat he'd pulled in Comparisons?

Raleigh Marquette for himself, and all others take second?

"But there has to be a way." She couldn't let it go at that. "You haven't done an uplink since when, Raleigh? Fleet doesn't know about the moons. The atmospheric pressure. They're going to need to change the calorie loads and increase the rations or First Colony won't survive for two years."

Which was how long the plan called for First Colony to live off what it could bring with it, before the colony could start to self-sustain. Two years and emergency reserves, none of which would be adequate unless they could get their data through in time.

"And it's cold. It's not warm. It's uncomfortable. First Colony will need extra food, extra fuel, extra shelter to support them while they adjust. And without all that First Colony is doomed, Raleigh, there's no chance unless we get the word back to them somehow."

No chance. Well, maybe there was a chance, but it was such a big risk to start out with—putting a colony on an alien world, howsoever carefully selected. If it was an experiment it would be marginally worth risking, and with volunteers. First Colony was not an experiment. First Colony was the future of the human race as they knew it.

Because Waystation One was here, now; and if Waystation One was as different from what they had expected, who would gamble the survival of the species on the chance that Waystations Two through Five would be more like what had been expected, and easier for a colony to adapt to?

Raleigh was shaking his head. "You're punchy, Brane. Your lover just let you take a hit with a full load of prefab, remember? You should rest."

Trying to discount her concerns. Trying to nullify her claims. He was frightening her, that was true, but she couldn't afford to surrender to Raleigh's self-righteously twisted view of the world.

"I may be punchy, but I can still think straight." She had shuddered beneath so heavy a sense of doom and dread before, and she had managed. She had derived a strategy. She had come up with a plan. True that the two situations could not be compared for seriousness; all the more reason she could not succumb to self-pity and despair.

At least not just yet. Later. Plan first. Strategize first. Collapse later. "There is too much at stake, Raleigh. First Colony deserves our utmost effort to make it go. We'll find a way. Cago, come on, we'll go back to *Goforth*."

Cago didn't want to let her stand up. But he respected her determination and gave her room. She was wobbly, but she could walk.

And it was time for her to do some serious polarizing of her own. "Mir, I need all the help I can get, Mechs, Jneers, everybody. We have to figure out how to get a message through. We owe it to First Colony. To the Colony Fleet. To the whole human race. Let's go."

All right; now she'd done it.

She moved around so that she had the Mechs behind her, facing the Jneers across the table upon which she had lain. As she turned she saw that Podile was standing there with Mir and Dela, among the Mech contingent. She'd always had Podile identified with Jneers in her mind—an artifact from her own Jneer upbringing, she supposed.

She was glad to have Podile behind her. "The information we have to transmit is life or death for the colonists. I'm going back to *Goforth* to figure out how we can find Fleet without a course. I could use your help. Mir's right, it doesn't matter now why or when the course correction module got broken—" Although that was the crucial element in deciding how to evaluate Raleigh's claims. "We just need to fix our problem and get back with the data. I hope to see you all when we reach the ship."

Five miles' walk, and her with shaky legs. No way of knowing how much of her trembling was physical trauma, shock, and how much of it was pure adrenaline . . . fury at Raleigh's irresponsibility, at his duplicity, horror at the realization of the nature of the situation that they were in.

Five miles' walk, and it was going to be cold.

People didn't think well when they were cold, when they were starved, when they were physically exhausted from the strain of merely carrying the extra weight Waystation One gave to their flesh and bone. But they would be back in familiar surroundings, and *Goforth* could be secured to conserve internal warmth. Once the computing systems were on line it would take the chill off. Gradually.

She stumbled from the mess building into the encroaching twilight; shadows had grown longer since the accident down by the river. Well, *Goforth* could be spotted in the dark by the white unnatural foundation of its autolaunch platform. So long as they kept the camp at their backs and marked on some star for an index they should be all right.

Not minding who was following and who not, too tired to really care, secure in her confidence that her own crew at least would humor her, Hillbrane set out to find her way back to *Goforth*.

There had to be a way.

And they had to find it soon enough to give the Colony Fleet the time it was going to take to react to the news they had to report.

It was that or doom First Colony before it started; and Hillbrane had no intention of letting that happen.

NINE

SEEKER

Cago stood his ground as Aitchel left, willing Marquette fixed to the ground by the force of his concentration. None of the Jneers seemed to want to move without permission from Marquette; so Marquette had to be faced down. No, Marquette had been faced down, and Aitchel had done it. It just wasn't as obvious to the others that Aitchel had won the clash of wills.

"Well?"

He could wait to take up his quarrel with Marquette. Aitchel's mission could not wait. Aitchel said so; Cago believed her. He wasn't sure he understood her sense of urgency, because he couldn't quite see how they were going to get a message off the planet without a course himself. But he was a Mech. He and Aitchel were crewmates. That was all he needed to know to understand that his place was to back her up.

"Maybe with you Mechs out of the way we can get some work done," Marquette said.

Well, if that was the way he was going to be about it. One of the Jneers was on his way out the door, that was a good sign. But most of them were not moving, though one of the Jneers behind Marquette spoke up, sounding a little uncertain. Almost frightened.

"Raleigh. What Brane said. Shouldn't we be helping?"

Marquette rolled his eyes at Cago, as if inviting him to share a joke at the Jneer querant's expense. Cago kept his face straight. He wasn't playing Marquette's game.

"You want to go work with Brane, Tyler, sure. Fine. Go right ahead. Waste of time, and we need to get the food line up and running. But—hey—if that's what you think you should do, I'm fine with it. Really."

No, Marquette thought it was the single stupidest suggestion he had heard in a long time. He had a genuinely enviable control over the inflection of his language. It was beautifully done.

And it worked.

Tyler subsided as if into shamed silence.

Marquette waited for a moment, apparently to assure himself that there would be no further challenges.

"Now if you don't mind, Cago, there's work to be done, and a long time before we'll get relief from Fleet. We'll be glad of your help. Once you and Brane have made up your minds to stay, that is, because you'll be staying, one way or the other. Get used to it."

Marquette could be right. But they'd try Aitchel's way first. He could afford to let Marquette have the last word. It didn't really matter; one of them was right, and one of them was mistaken, and only time was going to tell which one was which.

Cago left the growhouse, beckoning the Mechs to come with him.

They were going to need to hurry if they meant to catch up with Hillbrane.

After a while the mover came up behind her, and someone pulled Hillbrane onto the broad fender so that she could ride. Cago. He held her so that she wouldn't fall off, and she fell asleep with her head cradled against his chest only to wake once again in what seemed two heartbeats' span.

Goforth.

Ghostly in the near-dark, looming atop its autolaunch platform, silent and waiting. Climbing up into the black belly of the ship was almost more effort than Hillbrane could muster; she was glad of all the help she could get.

Mir was already there, Ivery and Neyrem with him. Once she was inside she could see dim lights from the Direction room, and stumbled aft to see what it was.

People crowded after her until the room was packed—there had to be twelve people there. More. She was dimly aware of the heavy resounding reverberation of the secures clamping into the access; they were alone.

She looked around.

Low light for energy conservation. Cold, but warming rapidly with the concentrated body heat of a dozen souls.

Someone sat down on the floor.

That was a good idea.

Hillbrane sat down too; and soon only Mir was standing.

"This is bad," Mir said. "I never would have dreamed anything gone so wrong. Okay. First things first. We have to get word back, and that means finding Fleet somehow. Chelbie. The others."

Hillbrane blinked. Was there a question?

"Marquette says he'll stay. Those rations were supposed to be for the advance party. Will they last him?"

Oh, this was too much to have to think about. She had such a headache. And her horror of what they had all heard from Raleigh weighed on her mind like a nonconducting field, through which rational thought could struggle only with difficulty.

"Advance party. One hundred and twenty-five people. Three weeks prior to the arrival of the main party. More than thirty weeks' rations for twelve people. Theoretically."

"We're using them up too fast." That was Podile. Yes. Hillbrane recognized her voice. "The rations that were for us are almost gone. Seven and a half months' rations may only last seven months, six and a half months. Possibly less."

Less, if the Jneers would not learn to eat everything on their plate whether they wanted it or not. But that wasn't her problem. Was it?

"The advance party is due within four months. So long as we can get through to Fleet, they can bring food with them. If we fail they'll come expecting food that isn't here, and there's the risk that the ponics won't be up and running in time to make up the difference. So we won't fail," Mir said, and it sounded so clear and simple, put that way.

No.

They would not fail.

They could afford to leave Marquette on Waystation One, he wouldn't starve.

They could not afford to fail to get the information they possessed to Fleet.

"Podile, I know you've been working hard. I hope you can manage the galley, all the same. Someone here can help you, maybe, since I don't see Vince."

Hillbrane didn't see Vince. She saw Kovacs, though, and wasn't he a little out of place here? Kovacs was a Jneer. Well. Good for Kovacs. But Mir was still talking; she had to pay attention.

"Chelbie, I'm sorry, but you're going to lie down to give yourself time to recover before we start working you. Now, there should be two days' worth of navigation in the short-term backup. Where could we find navigation information on this ship given that the course correction module is not available, and the index sets are compromised?"

Brainstorming. This was something Mechs were good at. Their whole lives were workarounds.

"We know our angle of approach to orbit," Kovacs said. "We know the orbit. We know how long ago it was. So we know where it was we took that angle to intercept. The back angle should get us out of system—"

"But it's not a back angle. We curved in on it." Ivery sounded thoughtful. "Maybe there's a chip in the steering rockets system that remembers what that was. If the trace hasn't decayed."

She could sit and listen to this all day. But Cago wasn't going to let her. Cago came and lifted her up from the floor, picked her up and carried her out of the room, down the corridor. Down to the shower room.

That romantic devil.

Hillbrane sat down on the soaping-bench and started to undress, but it hurt to undress, so she let Cago do it.

The water was warm and soothing. Cago was there to take care of her.

The last thing she remembered was the sound of the cycler and the welcome warmth of the shower stream; she was asleep before Cago tucked her into her bed in quarters.

Within the space of fifty hours Hillbrane Harkover slept and rose, puzzled, fought, wrestled with the data, and slept again to wake and start all over.

They could get the *Goforth* into orbit. That was short range.

Once they had gotten *Goforth* into orbit they would be able to break out of system, because the last set of registrations had not been overridden in temporary stores, and they all had a general idea of which direction they needed to be going in. They could correct for the changes in Waystation One's position along its orbital path without too much trouble. It had been less than four weeks. Waystation One had not traveled far.

But once they had cleared the system there was only the most basic route information recoverable from ship's navigation systems; Raleigh had been wiping and rewriting as they went along. That was what he had been doing after hours on the navstation. They could calculate what their angle of approach had been; they could come close to a figure for how much extra time it had taken them to get here, how much distance they had added to what had originally been expected to be a direct route. There was a cone of space that opened up from Waystation One and widened as it went, a cone that contained in its great sweep all of the potential starting points they might have come from.

There was too much space out there.

They had to find the Fleet, and they had to do it soon or it was as good as never. They could not afford to quarter and requarter all that emptiness in a systematic search; nor did they have the signal power to project a call over so wide an area and hope against hope for an intercept.

Too much.

The sense of urgency had not faded. The desperation of the quest had not dulled, not one fraction. But in fifty hours, working together, trying every idea for any possible hope, they had found no hope.

They could get up and get out, but they had no way of reaching the Colony Fleet in time for their message to be useful to anyone. If Colony Fleet was seeking them in turn, there was no sign of it happening. They didn't know where to direct a transmit or a receive. The Fleet was probably wondering why there was no answer to its call.

Fifty hours. One long day, and the most part of the following night. It had been sundown when she had come back to *Goforth*. It was short of sunrise still when Hillbrane gathered with the rest of her crew beneath the belly of the ship to climb down to the ground and trek back to their little settlement.

Raleigh would be vindicated, but that was not what wrenched Hillbrane heart and soul.

She was convinced that without the information that they had to relay the First Colony would fail, and the Colony Fleet itself would be able to rescue them only at the cost of the other planned colonies—if it would be possible at all.

The gravity was set too high; their bodies were condemned to ceaseless hard labor, and that was just to breathe. The air was too thin, and it was colder than they had expected; that, or they could not bear the cold as well, needing as they did so much extra food to fuel the work required to walk from place to place. It was the cumulative effect of it all that was so insidious. How could they hope to survive if the plans were not adjusted to account for the unexpected facts of life on Waystation One?

The crew was gathered all around her, the Mechs, Podile, and one of the Jneers—Kovacs. No other Jneers had come. No Mechs had not. The others had apparently evaluated Raleigh's argument and found it to be sound. The Mechs had less focus on the value of a particular analysis than on the importance of the group gestalt, and would work toward the common goal until consensus grew that said that it was time to give it over.

It was time.

They'd done everything they could.

There was nothing left but to accept the situation they were in and make the best of it, and Mir—gazing up at the sky— made that implicitly clear even as the discouraged group set out for the encampment.

"Look at those stars." The night sky was as deep as space itself, as bleak and huge. "We'll all get to make up our own constellations. I'll start. I name that curved set—there—'Footfalling.' Because we're on foot. And I'm falling."

He would fall, if he didn't watch where he was going. There was little ambient light, though both moons were visible. If she strained her eyes toward the eastern horizon Hillbrane could almost persuade herself to imagine that she saw the long opalescent reach of coming dawn. Her imagination. There was no cloud cover to catch and scatter the light of Waystation One's small red sun.

She stopped—and stared up, straight up, into the sky. Nobody was in a hurry to get back to the encampment, though it was cold. They all stopped with her, and Hillbrane struggled to get her words out, fought to ferry them over the rocky shoals of her emotion so that they would make sense when they found the air.

"Wait one."

What was she thinking?

She almost had it.

Clouds.

There weren't any.

There weren't any clouds.

"We've been trying to figure out where to find the Fleet. We don't need to find the Fleet. If we can find out where the Fleet's been we can find the Fleet."

No takers. Hillbrane pushed on, desperate. "We can find out where the Fleet's been, we can, we just need to look for nothing. Ivery. That test piece that Rena and you made for me for the lab. My plasma net generation simulation model."

Silence. Then Ivery put her hand to Hillbrane's shoulder, carefully. "It's okay, Chelbie. We can make you another one. Just as good as the original. Come on, it's cold."

"*Can* you?"

She didn't mean to challenge Ivery. But this could be it. This could be the answer. This could be the key. They would see it. They had to see it. If they didn't see it, it wasn't there— but that was the whole point. Something not being there.

Ivery was choosing her words carefully, but she wasn't making them up in an attempt to humor a worker possibly gone made. No. Ivery was thinking about it.

"It would take a few hours. We could use some of *Goforth*'s—Oh. Oh."

Ivery had seen it. And Ivery could only stammer. "Chelbie. Damn it, Chelbie. It could work."

Because the Colony Fleet not only traveled through the emptiest space that it could find. The Colony Fleet swept space before it to protect itself, captured space debris and dust particles and left a trail of emptiness in its wake that could be mapped, as a void could be mapped by marking everything around it.

The model Ivery and Rena had built for her had been designed to test how well a particle escaped her plasma web at varying rates of spool. They could use the same concept to map the clutter of space within the cone of potential points of origin until they found the place where space was dead empty. Once they had found the place where there was nothing, they would know where the Colony Fleet had been.

Then they could find the Fleet itself.

It could work.

"Sonar," Delacourt said. Staring. With wonder and comprehension dawning in her voice, and all of it in just one word.

"Space sonar," Cago confirmed. "Only what we want to find is what isn't there. It'll be risky."

Because they didn't have access to the kind of power they would need to get a no-echo at the distance between Waystation One and where *Goforth* had come from. There would be guesswork. But the further out they could get from Waystation One the better their chances would be, and they knew that they had followed the path of least resistance. That would help to reduce the number of choices they would have to make. They could afford to take some chances.

"Back to the box," Mir said. "Farsi. Take the mover and get back to the encampment. Tell them we leave as soon as you get back. Find out if anyone else wants to come."

"Er, what if they try to keep him, Mir?" Neyrem asked diffidently. Ivery and Delacourt were already scrambling back up into *Goforth*, and Hillbrane was hungry to follow them, but this needed her attention.

"Don't say when Farsi gets back," she suggested. "Say in four hours. Say at seven." It wasn't an optimal launch window, but they had no time. They could clear atmosphere and exit the system while Ivery was still building the test model they needed. "They won't have any motive to keep him, then. He'd just be an extra mouth to feed. It'll be okay."

She was almost sure.

And wasn't that the difference between Mechs and Jneers right there, when it came down to it?

Jneers were almost always sure. Whether they were right or not.

Mechs were almost never sure, but more frequently turned out to be right.

"Come on then," Cago told her. "Into the hold. We have work to do. Storage. Calculations. Prelaunch."

It was Wyatt in the maintenance hull all over again, but now Hillbrane understood it in a way she never had before.

It could work, it could. It could. It could.

And if it did nobody had to die. First Colony would arrive well prepared to establish itself and flourish.

And if it didn't, they had at least tried their utmost.

"Hsst. Raleigh. Wake up."

It was the voice of Vince, on nightwatch. Raleigh shook himself out of an exhausted sleep with an effort. Vince's voice was full of suppressed excitement—with a certain degree of emphasis on the "suppressed" element. Something Vince wasn't sure should be shared, then.

"Coming directly." It was warm and comfortable in the dormitory, and the sound of the heater running was a note of reassuring familiarity in this near-silent environment. But duty called. Raleigh rolled himself out of the seductive embrace of his bedding and set foot to floor with determination that gradually overcame his inclination—which was to fall back on his cot and go back to sleep.

He felt awful.

That was all right, though, because when he felt awful he looked worse. Everyone would be able to see how hard he had been working for the common weal, just by looking at him. He was working much harder than any of the others, but he had no complaints. He was running the mission. Yesterday's little dustup had just proved that to everybody. He would be firmly in control when the First Colony's advance party got here, and from there he would be in a very good position to leverage his influence to maximum benefit.

Extra effort now.

A life of influence and prestige, opening up before him, status he had hardly dared even dream of before.

It was a reasonable trade. Raleigh stumbled out of his room in the dormitory and followed Vince out of the building, buttoning his shirt as he went. With luck it would not take too long, and he would be back indoors soon.

Before he got cold.

He could put his jacket on, right enough, but that was too

much of an effort for a sleepy man to face. It was hard enough to keep the buttons and the buttonholes on his shirt aligned, as loose as his shirt was getting. As loose as his clothing was getting. Something in the air must be stretching the fabric, or else it was just wear.

Once outside the dormitory Vince stopped and pointed. At what? It was not yet dawn; there was an odd light out on the plain, between them and where *Goforth* rested. Oh. The headlamps. On the mover. All right.

The mover stopped short of the brown dirt around the dormitory, the rough circle of stamped ground worn bare by foot traffic since they'd arrived. It was Farsi and Podile. She slid out of the mover as soon as it had stopped, heading out for the mess dome; for rations, Marquette supposed.

Farsi sat in the mover for long enough to sound three long ear-shattering shrieks on the machine's siren, then got out. So much for controlling the situation, Raleigh thought grimly.

"Farsi. What brings you? Ready to move back home? We've been expecting you."

People were rushing out into the cold, clearly at a loss as to what the siren might mean. Farsi waited until almost everyone was present before he spoke.

"We think there's a way to find the Fleet without the course correction module. We're going to try. *Goforth* leaves in three hours, that's zero seven by standard chronometer."

That didn't make much sense. Was it just because he was asleep? "Farsi, that's crazy. You can't fly *Goforth* without the right course data. You'll be lost forever. That's no way to die." What was Farsi suggesting?

Farsi's answer was indirect, and aimed as much at the others—Raleigh realized—as it was at him. "It's a pretty good chance. Fleet absolutely needs the info we have, and this is our only hope of getting it to them. Anyone who wants to come can return to the ship with me, but there isn't much time."

Ridiculous. And ill-advised, as well, Raleigh realized. Farsi was not going to get much cooperation from this lot. They were all tired. They only wanted to go back to bed. He wanted to go back to bed.

"All right." He'd try reason. "Let's assume you're correct, and you can fly the *Goforth* without the course correction module. A crew of Mechs will do what a crew of Jneers couldn't. But we'll assume that, for the sake of the argument."

He knew the *Goforth* could not hope to find the Fleet. He knew it. It was up to him to protect the others from making a mistake. He continued.

"Here are our choices. Join *Goforth*, maybe find Fleet, maybe die. Or, let you go off with *Goforth*, since you're confident of your chances. Maybe you find Fleet and maybe you don't, but we stay here to get ready for the First Colony party. Now, what is gained for me if I leave on *Goforth*?"

Farsi was looking confused. "You don't think the data is important?"

"I don't see what difference my presence on *Goforth* makes. It seems to me that *Goforth*'s mission is independent of my being there. So my choice is to maybe die, maybe get back to Fleet, or make sure things are ready here for the First Colony when it arrives. Now, which of these two choices looks like the responsible one to you, Farsi?"

He was enjoying this. He was. Podile was coming back from the mess dome; what was she carrying? Survey data sheets. Oh. Yes. Of course.

"You make your own choice, Marquette." Farsi's voice held the resentment Raleigh had come to recognize as common with Mechs who knew that they'd been out-reasoned. The argument was sound. Farsi could not refute it. "We're leaving at seven. Anyone who wants to come, should come with us. Now."

"What is this 'us'?" Raleigh challenged playfully, pitching his question at Podile as she passed. "Surely you're not going to desert me, Podile. It's a fool's mission. Or a Mech's mission, which I suppose amounts to about the same thing in this case."

She was just loading the survey sheets on the mover. That was the explanation. It had to be.

"It's like this, Marquette," Podile said. Raleigh was unpleasantly surprised by her tone of voice. "Subject this to analysis."

And she used a casual form of address with him—neither the intimacy he had invited nor the polite *Ar Marquette*. It was a bad sign.

Maybe it would be just as well if she went after all.

"If I stay here I join First Colony by default, and I never see my daughter again. If I leave with *Goforth* maybe I die and maybe I get back to Fleet, and if I die I'm no worse off, but if I get back to Fleet I get to be with my baby girl. I think the choice is obvious."

Hardly. If *Goforth* didn't find the Fleet, Podile would die. This so-called choice of hers was between living without her daughter and dying for the chance to be reunited with the child. It was insane. She could have other daughters.

But arguing the issue with an Oway would only raise potential doubts in the minds of his fellow Jneers as to the quality of his analysis. He had his pride. Raleigh yawned, and stretched himself.

"Suit yourself." Let her have the last word. There was no need to give this insanity any more importance than it was worth. "More rations for us, I suppose. I'm going back to bed." It was too bad of her to take that line. He would miss her support in the coming weeks. And Hillbrane's as well? He supposed she would be leaving on *Goforth*, since it was her idea. Could he really ever have wanted her again, once she stooped to take a Mech for a lover?

The whole thing was irrational. It would all come to nothing. At most *Goforth* would take off and be forced to land again within a day or two, once the cold hard facts of their situation became impossible to ignore.

Someone had left the door to the dormitory open and let the cold in. He could hear the forced-air fans straining to move enough warmth through the building to compensate. They would have to be more mindful of things like that, it wasted resources which—though plentiful—were limited. It would give the wrong impression to the First Colony advance party if resources were excessively depleted when they arrived, rather than carefully husbanded and in place to support the newcomers.

Maybe they would have to have a meeting.

But it would wait.

There was no sense in making any elaborate adjustments until *Goforth* made its little excursion and returned, admitting defeat.

Three hours later Raleigh was roused again from his sleep, this time by a distant thunder.

He sat up.

Thunder was something they'd not heard here yet. An atmospheric disturbance of some sort might explain the uneasy dreams he'd had, though—something about Hillbrane, about Podile, about *Goforth*. Something about abandonment, being left behind, a fearful stressful dream that reminded him too much of how he'd felt when Brane had failed Comparisons and left him behind on Stiknals.

People were running through the dormitory halls outside his cubicle.

The thunder wasn't rolling, and it wasn't fading. It was a constant roar, muted but unvarying, and as Raleigh puzzled to make sense of it in his mind, Wybrandt opened the door to his cubicle—without knocking.

"Marquette, come quickly." Wybrandt was out of breath, and in his underwear. Sleepwear. Only half dressed. "It's the ship. It's *Goforth*. They're leaving."

Nonsense.

It all came back to Raleigh now, and he pulled his dusty boots on over his bare feet and half-laced them hastily. There was his shirt, where he'd dropped it just a few hours ago. It didn't take him more than a moment or two before he joined the others outside the dormitory, cinching his belt up another notch absent-mindedly.

Goforth could fire its engines all it wanted.

They weren't going anywhere, not in the long run. Why, even if they achieved an orbit they'd be forced back down, because there was nowhere for them to go—

The sun was still quarter-arc on its daily path, well clear of the horizon but far from midheaven.

Raleigh could see a pinpoint ball of searing white intensity from the place where *Goforth* rested, or had rested. They had deployed the hydraulics, so much was obvious. *Goforth* had no hope of lifting from its landing position: the hydraulics would raise the ship on its launch block to its ground-launch attitude, its engines positioned to thrust against the autolaunch platform itself.

"Raleigh, you said it couldn't happen—"

It was Vince, the Oway, who sounded near-hysterical. Raleigh frowned. He didn't know the man very well, but he did know that he had to quash that line of thought immediately.

"I said it was pointless if they did, and made no difference to us." His tone of voice was sharp, but not unnecessarily so. He needed to avoid ambiguities in the chain of command. The more he realized how much he'd sacrificed to gain his current position, the more important it became to him to keep hold of the prize. "They'll be back down in two days. If they're not—"

The white pinpoint of searing light blossomed and grew, pushing great billowing petals of black smoke in all directions as it unfolded. Raleigh shut up, aware that he would not be able to make himself heard over the suddenly much louder roar of distant engines. Nothing. They could see nothing but the intense fireball from *Goforth*'s engines; there was too much smoke.

Then Alsop pointed and cried out. "Look there!"

Goforth, rising from the heart of the black rose.

It moved so slowly.

Raleigh felt an increasing rush of blind panic. The gravitational pull of Waystation One. Hillbrane had said the planet pulled harder than they were used to; had they taken that into account in their calculations? Had they gotten the right vectors into the ship's navigation systems? Would they clear atmosphere?

Slow but stubborn, as if struggling with fierce determination against the cloying blanket of thick air, *Goforth* pressed on into the sky. Smaller by the moment. So small. So pathetically insignificant against the great bell of Heaven.

Black spots swam in front of his eyes. Raleigh blinked twice, and realized that he was holding his breath.

It was hard to see *Goforth* at all, now. Only the pinpoint of light, the incendiary fury of *Goforth*'s engines was still visible.

Then even that was gone, lost in the greater brilliance of Waystation One's sunlit sky.

Silence.

Raleigh took inventory, waiting for the first person to speak. Tyler. Sonaman. Alsop, Brent, Wybrandt. Fisch, Riatt, Gilrath, the Oway Vince, and there was himself as well—where was Kovacs?

Alone. They had come to Waystation One with twenty-four people, twelve Mechs, two Oways, ten Jneers. There were ten people here, and Kovacs was bound to turn up. It was unthinkable that he had thrown his lot in with the Mechs.

All Jneers. Well, no Mechs, at any rate.

Poor Brane, Raleigh thought, in a moment of sympathetic appreciation for a well-intentioned effort gone to naught. She had tried so hard to integrate them, and it had been working, but in the end they were still Mechs and Jneers, even if the Oways had ultimately proved divided in their loyalties.

"Well," Fisch said, with the strain of forcing a positive tone clear in his voice. "There's that many more rations for that fewer people."

Good man, Fisch. And a good point. Now that Fisch mentioned it, Raleigh was hungry. Podile had tried to convince him that they were going through their rations too quickly; now it didn't matter if she was right. There was plenty of food.

The advance party would be here inside of four months, and they'd have the production system on-line well before then to account for any excess food they might eat during the initial phase.

A really good feed would be a welcome treat as well as good preparation for the day's work. Maybe they would take the day off, have a rest day. They had certainly earned one. No question about that.

"And I say we go take up some slack in the rations department. I could eat a day's-issue all by myself, my belly's that empty. No work no food, but no food no work either, so let's go."

They might be subdued now; they were all in shock. He was in shock. They were all facing the possibility that they might never see *Goforth* again. Even while they recognized the benefits to them, there was no getting around the fact that the crew of the *Goforth* might have gone off to die. He was distressed by that himself.

They needed a break.

They'd have a feast and a rest day, and *Goforth* would be back—admitting defeat—before they knew it.

And if it wasn't?

Then it would be best to gloss over that tragic possibility in silence, unspoken, unacknowledged, something for them to deal with privately.

Engine start. Ignition. Launch thrust. Escape.

The beautiful world of Waystation One shrank steadily on-screen, and Cago Warrine watched it go with mixed feelings of relief—of gratitude—of regret, and of fear.

All right. They had escaped. They were away. Aitchel's navigation packet took them on a direct line out of system; they had no time or need to go to orbit, not now, not on their way out.

Nobody spoke.

Long moments passed, till the forward edge of the first of

Waystation One's moons approached, far in the distance, well behind the planet itself.

That was one.

Goforth's arc of transit altered subtly in response to navigational systems commands, and Cago saw the second moon, no closer to the *Goforth* than the mountains had seemed from *Goforth*'s landing site.

Two.

The transit arc was clear for them out of system now, and Cago decided he was clear to relax. To try to relax. His hands seemed frozen to the arm grips of his clamshell. He couldn't move his fingers.

"Delacourt."

Mir's voice was a welcome note of normalcy, though Cago thought he could detect the strain even in Mir's voice. The commonplace sound of it gave him the psychological leverage he needed to get his fingers loose of their grip on the armrests.

"Nothing yet." Delacourt's cheerful acknowledgment was not disturbing. Nobody expected that it would be easy to locate Fleet's track. Simply that they were going to be able to do it. "I might have a trace on our inbound. It's possible. But we're too small to have made much of an impact. Calibrations are great."

She sounded almost confident, and that heartened Cago considerably, even though he knew what the odds were. Theoretically they were solid. In practice?

But she was happy with how the scan was performing, and that was a good part of the battle right there. Cago flexed his fingers, interlacing them, stretching them. He hadn't realized he could grasp anything quite so firmly. Surely there should be dents on the armrests, but when he checked he found none. Amazing.

"We won't clear system for another five hours." Aitchel's voice was small and quiet, but fairly calm. She was taking it all very personally. Still the Jneer, in a way—feeling personally responsible for the success of the mission just because it had been her idea. They had all gone along with her idea, though, and not just because it was *her* idea. That made it a matter of individual choice and free will. "We can test the scans as we go. Maybe even get a directional. Maybe."

It was only human to feel a little extra stress when it was your idea, though. Cago could understand Aitchel's intensity. Once they were through this, they could have a long talk about it. If it worked nobody would grudge Aitchel the leader's share of the glory, and it could work.

They had a very good chance.

He could support their chances best by saving a conversation about trust, and team venture, and personal responsibility for some later time when it would all be academic.

"Coffee," Cago said, instead of everything else that was on his mind. "I'll go see if I can give Podile a hand. Seven here? Seven it is."

Not that it mattered.

Nobody was going to be able to sleep for hours, coffee or no coffee. Farsi had already brought a stack of bedding into Direction and piled it at the back of the room for use as required.

He'd be back as soon as he'd got coffee.

The best way to manage the dread knowledge in his heart of what odds they faced was to sit at the rim of the gambling-table and cheer Delacourt on while she threw the dice.

Podile sat huddled next to Harkover in Direction with her eyes fixed to the scan screen. "Is it getting darker out there?" she asked low-voiced, watching the scan. "Or am I misinterpreting something?"

It was quiet and dim in Direction; some of the crew were sleeping. Everybody got to take a turn at watching the scan screen. This was her turn to watch, with Harkover as her partner.

Ironic.

The first time she'd met Harkover had been at Comparisons. Harkover had been an earnest young Jneer, then, no different from all of the other Jneers on the floor—or so Podile had thought.

"You're right. I believe you're right. Let's take a quick peek. It can't hurt."

Now she was the one who was anxious and insecure in an alien environment, and Harkover was the one working with her to put her at her ease. Harkover had changed. She was still young, but she was no longer so Jneer. Still a Jneer, and she would always be a Jneer, though self-identified as Mech. But she'd gone from insecure and uncertain to grown woman, confident and in control, in less than a year.

Podile watched the scan.

Delacourt had found the first track-point hours ago, less than a day since their departure from Waystation One. Podile had had only so long to be really convinced that she was going to die on a fool's errand after all. They had gone on rotation shifts soon after that: two people, four hours at a time. *Goforth* was on course for the first registration point, but while they went, they watched to see if they could find the path on which the Fleet had tracked through space.

A progress line.

A transit arc.

Anything that would give them more information than the initial single point, because it would do them little good to cut the track of the Colony Fleet too far behind. Every hour that it took them to make contact with the Fleet was an extra hour that Fleet would not be able to use to replan the colonization party's supplies and composition in response to the data *Goforth* carried.

Left shift.

The noise level on the scan dropped off, but it was hard to tell. Harkover stared at the scan screen. After a moment Podile reached out and tracked the seeker pulse left, and the screen cleared, but then it started to fill up again with pushback responding to their signal. Dust. Dust, debris, small wandering chunks of rock; if this was the track, it didn't go left or right.

What about below?

South, in the artificial compass *Goforth* used to orient itself. South was down. It was just a way to talk about direction, but Podile had always had a little trouble with the concept. And what if the track actually led behind them?

Nothing was coming in from south.

Hillbrane reached out and redirected the scan. Podile shot a quick glance at Hillbrane's profile in the soft light from the scan screen. She was frowning, but in apparent concentration, not concern.

So she didn't think something was *wrong*. Exactly.

Was something right?

Because when the scan tracked in all directions the little bits of dust and matter adrift in the empty void of limitless space sent back their greetings to *Goforth*, but the south quadrant held itself aloof and did not answer.

"Hey," Harkover said, and nudged Podile with her elbow, but gently, so as not to attract too much attention. "Hey. Podile. You may be right. This could be it."

Harkover's excitement made Podile nervous.

They needed that second registration point.

They especially needed it if they were actually heading away from Fleet, but there was no way to tell one way or the other without at least two registration points.

"I hope you're right. Let's try it. But we should look a little further before we wake everybody up, don't you think?"

Cago Warrine hadn't been sleeping. He had noticed something going on; now he unfolded himself stiffly from his clamshell and came over. Of course Warrine would notice. Warrine and Harkover had developed that invisible link between them that ensured that each of them always knew where the other one was, what the other was doing. An underground stream of a psychic sort. Something like that. It happened to people who had made a good partnership.

Harkover scooted over to one side so that Warrine could see over her shoulder, leaving Podile to direct the scan. It had been her call. Now they were letting her confirm her find. It was un-Jneer of Harkover to step back that way, but Podile rather more appreciated it than otherwise.

The dead space to the south of her index point stayed dead. There was nothing there.

It was a pocket of black space still days of travel off, but Fleet had been there. There could be no doubt.

Carefully Podile eased the scan out at an oblique angle. Something like south by south–southwest. No. South by south-southeast would be better. Yes. That was a nice angle, that was a good angle, that was an angle into empty space. So her next track should be at—

It had gone dead quiet in Direction.

One point.

Two points.

A false hit, and another; but then—three points.

They knew where they were going.

She knew where she was going.

A great rusty gate in her heart swung open and admitted a flood of joy into her bosom, the pure joy of a reasoned guess proved valid.

Was this how her daughter felt, working her analysis cases?

Her baby had to have gotten it from somewhere—

And they were letting her do it, letting her go with it, letting her be the one to find the way.

She would not have sold this moment for anything.

Now for the first time in her life Podile realized what it was to be a Jneer.

TEN
FIRST COLONY

Even with the louver-vents full open it was oppressively hot in the growhouse, and Raleigh wiped the sweat off of his forehead with the back of one greasy, dusty hand.

"Right. I think that'll do. Ask Wybrandt to go ahead and punch the button."

Tyler nodded wearily and went off down the long aisle to the control station at the other end of the growhouse. Raleigh watched him go, his mind too numb with fatigue to do much more than stare at the baked brown beds that lined the walls, brown and sere, and smelling sweet as dried hay. He remembered hay. He'd had hayrides on Temperate when he'd been a little boy. He and Brane.

The growhouse beds had been thick and lush with foliage just yesterday. They had been on their way to a first harvest, but the water pump had jammed. The growhouse system used the water stream to operate the louvers when its autosensors told it that it was getting too warm.

Without the pump to provide water for moisture and pressure to open up the vents, the growhouse had sat in the sun and baked under its solar panels all day, all of a long long day, and there wasn't much nutritional value left in vegetation that had baked to dust in a slow oven for so long.

If there had been fruit it might have dehydrated and they could still have salvaged something. But the blossom had just

264

been coming on. It would be ten days easily before they would have ramped up to that stage again. All lost. All three growhouses. One pump system. No redundancies, because they'd been busy with everything else.

It was a bitter lesson.

And it had taken all night to bring the pump back on-line, but Raleigh hadn't dared to set the task aside for a rest period. There was food, yes, there was still plenty of food, but there was much less of it than he liked to see. Podile had been right about the rations.

The trend was disturbing.

What he couldn't understand was the fact that he was losing weight even eating double rations. They were all losing weight. Fisch in particular was beginning to look out and out unhealthy.

The growhouse lights dimmed fractionally for a moment as the current channel engaged for the pump, brightening again as the solar batteries compensated. Raleigh threw the switch and the pump started running, sending a fine mist of water cheerfully into the now-dead atmosphere of the growhouse. Well, it worked. It had been a real puzzle trying to deal with it, too, with no Mechs on site to perform that kind of maintenance.

He wasn't about to take any chances on running the pump dry, so soon after he had got it working again; he'd have to go let Alsop know it was safe to reconnect the water suction lines.

He switched the pump back off and stood up slowly.

Every bone in his body ached.

Tyler was on his way back now with Wybrandt, and Raleigh waited for them to get within comfortable speaking distance before he opened his mouth. No use in shouting. That took air. He didn't have enough of it. It was working in the growhouse that did it, perhaps; the atmosphere seemed so still and close and lifeless, with all of the plants dead.

"Let's go on down to the river." Alsop had volunteered for the messy chore of disconnecting the suction lines and cleaning them out. A clog in the system might have had something to do with the pump's failure; it might not have, but Alsop had needed to get away. "Alsop must be ready for company by now. We don't dare let the pump run without checking that the lines are all in place."

Alsop was the one who who had been scheduled to check the growhouse at midday. He'd fallen asleep instead. Maybe it wouldn't have made any difference by then, but Alsop had been visibly distraught at the disaster that had occurred during his watch.

Midmorning.

It had been a very long night.

He'd sent everyone who wasn't needed off on one chore or another to keep their minds off things; there would be some serious damage control to do. Later. He knew his priorities. Get the pump back on-line first. Find out people's emotional states of mind later.

Gilrath had taken a work crew to the far end of the encampment to continue work on the permanent residences. Raleigh was glad to see it. Once the permanent residences were in place they would be able to keep warm much more easily, and in the meantime it was something to do, something to occupy one's mind. Well, maybe not. But heavy physical labor did have a way of turning off a person's mind. It was an interesting phenomenon.

Down to the river, and there were sections of suction line hoses everywhere. Clots of muck lying on the grassy bank, except that it wasn't grass, it was some low shrubby green twiggy sort of stuff. It was clear enough that the suction hoses had needed cleaning, whether or not that explained the failure of the pump.

But where was Alsop?

The light set that illuminated the riverbank and the litter of hoses was still running at full power, though it was broad daylight. Several of the sections of hose had been reamed out, rinsed out, cleaned and stacked ready for reconnect. But as many more sections still lay in disarray, black muck bleeding from their gleaming chrome-ringed couplings.

No sign of Alsop.

Tyler opened his mouth and took a breath to shout; Raleigh stopped him, one hand laid flat to Tyler's chest. No. He didn't want to raise an alarm. He didn't want to attract any attention.

"Let's just look," Raleigh suggested, his voice shaking only slightly though fear possessed him. "Quietly. No need to bother the others, not just yet."

There was a worn place on the riverbank, downstream from the unfinished pumphouse, where the suction hoses had been laid; a place where they'd cut steps through the earth down to the level of the river. The steps had lost some of their definition over the weeks of use they'd had. It was more of a ramp, really, but it was a steep ramp, and right now Raleigh could almost believe that there was a long slip-streak in the black mud from the suction hoses, a slip-streak that creased the ramp down to the river.

"Turn off those lights."

Silt and river bottom, that's what it was. Black silt, decaying vegetable matter perhaps, drying now under the sun into caked earth. Raleigh approached the ramp with exaggerated care, half expecting to see something horrible as he peered downslope.

But there was nothing.

Streaks and scrapes along the ground, but who was to say that those had not been made by Alsop hauling suction line hoses up out of the river?

Nothing.

The pumphouse foundation stood bare and open to the sky, and there was nobody there.

Raleigh climbed down to the water, and stood for a long moment watching the swift water rushing by.

It was a very self-assertive little river. There were no such currents to be found on any Noun Ship. They had all learned to swim at an early age, of course, but in pools and artificial lakes. Nothing like this.

Tossing a bit of broken vegetation out onto the surface of

the water, Raleigh watched it travel downstream, out of sight even before it sank. It was that light. Only the fraction of an ounce. Anything with more of a cross-section would be hit by that current with an impact like being hit in the face by a blast door. A man would have to have his wits about him, and have plenty of strength on reserve for an emergency.

None of them did.

They were all tired, and weakened by heavy labor, not enough food, the ever-present and insidious chill in the air, the thinness of the air itself.

"Well, maybe he's just gone to the toilet," Wybrandt suggested. But Wybrandt didn't believe it. It was too obvious. Nobody would bother with the toilet with the river right here, no matter how carefully they encouraged each other to minimize taking shortcuts with hygiene.

"Yes. Maybe that's what he was doing." Alsop was probably nowhere they would ever find him. The evidence was all circumstantial, but it was persuasive. Maybe that slip-streak hadn't been Alsop, starting a fall down the ramp to the river. Maybe he had simply decided to run away. Maybe they'd find his things gone, when they got back to the dormitory.

Maybe he'd go and take some of Alsop's things, and some food, and cache them somewhere, so that they could all believe that that was what had happened.

"Let's keep this to ourselves for now." That would give him time to set it up. If everyone was out on the work crews it didn't have to take him very long. Tyler and Wybrandt might guess at what he was going to do, but they would keep it to themselves for the sake of group morale. If either of them had gone with Alsop—last night—

There was no sense even thinking it. "Go and borrow some people from Gilrath, we've got to get this pipeline back up. I'll go search the dormitory and the other areas. We can decide what to do when we know for sure what's happened."

That would work.

Wybrandt set off for the work crews; Raleigh for the dormitory, and Tyler just stood there on the riverbank staring at

the slide marks in the drying mud at his feet. Where someone
had slipped. Where someone had fallen.

There would be no trouble with Wybrandt and Tyler.

Then when the First Colony came they could all agree to
pretend that Alsop had drowned, to cover the fact that he had
run away; Alsop would be First Colony's first martyr.

That would be a good joke, really.

If only Hillbrane had not gone, he could have shared it with
her.

"**G**oforth seeks Fleet. Precise bearing unknown. We need
a transmission lock, please respond."

When everything was said and done they had a very good
chance of making timely contact with the Fleet. But it was
still only a chance, and uncertain by definition.

"*Goforth* seeks Fleet."

They had been ten days bearing on the track. It had been
nearly two weeks now since they'd left Waystation One.
They'd made better time outbound, but then they'd had a
course.

"Precise bearing unknown. We need a transmission lock,
please advise."

Another fifteen minutes and she'd close transmission for
another shift. Twenty minutes every two hours on a wideband
sweep, aiming in the direction they thought Fleet was in, hoping for an accidental intercept. Fleet was probably trying to
reach Waystation One. Wondering why there was no response.

Would they send a relief party?

It hadn't ever been part of the design. There were other
scoutships—reserved for Waystations Two through Five—but
it would take weeks to bring one of them on-line from long-
term storage. Then they'd have to find a crew, and put the
scout through its proving-cruise, and by the time all that had
been accomplished and a relief party could be sent, too much
precious recovery time would have been lost. Fleet needed this
information as soon as they could deliver it.

"*Goforth* seeks Fleet. Precise bearing unknown."

Direction was as empty as it had ever been. People had gotten tired of maintaining a constant level of concentration. It was one thing when their task had called on all of their combined efforts; but now all they were doing was checking that the automechanics were working correctly and trying to call Fleet. There were only five people in Direction beside her. And they were all busily minding their own business.

"We need a transmission lock. Come on, Fleet."

Sooner or later Fleet would have to hear them. Have to. Unless they had calculated incorrectly. Unless they were on the wrong track. There could be some unsuspected anomaly in the scan that Delacourt and Ivery had built. This could all be one gigantic mistake.

Sure, the theory was sound.

But theory was only theory, as a chance was only a chance. Reality had an irritating way of coming up with outlying events. Theories could never really be proven, only not disproved, because no matter how long the theory remained in place there was always the one spoiler event waiting somewhere for some unsuspecting soul to stumble over it.

"*Goforth* seeks Fleet. Precise bearing unknown. Please respond."

Well, that was it for another shift, then. Hillbrane yawned and stretched, wondering what was for supper. Casserole, she thought. It should be casserole day.

Then the sudden surge of power over the transmission lines flooded Direction with a burst of static, shocking Hillbrane fully alert in an instant.

Goforth. Goforth. *This is the forefront ship* Deecee. *What is your status, please advise.*

Fleet.

Every soul in Direction sat frozen for a moment, Hillbrane not excepted. It was dead quiet. They were all stunned. They had been waiting to hear from Fleet for days, and now that it had happened Hillbrane did not know what to say.

Goforth, *this is the forefront ship* Deecee. *Come on. You were just there.*

Hillbrane leaned forward slowly. As soon as she moved Neyrem ran from the room, and Delacourt jumped to set a lock on the transmission; as if one small gesture had broken the group paralysis. Where had Neyrem gone? To get the others, perhaps. He could have used ship's comm. Maybe he didn't trust his voice to speak.

"*Deecee. Goforth* here. It's good to hear your voice." Well, in a manner of speaking.

Where to begin?

"Ten crew have remained on Waystation One, we are returning with fourteen. We have vital information concerning variances between expected and as-found situation. Please patch through to Subarctic for data dump."

The most important thing was to get the news about the moons, the gravity, the air—the atmospheric pressure—into the hands of the people who would have to make the changes to the First Colony's plans in response.

Yes.

But they had found the Fleet.

They had done it.

And once the full story was told, the mission of the *Goforth* in and of itself would be more persuasive to the unconvinced than anything Hillbrane could have thought of to say about why First Colony needed as many Mechs as it could safely absorb, if they were to hope for the long-term survival of the colony.

Raleigh Marquette fled from the room into the hall, pursued by the implacable sound of Gilrath's screaming. Closing the door helped only a little, not nearly enough; sinking down to sit on the floor Raleigh pressed his palms against his ears as hard as he could in an attempt to shut out the hateful din.

It didn't work.

He could still hear Gilrath screaming. *God. Oh, God. I can't stand it. You've got to help me. Raleigh. Why don't you help me? Why doesn't anybody help me, can't you see I'm dying?*

After a moment Riatt came out of Gilrath's room after Raleigh and closed the door again behind him. Raleigh looked up. They were all standing around in the corridor, white-faced, thin-lipped. Staring at him.

Why were they staring at him?

Was it his fault that Gilrath had eaten the seed grain?

"Nothing in his stomach," Riatt announced grimly. "There's no help there. It may have been days ago, for all we know."

Days. Days and days, and days, and more days. Every dawn brought renewed awareness of how hungry they were, and every day ended without relief. This wasn't the way he had planned it. It wasn't his fault.

"No." Wearily Raleigh rubbed his face with his hands; wearily he pushed himself to his feet. "It's got to be in his system. Nerve poison. The seed grain is dusted with it to prevent insect contamination, and the stuff is harmless after it's been metabolized in the growth cycle. But you're not expected to eat seed grain. Why did he think it said 'Poison' on the hopper?"

No answer. Well, it had been a rhetorical question anyway. Gilrath might have assumed the warning was there just to prevent accidental consumption, not for real. If Raleigh had thought about the seed grain before this he might have tried it himself, and then it would be him inside there, screaming in agony as his intestinal tract slowly disintegrated.

"What are we going to do, Raleigh?" Fisch asked.

He was the leader.

He was expected to find a fix for this.

"I can't hear myself think." The dormitory building had never been intended for long-term occupancy, and it wasn't the least bit soundproof. He didn't know how any of them could stand the sound of Gilrath's voice. It made him sick to his stomach. Thinking about what came up with Gilrath's bile only made it worse. "I've got to get out of here. Let's go think about this."

"Gilrath—" Wybrandt started to say, but Riatt shook his head and cut the question off.

"It doesn't make any difference. There's nothing we can do about this. Nothing. There aren't enough pain meds in the stores to deal with this kind of thing, not unless we make up our minds to a lethal injection."

Well, at least Riatt was thinking what he was thinking. The only help for Gilrath now was to die, and someone would have to help him to it. But nobody wanted to be the one to make the suggestion, for fear of being tasked with the chore.

There was a lull, a respite, a short break, but then Gilrath started in again, and louder this time. Raleigh could make out every word all too clearly, and he didn't want to.

Help me. God damn you, what's the matter with you? Can't you see I'm suffering? Oh, God, oh, God, please. Help me.

"Out," Raleigh ordered. They were glad enough to follow, but they would not make a move on their own. There were drawbacks to this leader business, and Raleigh meditated on the issue bitterly as he limped away from the dormitory. The sprain he'd sustained during *Goforth*'s landing had never healed quite right.

If he wasn't careful he was going to run out of pain tabs, not as if it made any difference to Gilrath—the only medicine they could give Gilrath would have to be injectible. And he wasn't even going to think about what the poison had done to Gilrath's face. No.

He led them clear out to the foundation they'd been building for the permanent residence before he was sure he was safe from the sound of Gilrath's voice. Work on the residence had slowed in the past week or so. Alsop's disappearance had been a profound blow to morale, and it had gradually become impossible to ignore the fact that they were all starving.

Losing muscle mass.

They tried to keep order and ration the food stores, but it was so hard when they were so hungry—and starving to death by long slow degrees was more unpleasant than he ever could have imagined. It was the oxygen, he supposed, oxygen was needed for metabolism, and when there was less of it the food that they ate was less nourishing, and a full stomach did not satisfy.

He sat down on the third course of a foundation wall and looked back over the encampment, brooding.

Gilrath was dying too, but not quickly enough. The only thing for it was for someone to help him through. He kept asking for help, that was true enough. But Raleigh could not quite make up his mind to suggest such a thing, and he didn't dare try to make it an order. He would have to do it himself. That was what they all wanted him to do.

He couldn't.

First things first.

"Has anybody gone back to run an inventory in seed stores?"

He doubted it. It had been such a scene of horror, the store room in disarray, blood everywhere. Gilrath, writhing and foaming at the mouth, thick white sputum sickeningly streaked with blood. Raleigh didn't even want to think about it. And that had been *before* Gilrath had started screaming.

"I didn't think so. Well. It'll be dark soon. What are we going to do about Gilrath? Suggestions."

Nobody had any. It was too obvious—and too unthinkable. There was nothing to be done to make it any easier for the patient. The best thing they could do for him was murder.

"Come on, we're all grownups here. I don't want to go back to that hellish racket. It's more than anyone should be asked to endure."

He was getting tired of talking to himself. At last the Oway Vince opened his mouth to speak, and not before time either. "But . . . shouldn't someone at least be with him? Just in case."

It was a humane impulse, one to be appreciated. "We would all like to think that there was a 'just in case.' But there isn't. Nobody deserves to suffer like that. But the stuff's nerve poison. There isn't an antidote, not once it's started to work. I don't know what good it would do to force yourself to sit with that, but if you do you're more of a man than I am, Vince, I admit it freely."

There, that was what they wanted from him. Permission. Permission to be afraid, to turn their backs, to cover their ears. Someone would have to go and strangle Gilrath if he didn't shut up soon.

He'd get them all away from the dormitory for the night.

And if he was lucky Gilrath would be dead by morning, because as clearly as he knew that the only humane thing was to put an end to Gilrath's suffering, Raleigh simply could not face the prospect of being in the same room with him. The effects of the poison were beyond horror.

"Well. I guess the person on fire-watch could just look in on him. Every hour. That way we'll at least know if there's a change," Wybrandt said, a little diffidently. As if afraid that his suggestion would be too transparent. What was there to be afraid of? They were abandoning Gilrath, yes, because no one had the nerve to kill him, and they all knew it. Nothing need be said. The polite pretense would cover all.

"Good thought." And it would be functionally the same as sitting with the dying man. Really. It wasn't as though Gilrath himself would know one way or the other. It wasn't too hard to believe that Gilrath was already dead, in a sense, gone out of his mind with pain, and only a shell left to mewl and howl and ooze blood. Yes.

That was good.

Gilrath was already dead.

Poor old Gilrath.

What a price to pay for being hungry.

"We'll need bedding," Brent noted. "From the store room, maybe. We can put up a tarp for a roof. There's no sense in any of us trying to rest with Gilrath there."

Precisely so. "Well, you could take Wybrandt and see what you can scavenge," Raleigh suggested. Ordered. The fact that he was unquestionably in charge—that they all looked to him for guidance and decisions—was not as comforting as it might have been.

"Tyler, you and Riatt could carry up some rations. Wybrandt, you go with Larson to haul a heater out, it's going to get cold tonight. Sonaman and I will set some of this temp wall back up—" because the temporary portable wind shields had fallen, over time, and been left on the ground. "—and we'll get comfortable. Camping out."

It'll be fun, he could have said. But it wasn't going to be fun. It was so far from fun that he couldn't imagine anything less like fun and more like utter misery. This was all Hillbrane's fault. She should not have taken *Goforth* away, and left him here alone. That had been wrong of her.

His crew dispersed to do his bidding. Slowly Raleigh stood up; Sonaman was waiting for him. They needed to get the temp walls leaned up against what foundation walls there were.

Camping under the stars.

Was one of them *Goforth*?

Had *Goforth* found the Fleet, or hurried off into oblivion?

Wearily Raleigh limped over to where Sonaman stood ready to start work.

He didn't care anymore if he got a good place in the hierarchy of the First Colony when it arrived.

He only hoped he'd be here when they did.

The water lapped against the sides of the hull with a soft coursing sound as the flower-boat swam slowly into Stiknals' aquatic gardens. Hillbrane sipped from a cup of jasmine tea; Cago, sitting beside her in the salon, seemed a million miles away, staring out at the lush greenery on the banks of the canal. Cago had never been to Stiknals, and Hillbrane had to admit that a flower-boat was a much nicer place to meet with Speaker Girosse than a cold room in the kremlin in Winter Quarters on Subarctic would have been.

Speaker Girosse sighed, setting a report down on a low tambour beside her. "No, nothing from Waystation One. Of course it's possible they never set up the commstation. Believing it to be no use."

Speaker Girosse was clearly reluctant to engage in speculation. Hillbrane had no such reservations: she was worried. She had been worried since they'd left Waystation One, but she had had no extra space for her fears concerning the Jneers they'd left behind. There had been too much energy required to manage more immediate fears about her own immediate survival, and that of the rest of *Goforth*'s crew.

She had been recuperating with the rest at Stiknals for these three days now. She was rested, relaxed, and worried sick.

She set down her cup.

"Maintenance says *Goforth* will be fully loaded and ready to depart in two days, Speaker. The only way to be sure is to go. And we can carry specialists, now that we know more about the issues we're to face."

Ironically enough if they could get past the difficulties of orbiting a Noun Ship with two moons already in evidence, Raleigh's idea was slowly becoming clearly the better idea after all. It would allow a sufficiently gradual transition from the lower gravity they had lived with all their lives to the sterner demands of Waystation One. And it would provide refuge in the event that the orbits of one of those moons proved to be unstable.

Raleigh had been right.

He'd be insufferable.

But she'd become too much of a Mech to discard the idea just because its source was personally distasteful to her.

"Chelbie," Speaker Girosse said. Cago gave a little start, beside her, to hear the Speaker call her that. "I wish they had not stayed." Speaker Girosse's choice to use a first name—Hillbrane's Mech name at that—was a precisely calculated signal. Hillbrane got the message: Speaker Girosse was reaching out to her.

"You couldn't have forced them, no, and we're lucky you were able to run the ship on short crew as it is. But I wish they'd come with you. I don't think any of us will be quite happy until you get back to Waystation One and send us word."

"We'll be leaving as soon as we can, Speaker." All except for Delacourt; Dela had been carrying around a hairline fracture in her shinbone for all of this time, and not telling anyone that she was in pain. The gravity of Waystation One was particularly hard on hearts and other muscles and bones.

Their bones had all been formed and hardened under less stress; Waystation One would breed new people with higher bone density. They would need much more calcium in their diets all around, and the first generation of pregnancies would be particularly delicate. Such a little thing to make so much of a difference. Of course that was why the Speaker was worried about those Jneers. "Has a decision been made as to which Noun will be used?"

The Speaker seemed to grimace, a humorous expression dimly glimpsed in the diffuse light of the salon. "The debate continues. If we'd had more advance warning we could have terraformed one of the moons on site. Just another note for our lessons learned files. We'll send an away party ahead to Waystation Two two years out rather than just six months."

It was so obvious now. But all of this time they had been thinking of the colony as a completely self-contained installation to the exclusion of needing any extensive prearrival investigation. In a sense they had been ready for so long that they were not ready at all. Paradox.

"We're ahead by this much," Cago said. "The scoutship's going back. And using the Noun builds some slack into the system as well. It should help."

So he'd been listening, after all. He had seemed to be totally abstracted, distracted by the beauty of the scene, the sheer volume of disparate sensory inputs. It was nothing like life on the Mech ships; did that have something to do with the Mech talent for improvisation? Hillbrane wondered suddenly. Were the Mechs as good at seeing minute clues to complex solutions as they were because there was generally speaking so much less distraction in their normal environment?

A small skiff had come up alongside the flower-boat. Speaker Girosse rose to her feet. She was dressed in a silk wrap-shirt and a sarong, rather than the heavy silk winter kimono of Subarctic; but the fluid grace of her movements was the same as it had been under all those clothes.

"Quite so. I understand your courier leaves tomorrow to rejoin *Goforth* in refit, for departure. Excuse me. I must return to Stiknals. The boat is yours. I'll see you in the morning."

Well, this was certainly unexpected.

She didn't know quite what to think.

Two of the flower-boat's crew came in as the Speaker left and set out hot tea, trays of tidbits, and the clean white linen wraps one wore after one's wash, decorating the cabin as they went with the bright red blossoms with their gilt-streaked throats that served as Stiknals' signature flower. On the trays. Among the folds of the garments. Artfully arrayed in careful confusion on the mats themselves. Cago was staring, clearly confused; but Hillbrane was beginning to realize that she knew exactly what to do.

The showers on these flower-boats were small and low. It was going to be a real challenge to get two people into one of them at once, especially when one of them was Cago. Because he was a man, and there was more mass to him, in a sense. More bone to his bone. More muscle to his muscle. More "him" to him.

Awkward.

There was bound to be a very great deal of unavoidable physical contact, and the soap and water would just make things even more ridiculously impossible.

Mechs were good at impossible.

Cago was particularly good at being Cago—

Hillbrane stood up and took Cago by the hand to show him what was next. She was grinning like an idiot, and she didn't care.

The morning would come when it came.

She was going to thoroughly enjoy herself in the meantime.

*   *   *

They'd lost track of the hours almost as soon as *Goforth* had left, because someone had fallen asleep and let the chrono go uncorrected, then reset it to zero instead of taking the reading.

They'd lost track of the days themselves days ago.

There was no telling how long they had been here but by how quickly the rations were going, and that was no reliable measure. Not with as hard as they tried to ration, and as hard as it was to stop eating once they started, and not being able to tell exactly when Alsop had stopped pulling rations.

When Gilrath had died.

When Brent had run away, when Riatt had stopped eating, when Fisch had taken one too many pain tabs and fallen into a coma. Kovacs had never shown up. Raleigh still couldn't believe that Kovacs had betrayed his kind and thrown his lot in with Mechs; but he wished himself in Kovacs' place, wherever that was. He didn't care any more whether he got to run First Colony or not. He only wanted to get warm, and have enough to eat.

Now Raleigh sat in the empty shell of what would have been the permanent residence building and spent his day brooding. No one had gone back to the dormitory since they'd left Gilrath there. Nobody.

The watch had been supposed to check in on Gilrath at first, but Raleigh hadn't had the courage, and he was sure none of the others had—unless that was where Brent had gone. But if it was, he hadn't been back for more food, and the stink had grown too much to be tolerated. It had been ten days. It had been at least ten days. It had been ten days by the time Raleigh had realized that he'd lost count, again, and had no real idea of how long it had been.

By the time the advance party got here the body should be rotted, and the smell tolerable. At least Raleigh supposed so.

It was getting dark.

There were only five of them left, if he didn't count Riatt

and Fisch. He couldn't count Riatt; Riatt had set up his solitary camp out by *Goforth*'s abandoned autolaunch platform, and nobody had heard from him for a while. Fisch lay on the benches in the mess dome, still breathing, but less certainly every day.

Raleigh was worried about Fisch.

If Fisch died in the mess dome, they were going to have to move him somewhere before he started to stink as Gilrath had. Maybe they'd move him into the dormitory. Maybe they'd find Brent there if they did.

Maybe they'd just hold their breaths and dash in and out as quickly as possible, but no, that wouldn't do. A rotting corpse in close proximity to their foodstores could not be healthy.

Who had the energy for corpse-hauling?

Raleigh frowned at his heater and nudged the output up a notch. Cold. Somewhere in the back reaches of his mind he could hear a voice telling him that Hillbrane had tried to tell him that low oxygen in combination with a low atmospheric pressure meant less fuel available for the body to burn for heat. But he had no time to listen to Hillbrane. They were as low on Waystation One as they could get, it wasn't like this prairie was more than a few hundred feet above sea level. Hillbrane could just shut up.

The breeze from the river blew across the open unfloored space where Raleigh sat, and he scowled and huddled more deeply into his makeshift bedding. He had a flexsheet of insulation between two layers of blanket to keep warm. The others—Tyler, Sonaman, Wybrandt—had abandoned him to his own devices days ago and fled to the growhouses. Vince had gone with them, the ungrateful Oway; but Raleigh no longer had the energy to harbor a grudge against anyone.

Raleigh couldn't bear the growhouses, warm though they were. It was too much pain to be in the middle of all of that lush fertile growth and still be hungry. It wasn't vegetables, it wasn't fruit, it wasn't grain they needed. They needed fat to feed their hunger. There wasn't enough of it.

Maybe someone had prestarted some of the animals, nurturing them in vitro to help populate the new world. Maybe when the advance party arrived they would bring some sheep or some goats with them. A cow—no. A cow was too big, too much to hope for.

The atmosphere in the growhouses was oppressive.

He was better off out here, by himself, all alone, with no one to whisper behind his back about Alsop or Gilrath, no one to second-guess his claims about *Goforth*'s chances, no one to stare at him with dull resentment blaming him for everything and waiting with dumb patient desperation for him to make it right at one and the same time.

He closed his eyes.

When next he opened them again it was bright daylight, and he was so warm that the sweat ran off his face in rivulets. Raleigh awoke with a cry of fear and alarm; the heater was still running at full power, and he didn't like to run it all the time, he didn't want to take a chance of it breaking down. He switched it off. Thirsty. Sweating was not good, it robbed the body of water, and water was by no means available on demand.

He would have to go down to the water treatment plant at the back of the growhouses to fill his water can and refresh himself. The reservoir would be full; he could tell, because the pumps were off.

Was that a problem?

Had there been a problem before that had had something to do with pumps gone off-line?

He couldn't remember. He needed a drink of water, and some rations. Maybe the men in the growhouses would have pulled his share during their last foray into the mess dome. He hoped they hadn't eaten his share already; he'd have to get past Fisch's dying body to get more.

Fear gave him strength to stand up and stagger stiffly across the bare dirt to the water treatment plant behind the growhouses.

The growhouse walls were misted over from inside. There was no seeing in, but the moisture evident on the thermal glass was heartening evidence that the growhouses hadn't baked dry, as had happened before. So that was not a problem.

It was very quiet, though.

He opened the lid of the dipping-trough and washed his face in the sun-warm water, careful not to drip any of the soiled water back into the tank. It was funny how the air could feel cool and still things could get warm under the direct influence of the sun: his blankets, the water. The growhouses, of course, and the solar panels only increased the effect.

He had a drink of water, and another, and sat down on the damp earth beside the water tank for a while. Until his headache faded back a bit. He'd taken a slight case of sunstroke once when he'd been a child; it had made him susceptible to excess heat all of his life.

After a while things were better, but he still didn't hear anything. Anything at all. Maybe a subtle sort of dripping sound from inside the growhouse, as condensed moisture plashed down from the roof; but that was all.

He had another drink of water.

It was too quiet.

He didn't want to have a look, but he had to know what was going on. It took him another little while to make up his mind to it, but in the end he opened up the door and went into the first of the growhouses.

It was stifling.

But not the way it had been before, not dry and brown and dead; this was a growhouse full of rampant vegetation, moist, warm, healthy, thriving.

A little too moist maybe.

It was difficult to breathe, the air was that thick.

He limped from one end of the growhouse to the other as swiftly as he could; the crops were coming along beautifully, but there was no one there, and the heat from the sun on the solar panels overhead seemed magnified by the moisture in the air to unreasonable and unbearable levels.

It took him a moment to catch his breath once he got out. And then he was cold almost immediately. The moisture from inside the growhouse clung to his clothing, and the sweat from his body had only compounded the issue; the moment he stepped out into dryer air the cooling from the sudden evaporation chilled him through and through.

Was there no happy medium to be found in this place at all?

Was he always to be either too hot or too cold?

He had two more growhouses to check through. Now that he knew what kind of an environment he was to enter he could be prepared; he took a drink of water from his water can and went through into the second of the buildings.

It was like Tropical, but Tropical out of control. The humidity was inhuman, and the temperature was well in excess of the comfort range; why had they chosen to come live in here?

Because there they were, Vince, Tyler, Sonaman, and Wybrandt. They'd made a little camp in the middle of the growhouse with beds laid out atop planks set over boxes, packing-crate furniture. A pantry box cobbled together from surplus building materials. There seemed to be plenty of ration packs left in that pantry box, if his eyes did not deceive him at a distance. Raleigh wondered whether they would share, or make him go to get his own breakfast. Lunch. Whatever the mealtime was.

They hadn't noticed him. They were all sleeping; the excess warmth of the growhouse would have waked him by now— it was uncomfortable—but maybe it encouraged them to sleep.

He noted a packet of sleeping pills on a box table at the foot of one bed as he neared the little group of sleeping bodies. That would do it, too. It was a temptation to take sleeping pills, because while you were asleep you weren't as conscious of the fact that you were hungry; but it was too easy to overdo it and sleep late.

The medicine had a greater impact on them in their weakened state than it might otherwise have had. He didn't trust it, himself.

Nobody was waking up to challenge or to greet him.

None of those sleeping bodies had moved.

Sleeping bodies weren't supposed to be so still. People moved in their sleep, they shifted and twitched and grumbled to themselves—

He didn't want to take a single step further.

But now he had to know.

He stepped close to the nearest plank-bed and turned down the blanket covering the man who lay there. The blanket was heavy with moisture and warm to the touch. For a moment Raleigh felt glad relief; blankets covering sleepers were supposed to be warm, warm with body heat. Yes. Good.

But as soon as he felt better he felt worse, because everything in the growhouse was the same rather too warm temperature, and the body beneath the blanket was no more alive than the blanket itself.

Wybrandt.

Wybrandt, and there seemed to be no sign of distress or injury, though the corpse's skin was not cold. Warm, as everything else in this place was warm, and yet somehow still clammy to the touch in a sense; already bloating. Dead. No breath. Dead white. Wybrandt was dead.

And he was getting light-headed himself, it was so hot in here. With this much moisture in the air it did no good to sweat, sweat only cooled when there was evaporation, and there was no hope for evaporation in this humidity, so all sweating did was promote dehydration. When sweat lost its ability to cool, the body lost control of its ability to regulate the temperature of its core.

He had to get out quickly.

He made it to the entrance only just in time, falling to the ground a few feet from the goal but successfully crawling the rest of the way. He didn't go outside. He lay in the doorway blocked open by his body and let the air play over him, cooling him, reviving him. He had another drink of water. He was going to need to refill his water can soon, at this rate.

What had happened to Wybrandt?

Had he had too big a meal and fallen into a stupor? Had he

misjudged the desired dose of sleeping pills? Had he just gone to sleep exhausted, and been too deep asleep to wake when his body temperature started to creep into the danger zone?

Heat prostration.

Wybrandt was dead of heat stroke.

And the others?

Raleigh crawled out of the growhouse and let the door close behind him. For a long time he lay on the bare parched earth, paralyzed with grief and desolation.

He was alone.

This was too much for him.

Everywhere he could go for shelter, everywhere he could go for food, there were dead bodies; neither did he have the strength in reserve to bury them, not even for simple hygiene's sake.

Too much.

He was the man who had been responsible for the course correction module, and he had let it become damaged beyond repair. Because of that he was the man who had convinced the others to stay here rather than chance their lives on *Goforth*, sure as he had been that *Goforth* would not—could not—leave. And *Goforth* had left; and one way or another all of the people who had listened to him, rather than to Hillbrane and the Mechs, were dead.

It was his fault.

How could he bear the guilt?

The advance party would come, the First Colony would arrive, how could he bear the life-long shame?

To live, to be the only one left alive when everyone who had believed in him was dead—it was an intolerable idea.

But he knew what he could do to cleanse himself of the stain that the deaths of all of his peers left on him, body and soul.

Now that they were all dead he had no further business surviving. It was all over for him, now and forever.

He would go down to the river to wash his guilt away.

The river would take his life along with it, and carry his

wasted future far away from him, to be lost for all time in the waters of the sea.

There was only one more thing that he had to do before he could submerge his shame forever.

Goforth came in low over the prairie on its approach run, so close that the encampment was clearly visible onscreen.

There was no sign of any movement.

They'd been monitoring at extreme tolerance since they had come into range, and it was wonderful to see what had been accomplished since they'd been gone—growhouses, even the foundation for the first permanent residence.

Yet the closer they got the more confusing the picture became. The work that had been done on the permanent residence building seemed to have been abandoned at an early stage. And no matter how long they watched, no matter how discrete the scan, in the twenty hours between first sighting and arrival there had been no sign of life at the encampment. None at all.

Hillbrane didn't like it.

It was too incredible to believe that the unthinkable might have happened, but what were they to make of the apparent desertion of the camp?

The first hint came as *Goforth* made its last approach to its autolaunch platform. There seemed to be a clump of something at the side of the platform, and anything that stuck up from the plain like that had to be alien in this world. Nobody there to stand and wave and greet them, but it was something, and as soon as they could safely leave the craft Hillbrane and Cago and some of the crew went to find out what it was.

They found the body.

She couldn't tell who it had been; she hadn't known the other Jneers so well. Raleigh she could have recognized, she was sure, no matter how strangely changed his body might be by the organic processes of decaying flesh. In the absence of specialized corpse-handling insects—maggots, blowflies, the

complex system of corpse attendants spoken of in the books—
the body lost coherence more slowly than it might otherwise
have done, but the normal processes of endemic bacterial life
continued to work on flesh no longer alive, and the body could
not be identified.

There were a few clues.

Someone had made a camp here, there was water, but there
was no sign of any food, no ration packs.

What were they to think?

There were smears of dust on the wall of the autolaunch
platform. Someone had tried to put a message there, written
in mud it seemed. But the mud had dried and flaked off, and
what traces had survived had been destroyed by the heat and
the vibration of the *Goforth*'s landing.

Huddling together at the camp, Hillbrane and the others
with her—Cago, Mir, Ivery, and a Jneer scientist named Hostine—tried to come to a decision as to what to do.

"There's no sign of any infection." Hostine shrugged, peel-
ing off her examination gloves. "All of the microflora and
microfauna seem imported. It doesn't look like an alien
plague, but how would we tell?"

Something that had lain in wait and only attacked once people had been on the planet's surface long enough, perhaps.
The Mechs had all been exposed, and none of them were dead,
and quarantine had not found any traces of potential biological
contamination on *Goforth* or within them. But it was a risk.

"We're on the ground," Mir pointed out. "Let's take the
mover and go on. The others can all stay in protected atmosphere until we have more information. There's plenty to do
here without leaving the ship."

Well, it would be hard. Hillbrane remembered how eager
they had all been to step foot to this promised land. But they
couldn't risk the others so long as there was a chance that
some unexpected plague had taken the Jneers who had stayed
behind.

She helped Hostine and Cago isolate the little campsite under a quarantine sheet while Mir relayed instructions up

through the open passenger port, and waited for the crew inside to unship the mover. She was not so much frightened for their sakes as worried about the others; she and Mir and Cago had been and gone and come back, after all.

What was it that had happened here?

Why were there no rations at this camp?

They made the journey to the encampment in grim silence, and no one came out to greet them in response to the alarm horn Mir sounded. Hostine had issued biological contamination gear to one and all, and it was warm rather than cool inside the protective garments. Cago headed for the mess dome right away, so Hillbrane followed him; she was glad of the respirator mask she wore, because there was another body here, and the first corpse they'd happened on had stunk.

But there were rations here.

Depleted, yes, but rations left in relative plenty; no one had had to starve for lack of food. For lack of enough, for lack of the right kind of food, perhaps; the nutritionists were hard at work even now recalculating the food to be prepared and sent out in light of the specific information that *Goforth* had been able to supply.

What had whomever this had been died of?

They met Mir and Hostine outside the mess dome. Cago pointed to the dormitory behind them; Mir and Hostine had gone there, and Mir just shook his head and held up one finger. One corpse, Hillbrane guessed.

Three bodies.

But there had been ten people.

The growhouses were next to search, and the growhouses were a wonder. There was a beautiful crop in the first one: root vegetables and squash, ripening and all but ready to eat. Just another indication that there was food, but they would not be able to dare release this crop for actual consumption until they could be sure of what had happened to the people here.

There were two more growhouses.

One of them held four more bodies, all apparently lying in makeshift beds, none apparently dead of wounds or injury.

There was food there, again, uneaten rations. The heat inside the growhouses made the smell of rotting meat almost overpowering, even with the protection of the quarantine mask. Cago, picking his way carefully through the little cluster of the dead, lifted something from a makeshift table: a document. There had been writing on it once, but now there was nothing but a sodden lump of pulp stained with ink too far diffused to retain any coherence whatsoever.

Damn.

And that made seven out of ten, dead and accounted for, even if they still did not know which seven it was. Testing would show. Genetics would give them the answer, and autopsies would have to be done, to see what information could be gleaned from bodies in such varied states of decay. They had more medical staff with them on this pass, and one of the Jneers was a physiologist; they would get the answer. Or at least some parts of the answer.

The answer might not even explain this—

The third growhouse was like the first, full of green and growing things, but empty of clues about the fate of the Jneers who had planted them. In the third growhouse some of the crop had been left too long and had gone to seed. Radishes. Lettuces. Ruined, but in a positive way, really. More good fodder for the botanist on board, great experimental data, and completely useless to anyone until they could decide if it was safe for the botanist to leave the ship and have a look at the raw material that awaited her analysis.

Coming out of the third growhouse Hillbrane found Mir standing with Cago, looking off toward the banks of the river.

The suction pipes led from there to the water treatment plant at the back of the growhouses, but there was something else there, something strung up on the light-set that stood over the place on the riverbank where the hoses ran down to the water. Something tagged with streamers of bright red-orange cloth that might have been torn from the distinctive covering of the emergency medical kit.

All right.

They'd go find out.

They went together by unspoken agreement, and Hillbrane knew she was as afraid to see what the thing might be as she was anxious to discover it. No bodies appeared as they approached, and she was glad of that; but no live person appeared either.

A document.

A document, suspended between two poles of the light-set, carefully wrapped in weather-resistant waterproof fabric, its base weighed down with stones in the bottom of the packet—so that if it blew down it would not blow into the river, Hillbrane guessed.

She wasn't going to be the one to touch it—

But Hostine appeared to have no such reservations, and reached out to take the packet down and open it. Hillbrane couldn't stand the suspense. She walked on past the light-set to the riverbank; there was a pile of clothing there, neatly folded and stacked on the side of the bank and weighed down with more stones. A man's clothing, by the undergarment that was uppermost. The boots were there. Socks. She wondered if she recognized the pattern of the shirt, or whether her imagination was running on too rich a fuel-to-motivation mix.

Cago came after her with the document; Hillbrane took it carefully and looked it over. Standard report format, filled out in a meticulous but curiously crabbed hand. Incident report. Written up as though it was some lab experiment's results, submitted in support of a theory paper. The abstract came first: *A party comprised of nine Jneers and one Oway attempting to wait for advance party on Waystation One proved unable to overcome unanticipated obstacles inherent in the environment. The experiment must be considered a failure. Do not repeat without a more heterogeneous test group and/or revised resources.*

And below that—precisely two lines of spacing below that—the tabular summary of data, tragic and heart-wrenching in its dispassionate catalog.

Kovacs, unaccounted for, may have left station with Go-forth.

Alsop, accidental death by drowning.

Gilrath, accidental death by inadvertent ingestion of poisonous substance.

Fisch, presumed dead of systems failure following prolonged coma resulting from accidental ingestion of excess medication (overdose).

Vince, Sonaman, Tyler, and Wybrandt, accidental death of heat prostration due to prolonged exposure to high heat and excess humidity while unconscious/asleep.

Riatt, refusing food, and fasting for an undetermined period of time, presumed dead.

Brent, missing and unaccounted for, presumed dead.

Marquette, self-terminated, death by drowning.

It was a horrible list, achingly painful to read for all its clinical and removed language; and at the bottom of the page, where the research team would normally be listed, a single scrawled message—the handwriting still more crabbed than the rest, as if it was an afterthought, a final message. *Oh, name one of your babies after me, Hillbrane, I always loved you. I was wrong, but never meant you harm.*

It could only be Raleigh.

If she squinted she could almost recognize his handwriting.

There was more to the document; he'd written the report, it was all there, but she knew all she felt she needed to know for now.

Hillbrane took off her quarantine mask and wept over the sad pile of clothing on the banks of the river Deecee, with Cago crouched down behind her back for moral support.

Who would ever have dreamed that it could go so wrong?

EPILOGUE
REUNION

It had been fifteen years since she'd come to Waystation One, but right now Hillbrane Harkover felt as though it had been fifty at least. She was tired. The baby had colic. She supposed she was lucky that this was the first colicky baby out of the five that she had, but all in all she felt she could easily have foregone the experience entirely.

Observations was dark and quiet, but far from asleep, unlike most of the rest of the city of Newstart. Hillbrane stifled her yawns and blinked at the observation screen, trying to concentrate.

"At first we thought it was just a ghost, in far sector."

Axel was a few years older than she was, one of the people who had come with First Colony as an adult. Not so the people around them; this was Axel's advanced astronomics class, and these were all people who had arrived as children. They had made good progress in building a permanent colony here. And they had worked for it, too.

Axel pointed, and the young woman who sat at the controls called up a magnification. "But then Byrnie, here, decided to see if she couldn't box the ghost, just for demonstration purposes. Calibration exercise. And she found this."

There wasn't anything to see but a minute point on the gray screen. It seemed to vibrate a little; Hillbrane swallowed back another yawn. She had just gotten the baby to bed. It was the middle of the night. It was times like these that she was half convinced that Cago was right, that it was time for her to insist on being relieved of her position as Administrator of Newstart so that she could return to a quiet life in bamboo applications research and development.

"It's coming faster than anything we've ever seen," Byrnie explained—Podile's daughter, now twenty-something, with her hair done up in dozens of tiny braids that took her fond mother hours to plait. "Not only that. The spectroscopy is highly speculative at this point. But it's not throwing anything that would be consistent with any of the drives that we know of."

Podile's daughter. Something stirred at the back of Hillbrane's mind.

"Incoming." She'd meant to ask it as a question, but it came out declarative rather than interrogatory. So part of her brain was actually working. That was good to know. "It's manufactured."

Well, yes, that was obvious.

And impossible.

Axel was nodding slowly, as if in full understanding of all of the different things that this chance interception could mean.

"It says it's an autonomous scanner, self-identifying with a long string of code. Mira's still working on the decodes. It speaks our language, just not exactly."

Autonomous scanner.

They didn't call their probes autonomous scanners.

There was no such usage as "autonomous scanner" in the Colony Fleet.

"Where did it come from?" she asked, in a voice half-strangled with the immensity of the implications. "Can we tell?"

Podile's daughter looked up at Hillbrane over her shoulder. "System of origin," she said, and for a moment Hillbrane couldn't tell if she was rephrasing the question or answering it. "Our system of origin. Pluto colony. That's what it says.

And that's where it seems to be coming from. System of origin. Earth-based."

Hillbrane sat down, because her knees gave way beneath her suddenly.

System of origin.

"Byrnie. You're your mother's daughter." Podile had gone out on instinct, and found the track they had needed to identify in order to find the Colony Fleet. And because of that *Goforth* had not vanished into oblivion, with its crew and the critical information that it carried; and because of that First Colony had not arrived at Waystation One so woefully unprepared for the unique challenges it would face that its failure would have been much more likely than its survival.

Because Podile had had a thought and followed it.

And now this.

Byrnie looked down at her display. It was hard to tell, because it was dark in Observations, and Byrnie's naturally brown skin had taken the sun of Waystation One like a dear friend and shone a deep rich gold with it. But Hillbrane thought she was blushing.

Hillbrane hastened to divert potentially embarrassing attention from Byrnie. Byrnie was going to be getting enough attention and more, in the next few days, as the person who had made the first hit. "How long has it been since it left?"

Because if they knew where it purported to come from, and since they knew how fast it was traveling—

"Less than three hundred years." Axel had already asked that question. Obviously. Because he already had the answer. "Maybe as recently as two hundred and fifty. After they stopped talking to Fleet for sure. And maybe Fleet stopped listening too soon after all."

All right.

"Make a global announcement on morning meeting, Axel. Just the facts as we know them. We can all speculate on their meaning for ourselves. Have Byrnie read it."

After so many years, to discover that their home system—

the cradle of their species—might not be lost to them forever, after all—

"And we'll have to send after Fleet. But we can wait a few days to get a full data set. Byrnie, you and your team get alpha priority on resources from now until Weekly Meeting. We'll need to decide how to make contact with the messenger, if the vehicle itself hasn't told us by then."

But as huge and powerful and poignant as that was, Hillbrane knew that it didn't matter as much as it might have done had they made this intercept just twenty years earlier.

The Colony Fleet had fulfilled the first and single most critical portion of its mission. It had remained on target for four hundred years; and though unexpected social developments over time had ultimately threatened to degrade its long-term viability, it had demonstrated the ability of a healthy organism to self-correct as it continued on toward the next planned colony. First Colony had made a place for human life on Waystation One, and was thriving even in the adversity of an environment that—howsoever Earth-like—was alien to them, after four hundred years in transit.

First Colony could call back to the world from which they'd come as a self-sufficient people of significant accomplishment, and let the unknown descendants of their mutual ancestors know that they had honored the hopes and dreams of the people who had sent them here by fulfilling them.

True to the Founders' intent, they had stayed true to course. Now they were home.

Get ready for

EosCon IV

The original publisher-sponsored,
online, realtime science fiction and
fantasy convention

January 6, 2001

Meet your favorite authors online
as they discuss their work, their worlds,
and their wonder.

(Hey, it's the first sf/f convention
of the <u>real</u> new millennium!)

www.eosbooks.com

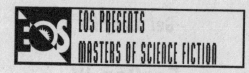